THE ROYAL NANNY

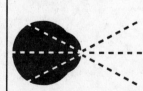

THE ROYAL NANNY

KAREN HARPER

THORNDIKE PRESS

A part of Gale, Cengage Learning

GALE
CENGAGE Learning·

Farmington Hills, Mich • San Francisco • New York • Waterville, Maine
Meriden, Conn • Mason, Ohio • Chicago

GALE
CENGAGE Learning®

LIBRARY OF CONGRESS CATALOGING-IN-PUBLICATION DATA

Names: Harper, Karen (Karen S.), author.
Title: The royal nanny / by Karen Harper.
Description: Large print edition. | Waterville, Maine : Thorndike Press, 2016. | Series: Thorndike Press large print romance
Identifiers: LCCN 2016024573| ISBN 9781410492555 (hardcover) | ISBN 1410492559 (hardcover)
Subjects: LCSH: Bill, Charlotte, 1875–1964—Fiction. | Princes—Fiction. | Nannies—Fiction | Large type books. | GSAFD: Biographical fiction.
Classification: LCC PS3558.A624792 R69 2016 | DDC 813/.54—dc23
LC record available at https://lccn.loc.gov/2016024573

Published in 2016 by arrangement with William Morrow, an imprint of HarperCollins Publishers

Printed in Mexico
1 2 3 4 5 6 7 20 19 18 17 16

Thanks to Don for going on
all the British Isles treks.
To Sandra Byrd for helping to
plan our excursions to
Buckingham Palace and the
Victoria and Albert Museum.
Especially to Annelise Robey and
Meg Ruley for finding this book
a great home with Lucia Macro,
who loves the Edwardians too.

NAMES AND TITLES OF MAIN BRITISH ROYAL CHARACTERS

A note on the royals and their names:

Although it can be confusing, the names given to the royal children of Queen Victoria, King Edward VII, and King George V at their christenings were often different from the names used by their families. This was a family who loved nicknames. And to makes things even more confusing, when ascending to the throne, they could choose a new name. Hopefully the following will make navigating the royal family tree a bit easier.

Queen Victoria, called Gangan by the York children

Edward, Prince of Wales, later King Edward VII, son of Queen Victoria. His birth name was Albert Edward, and his family nickname was Bertie. Father of George, Duke of York, and grandfather (Grandpapa) to the York children

Alexandra of Denmark, Princess of Wales, mother (Mother dearest) of George, Duke of York, and grandmother (Grannie) of the York children

George, Duke of York, son of Edward and Alexandra, later King George V

May of Teck, Duchess of York, later Princess of Wales, later Queen Mary. Mother of six York children:

David, Prince of Wales, full name Edward Albert Christian George Andrew Patrick David, later King Edward VIII, later Duke of Windsor.

Bertie (another one!), second son of King George and Queen Mary, full name Albert Frederick Arthur George. He later took the name King George VI, and was father of Queen Elizabeth II.

Mary, only daughter of King George and Queen Mary. Full name Victoria Alexandra Alice Mary.

Harry, fourth child of King George and Queen Mary, later the Duke of Gloucester. Full name Henry William Frederick Albert.

George, fifth child of King George and Queen Mary, later the Duke of Kent. Known as "George" as a child, he is sometimes confused with his brother George VI. Full name George Edward Alexander Edmund.

John (Johnnie), last child of King George and Queen Mary. Full name John Charles Francis. (Were they running out of fourth names at this time? Of course, the heir to the throne has seven given names.)

PROLOGUE

Monday, April 6, 1959
Sandringham Estate, Norfolk, England

"Here comes trouble," I said aloud instead of just thinking it to myself as in the old days. Indeed, here came one of my dear loves and my worst failure.

I opened the door and waited for him to exit the chauffeured Daimler. My life had been plum full of breaking bad habits in others, but I'd never been able to really calm or control him. There was one thing I could never forgive him for, though I'd tried, and it wasn't his continued smoking.

I watched as he took a big drag of his cigarette, then ground the stub under the toe of his shiny shoe. Good gracious, I wished this estate, where he'd been reared, would comfort him rather than make him more nervous.

As he came up the walk of my small grace-and-favor flat, I glanced over my shoulder at Johnnie's portrait. Oh, I'd hear about that again, though I'd removed my precious, framed, handwritten note and the agate statue of the grouse from the mantel. Queer how childhoods could make or break the best and worst of us, even my two kings.

I swung open the door but felt I was opening the past again — the pain, the fear — oh, of course, the good and high times too. Everything rushed at me as if I were coming here for the first time to live it all again. The graves out by the church opened, and the beloved ghosts walked in my mind and heart. I wanted to flee, down the familiar paths of Sandringham, down the paths of time and memory to begin again. But I stood firm and let him in.

■ ■ ■ ■

PART ONE

1897–1901
LONDON TO YORK COTTAGE

■ ■ ■ ■

CHAPTER 1

Friday, April 2, 1897

Of course I'd been out on the for-hire steam launch on the Thames my father captained, but in the railway carriage, I felt I was flying. It was noisy too, here in third class with the huge engine just ahead, huffing and blowing smoky steam that dashed past the windows. Where I sat was quite plain, with the leather seats a bit worn and cracked, but I felt I was in a magic cart to the moon anyway. My father had said the tracks would be well kept since this was the route the royals themselves used to get to their Norfolk estate, which is where I was headed. But when he'd put me on the train, he'd been disappointed that none of the royal carriages were on this run.

I was about to become undernurse to the royals at York Cottage on the Sandringham Estate, and it was my first time in a railway carriage and so far from home. I was going one hundred twenty miles from London, and didn't have to pay for the passage ticket either! Maybe that would be one of the grand things about being in service to the royals, because Mama said they were all rich, rich, rich. Honestly, I didn't care a whit about that, just that I could better my station and send some money home in these tough times, but how I missed my former and now grown toddlekins from Dr. Lockwood's family in London. They didn't need a nurse anymore, all grown up to only need their new stepmother.

Truth was, I used to wish the widowed Dr. Edwin Lockwood, my former employer, would marry me, though I knew that was quite out of the question. But when I first went to work at his house as nursemaid, I was only thirteen and such a dreamer. People think I'm a no-nonsense person, but I still harbor flights of fancy in my head and heart, and to mean something to someone else is one of them.

But in the nearly ten years I worked in London, I knew it was not that I loved the doctor, but that I loved his two little daughters and hated to leave them, especially after I'd been promoted to nurse after five years there. Now his new wife didn't want me about because her stepchildren doted on me. But the doctor gave me a good character, which the Duchess of York's friend Lady Eva Dugdale had somehow seen. So here I was, headed to the Duke and Duchess of York's country house to help the head nurse of two royal lads — one called David, nearly four years of age; the other Bertie, a year and a half — and a new baby to be born soon.

I beat down the butterflies in my belly and practiced saying "Your Grace, milord, milady, sir, ma'am" and all that. What if Queen Victoria herself ever popped in for a visit, for the duke was her grandson — well, there were many of her offspring scattered across Europe in ruling houses, but he was in direct line to the British throne after his father, the Prince of Wales. And since the Prince and Princess of Wales often lived on the same Sandringham Estate, so Lady Dugdale said, I'd wager I'd see them, right regular too, that is if the head nurse, name of Mary Peters, let me help her with the royal children when their kin came calling.

"Ticket, please, miss," the conductor said as he came through the carriage. I had a moment's scramble but handed it to him and had it marked. When he passed on, I put it as a keepsake in my wooden box of worldly goods, which sat on the floor next

17

to my seat. The carriage wasn't too full, not to Norfolk with its marshy fens and the windy Wash my papa had described to me. Oh, I was so excited I could barely sit still. I was to disembark at a place called Wolferton Station, where someone was to meet me. I was just so certain everything would be lovely and fine and grandly, royally perfect.

The three-hour railway ride took some of the starch out of me, but I ate my biscuits and had lukewarm tea from the tin flask Mama had given me. So I perked right up when we steamed into the tiny village of Wolferton a few miles from the great house of Sandringham, though I'd been told my final destination was a smaller house nearby called York Cottage. It sounded quite quaint, and I pictured a low, thatched place with rambling roses. Lady Dugdale had said it was much smaller than the Big House but it had been added onto to allow space for Duke George and Duchess May's growing family. Of course, she'd said, the household moved to London, Windsor, and Scotland on a regular schedule, so I would get to do more traveling too. But, mostly, for the children, the Sandringham Estate was home, and now my home too.

"Wolferton Station, miss," the conductor told me as he passed through again. He helped me lift my box, then set it on the platform. Toward the back of the railway cars, men were unloading barrels and boxes and what looked to be crates of coal. My legs were wobbly after all that moving and swaying. As I took a few steps, I hoped whoever was sent to fetch me would be here soon. But the brisk breeze felt good on my face, shifting my hat veil and long coat and skirt.

I'd worn my only walking suit, blue wool and a bit scratchy for such a nice day. The jacket had a stand-up collar that chaffed my neck, and my new, pointed shoes pinched, but I knew I'd soon be wearing the daily work or dress uniforms of my new position. Both my sisters had said I was to write them all about what the fancy folk wore.

"Miss Charlotte Bill?" a voice called, and a young man appeared looking hale and hearty as if country living did him good.

"Yes. Are you sent from York Cottage?"

"Jack of all trades on the estate, all seven hundred acres of it, not a better place to be. Chad Reaver by name, sent to take you to the Yorks. Ah, good, you are a sensible one," he said with a smile as he shook my hand and nodded at my box, which he easily hefted onto one shoulder. "You should see the massive trunks the prince's London friends arrive with for their fancy Saturday to Mondays, clothing boxes so big we call them Noah's Arks."

I smiled at that picture. Chad Reaver looked to be about my age, early twenties, maybe a bit older. His square-jawed face was sun-darkened, and his brown eyes almost matched his hair. He was clean-shaven, muscular, half a head taller than me, dressed in work garb, and if I had to describe him in one word, I would say *solid.*

"I apologize for bringing you in with the lading," he said as he led me to a wagon being loaded with crates from the platform. He put my box under the seat and helped me up to sit beside him. "I'll make amends someday," he promised, "and take you and the little Yorks for a ride in the estate omnibus . . . if we can pry her ducklings away from Mrs. Peters."

"Oh, their nurse. I'm to be her under-nurse."

He nodded, yet looked a bit grim. As we rode the long, uphill, pine tree–lined drive from the station toward the house, he became my guide, and, in my heart even then, my friend.

"Over thirty years ago, it was, when

20

Queen Victoria's husband, Prince Albert, bought this place for their heir, now Prince of Wales," he explained. I was entranced by the slight burr to his voice. " 'Course, Prince Albert picked it because he thought it would be out in the country, away from the temptations of London. But, as Prince Albert is long dead and the prince's fretful mother the queen's at a good distance, the prince imports his parties, though that's all in the Big House, not the cottage. Himself and the Princess Alexandra love being near their grandchildren, that's sure. Just sit back now and look around. It's a three-mile drive to the residence. I tell you, this place has been so changed and improved over the years."

"Does Her Majesty ever visit here?"

"At her age, they go to her. Look — a ruffed grouse taking wing," he said, pointing at a flapping, russet-hued bird and sounding more excited than when he'd mentioned the royals. "They're rare here as it's mostly pheasant and woodcocks, partridge too. I'm the head gamekeeper's son, you see."

"So you hunt game for the royal tables?"

"Oh, no," he said looking at me more than serious — almost stern. "I never shoot them myself. We feed and protect the birds for the family and their guests to shoot. Meanwhile, we keep a good eye out for poachers. Guns make such a bang that the thieves use snares attached to sticks or canes, but I know their shifty ways. This spring you'll hear the grouse males make a drumming sound by beating their wings to attract their female friends, but that can attract poachers too. We feed and tend the birds, or they'd eat the buds off the trees. We must always take the bad with the good, you see."

I nodded. So much to learn here. I did admire the beauty of this place with its scattered woodlots and encircling, deep forests, vast fields, and a few small, distant villages surrounded by fens and the marsh beyond. He pointed out to me the nearby village where he lived, West Newton by name. It was tiny, a mere score of houses edged by fields and trees with a fine-looking church nearby. And ahead, at the end of this straight road, loomed a grand house and a smaller one.

"That gray slate roof up ahead . . . the Big House," he told me, pointing. "That's what we all call it here. It has as many rooms as there are days in a year, pretty fancy ones. I'm sure you'll get to see them eventually."

I couldn't hold back a gasp at the sight of

it. And this was called a country house? As we drew closer, I saw it was red brick with an imposing front and wide lawns and terraces. "Don't fret if you hear dogs at night too," he told me. "The Big House kennels hold some fifty hunt hounds."

"I shall listen for them, and the drumming of the grouse wings, but mostly, the even breathing of my little charges at night."

"Well, from what I've seen, Mrs. Peters keeps a good watch on them, 'specially the heir, of course. And that," he said, pointing again, "is York Cottage."

"Oh, it's on the banks of a pond, very pretty."

"Righto," he said, looking sideways at me, "very pretty."

I caught his gaze and started a big blush that crept up my throat to my cheeks and temples. I looked away to study the house that was to be my new home, a fairy-tale place with gabled roof and lots of chimneys, not what I would call a cottage at all. Not as grand as Sandringham House or Buckingham Palace, where I'd taken Dr. Lockwood's girls to peer through the iron fence, but it looked lovely to me, reflected in the little lake with wild ducks and two small, strangely antlered deer drinking. So peaceful, so perfect under a spring sky with clouds like clotted cream.

Chad Reaver helped me down and put my trunk on his broad shoulder to escort me to a side door. I was glad that he was with me and wanted to thank him for the tour and tidbits he'd shared. But, sadly for me, the moment he rang a bell and a middle-aged woman appeared, with a tip of his cap and the words "Mrs. Wentworth, the new undernurse from London, Charlotte Bill, delivered safe and sound," he was gone.

Mrs. Wentworth, the York Cottage housekeeper, gave me time to wash and compose myself in a small attic bedroom, then took me on a tour of the house — that is, the servants' area and the staircases and hallways, for I saw many closed doors she called "the private rooms." I was a bit disappointed she didn't take me straightaway to see the children's quarters.

"York Cottage was built higgledy-piggledy, first as a place to put extra guests when the Big House parties overflowed," she explained. She had a kind face but had a habit of standing so erect that her gray eyes seemed to be looking down her long nose. Her black skirts rustled when she walked.

" 'Twas called Bachelor's Cottage until the Yorks came here for their honeymoon and made it their country home. It's small enough that everyone can get underfoot," she told me with a lift of her silver eyebrows that matched her hair. "But His Lordship likes small rooms, from his navy days, you know, like on a ship."

"Oh, yes. I'm used to small rooms and lots of people from my own home."

"I warrant we'll see a large family from the lord and lady. Why, three children close together, if you count the one coming soon," she said, her eyebrows rising even higher. "So you are used to a large family?"

"My sister Annie is two years older than me. She was in service but is now married to a river man. Then my brother Ernest, three years younger than me, and last Edith, three years after Ernest."

"Years apart at least, instead of a bit over a year. I'll soon introduce you to the children's nurse, Mrs. Peters, as I believe she'll have the lads down for a nap now. Of course, in this small a place, it's a challenge for the young ones to be seen and not heard — not even seen sometimes. But they are presented to their parents at teatime each afternoon promptly at four when the duke and duchess are here."

Presented to their parents? I thought. Well, I guess people were presented to royalty, evidently even their own flesh and blood.

"And today," Mrs. Wentworth went on, with the keys on her waist chain jingling as we went downstairs, "her ladyship has asked that you be brought in with the children so that she can greet you, but don't speak unless spoken to first, of course."

I was starting to lose track of all the *of courses,* though I knew things would be done differently here and I must learn new ways. She showed me how to use the back stairs when I fetched things from below. She introduced me to the servants, though their names didn't all stick at first, and I thought I'd be taking my meals with the children anyway.

But one of the servants, who all seemed eager to catch a glimpse of me too, gave me a sweet smile as her eyes swept over me, hat to shoes. I caught her name — Rose Milligrew, lady's maid to the duchess — since she seemed so welcoming, even without saying a word. Rose, so blond and pale that it seemed she had no eyebrows or lashes, was sitting at a table in window light, mending a taffeta and net evening dress in a rich amber hue that shimmered and nearly took my breath away. Oh, I'd have to mention that garment in my first letter home.

Upstairs again, but not the attic where the

female servants — including myself when not on duty — would sleep, but this time at the back of the house, with a green baize swinging door shutting off their parents' chambers, where two small rooms were set apart for the children. I found it hard to fathom that Dr. Lockwood's daughters had far more room to play, sleep, and roam. I learned there were two newfangled bathrooms in the house, but both were for the use of Their Graces.

"The children, you see," Mrs. Wentworth added, "are bathed in their nursery each Saturday evening, and that is a lot of water for the nursemaids to tote up from the kitchen. There are two of them to help, at least, though Mrs. Peters has them down in the basement washroom, fetching and ironing right now, Martha Butcher and Jane Thatcher. They go by their given names as the duchess didn't care to hear a Butcher and Thatcher were caring for her children."

I wasn't sure if that was a jest or not, but she was off on another turn, both in the hall and in her talk. I tried to keep track of all the new names.

At the second door, she whispered, "The day nursery." Mrs. Wentworth opened the door a crack and "a-hemmed" without sticking her head in. Out came a square-jawed woman with her hair parted in the middle and pulled so hard back that it looked painted on beneath her lace and linen cap. Under her thick raven brows, her dark eyes looked me over.

"You'll be called by your first name, Charlotte, like my other workers," she told me, "since I hardly need an undernurse called Bill. You and I shall talk after I tuck up the children tonight, about rules and regulations, timing, behaviors. I am the boys' head nurse. Besides the nursery footman, Cranston, I have two nursemaids. But couldn't see promoting the likes of them to undernurse, and Her Ladyship Mrs. Dugdale says you come recommended."

Though surprised by her cold manner, I knew I had to manage a proper reply. "I tended two girls for five years as head nurse and was nursemaid before that."

"Well, then, the demands will soon be much greater as we're about to have a third child. The baby will need close watching by you, while I tend my boys, especially the heir, a delicate, darling child. Poor duchess," she said, lowering her voice to a whisper, "doesn't like pregnancies any more than, they say, the queen herself did, but that will be over soon, and you'll be very busy. I'd best get back in to my boys, prepare them

28

to meet their parents at tea, for which I hear you are to tag along. I usually take a nurse-maid to keep an eye on Bertie, but you can do that now, and when the new baby arrives, you'll carry him or her."

"I'm sure it will be a special time for the lads with their parents."

"We'll see," Mrs. Peters said and, without further ado, went back into the day nursery and closed the door.

I felt crestfallen, and I'm sure Mrs. Wentworth knew it.

"She becomes overtired," she told me, patting my shoulder. "Poor thing works so hard and never agrees to take even a short holiday, so it's good you are here. And she's so protective and concerned that all goes well with the boys, especially David, but both lads have problems."

"Problems? Such as what, Mrs. Wentworth?"

"I'd best let her tell you. How about you come down and have a spot of tea with me in my room to buck you up after your journey? Of course, you won't take tea with Their Graces, just stand back to tend to the children lest they roil their father and have to be removed."

Removed? Presented and then removed? I had been so certain that royal children would be well behaved and that the nurse who tended them would at least be welcoming. Suddenly, I missed my Lockwood charges terribly and, for the first time in years, was homesick for my own family too.

CHAPTER 2

Teatime was fast approaching, and I was on pins and needles. Soon I would have my first real glimpse of royalty, because when I'd tried to see Queen Victoria during her Golden Jubilee ten years ago, the crowds were so huge near the Abbey that all I saw was her gilded carriage and six cream-colored horses. The press of people, that's what I remember from that day. But to see members of the royal family close, to speak to them and hear their voices . . . well!

At least I was to meet little David and Bertie before "being presented" to their parents in the queen's boudoir, as was evidently customary before the elders dressed to dine each night. I knocked on the day nursery door. Would I ever learn the twists and turns of this place with all its corridors and corners? I'd lost my way twice between my attic chamber and this hall.

"Enter," came Mrs. Peters's crisp voice.

31

Of course, I was to call her Mrs. Peters or Nurse Peters, however closely we would work together, not by her given name of Mary.

I went in to find two sweet-faced boys who greatly resembled each other, the youngest in a white dress with lots of flounces and lace, the older in a sailor suit. To my dismay, it appeared the little lads had been crying as she washed their faces none too gently. Both tried to flinch away, though she held their chins firmly and scrubbed at their already rosy cheeks.

"My dears," she told them, still not looking my way, "this is my new helper, Charlotte. Say hello to Charlotte, David and Bertie. Char-lotte."

"Miss or Mrs.?" David asked.

"Just Charlotte," Mrs. Peters said.

"Good day, Charlotte," he said with a nod but not a smile.

"Lala," said little Bertie. "She Lala."

"Well, we'll have to work on that," Mrs. Peters said, tossing her washcloth in the basin.

Despite still wearing my walking suit, I went down on my knees to greet the boys.

"You needn't kneel to them — not here!"

"I'm only making their acquaintance on their level," I told her, smiling at them, for it seemed smiles were in short supply. "I know a new person can be daunting to little ones at first. Hello, David, and hello, Bertie. We're are going to be friends and have lots of fun."

Mrs. Peters snorted so hard I thought she was going to sneeze. "You, just like me, had best follow orders here about, Their Graces' wishes and mine, and that doesn't mean games."

"Of course, I will follow orders and help you," I promised as I shook hands with these two solemn, little boys, though I yearned to hug them. They kept looking nervously at each other and then up at their nurse, so I got to my feet and decided to bide my time for full introductions. The little poppets were blond beauties, and I was sure their parents would be even more handsome than the drawings I'd seen of them in the gazettes at the Lockwood house.

"I always take the heir," Mrs. Peters told me and lifted David into her sturdy arms. "You bring Bertie." Strangely, David looked upset, when most little ones loved to be cuddled and petted. Nurse Peters was rubbing his back and arms, patting him on his bum.

Though Bertie was walking well, even with his soft leather shoes, petticoats, and skirts

— for he had edged away from me — I picked him up, bounced him once and held him close. To my surprise, under all that fancy fabric, the boy seemed thin, almost bony. We went out, down the hall, and through the padded, green baize door. I followed Mrs. Peters with David looking back at Bertie and me. Bertie put his arms around my neck and clung close.

David stretched one hand back toward us, probably trying to reach out to his younger brother. Or to me?

"You wait right there 'til summoned," Nurse Peters told me at a turn of the hall and carted a wide-eyed David around the corner where I couldn't see them.

"I hungry," Bertie told me. "Lala, I hungry."

"I'm sure there will be something good when you see Mama and Papa," I told him. He stayed solemn, even as he held harder to me, seeming to stiffen as if waiting for something.

From down the hall came a high-pitched shriek. Good gracious, could she have dropped David? Though I'd been told to wait there, holding Bertie to me who clung so hard he almost cut off my air, I rushed around the corner and down the hall. David was crying and evidently Mrs. Peters was shaking him. I hurried to her and started making funny faces and meowing and chirping to distract the child, but he still cried. Oh, this was going to make a terrible impression on his parents and on my first meeting with them!

I heard a loud male voice on the other side of the door bellow, in a voice that carried over David's wails, "Not again! What is wrong with that boy? Must he always be caterwauling?"

I was thankful that made David's cries subside to sniffles. Whatever had set him off like that? Just being momentarily separated from Bertie? Fear of his father's booming voice?

A woman's tense tones wafted through the door. "Let's bring them in and feed them. After all, it's their last meal of the day."

"At least my stamp collection doesn't shriek. Even my hunt dogs don't bark like that. We'll never make a man of him."

"My dearest, he's not even four. I can't take it either, not with this wretched state I'm in. I just want it to be all over, this waiting, this birth."

I was tempted to take Bertie and flee, but Mrs. Peters rapped on the door, then opened it herself. In she swept with David starting to cry again. Could he indeed be afraid of his father? I did not know whether to wait until summoned, but I went in too, following Mrs. Peters's lead to curtsy. When I tried to put Bertie down, he clung so hard I kept him in my arms.

The room was exquisite with satin draperies in pale greens that matched the full, embroidered robe the duchess wore over her form in her delicate condition, *en negligee,* Dr. Lockwood's new wife had called that style. No corsets, no petticoats beneath. All sorts of photographs and bric-a-brac clustered on tables. May of Teck, the Duchess of York, had dark hair swept up beautifully and a regal bearing despite her big belly.

I was surprised that the duke was my height at five feet and a half. He had a brown beard clipped tight and stood ramrod straight with his teacup in one hand and cigar in the other. Could the strong smoke from that be something the children disliked, and so they protested these visits? It did rather sting one's eyes.

"If that boy can't be quiet, take him out, Mrs. Peters," the duke said over David's renewed sobs. His voice cut right through one, as if he were speaking to an entire shipload of men, for I'd heard he still considered himself a Royal Navy man. "How you manage him, I don't know. Her Grace doesn't need to be upset now."

To my horror, Mrs. Peters curtsied and carried David right out, leaving me with Bertie facing my new royal employers. I bobbed another curtsy and put Bertie down, hoping he would go to his mother, which, thank the Lord on high, he did.

With a weary smile, the duchess said, "My friend Lady Dugdale and her London doctor recommended you highly. We hope you will be happy here. As you must know, there will be a third child soon." She had a unique way of pronouncing her words, sharp with rolled *r*'s, which I learned later were traces of her German accent.

"Yes, Your Grace. I'm honored to serve here, and I love children."

"Well, good," the duke chimed in, "because these two are hard to love at times. Not since they've been babies, when we doted on them. I will leave all this to you, dearest," he said to his wife, "and be in my library with my stamps."

He made a hasty retreat. I didn't hear David's cries anymore so I hoped Mrs. Peters would bring him back in, but perhaps she had fled. To hear this had happened before was most unsettling.

"Excuse me, milady," I ventured, "but

Bertie said he's hungry." The moment that was out of my mouth, I was appalled. I hadn't been spoken to first. And had I just indirectly criticized Mrs. Peters or demanded something?

"He's always hungry yet doesn't seem to grow. So what do we have for you here, eh, sweeting?" she asked the child, and his face lit. "Why don't you sit on this stool and put him on your lap," she said to me. "I don't have a lap right now to hold him right, and he can have some grapes, muffins with jam, and milk. Ah — what is it you will be called by here, Miss Bill? Not Mrs. Bill, I'm sure since you aren't the head nurse, and I believe Mrs. Peters didn't want to use Bill at all. I recall that her husband who died years ago was Bill."

"Charlotte, she decided, milady." I had been told by Lady Dugdale that after addressing the duchess the first time as "Your Grace," I could switch to "milady," so I hoped I was doing that proper.

"Charlotte it is, then."

"Lala," Bertie declared with his mouth full of grapes. "She Lala."

Feeling a bit softer toward Mrs. Peters for her being a widow, I sat on the stool and held Bertie while his mother fed him as if he were a little bird — a ruffed grouse with all his fancy baby garb. And he did seem starved.

"I do hope you will be able to help Mrs. Peters deal with David," the duchess said. "I do worry so for his delicate nature, since so much will be expected of him. And I must keep reminding myself that his father will someday be his king too."

I was so relieved to find the children's mother a sweet and caring parent. And here I sat with her in intimate conversation.

"I will do my very best, milady."

"As must we all, in any circumstance and station," she whispered as if to herself. Her jaw set, and she blinked back tears. From that moment on, whatever might befall, I admired her.

CHAPTER 3

I soon came to understand how Nurse Peters could be so stern and possessive of the children, yet so well tolerated by the staff and the royal parents. Rose told me on the sly that she had actually saved the duchess's mother, Mary Adelaide of Teck, from a dreadful fall on the front staircase. Quite a feat, since Rose said the woman was cruelly nicknamed "Fat Mary," and must be three times the size of her pregnant daughter. So the Yorks felt they were beholden to Mrs. Peters.

"I vow, Charlotte, poor 'Fat Mary' would have been a hard one to dress and care for her garments," Rose had whispered with a roll of her light blue eyes.

Though Rose was almost ten years older than me, she didn't seem it. I liked her partly because she told me she had also gained her position here through a recommendation from Lady Dugdale. Rose longed to design fine ladies' garments, though she knew her true lot in life was to care for them. I think she was lonely, caught between spending a lot of time with the duchess upstairs, traveling with her, but supposedly living downstairs with the servants. Anyhow, we got on splendidly.

From Rose I learned there had been an even earlier nurse who had been dismissed before Mrs. Peters, for somehow insulting the duchess's mother, who used to be much about before her current illness kept her confined to White Lodge at Richmond Park in London. That was the location of David's birth, though Bertie had been born here.

In short, the staff, including Rose, all felt they were skating on thin ice. As one of the footmen put it, no one wanted a "fall from grace" since the Yorks were quick to sack anyone who stepped out of line. And so, more than once, I saw the butler on down to the nursery footman merely roll their eyes and keep their heads down, however brusque Mrs. Peters acted and however much David howled and Bertie cowered.

I, who worked closer than anyone with the woman, felt ill at ease with her all the time, so what must her little charges feel? Both were tense and skittish. I'd been in service at York Cottage for twenty-three days to be exact, and I feared Mrs. Peters might get me sacked for my cheery and affectionate way with the boys — Bertie, at least, since David always seemed off limits. The fact I was appalled at David's behavior more teatimes than not didn't sit well with her either. She mostly kept me at bay and treated me more like another nursemaid than undernurse, but I hesitated to complain.

Today was Sunday, April 25, and we'd been to St. Mary Magdalene Church on the grounds, though without the duchess in her usual place since the birth was so close. Day of rest or not, that afternoon I planned to store a pile of clean nappies in the day nursery in preparation for the birth of the new royal baby. Arms full, I walked right into the day nursery without the required knock.

I thought Mrs. Peters had taken the boys outside in the spring air. Bertie wasn't to be seen. But there she stood, leaning over David who was bent facedown over his bed. She was spanking his bare bum with the bristle side of a hairbrush!

"You'll learn, you bad, bad boy," the woman muttered. "You are my boy, aren't you? Aren't you?"

The child's hysterical cries were muffled by a pillow pressed against his face. In that moment, all the strange and horrid pieces of the puzzle flew together for me. She must have pinched and scratched the child before taking him in to see his parents each afternoon, then carried him out in triumph as if he were hers alone to comfort and cuddle. Bertie and David both feared her, yet were coerced and groomed — like this — to think she loved them and they must love her. Love demanded by pain — so wrong.

"Stop it! Unhand that child!" I shouted, though I knew the moment I spoke that my time here was doomed. I dropped the nappies on the bed, ready to leap at her. I wanted to seize that brush and hit her, but she stopped and yanked the child, clad only in his shirt, to a sitting position on his bed.

"You, leave at once!" she cried, advancing on me, keeping her voice down as I had not. "He's been naughty. He's in my charge."

Her expression terrified me. Her gaze seemed askew; her features twisted, unnatural. Could she be not only cruel but demented to treat the future heir to the throne like this? And she had gotten away with it?

"Where's Bertie?" I demanded.

"None of your business, which will soon

43

be ended here," she snapped and threw the brush at me. It bounced off my shoulder onto the floor. I felt sick to my stomach, for the boys, and yes, for myself.

Tears streaking down his face, behind her back, David pointed to the cabinet where we kept extra clothing and where I'd meant to put the nappies. I marched to the cabinet and pulled the door. Locked! The boy was locked in here? I grabbed the key from off the top shelf, unlocked the cabinet, and opened the door wide. Bertie was doubled up inside with his eyes screwed tight shut and his hands over his ears.

"Come on, poppet," I said and stooped to pull him out, but he'd gone rigid as a statue. "It's Lala, come on now." As I lifted him into my arms, he clung hard to me. I'd made some inroads with him at least.

"You'll be out of here now," Mrs. Peters said, propping her hands on her hips as if to keep me from seeing David, who peered around her. "My husband wouldn't give me babies of my own, but these are mine."

"We'll see about that," I told her. "I'm taking them outside for some fresh air as you were to do, and if you make a fuss, I'll tell Her Grace what I saw. You have lost your mind and —"

She began to make great, sucking sobs

where she was standing. Her shoulders shook and heaved. "Three years . . . since he was born, not a day off . . ."

"But everyone has their time off here, so —"

"I didn't. Couldn't leave him, not for a moment. He wants me, not them." Hysteria convulsed her.

"David, come here to me," I told him, and he scrambled around her with his thin white legs sticking out the bottom of his shirt — legs with black and blue bruises. "Where are your trousers?" I asked. He pointed to the floor where they'd been thrown. "Pick them up and bring them." He still wore his shoes, so I grabbed a tweed coat for him and one for Bertie, who was hardly dressed to go out either. I took the washcloth from the bowl, dripping wet, and grabbed a jar of salve from medicines I'd recently arranged on top of the cupboard. My arms full, and without another word, I took both boys out into the hall and closed the door.

I put Bertie down, though he pressed himself against me as I knelt next to David and gently washed his crimson pinprick cuts and blue bruises on his little, white bum. He was trembling but didn't cry. God help me, if someone came upon us in the hall like this.

"I know this hurts, but this will make it feel better soon, I promise," I told him and smoothed the aloe ointment on his bottom. He barely winced. Could he be used to this? I prayed he did not think I meant to treat him as she had. Why had I not realized she was pinching and bruising him each time we went to visit his parents? Why didn't they?

"Get your trousers on, here, help me," I told David, and he instantly obeyed, putting a hand against the wall and stepping into them though we didn't have his drawers. "We'll put your coats on downstairs, both of you. Come on." I picked up Bertie again and led them through the green baize door, down the hall, past their parents' private rooms — I heard muted voices inside — toward the front staircase. Bertie clung, and David stuck so close he almost tripped me.

"Hitchetty-hatchetty, down we go," I said in singsong fashion on the steps, but what tormented me were lines from the nursery rhyme I had recited to Bertie just last night: *When the bough breaks, the cradle will fall, and down will come baby, cradle and all.* I had no doubt their little world had crashed, but I was determined — if I could find a way to stay here — they would not be broken.

It was a glorious spring day. I had no coat, but I didn't mind. Outside on the steps, I put their coats on, then we went round to the side of the house where their pram was waiting. Though David usually walked, I decided to put them both into it, Bertie between David's legs with the pillow under his sore bottom. He was still shaking. I bent to hug him, held him a moment, then put my arms around both of them.

I needed time to think how I would handle this. Inside, Mrs. Peters might be tattling on me or might have collapsed, but I had to decide whom to tell the truth to and when. Their mother — I would have to risk telling their mother, but she was going to be delivered of a third child any day now. Could I convince her to keep me on until, hopefully, they would bring in another head nurse? If it was the last thing I did here, I must be certain Mrs. Peters was dismissed.

"We're going for a nice ride," I told the boys, who hadn't said a word. "And later we're going to talk to your mama about Mrs. Peters taking a long rest away from here. David, you may have to help me explain that Mrs. Peters hurts you."

"I can't, Lala," he said. "Then she will hurt me again."

"We'll just see about that. But right now

47

we are going to have some time just to be together."

With a helpless feeling — exactly what these little ones must have felt with that woman — I pushed the pram out toward the gardens, where I nearly ran down Chad Reaver, whom I had not laid eyes on since the day he'd brought me here. I'd thought of him, though, especially when I'd heard the drumming of the ruffed grouse's wings at night, calling for his "lady friend," as he had put it.

"Oh, Mr. Reaver! I didn't think to see you here!"

He had papers in his hands. He doffed his tweed cap and shot me a smile that didn't calm me down but stoked my emotions even more.

"Hello, Miss Charlotte Bill, and my favorite young men! And, ask for Mr. Reaver and you'll get my father, so call me Chad, eh, but never Chadwick, which my sire named me." He rolled his eyes and bent down to make a funny face at the boys.

Then he straightened and said to me, "The duke asked me to bring a reckoning of pheasants and grouse, but Mrs. Wentworth said to come back later. You see, she just told me, what you must already know." He turned away from the boys and began to whisper. "About keeping the lads away today, because the duchess has gone into labor."

"Oh, I didn't know . . . yet."

"What's labor?" David piped up, the first time I'd heard him so much as ask a question, despite the sharp mind I was sure was buried in there somewhere. He'd been so scared to move or speak that his father thought him quite the ninny.

Before I could think how to explain childbirth to the lad, Chad told him, "It's hard work for something that's good, something important, like I'm going to go hitch a horse to a wagon and instead of you lads riding in that perambulator, we're all going for a ride round the pond, down to the church and back."

"Is that all right with Mrs. Peters?" David asked me, which nearly broke my heart.

"It's all right with *me*," I declared, figuring I might be gone tomorrow anyway.

Bertie almost cheered, "Lala says yes! Lala says yes. Get a horsie."

"Righto, my lads. If Lala says yes, that's it then," Chad said with a laugh and wink at me.

As he started away toward the stables, he ruffled David's hair. It might have been the first time a man had touched him playfully.

The corners of his mouth lifted in a hint of a smile.

I vowed I wouldn't go without a fight. New baby or not, these beaten and beaten-down boys were never going back to Mrs. Peters. And for an hour or so, I was going to love them and be with Chad, even if it was the last day I ever spent at Sandring-ham.

CHAPTER 4

"I'd best get back in case they need me," I told Chad as we rode on our second loop toward York Cottage. Bertie was on my lap, and David held on to me, standing. I knew why. All the times I'd seen Mrs. Peters pat or rub his bum — was it a reminder of a previous beating, of her warped "love" and power over him? I dared not think it could be more, that she had abused him in other ways.

Despite Chad's banter with the boys and the sunshine on my face, my stomach was still in knots from what I'd seen and done today — and what must be next to come. Would I be sacked before I even saw the new infant, one who was to be in my care and I'd been so excited about tending?

"So, Master David and Master Bertie," Chad was saying, "are you hoping you will be blessed with a brother or a sister?"

"We don't have a sister," David whispered,

as if that were some sort of secret. "I say a sister, so she won't ride my rocking horse. Bertie wants to, but he's too small unless Lala holds him."

"Unless Lala holds him," Chad echoed and shot a smile my way. "Sounds worth the rocking ride to me."

He was flirting with me and didn't know his timing was terrible. Could he not tell I was distraught? Besides, one of the rules for women in service was no followers at the door, taking one's mind off one's duties. I only assumed Chad Reaver wasn't wed or at least betrothed. If I were a village girl, I would set my cap for him.

"Carriage coming from behind," he said before he even looked back on the road. "Lady Dugdale's been sent for to attend the duchess, and the regular house driver's gone to fetch her. I heard her train come in. Next time we'll ride to watch the trains come in, eh, lads? Meanwhile, you, Miss Charlotte Bill, were honored to have me and a coal wagon when you arrived."

"Lady Dugdale interviewed me in London and hired me for the duchess, and I liked her very much. Chad, will he let her off at the front door? I need a quick word with her."

"Probably not the best of times, but I

hope not the worst. Righto, we can draw up there when she does."

I'd been agonizing over whom to go through to tell the Yorks that Mrs. Peters was abusing the boys. I'd considered Mrs. Wentworth or my friend Rose, though I didn't feel it was fair to put them in the middle of this. I dared not try to face the duke, but I wasn't giving these boys back into that horrid woman's care. And I wanted to keep my post here.

Chad pulled us round near the front steps as a fine-looking landau with its top thrown back arrived. Lady Dugdale and a woman who must be her lady's maid sat inside. Despite wearing a brimmed bonnet, her ladyship held a parasol against the late April sun. And here I was in a nurse's plain gray linen day dress and white apron with no coat or bonnet since I'd grabbed the boys and come out so quickly.

Still, I knew this was my best chance to have an ally, an influential one with the duchess, one who had once recommended me. It seemed she was a gift from heaven.

"Boys, you sit here with Chad and be very good," I told them but my voice wavered as Chad gave me a hand down. On shaky legs I walked to the carriage and curtsied.

Eva Dugdale was petite and pretty but,

I'd heard, a formidable force in the Duchess of York's life with the title lady-in-waiting, however much she came and went. I'd been told by the maid at the London home where I had been sent for an interview that her ladyship was the only daughter of the 4th Earl of Warwick and had been reared in a castle, no less. She was wed to a great friend of the duke's, but she and the duchess had known each other for years. Their mothers were good friends, and they had played together as girls. She had seemed kind to me when she had hired me for the York household, and I silently prayed she could help me now.

"Why, it's Miss Bill with the boys," she said as she was helped down from the carriage by a York Cottage footman. "Good to get them out with all that's going on inside. I hope I'm in time. Any news yet?"

"Not when I brought David and Bertie out, milady. I know you are sent for but, please, just a quick word with you."

"Aren't things going well? You look distressed."

"Milady, have the duke and duchess told you how David bursts into tears when taken to them at teatime? How Bertie's always jumpy and scared . . . and hungry?"

"Something about the boys? Come over

here," she said and led me a few steps away from her maid and the pile of her luggage the driver and footman were unloading under the watchful eye of the house butler. She squinted toward the wagon. "They're not ill?"

"Milady, their head nurse, Mrs. Peters, is not well . . . in her mind. She's been mistreating them, tormenting David and ignoring Bertie, even not feeding him regular, I fear. She kept me at arm's length and tried to browbeat me, but she did beat David. I saw it today, and she seemed quite demented. He's black and blue, has bruises I'd seen before, but she told me he fell. Please, can you help me protect the lads from her? I brought them outside in a rush but —"

She reached out to squeeze my clasped hands with her gloved one. "Oh, no. I found her for them too, and they've had such trouble with nurses. They . . . surely, they must not know about this."

I shook my head, thinking *Surely, they should know* but I said only, "Mrs. Peters had the boys scared to death and the staff afraid to make a peep."

"But you, brave girl, have done so. The timing's dreadful, but I know how they are," she said with a quick sideways glance at York

55

Cottage. "Busy, wrapped up in duties, even each other. But this must be kept quiet at all costs. You may have to explain it to them when the happy news of the baby is over. For now, I'll take care of this, and you take care of the lads. I must go in now. Stay out a few minutes more, give me time to clear things for you to watch them and get Peters away. I must go in now," she repeated.

Worry lines etched her face. Tears gilded her eyes. She still held my hand, which she squeezed again before moving away. She stopped at Chad's wagon and reached up to pat both of the boys' hands that gripped the wooden sides. They had twisted around as if to not let me out of their sight.

"David, dear, how are you?" her voice floated to me as I followed her over. "Do you like Miss Bill?" she asked with a nod my way.

"We call her Lala," he told her solemnly in his thin, high voice. "She won't let anyone hurt me, ever again."

"Lala she nice," Bertie chimed in. "I hungry."

"And I shall see that you have some good food sent to the nursery in a few moments," she told them. "Lala can eat with you, and I don't think Mrs. Peters will be back. Would that be quite all right?"

56

Bertie nodded so hard I thought he'd hurt his neck. David, bless him, told her, "When Mama is better, I want to tell her Mrs. Peters is naughty, not me."

Lady Dugdale looked back at me, nodded, then marched up the steps and in the front door the butler was holding open.

Less than an hour later, I sat with David and Bertie in the day nursery eating our generous tea of biscuits, jam, porridge, milk — tea for me — and, to the delight of the boys, rice pudding. We halted our chatter at a knock on the door.

"Please come in!" I called out, not wanting to copy Nurse Peters's brusque "Enter!"

Mrs. Wentworth popped her head in. "Lady Dugdale said to tell you and the lads that they have a baby sister named Mary. All is well. And the duke himself may drop by. Busy now, all of us," she said and was gone.

"See, you both have been blessed with the sister you wanted," I told them with a little pat on both their heads. David had scooted his chair so close to me I kept bumping him with my elbow. He was sitting on a down pillow and seemed taller than usual. Bertie had not stopped eating, so what I had sadly surmised must have been true: the child had been ill fed, and maybe some days not at all, because Mrs. Peters had been so possessive and obsessed with David.

I couldn't fathom the duke might make an appearance here, but I rose to fold and put away my clothes that had been delivered while Mrs. Peters's goods had been hastily taken out. I shoved my half-empty box under the bed I would now sleep in until a new head nurse was hired. I had hopes I was to stay and tend to baby Mary.

I sang the boys nursery rhymes I'd learned at Dr. Lockwood's house, to tunes I made up on my own, but I carefully avoided "Rock-a-bye Baby" this time. When there came a sharp *rap, rap, rap* on the door, I bounced up and both lads came to attention as if they recognized the knock, David standing, Bertie stopping after three muffins, which I should not have permitted, but I felt so for what he'd been through. Time enough to establish my own timetable and rules for them, until another head nurse arrived.

In case it was the duke, I hurried to the door, for no shout to enter would do.

Indeed I opened the door on him and dropped a curtsy. "We are honored to have your father here, boys. Bid him a good evening."

David parroted, "Good evening," and Bertie, his mouth still full, managed "Good."

Despite the momentous news of the new baby, the duke still stood stiff and stern. He took only one step inside. "You two have a sister now, and I'll expect you to help your new nurse to take good care of her."

"Yes, Papa," David said. "I wanted a sister — Bertie too, because we don't have one."

The duke almost smiled at that. "Well, there's some news. Mrs. Lala," he said, turning to me, "I hear we've had some rough seas, but you acted decisively, as you should."

"Yes, Your Grace."

"Well, you'll need help keeping things shipshape here with the new baby and the boys. But a new undernurse, two nurse-maids, and a nursery footman will help. You will help, too, won't you, lads?"

David managed a proper "Yes, sir," and Bertie, with his jam-smeared mouth that I should have wiped, nodded.

"I'm pleased to have peace and quiet here," the duke said and started out.

I could hardly find my voice. He'd called me Mrs. Lala! Good gracious, he must have meant I was to be the head nurse for all three children. I felt tongue-tied at the mere thought.

"Ah," he said, turning back in the hallway. "Lady Dugdale mentioned your father captains a launch on the Thames, Mrs. Lala."

"Yes, sir. A small boat for hire, and I loved going out on it."

"Then you know something of seafaring discipline, so be certain these lads learn that. They will both eventually follow me into the Royal Navy, the best in the world for building men and the empire. Good night, sons. As soon as they're tucked up, Mrs. Lala, best leave them with a nursemaid and come to the duchess's bedroom to have a peek at the baby. The doctor's here for the night, after which you will take over."

I was hoping he would hug his sons or at least ruffle their hair the way Chad had, but his visit and his words would have to be enough. And so was I truly, at age — well, after all I was twenty-two! — to be head nurse to three royal children.

In the duchess's bedroom, the duke and doctor were not in sight. It was such a beautiful room in lavender and pale yellow, which made its modest size seem larger. A flower-patterned carpet was soft underfoot. The silk, tasseled drapes were closed. Family photographs crowded the dressing table.

Lady Dugdale sat in an upholstered beige silk chair near the large, canopied bed. Her slippered feet rested on an ottoman. Rose busied herself in the far corner, though she shot me a nod and a smile. And, there it was, a white, frilly bassinette next to the bed. I came closer and curtsied.

Lady Dugdale saw me and stood. She bent over the duchess who had her eyes closed. She looked pale and wan but somehow radiant — or at the least, relieved.

"Baby Mary's nurse is here, dear," Lady Dugdale told her friend. "I believe the boys have dubbed her Lala."

The duchess's eyes fluttered open. "Come closer, Mrs. Lala." Her voice was hoarse and soft.

I did and bobbed her another curtsy. "Congratulations on your first daughter, Your Grace," I told her. I glanced toward the bassinette but couldn't see inside.

"And last daughter, perhaps last child," the duchess said with a deep sigh. "On top of the heir and the spare, yes, Eva?"

Lady Dugdale patted her hand, then held it, even as she had mine when I was distressed. Indeed, I knew childbirth was a terrible trial. I'd heard my own mother scream for hours, even curse in the pain of it. But once it was over, I thought the joy of it would cover all of that. Well, what did I know of it, virgin and caretaker of others' babes?

"Take a look at your new charge," the duchess said, turning her head toward the bassinette. "The doctor will give her over to your care soon, tomorrow, I think, though I've quite lost track of time. Say hello to Victoria Alexandra Mary, to be called Mary, my mother's namesake."

The infant was swathed in white satin and lace with only a pink face visible, crowned by a touch of hair so blond it looked white, but then many infants were born blond and went to brown. I could see no more of her, but I would, this precious bundle. She opened her little eyes — cornflower blue — to blink once at me before seeming to sleep instantly again.

"Oh, she's so lovely," I whispered. "David and Bertie will be in awe."

"Best they — and you — have a last good night's sleep," Lady Dugdale said. "The doctor may have a word with you, but he and the duke are at cigars and celebration drinks right now. And, oh yes, the proud grandparents from the Big House will be here tomorrow afternoon to see her, so best be ready for that."

"Yes, milady. Thank you," I said and curtsied again.

"And, Charlotte . . . Lala," Lady Dugdale said, "the duke and duchess are grateful that you have taken good care of their sons. Your concern for David and Bertie is well noted. And I must tell you what the upper and downstairs staff have already been told by Mrs. Wentworth. Mrs. Peters has become very ill. She has been taken away to get the care she needs. So that will be all for now — as that is quite enough for one day."

With a last glance at the new child someday destined to be a princess, I walked away, but I could have soared.

CHAPTER 5

Things were happening too fast, but surely nothing could go wrong now. At least, that is what I kept telling myself the next day. And I was to take the three children, all washed and dressed up, to meet their grandparents, the Prince and Princess of Wales, downstairs straightaway.

My only worry was that since David was now sure that Mrs. Peters had gone away for good, he had turned into a bit of a terror, riding his rocking horse wildly, shouting and bossing Bertie. I could tell he resented my carrying baby Mary about. Setting down strict rules and regulations was of immediate necessity, lest he think punishment of some sort was a thing of the past. Yet how I wished I could give both boys a little holiday from all they'd been through. I reckoned I'd also be giddy with glee to have escaped Mrs. Peters's clutches.

"David, keep your voice down and don't

muss that new sailor suit. We do not want your grandparents to hear you shouting right through the padded door and clear down the stairs."

"I call them Grannie and Grandpapa," he told me, fidgeting with his starched collar and coming over to pat the baby a little too hard on the head, through her frilly bonnet. We were awaiting the summons to take her and the lads down into the drawing room.

"Gently, gently with the baby," I told him. "And remember, it's not good for any of you to be crying when we see your father, so don't you get little Mary all stirred up."

That mere reminder seemed to settle him, though I hated to invoke the ghost of Nurse Peters. He needed to learn discipline from within — on that much, I'm sure, I agreed with his father. A naval career and making a man of him were the farthest things from my mind. Secretly, I was overjoyed this new child was a girl, because I had no doubt that these lads would too soon have a male tutor, their own valet, and be reared quite away from the nursery. With a girl, it was always different.

I was appalled that, the minute I entered the drawing room with the three children, David vaulted past his father and threw his arms around his grandfather's knees. The duchess wasn't present but the duke frowned and cleared his throat as if that would calm David. Still holding Mary, whom I intended to hand to his grandmother, Alexandra, Princess of Wales, I cringed. But, evidently to the duke's chagrin and my relief, the Prince of Wales, a huge man, picked the boy up and hugged him close.

"Oh, my," Princess Alexandra said, "I hope that didn't startle the baby. David, my dear, you are not one of those wild Indians that Buffalo Bill's show brought to London and paraded through the streets, you know."

"Yes, Grannie."

"Oh, let the boy be," Prince Albert said and bounced him hard. "He's glad to see his grandpapa, aren't you, my lad? High spirits, that's all. But let's have a look at your new sister. And there's my Bertie boy, eh?" he said and sat on the chintz sofa so he could lift Bertie up, one of them on each knee.

"Sit, Mother dearest," the duke said, "and let Mrs. Lala hand you the baby."

I managed a curtsy and bent to give Mary to Princess Alexandra. The little mite, praise the Lord, looked alert and was not crying. She even waved a tiny fist as if in greeting, for I had decided not to wrap her arms close to her body. I'd even given her a little kick-about time on a blanket upstairs. Now I arranged the child's voluminous wrappings and stepped back, relieved to watch what could be a normal family, oohing and aahing over their new addition.

The prince said, "A beauty, just like you, Alix."

Princess Alexandra said to the baby's hovering father, "Oh, my boy, I think this child resembles you more than she does May."

I didn't think the little mite looked like anyone but herself so far. Truly, babies don't, though everyone says so. I stepped farther away. This drawing room, which I had not been in, bespoke wealth but not royalty with its stuffed, flower-design, chintz-covered furniture and numerous bibelots and framed photographs, patterned carpet, big roses wallpaper and a huge looking glass over the crowded mantel.

Oh, how I admired Prince Albert for his good cheer and open affection for the boys, even though he paid the baby little heed. And Princess Alexandra, whom the prince called Alix, was as lovely as the sketches I'd seen in gazettes at Dr. Lockwood's, but even more regal and elegant in the flesh.

Now in her fifties, she wore her dark hair, which looked to be woven with silver threads, swept up but fringed across her forehead, in a poodle style. She seemed grand even in her peacock satin day dress and three strands of big pearls clasped close around her long neck — a swan neck was how I'd heard it described. She seemed especially graceful and slender next to her big bear of a husband. Yes, I thought, the swan and the bear. I tried to study the scalloped inserts and tucked cotton roses on her embroidered lace inset bodice, because I knew Rose would quiz me about the gown the princess wore. Before I knew Rose, I would have just said she was in a pretty blue dress.

At least Duke George had calmed down, but what choice did he have since his parents were so entranced with his children? If only he could show some of the warmth they showered on them. He did look proud at least, when, in truth, the duchess had done all the hard work.

I wondered if I should step out into the hall to give them privacy but I stayed mute, blended with the walnut-paneled door, until the princess looked my way. "The new nurse's name again?" she asked her son, none too quietly. Did all three of these royals bellow?

"Charlotte Bill, Mother dearest, but the lads have dubbed her Lala."

"Oh," she said, smiling at me and talking loud enough that little Mary began to fuss, "like a stanza in a song. Mrs. Lala, the baby's great-grandmother Queen Victoria would like to see her soon, so we'll all be heading for London when the duchess can travel, but the christening will be here on the grounds at St. Mary Magdalene. We'll bring in the Archbishop of York — so appropriate, isn't it, George?"

"Yes, very good, Mother dearest."

He really called her that? I marveled. Each and every time he addressed her?

"Very good, Your Royal Highness," I told her and went over to lift the child from her lap, but my heart was beating hard. Not only to be so close to the Waleses, but to think I might catch a glimpse of the queen. "We will be eager and ready for that, won't we, David and Bertie?"

Bertie nodded, mumbling something about jam tarts. David, thank heavens, politely informed me, "Great-grandmother, the queen, we call her Gangan."

"And," the prince puts in, "she likes that name, Mrs. Lala, so don't scold them for that."

"Yes, Your Royal Highness. I shall scold them as little as possible but try to keep them, as His Grace, their father, says, ship-shape."

I don't know if I had dared to say more than I should, but the duke nodded and managed to pry David from his grandfather's knee. He turned Bertie about to head him toward the door after me.

"And you just bring all three of them to see us at the Big House tomorrow for tea," the princess called after me. "George, you too, if you wish, though it will be a bit too early for their mother to be going out."

"I may have to send Eva Dugdale over with them as I have business with some of the estate staff."

I realized that all three of the adults had been intentionally raising their voices. The duke often shouted, as if giving orders, but why did the princess too? Perhaps she or the prince were hard of hearing. My grandmother had been. Yes, I recalled Princess Alexandra had cupped her hand behind her ear before she held the baby.

As I went out, the butler and a footman were carrying in silver trays with tea and little sponge cakes and raspberry scones, so I was grateful Bertie was too short to see all that. "Come on then," I told them, being mindful of my long skirts as I climbed the front stairs with Mary held close. "David, take Bertie's hand since I can't right now, and we'll have our tea upstairs."

"Rice pudding?" Bertie asked.

"I think that was special just for yesterday," I told him.

"Because Mrs. Peters left," David said. "And she's going to the same place some lady named Mrs. Mordant got locked up for going to the fair with Grandpapa."

It took me a moment to unscramble what the child must have overheard, and I couldn't hold back a gasp. Not "going to the fair," but "having an affair"? I blushed to think what might have happened if he'd blurted that out back in the drawing room. Rose had said that for years Princess Alexandra had bravely borne her husband's marital infidelities. And, I'd heard, his longtime mistress was named Daisy Warwick, and, I figured, she must be sister-in-law to Eva Dugdale, who was sister to Daisy's cuckolded husband. I'd only meant to concentrate on the children here but the adults came with tangled strings attached.

"Who did you hear say all that about Mrs. Mordant?" I asked David as we reached the second floor.

"Nursemaid Jane. She said so to Nursemaid Martha," he told me, his voice almost belligerent.

So I now had to put a stopper in three mouths, and one of them who would only be too happy to say bad things about Mrs. Peters and Lady Mordant. To his parents? Grandparents? The queen?

"We see Mama today?" Bertie asked as we passed the duchess's bedroom door.

"I bet we see her tomorrow. She's sleeping today."

"And that's what Mrs. Mordant did with Grandpapa," David declared. "Took a nap."

Oh, dear. At least the boy must have interpreted "gone to bed with" or "slept with" as took a nap. If I didn't want to cry, I could have laughed.

As we went through the green baize door into the back hallway, I hesitated to scold him, but how to explain that some things were not to be repeated, even if he didn't really understand? Mrs. Mordant was one of several women rumored to have had an affair with the prince, whom the gazettes liked to call "Edward the Caresser" for his dalliances, and that one, though some years ago, so I had heard, had nearly blown up in his face.

There had been a public divorce scandal between the Mordants, during which the prince had been named as one of her paramours. Indiscreet but not, at least, damning letters had been found by her husband from the prince. Worse, the woman had borne a baby not her husband's, for he had been away when it was conceived. She'd then been declared insane and had been locked away in a lunatic asylum ever since, so that must be the connection to Mrs. Peters being sent to one. David must have overheard that too, for I'd only told him she'd gone away, not that she had been committed.

Well, I had to talk to my two nursery maids about gossip, and David too, so it didn't pop up as teatime talk tomorrow on the very first day I was going to visit Sandringham House.

"No!" Rose cried with a gasp, wide-eyed when I told her what David had overheard. "He thought someone said, 'took a nap with her' instead of 'slept with her'?"

We had a giggle over that. Sometimes children said the funniest things, even though what David had overheard was no laughing matter.

"I'm afraid so, on top of 'he went to the fair' with Mrs. Mordant."

"Out of the mouths of babes indeed!" she

said as the two of us continued to stroll round the lake near York Cottage. "You know, I've heard Daisy Warwick dresses like a dream, but Mrs. Mordant didn't have an ounce of fashion sense, and the prince's new love, Mrs. Keppel, is even worse. Well, I've seen that, so she must have 'other things' than clothing in her corner. Which reminds me, Her Ladyship has given me a castoff gown of hers that she thinks is plain, but you would not believe it! I'll show it to you soon."

"Is it damaged?"

"She said it didn't quite look right over the Paris lingerie she likes now that her stomach hasn't quite gone down from bearing number three."

"Lingerie — what? A combination garment, you mean . . . underwear?"

"Charlotte, your isolation with the children does keep you behind the times with things! Lingerie is all *très* French right now, and you know that's where the latest ideas some from. At least when referring to ladies, you must learn to say lingerie and not underwear or combinations."

"Well, pardon me!"

But she was hardly listening. "Oh, it's all so beautiful, the layers of what the luscious gowns and negligees hide these days," she

74

went on, as if enraptured. "I mean, I know you dress the little ones in layers but not six or seven of them, I'll bet, from the satin vest and ribboned corset, silk faille camisole. You should see the princess's newest watered silk and Valenciennes lace knickers. Granted, you and your nursemaids have to change the children's clothes now and again, but I change the princess five to six times a day, from skin out — more if we're on one of the king's Saturday to Monday gatherings here."

"And you treasure every bit of those lace and silken things. No, just give me a good linen or polished cotton children's sailor suit to put on the boys," I teased and squeezed her arm.

As time went on, I grew to consider Rose a good friend. We laughed a lot and sometimes argued. I would have hated to lose Rose, and I missed her when the duchess traveled for long periods of time. I never knew why Rose took such a shine to me from the first — perhaps I was her fashion project. I knew she loved that I believed in her, that, in her head and in her sketchbook, she could create fine fashions, even if she never got to make them real.

When I had a serious sit-down with David,

he'd promised me no more talk about Mrs. Peters or his grandfather and someone named Mrs. Mordant. He was not to repeat things he overheard, except to me. And I gave what for to my two nursemaids, making them repeat, as if they were children too, "Little pitchers have big ears. I will not gossip around the children. Little pitchers . . ."

Yet I was still a bit nettled as Lady Dugdale walked ahead of me, holding David and Bertie's hands, and I carried the new baby toward massive Sandringham House. I reckon I would have gone in the side door, but milady took us round to the front, of course. I fought not to feel overwhelmed by my new duties, by a mere visit to grandparents, and by this massive house and tended grounds. Why, it could have swallowed York Cottage for lunch with its massive red and blond brick facades, gables, and numerous chimneys. Mind you, I'd been reared in a small house with one chimney, and right grateful we were for our single hearth on winter nights.

Chad had said this many-roomed mansion wasn't all there was to see. Out back, where I had not been yet, stretched the estate gardens, stables, kennels, a model farm and stud farm, where the prince's racing Thoroughbreds were housed in fine style. Chad had also described glasshouses for vegetables and flowers and a pheasantry he and his father tended where thousands of game birds were raised for estate hunting.

Lady Dugdale said, "Come on, then, Bertie, don't dawdle. Mrs. Lala can't carry you and Mary too. You know how your grandfather is about being on time. Mrs. Lala, have you heard he's set his clocks an hour ahead to save extra light at the end of the day for his shooting parties?"

"I did hear. And that Princess Alexandra is the only one who dares to be frequently late."

"Lala," David said, turning back toward me. "Do not repeat what we hear others say. You said so."

"So I did, David. We shall talk more about that later."

"Good luck with that," her ladyship said. "Each level of servants has its own grapevine, not to mention juicy tidbits always flying round among the uppers of dear England and all those between who read the gazette rags."

"Yes, milady."

I would have straightened David's sassing me out promptly, but not with Eva Dugdale here. I felt momentarily overwhelmed by the task facing me as head nurse to the innocent in my arms and her two older brothers who had been abused by that horrible woman. But I vowed to heal them, to help them be the very best they could be.

Still, I could not help feeling the weight of this big house that cast such a huge shadow. I took a last breath of sweet spring air before we approached the front door, which swept open as if by magic and in we went.

CHAPTER 6

"Bertie, don't touch," I told the boy as he grabbed a carved animal statue off Princess Alexandra's side table. I was fretful something would go wrong on my first visit to the Big House — and baby Mary's first visit too.

"Oh, that's quite all right," she told me. "They are allowed to play with the Fabergé agate collection."

I'd never heard of Fabergé or agate, but I was relieved. So far, I thought our visit to Sandringham House was going well. I'd noted from the first that the boys' grandparents seemed to work wonders with them, and I soon learned the prince was not the only fun-loving one. Alexandra let them play on the flowered carpet with her zoo of exquisite agate animals, which looked carved from many-hued, veined marble. She held the baby again while Eva had tea with them, and I took my tea with the boys at a smaller table set up near the unlit hearth. Bertie had an agate lion with him that zoomed around the jam tarts, and David, a ruffed grouse.

I must admit I kept one ear cocked to adult talk, which, I suppose, proved big pitchers had big ears too. David had already reminded me that I too, especially when I was with Rose, could be a gossip.

"And how is your *dear* sister-in-law, Daisy?" I heard the princess ask Lady Dugdale.

The boys chattered on but I froze. Among the Marlborough Set, as the intimates of the Waleses were dubbed, there was only one Daisy. The noble beauty had even inspired a song, *Daisy, Daisy, give me your answer, do. I'm half crazy all for the love of you.* But surely, Alexandra knew Daisy Warwick was the prince's longtime lover, his semi-official mistress, some said, though I'd overheard at York Cottage — and Rose had said it was true — that he preferred a woman named Alice Keppel now. So was it a fact that Princess Alexandra abided his paramours? But poor Eva, sister-in-law to Daisy, to be put in the middle of that.

"How kind of you to ask, Your Highness," Eva said, her voice calm and warm. "I believe she is quite busy between her duties at the castle and in London, where she'll be for the season, entertaining. She loves people and, I'm sure, would love to see you there."

"Yes," Alexandra said, not looking at her husband, but her tone was cutting and her voice, as usual, loud. "I heard she does love people. Alas, I may have some Danish relatives here to entertain on my own at that time."

The prince said not a word but lit a cigar and came over to tell the boys, "Line those beasts up for battle on the floor, and we'll have a little war."

To my amazement, the big man sat down on the carpet with them, and they maneuvered carved mice and ducks, partridge and grouse, elephants and other little pieces by someone with that French name I could not recall.

Even after the princess's salvo at Eva, which was, no doubt, intended for her husband, it was decided Eva would stay for a tour of the stud farm and I would walk the children back with a Sandringham housemaid who was just returning from her half-day free. We bid good-bye to the doting grandparents, and I was pleased that the maid turned out to be sister of my nursemaid Martha Butcher. I carried the baby, she held Bertie's hand, and David strode a few steps ahead of us.

"I didn't know," I told Mabel, "that Martha had a sister close by."

"We're from Slough, Mrs. Lala, both come to the estate the same time, her at the cottage, me at the Big House. I may be the youngest housemaid but I mean to rise high, be housekeeper someday. I mind my *p*'s and *q*'s and keep my eyes open, work hard, I do. Bothers me a bit, though," she confided, lowering her voice, "that if Their Highnesses pass by in the hall, we're to turn our faces to the wall and stay still — mostly never to be seen. That's one reason I'd like to be housekeeper, because she talks with the princess real regular. You — with the royal little ones and all — that's the way with you, isn't it?"

"Yes, I talk with Their Graces, especially their mother, about the children. But you have the downstairs folks for friends and I really don't, except for one. I feel caught between both worlds and not in either."

"Oh, Martha never thought of that."

"No, she wouldn't, since she's downstairs fetching and fixing things nearly as much as she is up with me in the nursery, and she sometimes takes her meals with them downstairs too."

"I know Nursemaid Martha," David, ever all ears, piped up as he came back to walk with us. "I'm going to show her and Nursemaid Jane this before I give it to Chad."

From under his coat, he produced the agate grouse.

"Oh!" Mabel cried. "I dust the big lot of those every morning, every bit of them!"

"David, stop!" I ordered, and we all stopped walking. "I did not see your grandmother give you that."

"No, but she has a lot of them. We can play with them, but we can't with all of Mama's collections."

"You cannot just take things without asking, even from someone who has a lot, even someone in your family. You can tell that those mean a great deal to her because she has so many."

"Too many. She gives me things. She loves me."

"Yes, she loves you, but because you love her too, you will not just take something that belongs to her, something she paid for or was given as a gift, something she likes. We need to march right back and give that to her, tell her you're sorry and will not do it again."

He stuck out his lower lip and frowned. Was he going to buck me on this? "It's for

Chad," he said, shooting me a hopeful look. "He likes birds, and you like him."

I was once again shocked the child was so perceptive. No simpleton, little David, though his learning to recognize alphabet letters and write his name seemed to bore him at times. "That has nothing to do with this," I told him. "I know he likes birds, ruffed grouse too. But what if you gave it to him and someone found out he had an agate grouse instead of the real kind he loves? What if they thought he went into the Big House and took it, even if you gave it to him? You see, we can't just take things we want, because something bad could happen to someone we care about."

"Don't tell Father."

"I won't if you do the right thing, but I can't promise you that your grannie or grandpapa won't tell him."

He heaved a huge sigh. "They won't. They're on my side," he insisted and turned back toward Sandringham, dragging his feet so badly I figured the footman Cranston would have a terrible time polishing the toes of his shoes. But since I needed to pick my battles with this boy, I decided to handle the thievery first, scuffed shoes later.

Back at the Big House — the side door this time — I sent Mabel ahead to fetch the butler to announce that we were back because David had something to say to his grandmother. In again we went. I was grateful that the princess came out into the hall without the others and — it was the first time I noticed she limped — walked to us. I gave David's shoulder a little shove and, head hanging, he shuffled toward her.

"Look at me, Edward Albert Christian George Andrew Patrick David," she told him in an unusual stentorian tone. "You will be a prince and a king someday, God willing, so chin up. Now, whatever is it, my boy?"

He looked up at her. I wished I could see his face. "Grannie, I made a mistake and had this animal with me when we left. Lala says bring it back right now. I didn't think you'd miss it."

She leaned over to take the finely carved little piece. "Mrs. Lala was right to make you return it. Someday, I will see that you have it back with some of the others, but your grannie loves that Fabergé collection. Are you sorry you took it?"

"Well, I know I should be, and I do love you dearly."

"I believe you have told me the truth. But I do not expect you to take things not yours, and not to keep secrets, not from those who love you. Someday, you will be given much, understand?"

His blond head nodded, though I doubt if he fathomed that final thought.

Tears shone in Alexandra's eyes as she stooped to hug the child. It was the first day I realized that David might have learned more from his grandfather than just how to have fun. The prince evidently took women who were not his and tried, at least, to keep it a secret, but if word got out, he bluffed or charmed his way out of trouble. It was also the first day I warned myself against being manipulated by this boy, who would some-day be king. And I realized too that I wasn't the only one who would like to have given that precious ruffed grouse to Chad.

About a week later, I found David had hid-den two other Fabergé animals, a horse and a stag, under his bed, tied to the slats with string so the maids wouldn't see or hit them when they dusted. Clever boy, devious too at almost age four, since he'd obviously managed to filch them at great risk to himself while Mrs. Peters still ruled the roost.

I know I should have marched him right to his father or to the Big House, but I talked to him again and made him sit in a corner during outside playtime for two days straight, one for each stolen — yes, I used that word to him — animal. So there he sat, hurt and upset, glaring at the wall with Martha watching him while I took Bertie and the baby outside. It was not a punishment, I told him, but a reminder. I hoped the lecture about to whom much is given much is expected — right out of the Bible too — somewhat sank in that wily little brain.

That day I found his other loot, I took Mary and Bertie over to the Big House and, at the side door, asked to see Mabel Butcher. She'd promised to keep quiet on what she knew of the first theft, and evidently had, since her chatty, cheeky sister said naught of it.

When Mabel came to the door in her black uniform with white starched apron and cap, I said, "Mabel, we didn't have much time to talk before, but I think we can be friends."

"Oh, yes, Mrs. Lala. Martha says you're firm, but real kind to her and the children, and much appreciated, especially after — after, you know — that other head nurse," she said with a glance at Bertie who was turning in circles to make himself dizzy on the grass near the rose garden.

"When you dust the agate animal collection," I told her, "I'd like you to put back two other animals David had, but I don't want you to take a chance getting caught with them yourself. Go fetch the housekeeper please now so I can explain to her where I found them and that David has sent them back. I ought to let David take his medicine for this, but he's been through a lot, and we're building from here. Will you help me? And please call me Charlotte when we are alone, or even Char. My sisters call me Char."

"Thank you, Miss Char. I would like to have a friend — besides my sister, I mean."

So that deed was done. David learned he could not misbehave or pull the wool over my eyes, however much I lavished affection on him and his siblings. I kept quite calm after that, until word came that we were to all go to London to attend the queen.

CHAPTER 7

Queen Victoria's Diamond Jubilee was celebrated in London and across the nation and empire on June 22, 1897. The Waleses and Yorks were attending the London festivities, but the children were not included, so we didn't budge from the estate. In West Newton village, I watched the fireworks over the fields with David, Bertie, the baby, and Chad, though I had to go in early because the baby squalled at the noise. Soon after, I tried not to look crestfallen when I learned we were being sent to join the queen at White Lodge in Richmond Park instead of Buckingham Palace, but who was I to wish such things?

It was the first time of many, I supposed, when I would oversee packing for three children, though the nursemaids did most of that work. Chad trundled the nursery household to the railway station in the estate's omnibus, while their parents, who

89

had come to collect us, rode in a carriage.

I hardly had time to say more than two words to Chad, whom I had enjoyed seeing off and on. He shook my hand good-bye, gave it a special squeeze, and saved a smile just for me. Rides about the estate on my afternoon off each week were the only times we really had together, and that scarce enough because he was often busy. So I sometimes spent the time with Rose or Mabel if we could coordinate our schedules.

But when he could manage it, Chad always found me, and we visited the beautiful sites of the area while he pointed out the coverts with nesting birds. He fretted much over the fact that ladies who visited Their Royal Highnesses here liked to collect the nest, eggs, then prick the shells and blow out their innards and display them under glass amongst other bric-a-brac. If they destroyed the nests, he had muttered, how was he to protect and tend the birds until the ladies' husbands could shoot them at one of the duke's or prince's Saturday to Monday parties?

On my first journey to London from Sandringham, I took both nursemaids, though we left our nursery footman, Cranston, behind and would use one of the queen's footmen there, since he would know the place. But a lodge instead of the palace? I knew not what we'd find.

I should have known the lodge would be a mansion. With its grand, exterior staircase and elevated pillars, portico, and porches, the three-storied White Lodge stood stunning in the brightness of the June sunshine. Set in a finely trimmed lawn, this was where David had been born, where Duchess May — named for the month of her birth — and her brothers had been reared and her mother, a first cousin to the queen, now lived as a near invalid. So we would have grandmothers galore to look pretty for and amuse — and behave for.

I'd heard that the queen hated the new modern advances like electric lights and telephones. Yet I could not wait for my first close glimpse of the woman who had been on England's throne for sixty years. How exhausted she must be after all her Diamond Jubilee appearances. I'd heard they tired her so she could not even walk up the steps of St. Paul's for the celebration, but the people on the program had come down to her while she sat in her carriage. I hoped that she was better.

To my surprise, when our three carriages pulled in after collecting us from Paddington Station, she was pushed out to meet us in a rolling chair. Was she a cripple now? A heavy woman in face and form, she was swathed in layers of black, despite the heat of the day. The way she squinted and searched faces, I could tell that her eyes were weak, but she had no trouble picking out her son's big form.

"Bertie," she clipped out to the prince before any sort of general greeting, "I believe I suggested to you that one of the new child's names should be Diamond for the occasion, even though you have used Victoria."

"I mentioned it to George and May, Mama. After all, they are the parents. But Victoria — Victoria Alexandra Mary — it is, and she's a charmer. We've got lots of Berties too. I'm sure you want to greet everyone, especially David and Bertie the third, before scolding me again."

Shocked by this good-natured man's flip tone with the queen — and her scolding of him — I pushed the boys forward. True, I'd heard no love was lost between the queen and her heir, that she and his long dead father, Albert, had despaired of their son's modern, decadent ways. Some even said the queen had blamed him for Prince Albert's early death because he'd caught his fatal malady traveling to undo a mess with a woman their son had gotten into at Oxford.

I blessed Princess Alexandra for stepping forward to hover over the boys, who greeted their "Gangan" just as I had made them practice. Duchess May took the baby from my arms to show her to the queen, who pronounced her pretty and well behaved.

"We'll have a photograph later," the queen declared. "The children and I, and the Prince of Wales, George, and his heir."

"That's me," I heard David say.

"Me too," Bertie blurted.

Well, I thought, I'd need to explain that to Bertie sooner than later. David would be king, and then it would be David's heir, not Bertie, on the throne. I prayed he would not only accept that but welcome it someday.

Later, I too was in a photograph with the queen, though no one could see me any more than they could the small Pomeranian dogs she favored that hid under her skirts. Her Majesty was so shaky that I crawled back behind her and supported little Mary on her arm so the old woman would not drop her.

I thought then of Mabel, who was bothered by having to keep out of sight of her betters, and my own awkward plight of having to blend into the woodwork at times.

So much I learned about the reality of royalty that first stay with the queen. I overheard she could not even read the royal dispatches anymore, unless drops of belladonna were put in her eyes to make her pupils huge. Princess Alexandra told the duchess that the queen's daughter Beatrice — not her heir, the prince — was like a secret secretary to her, reading her important papers when she could not. And it was true that the queen lived in the past with a room in each house she had sealed off and dedicated to her beloved Prince Albert, who had been dead for decades. So in a way, she was a prisoner to her place and her duty, just as were we all, princess to lady's maid to housemaid to game bird breeder to head nurse.

But I was to learn even more that December at Christmas celebrations in the Big House. The royals and the rich were indeed different from what I had known and imagined, even from my days at Dr. Lockwood's house. Prince Albert and Princess Alexandra were not a bit like his stern mother. I, who was used to rather plain Yuletide celebrations with my family, was astounded at the "normal, usual" vast and exuberant display for the holidays. Like a child, I stood agape at it all. My first Christmas at Sandringham House stunned me.

Mabel had said that the princess did up the presents herself — multiple ones for each relative and guest, all wrapped in pretty paper with satin ribbons. And she oversaw the decorations. Well, my parents had done all that too, but usually one gift apiece for us — often an orange or small wooden soldier, doll or top — and the decorations were as sparse as the feast. A roast goose and plum pudding were luxuries when I was a child.

But here, I vow, I was as excited as the children, and all this for just the family and about a dozen of their closest friends. In the very center of the ballroom stood the Christmas tree, a fir cut from the nearby forest that, I swear, was taller than the house I grew up in. It smelled of brisk wind and sharp pine, all mingled with the aroma of food and scented candles. The electric had been turned off so that the tree glowed. I could hardly believe it — swags of tinsel, hanging glass balls, pieces of cotton to imitate snow. Good gracious, it was magic — a fantasy beyond my dreams. I'd fear a fire, but what was there to fear when everything shone brighter than — as Mabel put it — "the star over Bethlehem."

Round the room, under the watchful eyes of ancient, painted people in gilt frames, were laid trestle tables covered with white linen cloths, laden with gifts and food. Bone china emblazoned with the Prince of Wales's three ostrich feathers shone, and silver tureens filled with steaming soups gleamed. I saw Mabel was right: the children must sit through dinner and much talk before they were to open their gifts. If that didn't teach discipline among all this bounty, nothing would.

Besides the roast goose — four of them — there was boiled turkey, oysters in wine sauce, and cod's shoulders. Jellied eels and molded aspics shimmered in candle glow. The children loved the mashed potatoes and macaroni, as did I. This was the first time I had eaten a meal in the same room with the adults, because I was to watch over the children's table in the corner. The grown-ups' laughter sounded over the clink of glassware and china. Now and then, David and Bertie were summoned to the dining tables, so I made sure they went straight there and came back — mostly to be shown off by their grandparents, not their parents.

As far as I could see, we had everything at our little table, including the fabulous desserts — but not, of course, the array of wines. It was a bit of a shock to have house servants waiting on us, and to see the huge array of forks and fingerbowls set before us, but the children must learn their manners — and I too.

"Bertie, do not get those jelly pastries all over," I told the squirming boy. "Gently wash your fingers in that little bowl of water. No, do not make waves, because —"

"Lala," David interrupted, but I half forgave him, for they were all on edge, "do you think a pedal motorcar could be hidden over there? One with a steering wheel and real tires? Can I peek under those table-cloths near the tree? I think there's room."

"You will find out soon, both of you. Can't you eat the way Bertie is? You haven't touched your turkey."

"I'm too excited."

When the gift giving began, thank heavens, their grandpapa decided the children should go first and soon both boys were pedaling little motorcars around the ballroom while I kept an eye on them. Baby Mary was with Jane, but when she was brought in to let her mother hold her, she was given a silver rattle to shake and a baby doll nearly as big as she was. I had already been given gifts, a fur muff and a crisp ten-pound note, which would greatly supplement my thirty-five-pound-a-year salary.

But my eyes grew as wide as the children's when I saw the adults of the so-called Marlborough House set open their gifts to each other: watercolors, gilt or silver cigarette cases, cigar humidors, a jeweled inkstand, collars for the pet dogs, gold picture frames with family photographs, diamond pins and studs, and, of course, for Alexandra, agate animals. It seemed that these glorious people in their silks and satins and jewels glittered as much as the gifts and the tree. And to think, Mabel and Rose had both told me that more gifts would be given to the downstairs staff and estate workers in a week on New Year's Day, another time for celebration and a party.

But for me, among these glittering people who ruled the realm, a new year — a new life — had already begun.

CHAPTER 8

Three and a half years later, all seemed in chaos, not just the nursery. The queen had died on January 22, 1901. Since the twenty-third, yesterday morning, when the news had arrived, the entire York Cottage household had dressed in black garb, though the boys were still in their white flannel nightshirts this morning.

"Grandpapa is king, and Grannie is queen," little Mary said over and over. Her chatter annoyed David, I could tell. But truly, even in the best of times, he seemed to lord it over the other children. I wasn't certain if it was because he was firstborn or now knew he would be king someday — or because he wanted my attention all for himself.

"Which means," David interrupted before Mary could recite that again, "Papa will be Prince of Wales and Mama princess."

Mary asked, "What about me?"

He ignored her, so, as I tied a crepe bow in her hair to match her black dress, I whispered, "You are always special, Mistress Mary, quite contrary. Mama and Papa will explain later, but right now, they are in a rush to go to the Isle of Wight where Gangan died to help plan her funeral. There will be a kind of parade, a sad one, and a church service, things like that, in London."

"But I want to go too!" she cried. Though usually well behaved, she started to sob while David just rolled his eyes and Bertie became even more jumpy, something I'd worked hard to get out of him. But now I concentrated on comforting and shushing Mary.

York Cottage and the Big House had all the drapes drawn and edged with black. Even the village folk seemed draped in mourning. Earlier today, I'd seen Chad, with both arms black-banded, walk past and look up at the windows. I'd waved to him, but I don't think he saw me since the late January frost was so thick on the panes. I was in the sickroom where we'd kept David and Bertie while they had the measles, though they were well enough to be back in the nursery today. A crowded nursery it was, and I loved it, but that also was about to change, and I felt like wailing too.

All four children — David, now nearly seven; Bertie, at five; three-year-old Mary; and the new baby, Harry, nine months, formally dubbed Henry William Frederick Albert — were recovering from the German measles. I'd been told their grandfather had joked last week that they might as well have the German kind, since they were all related to more Germans — and Russians, and Danes, etcetera — than to British.

With tears in my eyes, I watched the children wave good-bye at the nursery window while their parents traveled in a closed carriage to the railway station and from there to London. It was bitter cold and snowing. In a few days, David and Bertie would go to Frogmore at Windsor for the queen's burial service, and we'd all be joining the family at Buck House, as they called it, after that. The coronation of the new king with all its pomp and planning was months away, scheduled for good weather in the summer. I wondered how much the queen's death would change the yearly routines of her heirs — and my life too, for I had come to accept the set pattern.

The royal York family I served was always together on the estate for Easter and Christmas, and the hunting season for the month of August — and any other time the prince or duke could bring a hunting party of friends here. During May and June, the social season, they were in London, but I was here with the children before the rest of the royal schedule took us far and wide: Frogmore at Windsor for the ten days of Ascot every year; autumn in Scotland at Abergeldie Castle near Balmoral, or York House at St. James's Palace in London; several weeks on the royal yacht *Victoria and Albert* each year, especially during August for the races at Cowes. Each place had suited the duke's schedule, but that might all be different now, especially if he were to be named Prince of Wales soon.

But there was another big change coming. Finch, the handsome, black-haired, and dark-eyed new footman who would soon take charge of David and Bertie, did his distinctive knock on the nursery door. "Come in, please, Finch," I called, and he entered.

Already, he had much more power than Cranston, who still fetched bathwater and most meals for the youngest Yorks. I knew Finch — Frederick was his given name — had been hired by their father and was being groomed to be David's valet. He was good at romping with them as he was strong and muscular, strict but good-humored, so I had no objection there. To top that off, all too soon, a male tutor and a French governess would arrive to teach the lads to whom I'd taught basic sums and writing. How fast these years had flown, but Victoria's death seemed to me the end of an era for my life as well as for England and the Empire.

"Back in bed, lads," Finch told them with a clap.

I say again it was difficult to get used to someone else bossing the boys. If they had not come down with the measles, I was sure Finch would have had permission to move them already to the new quarters he'd been preparing for them at the back of the hall.

When the boys lingered at the window, Finch said, "Your parents can't see you through the snow anyway today, and it's cold for boys who have been ailing to be standing at the window, eh, Mrs. Lala?"

"That's right," I said as I pulled Mary closer and bounced little Harry on my lap. "Back in bed, you two." At least Finch recognized my place with them, and I hoped that in the future the two of us could work together.

Once the boys were settled and I had tucked them up, Finch gestured me out into the hall, so I put Harry in the crib. The boys whispered to each other about going to London soon, while Mary looked through a picture book. She never had much to do with the lovely, painted, porcelain-faced dolls she had been given but seemed a bit of a tomboy, trying to keep up with her older brothers.

"Is everything all right?" I asked Finch when he closed the door behind us.

"Two things the duke — I mean our soon-to-be new prince — told me before they went. One, he thinks Bertie's looking knock-kneed and insists he wear iron splints to straighten his legs. He says you should order some sailor suits with wider trouser legs, because the splints will be ready soon. He'll sleep in them at night too. He won't have a knock-kneed sailor son someday, His Lordship said. And you're to sew up all the pockets in both boys' trousers so they don't stick their hands in them and slouch about."

Tears prickled my eyes. "Iron splints? Poor boy. And?"

"And he insists that the new tutor who's being brought in for the lads — and you since you taught them to read and write their *abc*'s — must force Bertie to write with his right hand, not his left."

"But I had a brother born left-handed. He could not do decent penmanship with his right. It fretted him something awful, and Bertie's delicate anyway. Good gracious, his little system never got over being fed so erratically by that woman, not to mention being locked in cabinets."

I had confided in Finch about Mrs. Peters, for somehow her ghost still stalked the halls. Neither lad ever spoke of her, but I swear David's combination of rebelliousness and clinging nature and Bertie's bad nerves and upset stomach were her dreadful legacy to them and to all of us.

"But the staff says you've done wonders with Bertie," Finch insisted.

"Which I don't want reversed."

"Well, his father has spoken, and that's that. No way to try to get his mother to weigh in, not a bit."

"No. Thank you for telling me. If you don't mind, I'll try to break it to Bertie — unless you feel you must."

"Let's try to explain it to him together. I know you have the day off — what's left of it, so tomorrow?"

"Yes, all right then. But my heart isn't in his wearing braces or the handwriting change, and he'll know it. I've always tried to tell them true."

"Time to stop coddling them, their father

says, you and their mother and grandmother too."

Nursemaid Martha approached, so I turned to her as Finch went on his way. She was probably thinking something about our whispering in the hall, for she had a soft spot for a handsome man. I could have told her, though, that Frederick Finch was dedicated to his career and to climbing higher in royal service. In short, an ambitious man, not an amorous one, and I thought the duke had chosen well with him.

"It's your afternoon free, Mrs. Lala," Martha reminded me. "Mrs. Wentworth said off you go — or just come down to her room since it's so cold out. But I see Mr. Chad Reaver's waiting for someone down by the frozen pond again, standing in the snow, he is."

"Thank you, Martha. I would never have seen this vast estate at all if it wasn't for his kindness, and he's always so busy during shooting and bird breeding seasons. By the way, I hope Mabel won't be going to London with the new king and queen. We've become fast friends, and I would greatly miss her. And, of course, Rose has gone with the duchess."

"Mabel's to stay here, keep Sandringham House proper for them, got raised to head housemaid, she did, because hear tell they took the other to Buckingham Palace. The prince — I mean the king — says they'll be back often as they can. Right now she's helping sheet the furniture in all the rooms. And guess what else?" she said lowering her voice. "The Big House is to have thirty flush lavatories installed by the Thomas Crapper Company while they're away. Mabel's to oversee all that."

"I tell you, we could use just one of those for the nursery, right, instead of the children doing their business in ceramic pots and you and Jane having to carry the night soil away. Well, maybe someday."

I talked Mary out of wanting to go with me, grabbed my coat, hat, and gloves, and left Martha in charge of the children. I hurried down the side stairs. Out I went into the cold, squinting into the swirling wind toward the iced-over pond, where Chad waited. The mere sight of him, trudging through the snow to meet me, warmed me. I had to admit to myself, if things had only been different . . . I not in service . . . dedicated to the children . . .

I could tell he wanted to kiss me but he did not. We had been affectionate to each other lately, holding hands, some quick good-bye hugs, but no displays of affection in such a public place as now. Oh, in private we had kissed on the lips, and I had loved that — felt it clear down into the depths of my belly, so that was something amazing and frightening too. After all, marriage or a physical union between us was impossible in our positions, however much I had moments where I wanted to throw caution to the winds. If we petted or kissed, it was in the woods or by the breeding bird pens.

"Thought we'd go to the glasshouse with all the flowers today," he said. "They have to keep it warm in there."

"So many important things are happening now the queen is gone," I told him, letting him take my gloved hand in his as we headed past York Cottage and along the side of the Big House. Through our layers of gloves, I could still feel the heat of him. "Just think," I rattled on, "she's been in mourning for years since she lost her Albert, and now, far and wide, the mourning is all for her."

"I'm sure she would have given anything to have him back — given up the whole kit and caboodle. Best not to waste time when one's in love, eh?"

"But I'm not sure she'd have given up her kingdom to have him back," I argued. "There's something to be said for loyalty to duty. I'm sure she felt the nation and empire needed her."

We stepped into the glasshouse with its warm, moist air. It smelled fresh and heady in here, the soil, things growing and blooming, and how I yearned for spring. I had to admit to myself at least, though it was exciting to visit new places, my favorite was Sandringham, and mostly because of this man. I did care for him deeply — yes, secretly loved him, wanted him as I knew he did me, so I was grateful he'd usually been restrained. I trusted him.

We stopped in an aisle of flowering bushes by two gardenia plants in pretty porcelain pots that looked ready to be moved indoors. The sweet smell was almost overwhelming. Chad seemed nervous, so unlike him.

"I have something for you," he told me, taking his knitted gloves off and throwing them amidst the pots.

"But you gave me these lovely leather gloves for Christmas."

"It's a picture of the fens and the forest all made from bird feathers sewn down on stretched linen," he told me before he even drew it from behind the pots and showed it to me with a flourish. It was in a narrow oak frame and covered with a piece of glass.

"Oh, it's beautiful. It shimmers in the

light. You . . . you didn't make it, did you?"

"My gran made it and several others before she died. This one is mine."

"How kind . . . how special it is, but I can't take it from you then."

"I was thinking we could share it, find a place in common to hang it." He took it back from me, put it down, pulled my gloves off and seized both my hands. My insides twisted in a knot, and I began to flush. "Charlotte, I know we haven't talked of this . . . couldn't really 'til now, but now is our time. You said the royal lads will be moving on to that new Mr. Finch. You've helped make Lady Mary the fine lass she is, and little Harry's so young, he'd adapt. You've served Their Graces well these last four years, but don't you want a life of your own, children of your own?"

I was so stunned that I just stared at him. I sensed what was coming, but it could not be. Oh, yes, I longed for a family of my own and, God knows, I cared for him, but he knew I couldn't leave the children and marry him . . . didn't he? Doing both would never work, wouldn't be allowed. I had thought that was unspoken between us. I'd even told him my parents needed the small amount of money I sent them twice a year.

"Charlotte, tell me you'll think about it

when they're away. Chad and Charlotte Reaver — sounds right, doesn't it? Mayhap for a while, before we have our own family, you could still work at Sandringham House or York Cottage, with the new head nurse in some way, and —"

"Wait . . . wait. I — This is all too fast. I've only met your father once, and you've never met mine — my family. And, I — You know I can't . . . we can't! The children still need me."

"But we're not children, my love. I'm twenty-six, and you soon will be too. Getting on, both of us, and you'd be such a good mother. I said, don't you want children of your own?"

"Yes, yes, I would love that, but I have them in a way. I couldn't just leave, even to live elsewhere on the estate. I've promised to tend them — duty, as I said."

"It's that new, handsome footman Finch, isn't it?" he demanded, dropping my hands. "Better taught, proper ways, more to your liking."

"No, it isn't Finch. I'd be out of there on my ear if I took up with one of the staff."

"Oh, I don't know. The duke and duchess think the world of you, and you told me you thought Finch and you could work to-gether."

"Yes, I hope so, but I didn't mean aught else by it. I said the children still need me, Finch or not, and however much the duchess doesn't like childbearing, there may be others to come."

"Are you afraid to have children of your own, because it's been hard for her and she detests birthing?"

"No, no, it isn't that. It's just that —"

"Duty is fine, but you are throwing your life away on children that are not yours, when you could have your own . . . with me!"

Tears blinded me. I swiped away a sheen of them from my cheeks when I hadn't realized I was crying. "Please understand, Chad. My whole life has led up to —"

"To leading me on! To want you. To hope for you. You'll regret this."

"Of course, I'll regret it, but I didn't mean to lead you on. You know your position — and you know mine."

"Damn it, you're choosing wealthy, coddled children — who have all the benefits in the world already — over me and the children we could have!"

"No, I'm choosing them over myself! Over what I want, would love to do, to be your wife and bear your babies. I must choose the children, at least for now, for today with all they've been through and have yet to face with their father the way he is. He's going to put braces on Bertie and force him to write right-handed. David has problems, and Mary would be so alone without me. Can't we talk about this tomorrow, and —"

"There won't be a tomorrow for us. What about all I've been through, waiting, biding my time, curse it . . . and curse you!"

He seized my shoulder in an iron grip and shook me once. "Charlotte Bill, one more time. Here's my asking you to wed with me. I love you, have since I first laid eyes on you, standing on the Wolferton railway platform, looking round for me to fetch you. That's what I meant to say at first just now before we argued. But if you don't see things like me, won't even give it a chance, there's a girl I've been putting off in the village, and I won't waste more time."

"A great honor but please understand, though I love you too —"

"That's a lie! I get the picture — and," he said, shoving me back, then lifting the feather picture and pressing it against my breasts so I had to take it, "you get this one. I waited nearly four years to speak, and that's long enough. I swear, you'll mourn this too, and it will come back to haunt you! I wish you well, then, Mrs. Lala."

I stood stunned as he turned around and stalked out. The words "Chad! Wait!" died in my throat. So there I stood in the jungle of flowering, fragrant plants with sleet tapping on the glass ceiling above me, sobbing.

CHAPTER 9

After that, I felt fragile — and haunted by his yelling at me and cursing me. I wrapped and put the feather picture away because I couldn't bear to look at it. I couldn't sleep and was short with the children as if I blamed them. Funny how controlled, calm Chad was really as deep and strong as the sea, and I hadn't known it.

For days, after Queen Victoria was memorialized and buried, until the new king and queen sent for us to come to Buckingham Palace, nothing moved me, mired as I was in private despair no one knew about but Mabel. I think the others believed I was mourning the queen or sad to have the older boys soon leaving my care. Oh, how I wished Rose was here, but she would have probably just tried to distract me by carrying on about how Duchess May had ordered black mourning lingerie for herself and little Mary.

But blast that man, Chadwick Reaver! I felt guilty each time Finch and I put our heads together about the boys. It had been decided — not by me — that when we returned from London, Finch would take over the care of David and Bertie. The perfect time, Chad had said, to make a break, but what was broken was my heart. Why had I not seen that friendly, proper Chad would want me for his wife? And had I made the wrong choice, the mistake of my life? I doubted myself, hated myself at times.

"This is a great place to run around in," David told us as our carriage pulled into the central quadrangle of the London palace the family called Buck House. "Now that he's king, Grandpapa will let us run in our stockings and slide on the long floors, I'll bet. Lala, why is he to be called King Edward when he was Prince Albert and called Bertie his whole life?"

Finch, sitting across the carriage with Bertie answered for me. That would have annoyed me before, but now he might as well assert himself with them. It was going to be an emotional separation and transition even though the boys would be just down the hall and I could see them daily. But it horrified me that my separation from

Chad — and the way we'd parted — was much, much harder. Yet I kept telling myself, these children need me more — in a different way at least, of course, they did.

"Because," Finch answered David, "a new king is allowed to choose the name he wants, and that's the one he likes."

"So he likes it better than his own father's name, Queen Victoria's Prince Albert, who died a long time ago?" David pursued.

"Let's just say this," Finch said. "So listen to me, you lads, and Lady Mary too. When a new king comes in, there are bound to be lots of changes. That's it."

I was glad Finch hadn't told the boys how much the new king resented his father's bullying and scolding. Too close to home for them.

On the ground floor of the palace, I tried to herd the children toward the large room we'd been given as a nursery on our other visits, but the boys — with Mary right behind — headed straight for the sweeping, wing-shaped grand staircase I so admired, with its ornate, interlocking patterns of oak and laurel leaves. It gleamed gold, though it was made of polished bronze. Oh, yes, I knew their plan, even if Finch didn't.

I explained it fast to him. We let our helpers take little Harry and the luggage upstairs and tore after the children.

I heard David shout to his younger siblings, "The Big House at home has only three hundred sixty-five rooms, but this place has almost eight hundred. Grandpapa said so, and now he's king. Let's go!"

His voice echoed. The times I'd been here, I'd tried to give the children an attitude of respect toward the place, though I had obviously failed at that miserably. Well, how could I expect them to look at these vast rooms and priceless treasures the same way a Cockney girl would?

The staircase had always looked like a golden, glorious bird ready to take flight. But I didn't want David and Bertie to be hurt — or caught — sliding down the steep, twisting banister, and I had forbidden that before. With the old queen gone, they must think things had changed — and so, no doubt, they had.

"Will you look at that?" Finch called back to me when he caught sight of the ornate, two-sided, two-floored staircase. "And those huge paintings of people as if guarding it."

"Queen Victoria's relatives," I told him, out of breath.

"All right," Finch bellowed to the boys, "no horsing around on that, not today."

"Grandpapa will say it's all right!" David

challenged.

"Then you may ask him later," I argued, getting into the fray. With his splints on, poor Bertie couldn't even keep up with David on the crimson-carpeted staircase, so I seized Mary's hand and Finch ran to scoop up Bertie. We hustled all three of them up the stairs, for I knew another way to the nursery from there.

"Well, then," David said as we turned away from the balcony to head toward our rooms, "let's go run through the Marble Hall or visit the throne room. Bertie and I sat on and hid under the thrones before."

But as we heard the new king's voice boom out below, Finch put Bertie down and quieted David with a hand over his mouth. Holding Bertie's hand tightly and with an arm around Mary, I edged toward the banister overlooking the entryway below. Finch kept a hard hold of both of the boys' shoulders, I made sure of that, before we all looked over, expecting, I think, to wave at their grandpapa.

But the new king was addressing a group of twenty or so servants, maids, butlers, footmen, who had quickly assembled and stood at attention like soldiers in their mourning black. I noted Queen Victoria's silk-clad, exotic-looking, beloved servants from India, who, I'd heard, had often attended her, were nowhere in sight.

"I want this morgue cleaned up," the new king told them in a crisp voice that echoed to the ceiling under which we stood. David and Bertie both seemed to stiffen. Ah, I thought, this was a grandfather they didn't really know. Mary was wide-eyed, peeking over, listening to every word.

"I want everything out of that closed-up room of Prince Albert's the queen kept like a mausoleum," King Edward ordered. He might be yet uncrowned, I thought, but he was ruling indeed.

"Cartloads of photographs and bric-a-brac, his clothes, away! For heaven's sake, the man's been dead for forty years! We'll soon have more modern plumbing and an extended telephone system in here and storage for motorcars as well as those old carriages, but we need to start from the bottom up. The seepage of coal smoke in here over the years makes this entire place look like it's in mourning! The queen and I will be entertaining over the years, have guests in, and I don't mean for afternoon teas or garden parties. Formal dinners, card playing, dances. We may all be in deep mourning now, but we are going to live in the present for the future, not in the past. That's all.

Get busy with it, then."

He disappeared, and the staff scurried away in a flutter of footfalls and whispers that echoed. Finally, Finch loosed his hold on David.

"Lala," the boy whispered, "is there a mausoleum here? But that's where they buried Gangan at Frogmore."

"It means a place the living must not live in," I told him. "Finch will explain. Come on boys, Mary."

I led them to the Buck House nursery suite, which — who knew? — might yet see more royal children. Amidst the grandeur of the palace as I had at modest York Cottage, I told myself for the hundredth time that I'd done the right thing to turn Chad down. After all, he had blindsided me with his declaration of love and proposal of marriage. I was Mrs. Lala, and blessed to be so . . . wasn't I? And the times were indeed new with King Edward VII and the children's father next in line to the throne and David moved up even closer to that honor — that challenge and burden.

Oh, yes, new times were here, and I must embrace them instead of a man and children of my own.

■ ■ ■ ■

PART TWO

1901–1905
YORK COTTAGE TO SCOTLAND

■ ■ ■ ■

CHAPTER 10

Thursday, June 6, 1901
York Cottage, Sandringham Estate

Finch's distinctive warning knock sounded on the door of the day nursery. We had several we used, and this one usually spelled trouble. It meant Queen Alexandra was on her way from Sandringham House to York Cottage again to take over, and the staff who tended her grandchildren were at her mercy.

With the wet, squirming, six-month-old Harry in my arms, wrapped in a towel and fresh from his bath, I hurried to the door, even as extra raps resounded. I opened the door to find not only a frowning Finch but an irate Helene Bricka, the boys' new French and German tutor who had been their mother's longtime governess and friend.

"Who is with her?" I whispered to them with a glance back into the room at four-year-old Mary. She still madly rode David's old rocking horse, which he had finally outgrown.

"Her friend Lady Knollys," Helene told me, stepping in front of Finch, "but the king's coming too. For once I'm glad David keeps bobbing up from reciting his verbs because he spotted them coming across the lawn."

"So there goes any discipline and lessons," Finch added grimly.

"My problem is she'll want to bathe the baby," I said, bouncing little Harry whose blue eyes darted from one of us to the other, "and I've just done that. He'll get all puckered, and the water's dirty. I'll send Martha for more. I can't fathom five more months of this, but I do understand their loving these children. And I know they like to escape London to entertain here. His Majesty still refers to Buck House as a mausoleum."

"Hmph," the elderly woman sniffed. "Her Majesty simply could not wait to convince the king to ship our dear duke and duchess off on a world colonial tour so they could cause chaos with these children, and you know who gets blamed for that then! And, I tell you, it's the queen who talked the king out of naming my dear May and the duke as Prince and Princess of Wales yet. Meanwhile, we'll just see about those rowdy boys getting off from their lessons again. I would like to personally tell Their Majesties that David and Bertie are occupied."

Off the petite, stout woman went with her rolling gait that made her old-fashioned curls bounce and sway. I had not liked her at first, as she was so opinionated with liberal leanings, but her devotion to the children's mother was so strong that we were soon allies. From their steamship called the *Ophir*, Duchess May had promised to write her dear friend letters from most of the places they were scheduled to visit: Gibraltar, Australia, Malta, Egypt, Ceylon, Singapore, Australia, New Zealand, South Africa, and Canada.

But to be so long away from the children! Still, I think it was perhaps good for David and Bertie in a way. With their father gone, they did not have to face his dressing downs, and Bertie's stuttering was not as bad. Ever since his leg braces and his writing with his right hand — well, no time for that now. An invasion by the king and queen always took some doing.

Already I could hear David and Bertie whooping it up down the hall that Grandpapa had arrived. I rushed back into the nursery and dressed Harry so that the queen could get him undressed again. I had tried to tell her the first time she did this that the child had just had a bath, but she was not to be deterred. At least, why could she not warn us when one of her whims to visit was in the offing? I could hardly leave this baby unwashed each day just in case.

Martha came running in with two buckets to take the used water downstairs. "Are they heating more in the kitchen?" I asked her.

"Yes, Mrs. Lala. We saw them coming too. Cook's upset as she needs the stovetop for lunch, but we'll manage."

"Mary, off that horse for now," I told the girl. "Your grandmother is coming while your grandfather visits the boys."

"What if they have another doll for me?" Mary asked with a sigh.

"Then thank them very sincerely for it and add it to your collection. Do not say you would rather have a horse. And please straighten your bed a bit. I asked you not to bounce on it because of that time you hit your head on the wall."

She pouted but did as she was bid. In swept the assault of Queen Alexandra, looking as lovely as ever, followed by four of her pet pug dogs, which Duchess May could not abide for all their yipping. Behind her also came her loyal friend and bedchamber woman, Lady Knollys, who had the same first name I bore, Charlotte, though, like the others here, I had begun to think of myself as Lala these last years.

Chad had been the only one who had called me Charlotte, and he was lost — that is, lost to me. He had quickly wed a village woman named Millie Chambers. When the bells of St. Mary Magdalene tolled for their union, I walked alone to the glasshouse where Chad and I had parted and cried. It did no real good, to get all red-eyed and nasal, but I guess it helped a bit. I felt haunted by the soul-rending regret that his bride might have been me.

As for now, I knew Her Majesty did not like me hovering, so I stepped away, just as fresh, warm water arrived. For a few moments, I watched as she and Milady Knollys fussed over giving Harry his second bath. Thank heavens he loved to play in the water. When I saw the child was not upset, I stepped out and went down the hall into the room where the boys were tutored. I found the schoolroom empty but for a sputtering mad Helene Bricka and a pile of French and German primers on the table. Her students' chairs were thrown back in disarray, evidently from when the boys bolted for the door.

She frowned at me across the table. Poor woman. She had preferred to tutor girls like Duchess May when she was young, then children at a girls' school. Though Mlle. Bricka was much more European in her experiences and thinking than I would ever be, as our friendship had developed, I had begun to call her by her given name.

"I have written the duchess more than once," she muttered as I sat across the table, keeping an ear cocked for voices in the hall that might mean I should head back to the nursery. "But what can she do from the far reaches of the earth? And it galls me to no end, my girl, that George and May have not yet been named Prince and Princess of Wales. The queen's doing, I tell you. She's jealous that the king admires May so much, even gave his permission for her to help the duke read the important documents in the official boxes the king shares with him."

Perhaps she is right, I thought, though I dared not voice it, for it seemed to me, even here at York Cottage, the walls could have ears. Alexandra resented May's interest in affairs of state because they were beyond her, and the king knew it. Or perhaps the queen's resentment of May stemmed from the fact she had some sway over her, whereas Her Majesty had no way to get back at the king's favorite mistress and advisor, Alice Keppel, who was known to also weigh in on governmental matters.

"Now about us getting shuffled off like this . . ." Helene began before her voice trailed off. She shook her head, and her curls bounced against her pink-powdered cheeks. "It's the way with us in service, isn't it, even those of us who are more intimate with the royals than, say, the scullery maid or hall boy? I often wonder if, in heaven, there will be these class differences. We are not good enough to mix with some of them, but good enough to bring up their children, the highest in the land too. It does not make people more loyal to be snubbed and ignored. Those boys should be here right now conjugating verbs! Why, I heard that George's cousin, Kaiser Wilhelm — Cousin Willie, they call him — might visit again, and I want David and Bertie to greet him properly in his native language. Oh, I despair of all these delays!"

I only nodded at first. Lately, though I kept it to myself — even from Rose and Mabel — I knew all about despair. I fought to keep my mind on the children. "At least Bertie's stuttering seems to be better lately, though he's so frustrated by those dreadful

131

splints he has to wear. Helene, he begs Finch to let him do without at night, and sometimes Finch agrees."

"Worse, soon we're to have a tutor to set up a proper schoolroom, and I'll only have a bit of their time then. Whatever are we going to do and whatever is this world coming to?"

We both froze as a shrill whoop from David sounded clear from downstairs where their grandfather was no doubt entertaining in fine fashion. Why, I'd heard at a formal dinner he'd brought the boys in and put butter pats on both of his pant legs, then let them cheer to see which would melt and run down first. It was so good to see them happy, but then we were all left with settling them down. The king was already promising them that they would be invited to his sixtieth birthday party and get to stay up late and eat anything they wanted. Now, that could be a battle royal with their father.

"Oh-oh," I said, popping up from my chair. "I hear Her Majesty's voice in the hall. Time to go and pick up the pieces. I had to do that literally last time. Harry grabbed and broke her three-strand pearl choker, and I had to fish them — big as chickpeas, they were — out of the soapy water."

I gave Helene's shoulder a little squeeze and hurried out and down the hall. "Mrs. Lala," the queen's voice boomed out, "we have dried and dressed little Harry and put him down for a nap. Mary is playing with her new baby doll. I do believe you have the most wonderful job in the kingdom, caring for those lovely children. Perhaps we should change places for a day," she said and laughed as I curtsied and edged toward the nursery door. "And I've kept count of my little menagerie of agate animals David so adores, and you've done a find job keeping him honest . . . you and Finch."

"Thank you, Your Majesty. I believe he is coming along nicely."

I noted her peacock blue walking suit and yellow silk parasol were both speckled with soapy water. Her beige mushroom hat with its cotton netting poufs had slipped to the side, and its three ostrich feathers were dripping water down her back. Rose had taught me well to record fashions for her while she was away. I even jotted things down for her, so wait until she heard this regal, elegant woman looked absolutely bedraggled after her water skirmish with Harry.

I noted too that she and Lady Knollys had left wet footprints behind them. I shuddered to think what I was going to find in the nursery.

I went in to see Mary had already put a fashionable, bisque-headed doll with her collection of them and had her nose in a book on horses, for she had taken to reading earlier than the boys. Water blotched the wall and the floor. Harry was indeed tucked into his crib, looking exhausted, no doubt from what must be equal to a swim across the channel.

Queen for a day, indeed. *Me?* Even as a joke? *Me?*

How Chad would have laughed at that.

Still in a tizzy over the king and queen's whirlwind visit, once Mary was down for a nap too, I left Martha mending the children's clothes in my chair in the nursery and went outside to calm myself. It was a lovely day, and I strolled to the botanical glasshouse with its riot of colors and smells. Although flowers were blooming on the grounds already, and I'd heard the ruffled grouse drumming away with their mating calls, I still needed to heal my loss of Chad. This seemed to be the nearest — and most challenging — place to do it.

I didn't fear I'd run into him here, for it was one of his busiest seasons stocking the coverts and fields with pheasant, grouse, and woodcocks. Too soon, no doubt even this Saturday, the air would be rent with the bangs of guns bringing down the birds Chad and his father raised. Massive numbers of them were killed at one of the king's or duke's hunting parties on the grounds by the male guests, while, during their midday break, the ladies, dressed to the nines, met them in the field for luncheon under a tent before more shooting.

Once I was in the door, I breathed in the moist, sweet air. A young, brown-haired woman with a cart that just fit between the aisles of plants was loading orchids and clove-scented malmaisons into it, no doubt decorations for the Big House. I'd seen that Queen Victoria's favorite begonias and petunias had been quickly replaced by more exotic, imported blooms. I'd heard that Queen Alexandra's favorite color mauve was taking over the old queen's favorite dark colors in drawing rooms and salons. French instead of German styles, they said, were all the rage. As for this woman, I didn't want to bother her or speak to anyone, but she turned as if she had sensed my presence.

"Oh," she said, with a little gasp. "It's you. I know who you are."

I did not know who she was, but I sensed it. Chad, Mrs. Wentworth had told me, had married the daughter of the man who kept the Big House in flowers, but I'd encountered no one here this late in the day.

I said nothing for a moment as we studied each other. *I know who you are,* echoed in my head. But sometimes, I didn't know who I was. Oh, yes, Mrs. Lala, head nursemaid to the royal children, and blessed to be so. But was I missing something, living here like a nun at Sandringham? Was it enough? Would I look back with regrets? I did now, so terribly torn between who I was and who I could have been.

"Then you have me at a disadvantage," I said, though it was partly a lie.

"I warrant I do now," she said cheekily and banged an orchid so hard on her cart, the flowers nodded hard in agreement. "My Chad wasted years on you, taking you all about the estate, but I'll make up for it now."

I wanted to say something pert, even hurtful back to her, but I held my tongue. For Chad. For propriety. For my own terror that perhaps I had done a stupid thing not to run after him in this very place and beg him to give me more time, to wait for me.

Instead, I said to her, "I believe you have a job here on the estate that you must love, just as I do. I wish you well, Millie Reaver."

I guess using her name or my kindness

took her aback. Her mouth dropped open. I turned to go, but wondered if I should send her the feather picture, or if Chad would be angry at that. I was upset she had ruined the glasshouse as my refuge. As I hurried away, one thing hurt even more than losing Chad. I pressed one hand over my mouth and one over my flat belly, for I had long ago learned to read the signs: Despite the dustcoat she wore over her dark green cotton dress, I saw Mrs. Chad Reaver was several months breeding.

Tangling with both the highest woman in the nation to the lowest flower girl, I'd had a difficult day. So I was happy when Finch let David and Bertie run down the hall to the day nursery to join Mary to recite the creed their father had wanted them to have memorized before he came back from his tour of the empire. Especially today, after coming face to face with Chad's wife, I took it to heart as first David, then Bertie — he stuttered yet a bit — recited it for me:

"I shall pass through this world only once. Any good thing, therefore, that I can do or any kindness that I can show any human being, let me do it now. Let me not defer nor neglect it, for I shall not pass this way again."

"Very good, both of you," I told them with a little clapping.

David said, "Bertie says his *b*'s too many times like 'human b-b-being.' "

"Well, then," I told them, "it's good that the creed has very few *b*'s at the beginnings of words. I think Bertie's doing much better with that."

Bertie beamed but David rolled his eyes. Despite their naughty natures, how I missed tucking them up in bed at night, being with them more. But Finch was good for them, Helene was necessary, and they would soon enough have a tutor for all else but the foreign languages.

"Lala," Bertie said, "how about a b-bedtime nursery rhyme song?"

I pulled both of them closer. Harry was on my lap and the ever-independent Mary hovered. "Well, now that you are both getting older, shall we say the Lord's Prayer together like we used to?"

David said, "Is the part 'Thy kingdom come' because Father will be king after Grandpapa and then I'm next? You know, this kingdom and the empire is to come for us? Lala," he added, lowering his voice, "the thing is, I don't want to be king and have a kingdom. Too much work, even if there are nice parties. I would rather have a bicycle."

I didn't know whether to laugh or cry, especially when Bertie chimed in, "Don't tell Father, but I'm glad I shall never b-b-be king."

"Listen to Lala now, both of you. Sometimes we cannot choose what we will be, and life can take a sharp turn or go too fast — like a bicycle going lickety-split on the hill to the station, David. I'm sure you will both be given bicycles soon. But just as you have to obey rules to ride a bike and make the turns that are already laid out on the road . . ." My voice caught. My own life and losses rushed at me. "Well, that's enough for tonight. Now let's say the prayer and then off to bed before Finch comes looking for you."

I was glad the three oldest closed their eyes for the prayer. I dreaded how I'd explain if they saw my tears.

CHAPTER 11

The first of November 1901 marked the first time I'd ever been to sea — I mean really out on the water where I couldn't spot land. Once each year Papa had taken us up and down the Thames on the steam launch he captained, but now we were in the English Channel just off the Isle of Wight. Mind you, this wasn't the real ocean but it seemed like it. Chad had said once he'd like to see the real ocean, far from the North Sea with its winds whipping into the Wash just beyond the estate's fields and fens.

I sighed. Chad would like to see the ocean, and I would just like to see him. To say I'm sorry. To wish him well. Maybe it would get me past being haunted, as he'd said, by making the decision I did, a decision I had to make, didn't I?

I was with the children and the king and queen on the royal yacht *Victoria and Albert* going out to meet the return of the steamship *Ophir* after its eight-month colonial tour. Despite our craft's seaworthiness, it was tilting through choppy waves. The wind yanked at my hair and hat, and the overhead flags flapped so hard it sounded like cannon shots. But, even as I held little Harry firm in my arms and kept an eye on Mary, I reveled in it all.

To think that baby Harry had not been walking or talking when the duke and duchess left for their tour, and now he was doing both. What a sacrifice, at least for the duchess, to have missed all that. Yet the letters she wrote to Helene, which she shared with me, were filled with a newfound sense of self-confidence. She had been welcomed and wildly cheered everywhere she went. The newspapers even commented that she was more popular than the solemn duke. Now we waved madly at the still distant *Ophir,* where the triumphant couple waved at us in return. I searched for Rose among the clusters of staff and servants, but could not pick her out.

"Too rough to tie up and board from ship to ship!" King Edward shouted to us. He kept his hand on David's shoulder. "We'll get on a steam barge to go on over to board the *Ophir,*" he told us.

But it was too wild even for that, so it was

decided that the barge and the ship would steam up the Solent toward Portsmouth for the reunion. Word of that soon spread, and we were quickly surrounded by pleasure craft of all sorts with people cheering both their present and future kings. As I watched seven-year-old David jump up and down, I saw that they even cheered their future-future king.

The harbor itself was lined with people six or seven deep. I must say, it was the first time since the death of Queen Victoria that I realized the reach of the monarchy itself, how its popularity was passed on. Bands played ashore — I recognized the tune of "Home, Sweet Home" — and the cheers were deafening.

Finally, when the ships docked, we all disembarked the barge and boarded the *Ophir*. The king clapped Duke George on the back and said something to him about soon being named Prince of Wales, that he had earned and not just inherited that honor. The duke seemed deeply moved as he actually embraced David, then Bertie, something I had never seen him do. Bertie managed to greet his father, fortunately without a word that began with a *b*. Four-year-old Mary smiled when she was handed some sort of Oriental doll by her mother, though she then went back to hiding behind my skirts and then her grandmother's. But when I tried to hand little Harry to his mother, the child clung to me and burst into tears and shrieks.

"Oh, dear," Duchess May murmured as tears filled her eyes. "It's Mama, my darling, it's Mama. Lala, I tell you, there is always a price to pay."

How well I understood that, but I only tried to assure her, "He'll be running to you in no time, Your Grace."

"He'll come to me, won't you, sweeting?" the queen asked the squalling child. She edged in between us and stretched out her arms as little Harry nearly dove into them.

It was then I realized what Helene had been grumbling about was true. Despite her power and position, the queen meant to hurt her daughter-in-law. I had also seen that, once Alexandra had become queen, she'd stood up to her husband by always being late to his promptly planned events, or not being there at all. She'd also scheduled visits to her native Denmark, leaving her husband behind and snubbing his closest circle of friends.

Of course, her increasing deafness made it hard for her to cope with a great deal of chatter, but it was her way of getting back at her husband for his women and his Continental ways. Oh, the French loved him.

Granted, the queen had also been hard on her own daughter, called Toria, keeping her home most of the time and fending off her suitors, but should she not be tutoring and building up May to inherit her position as queen someday? It was one thing to cleverly protest her husband's infidelity, but must she mow down Duchess May?

It was then I spotted Rose and managed to edge toward her. She kissed my cheek, and we hugged. "Oh, my goodness, I have so much to tell you, Char! My poor mistress was a triumph on land but spent the hours at sea sick as a dog — *mal de mer,* the French call it. And wait 'til you see the samples of silks I've brought home, and I'm making you a lovely embroidered bed jacket. You can't be dressed like a children's nurse all the time!"

In just over a week, November 9, 1901, we all celebrated King Edward's sixtieth birthday at Sandringham. I say we, for the event with all its guests kept the staff busy from before dawn to late at night. Even the children were on edge, for they'd been promised what their grandfather called carte blanche for the occasion, which I heard David tell Bertie meant they could have and do anything they wanted.

"Mind you, not 'anything'!" I corrected the boys. "You will get to meet all his guests and have some lovely cake and see beautiful decorations, but you are still to behave."

"Righto!" Finch told them. "No bouncing off the walls."

"We wouldn't d-do that!" Bertie protested, but my mind began to wander again. Chad had often said, "Righto." I felt a stab of pain over losing him at the strangest, random moments. But again, the children needed me. I knew the king's so-called *La Favorita,* Mrs. Alice Keppel, and her compliant husband, George, were coming too. Should I explain that to David so he didn't blurt something out if he was introduced to her?

"Mrs. Lala" — Finch's voice interrupted my thoughts — "I said, what time are we to take the children over?"

"Oh . . . yes. The king wanted them to be there for his investiture of the duke as Prince of Wales at eight."

"Goodie!" Mary piped up. "We get to stay up late. And what about Mama? She will be a princess and me too, someday, I vow I will."

"B-But," Bertie said, "I can't wait 'til

Grandpapa and Papa show us how to shoot. Chad's going to show us the good places to bring down b-birds, that's what he said, b-bring d-down . . . birds. Then I think we will have them for a b-banquet since they will be d-dead."

David rolled his eyes either at Bertie's naivety or his stuttering, which had grown worse since his father had returned. I swear, Finch looked at me as if he knew all about my agonizing over Chad Reaver. Of course, the belowstairs staff could have told him how we used to go about together.

As the boys hurried down the hall toward their room, Finch told me, "I wouldn't worry, Lala, about Chad Reaver being around much right now since he's in mourning."

"Oh, his father died? I knew he was ailing, but I hadn't heard."

"No. Mrs. Wentworth mentioned that he — that is, his wife — lost their baby, a month or so before it would be born. Of course, they are taking it quite hard."

"Yes, of course. I daresay."

"There's a service tomorrow at the village church. Not a small one, I warrant, because Chad is so popular, and the nearby folk will turn out."

"Finch, thank you for telling me," I said

and hurried back into the nursery. Trembling, I leaned my elbows on the windowsill from which I'd often watched Chad go by and wave at me the first few years I was here. I thought of Millie, loading flowers on her cart in the glasshouse where she had rebuked me for keeping Chad from her. And I recalled my father once saying that "People who live in glass houses mustn't throw stones." I had truly meant to give the feather picture to Chad and Millie for their child, but now there was no child, though I had no doubt they'd try again.

They say there's nothing worse than a dead child, stillborn or once living. But really, which was worse, to have never known the little laugh and cuddles or to have loved and lost? Heavens, what good was all this agonizing doing me? My children were down the hall and in this very room. A man who had once been very kind to me was lost in grief and lost to me and that was that. Or so I tried to tell myself.

Never a dull minute with the royals, and I was ever grateful for that. I had a ride in the king's newfangled electric car with the Prince of Wales driving. I had Harry on my lap and Mary next to me, pretending she was riding a horse. David and Bertie sat in the backseat with Finch. Soon we were all to go to London for the king's coronation on the twenty-third of June. The new tutor for the boys, an imposing tall man, I had heard, would be here soon, and that had us all on edge.

Princess May was now pregnant with her fifth child, so I had much to look forward to. "Well," the newly named Prince of Wales had said when he heard that news, "soon we shall have our own regiment."

"To fight in the Boer War in Africa, Father?" David had asked.

"No, to guard Sandringham," the prince had said, though he seldom joked with the boys.

"I think we'll need to have horses for that," Mary dared.

David said, "Or bicycles to guard the gate and the train station."

"Stop your wish list!" the prince had scolded. Even I had flinched at his sudden change of mood and harsh tone. Being named Prince of Wales had set him on edge, for he was truly at heart a country squire who didn't like meeting new people the way his father did. He would rather build up his bird coverts than build an empire.

When he'd stormed off, back to his stamp collection, I'd told the children, "If wishes were horses, then beggars would ride."

Mary spoke first. "We don't have beggars around here."

"It means more than that," David said. "Like wishing isn't enough to get what you want, right, Lala?"

"You are very right, David," I had told him. "Whenever your new tutor, Mr. Hansell, gets here, I hope he challenges that smart brain of yours, and Bertie's too."

"Let's go, lads," Finch had said. "We need to make very sure you have all the suitings you'll need for the coronation events in London, and we are going to review how we are to behave. Your grandfather loves ceremony and pomp, and we must all do him proud. He's in London already, practicing everything, but he'll want a good report of you."

I had backed up Finch on that, but right now Mrs. Wentworth stood in the nursery door, wringing her hands. Mary, Harry, and I were the only ones in the nursery. All I could think of was that something dreadful had happened to the princess . . . that the child she carried . . . like Chad's wife's baby . . .

I stood so fast, I nearly dropped little Harry off my lap.

"What is it?" I demanded of the poor

woman. Ever in charge, she looked like the world had turned upside down.

"The king. He's very ill, like to die, Princess May says. A phone call — he . . . he . . . Appendicitis something terrible, and they are going to operate on him, try to save him, right at the palace. The coronation — all postponed — for now. The children's mother is comforting the prince and asks you to break it to the boys. Prayers — prayers and hope," she added and burst into tears. " 'Tis complicated — the operation — the royal physician says, by his age and girth."

She had not seen Mary behind me, who now clutched my skirts about my legs so I could hardly move. She also began to cry.

"Mrs. Wentworth," I told her, fighting for calm, "please go down to the kitchen and send both of my undernurses up here to sit with Harry and Mary while I talk to Finch and the boys. I am sure all will be well. It has to be."

"Yes, Mrs. Lala. Yes, of course, it will."

I held on to that "of course," and held both boy's hands when I told them the news shortly after. David took it the worst of anyone, fuming, angry, balling up his fists and pounding the wall until Finch pulled him away, but the boy kept muttering, "He's my best friend! Loves me, not like father. Best friend, along with you and Finch, Lala, he's my very best friend, you know like Chad used to be to me and you, but now he stays away. But we can't lose Grandpapa, can't, can't, can't! Then father will be king, and I'll be next, we can't, just can't, Lala, can't!"

I knew how he felt. While Finch hugged Bertie, I held David as if he was young, like I used to when things first went so wrong in his little world. God forgive me, but how I wanted someone to comfort me.

CHAPTER 12

King Edward did not die, but survived his operation with royal colors flying. I overheard the Prince of Wales tell his wife a few days after the good news came, "I tell you, May, he sat up in bed the next day, big as you please, smoking a cigar and driving his doctors to distraction."

"As he does you at times, my dearest. Or rather as the thought of taking his place does to you."

"I know David claims he does not want to be king, but, in truth, I'm not sure I do either. I swear, I'd rather live right here, even in little York Cottage instead of the Big House, overseeing those working with the land . . . and hunting."

"But you know . . ." was the last of their words I caught as I hustled Mary past their door, which stood ajar into the hall. During the five years I had lived among the Yorks, now dubbed the Waleses, how much I had overheard of royal family secrets, of court life, of the wider world of politics. Right now, I had a moment's respite with little Harry balanced on my hip as I took him and Mary into the day nursery. But it was not five minutes later when Finch gave a knock on the door that meant we were to present the children before their parents. As I opened the door, I saw he had both boys nattily attired in their usual sailor outfits.

"We must not keep your father waiting, right, boys?" I asked.

"You're right about that," David said, tugging at his starched collar. "Lala, we're learning to salute just like we will in the navy when we first arrive and are called 'snotties,' Father said."

Snotties, indeed, for they'd been that in their nursery years. My gaze snagged with Finch's as he tried to stifle a grin. Thank heavens, he had a good sense of humor, and we hoped that Henry Hansell, the older boys' new tutor, who was due today, would too. All I'd learned about Mister Hansell so far was that he was thirty-nine, very tall, and as good at sports as he was at teaching history. The trio of Helene Bricka, Finch, and Mrs. Lala was about to add a fourth leg to take care of these children of destiny, who only wanted to have fun and friends right now.

As Finch and I stood behind the children in their mother's boudoir, their father clapped his hands and announced, "Good news all round! You already know that your grand-father's health has taken a turn for the best. His coronation has been rescheduled for the ninth of August, barely over a month away. We'll all go to London for it. You eldest three will be in the Abbey to see it all."

"Yes, Papa. Thank you," David said. I could tell he was trying hard not to fidget. He loved his grandfather so he was prob-ably ready to explode in cheers.

Bertie blurted, "Yes, P-P-P- . . ."

"Well, get it out, boy! Stop that wretched stuttering right now!" the prince ordered. Bertie recoiled as if he'd been hit.

Mary, bless her, put her arm around Bertie's shaking shoulders and said, "You can tell we're all excited about it, Papa."

Their mother put in a quick word as if to deflect the prince's attention from Bertie too. "We'll have kilts made for you boys, and Mary will have a new, lovely white frock with lace and ribbons. Harry will have to stay with you, Lala, but I believe you can see the parade and procession from the windows of Marlborough House."

I was glad Harry was only fourteen months so that being closed out of the momentous event meant nothing to him, though he was old enough to keep quiet in his father's presence. But when the prince went out to his study, Harry said, "Mama! Mama!" and put out his arms toward her. Oh, how hard I'd worked on getting him to go to her. With another royal child coming, I prayed that baby would not be without his or her mother's love in the earliest years.

Princess May held little Harry while her lady-in-waiting played on the piano all sorts of tunes from a Scottish songbook. And then came some American folk tunes like "Camptown Races," "Oh My Darling Clementine" and the Civil War song "When Johnny Comes Marching Home," which was my favorite. Princess May had taught us the words, and I must admit I had a good voice and had always loved to sing.

Soon, apple cinnamon scones, cherry tarts — I knew we were in for messy faces with that — and tea with lots of milk in it appeared. It was a wonderful hour, and I noted well that Bertie never stuttered his *b*'s or *d*'s when he sang. I believe I cherished those times as much as the children. And it helped me to convince myself I'd made the right choice to remain among them.

But when we traipsed toward our back section of the hall, there stood the prince outside the boys' schoolroom door. We all came to a quick halt. With him was a very tall, mustached man with a valise in his hands.

"David, Bertie," the prince said, "this is your new tutor, Mister Hansell, you've been waiting for. Hansell and I have decided you must know your country's history when your grandfather is crowned, so get to it."

"Mary. Mrs. Lala," he said as he passed us and gave a single, gentle stroke to Harry's little head. He seemed to always like the babies at least. So here we stood with a stranger as the prince's feet thudded down the hall.

"Greetings all round," Henry Hansell said, putting his fat valise down. "Boys, we'll start first thing tomorrow with facts about Westminster Abbey where your grandfather will be crowned, but I daresay we'll have time for football, cricket, and golf too, eh?"

"We don't know how to play those," David told him. "But I want to learn to shoot and ride a bike, Midder Hansell."

Well, I thought, the king had spit out Hansell's name quite fast, so David must have thought he said *Midder* instead of *Mister.*

Hansell looked down over his broad mustache at Finch and me, and his thick eyebrows lifted. "Now don't correct the lad, for I'll be doing enough of that. I hear the children have named you Mrs. Lala, and I warrant they've just dubbed me 'Midder,' eh?"

And Midder it was, ever after.

David and Bertie were soon reciting the kings of England and the histories of the Tower of London, the Abbey, and St. Paul's. It didn't surprise me that the prince had partly picked Hansell for his athletic prowess, for Finch told me he'd excelled in football at Oxford. I heard he could shoot with the best of them, but, sadly, had six handicaps in golf or something like that.

Everyone liked Midder Hansell except for Helene, who had to compete with him for the boys' time and often lost, however much she tattled to Princess May. Best of all, when he was not drilling facts into the boys, Hansell — usually with Finch — took them outside to run off extra energy, playing with a football or using a golf club on the lawn, though I heard their father had ordered them not to "hack it to death." When I told Hansell that the children never mingled with others their age and were quite lonely for that lack, he arranged a football game with some of the West Newton village youth.

"Mrs. Lala, leave the baby with an under-nurse and come down to see how they do, in the field between here and the village," Hansell called to me as the four of them set out, Finch carrying a hamper of drinks and food, the boys bursting with excitement.

So, when shouts and cheers reached my ears that late July day, I did just that, taking Mary to see her brothers play with the local lads. A crowd of villagers had gathered, mostly on the far side of the field nearest their houses. We sat on a bench to cheer our team on, but I soon saw there was a problem. The village boys ran way round David and Bertie so, I assumed, as not to hurt them. They never kicked the ball hard at them, almost fed it to them, even those on the opposite team.

"Here, sir," a redheaded lad said to David, kicking the ball gently to his feet, then backing away. "Your turn again. You can have the ball if you want it."

I could tell Hansell was frustrated. Finch, more than once, spoke to the local boys, I assume, telling them it was fine to really play a game and not mollycoddle the Waleses.

"A disaster," Hansell told me when he

158

jogged over to get a drink from the hamper at our feet. "The royal lads will get the idea it's a game for sissies. But if David and Bertie are not going to so much as shake a leg, I can hardly scold the village lads."

"I can," a familiar voice behind me said. "Let's you and I and Finch go at it then. We'll give the lads the idea that all's fair in love, war, and games, righto?"

Chad. Standing close behind me for who knew how long. I felt frozen in place, afraid to look him full in the face when I'd longed to see him. But what did it matter now, our days together, his hopes and my ignorance, however much he still, strangely, meant to me. I felt naked. The entire universe was screaming at me. I found I could not so much as reply.

"Mrs. Lala," Hansell said, "what do you think?"

I cleared my throat. Still looking off toward the waiting boys, I managed, "I think it's worth a try, and David and Bertie know and respect Chad."

"Ah," Hansell said, peering at me from under his tweed cap. "So you're all acquainted."

"Come on then," Finch said.

Without a glance or word my way, Chad went to the two leaders of the village team and shook their hands, then did the same with David and Bertie, who, evidently, had been named captains of the other group. Then Chad, Finch, and Hansell went at it: kicking, running, shouting, pointing, and ordering their opposing teams around.

David and Bertie at first just clapped and cheered — for Chad as well as the York Cottage men. Chad huddled with the village boys, and they started to treat the royals a bit more like real rivals. It seemed to me that Chad was especially hard on Finch, Hansell too. Mary shouted for Hansell and Finch, and David and Bertie began to catch on and not stand about like scarecrows. I kept mostly quiet, but for clapping for goals. Earlier, I'd expected David and Bertie to win by default since the others did not dare to approach them, but they finally got into the fray with flying feet and a goal. But the village team and Chad won in a final rally of rough and ready.

After the game, Chad, sweating, rumpled, out of breath, walked past me. "Always problems, yes, Charlotte, taking the bad with the good?" His brown eyes bored into mine. "The differences sadly mean that 'Never the twain shall meet.' But once, they almost did, they could have." He doffed his rakish cap to me and kept on walking. At least he had spoken, used my name as no one else did anymore but in letters from my family. But his words had accused and condemned me again.

He looked so good that day, sun-browned with strong chest and arms none of the men I saw daily flaunted. His deep voice raced from my breasts to my belly, the latter managing a huge cartwheel. Again, he'd helped my beloved boys. Though Finch had kept up with Chad, and Hansell's size had dwarfed him, Chad Reaver seemed the top man in that game, the one truly in charge. All during the coming fuss and flutter of activity for the coronation, I crowned Chad in my heart as the best and dearest man I'd ever known.

How hard I tried to get into the excitement of coronation day in London, the ninth day of August 1902. It had been a strangely cold and cloudy morning, but then the sun burst forth as if to herald a heavenly blessing. From the third-floor window of Marlborough House, I held little Harry up to the window from which we could see the Mall and Buck House beyond Green Park. My family would be in that crowd somewhere, and here I was, looking down at it all.

We could see the parade route with swags

of red bunting that nodded and bowed above the cheering crowds twenty deep. Troops, which had been camped in the city parks, paraded, row after row of dashing uniformed men afoot or mounted. The clip-clops of the horses' hooves mingled with shouts of *Hurrah* and *God save the king*!

I told Harry, "Grandpapa and Grannie are in the first carriage leaving the palace. Papa and Mama are in the next one. See the Royal Horse Guards riding with them?"

"Horsies! Horsies!" the little lad shouted.

Well, I thought, so much for grasping what was going on down there. At least David and Bertie were not just learning about pomp and ceremony today but observing it up close, for they, and Mary, were to be in the royal box with their mother and aunts to see the great display, which would begin promptly at five minutes to twelve.

Since this was only early August and Princess May was not due to give birth to her next child until December, I thought it unfair that she was not seated near her husband on the main floor. But I'd over-heard her tell Eva Dugdale that Queen Alexandra wanted "the stage all to herself." So once again the stubborn queen was try-ing to shift her daughter-in-law off to the side. She was defying her husband again

162

too, as he'd been adamant she wear a British-made gown today, but she had chosen one from Paris. Rose said it would be of glimmering gold, and the long train of her robe had been embroidered by some of India's finest dressmakers. She was to be absolutely ablaze with diamonds.

I knew more about Princess May's gown, though, since Rose was to dress her, and had described her coronation attire to the last silk rose garter on the lingerie. Unlike Alexandra's dress, May's was made entirely by British seamstresses. It was ivory satin, embroidered with four shades of gold and studded with pearls. The bodice bore a corsage of pearls and diamonds, no less. Over this she was to wear a robe of heavy purple velvet and an ermine cape attached with huge bows of gold and pearls, which Rose had fretted might come loose, since the robe and cape were so heavy. Ah, well, at least all I had to fret for today was making sure Harry could see his "horsies."

After the parade passed, I sang to him and put him down for his nap, then started pacing, not wishing so much I was there to see the splendor of it all, but thinking that the nation's shouts and huzzahs reminded me of how Chad had cheered on his village team of boys and yet supported the fumbling David and Bertie. I should have told Chad thanks for helping them when he walked by me. I should have told him I was truly sorry he had lost his child and what a good father I knew he would be someday. Or should I have told him he must come and take the feather picture back?

I know not how long I walked in such a daze, but hours later I heard the children's voices as they came running down the hall and burst into the room to find me. They were so excited that it did no good to put a finger to my lips and point to the railed bed with their sleeping brother.

David blurted, "You should have seen it, Lala!"

I herded them out into the hall where we stood under a huge portrait of one of the King Georges. "Tell me then," I said hugging each of them in turn and expecting to hear how they had been awed by the solemn occasion.

David told me, "Well, everyone yelled a bunch of words in Latin, which we didn't know, but don't tell Madame Bricka because learning French and German is hard enough."

Bertie: "And Princess B-Beatrice dropped her program out of the b-box and it made a b-big noise down b-below."

Mary: "Oh, Lala, you should have seen it. Her program plopped right into a golden cup below and people gasped, but we laughed."

David: "Until Mama made us stop."

"Good gracious, I would have made you stop too," I told them as Hansell and Finch, who had gone along in the carriage but not into the Abbey, caught up with them.

Hansell: "Beautiful, stunning, historic, especially the crowning."

David: "But the old Bishop of Canterbury . . ."

Hansell: "Archbishop."

David: ". . . stumbled going up the steps with the crown. Grandpapa — I mean, really King Edward VII — had to make a grab for him or he would have fallen and the crown gone flying."

"Oh, my," I said. "Grandpapa — King Edward — to the rescue again."

Bertie: "And another good p-part. P-Papa had to kneel before the king and say he would and ob-bey him."

"I can see why you especially liked that part," I told them as Mary grinned and David nodded. "But that does not mean that the way your grandpapa lives with his parties and fun is the way your papa must rear all of you."

"So," Hansell put in, "is *that* what they were thinking?"

"This is a special day," Finch declared, "but it's back to rules and routines tomorrow."

Finch and Hansell led the boys down the hall to their room, where they would have tea with Mary, little Harry and me joining them soon.

"Well," Mary put in and squeezed my hand, "I told them Father's vow of obedience didn't mean that, but it was fun to pretend that Father would be kinder and love us more."

"Mary," I said, my voice severe, as I sat in a chair and pulled her close to my knees so we were face to face, "your father only wants what is best for all of you, to learn to follow rules, especially for the boys, to toughen them up for the real world they will face someday outside of York Cottage and Sandringham. In his own way, he loves you very much."

"That's what Mama says. When he's king, he'll have to deal with all those people we saw today, but I think he's really as shy as Bertie. The Irish are a problem too I heard Mama say. Lala, they set off bombs and hurt people! They want what they call free home rule and independence, but doesn't everyone? David does, so Bertie does too. Even me, and I'm a girl."

As big as she was, I pulled her on my lap and held her close. "Everyone thinks it's an easier world for us girls, even for grown women, my dear, that we must be cared for and coddled because we are gentle and weak. But that's not true. We will face lots of problems, lots of challenges. But you are bright and strong, and you will be fine. And I do think it's time you had a tutor of your own."

She looked hard at me, then nodded and kissed my cheek. "Like that gamekeeper said to you at the football game, there are always problems, and we have to take the good with the bad?"

Chad. She'd sensed something between Chad and me. Out of the mouths of babes . . . well, Mary had always seemed older than her years.

"Yes," I managed. "Something like that."

CHAPTER 13

"Won't you go way up in the stone tower with us, Lala?" Mary wheedled for the third time. "We want to see the ghost, and Midder Hansell and Finch have gone deer stalking with Papa." She gave me her sweetest, good-girl smile.

Immediately after the coronation in August of 1902, the Waleses had taken us on the train to the Highlands of Scotland. Three miles down the River Dee from Balmoral Castle, the sovereign's Scottish home, Abergeldie Castle, was now in the possession of the prince, though it was rather an ancient, primitive place. The children were all convinced it was haunted.

The original granite walls were covered with gritty, white stucco. Finch ordered the boys to stop picking off pieces and flipping them at each other, but they still did it behind his back.

But now, since I believed it would be a

good time to prove to the children that there was no such thing as ghosts — except those who haunted the heart — and leaving little Harry behind with Martha, I followed the three eldest up a circular, worn stone staircase toward the wooden cupola of the tower. At the top David lifted the rusted iron latch and pushed open a creaking door.

"Eeeek!" Mary shrieked when a bat dove at her and flew down the staircase. "Bats are always with witches, aren't they, Lala? And this ghost was burned as a witch!"

We heard mice or rats skitter away, and I sneezed from the dust. Spiderwebs hung so thick that one laced itself across my face. "Ugh!" I muttered. Then, brushing it off my damp skin, I told them, "The bats are real, and people used to fear witches, but we know better in this modern age."

"Isn't this place grand?" David declared, looking around at the dirty, decrepit chamber.

"More like eerie and scary," I said, wishing now that I'd forbid this excursion. Mary kept close to me, but at least Bertie wasn't stepping on the hems of my skirt as he had on the way up the stairs.

"That's what I mean," David insisted, edging over to the open casement. "Look out these windows. I bet right here is where they caught her when she ran, then they took her to that hill over there and burned her at the stake!"

"It was a dreadful time of superstition," I told them, wishing Hansell was here to fill in the proper history. "Poor Kittie Rankie. Even now, I feel so sad for her."

"Me too," Bertie said, looking out. "B-But I want to hear those sounds of her crying and moaning here, like Father's two Scotsmen said."

On this annual trip, the prince had taken it upon himself to add two Scots to the household. One, Mr. Forsythe, played the bagpipes a bit before eight each morning. He stood under the prince's window but the music woke us all. Poor Princess May — pregnant as she was again and hating every minute of it — did not wish to rise so early.

From what I could tell, the other Scot, Mr. Cameron, drank too many "wee drams" every evening and was never up early. He told the boys tall tales of fighting in the Boer War. He also filled their heads with stories about local witch hunts.

But all that aside, I found the wide vista of the Highlands stunning. Now, as I gazed out from the tower, the purple haze of heather spread itself among the bracken, and, in the farther distance, the sky boasted three kinds of clouds. Birds sailed past at eye level. We could hear the rattling stream, looking like a silver ribbon below, as it bounced over granite boulders to feed the River Dee. Out the other way I could see the roads through the forests we'd traveled during carriage rides with Princess May to have picnics.

I'd wished Rose could have gone along on those, but such was not among her duties. Even here, she was often busy mending or overseeing the ironing of layers of Her Highness's clothing. Rose did not like the chatty Scottish girls who helped with that, which made me realize that her duties weren't always fancier than mine. Granted, I'd rather oversee a torn silk chemise or broken bone of a corset than a soiled nappy, but I'd also rather deal with naughty, loud children than silent, stunning silk dresses.

"Just like Lala, I don't believe in witches or ghosts," Mary said, though she still stuck tight to my side.

I did believe in the kind of hauntings of lost loves, but I assured her, "Good for you!"

At that, the old door blew shut with a bang. Everyone jumped. Even I couldn't muster up a laugh but went over to the door to open it. Enough of this place, I thought, despite the view.

But the latch would not budge. Had something caught when the wind — surely, the wind — slammed the door?

"David, come over here and help me lift this latch," I told him, trying to jiggle it.

We tried together. I peered through the keyhole for all the good that did. And I must admit there was a swirling sort of mist, surely the chill wind moving dust on the stairs, so I said nothing to the children. But my stomach began to cramp at the thought of an angry ghost in a white gown.

"I c-can hear her moaning," Bertie announced.

"Nonsense. It's the wind in the top of the cupola above us," I said, trying to keep calm, but I was getting annoyed — no, panicked. I had not told anyone where we were going, including the nursemaids, but had merely said we were off on a lark. Some lark, I thought, as another bat whipped past us and circled above our heads before darting out a window opening. If it weren't for that dratted deer stalking that went on for the six weeks we were here — alternating with shooting game birds, of course — Finch or Hansell would be with us. Now we would be late, actually missing, when Prince George returned and expected us to appear in Princess May's sitting room precisely at four.

I yanked again at the door, hurting my fingers, and then gave up. It took us an hour, taking turns shouting out the windows, before we caught the gardener's attention and he came up to let us out.

"Mrs. Lala, we have never had this tardiness problem before," the prince addressed me when we straggled in late — and sin of all sins, the boys were not pristine in appearance. I warrant I was disheveled and windblown too, but I'd hustled everyone here straightaway rather than be even later.

"The children were very keen to see the tower and the lovely view, and I know you appreciate their curious minds. But I regret that the door of the tower slammed shut on us and the latch caught," I told him. "We did our best, Your Royal Highness."

"It is not enough to do your best, but you must do what is necessary."

"Yes, sir."

He looked at me through narrowed eyes, and I waited for more of a dressing down. I knew now how the boys felt, for I'd often suffered with them in a royal rant.

"Well," he said, "at least their curious minds, as you call them, go to the heart of what I've decided today." He held up a stiff arm and open hand toward their mother to keep her from interfering. "In the immediate future, there are several things the princess and I believe will help to educate the boys and Mary. Some real-life experiences and a bit of exercise for the body as well as the mind."

"Yes, Papa, we're listening," David said.

In those few words, I could hear the excitement in the boy's voice. I'm sure he was hoping that the bicycles he and Bertie lusted for were coming, and Mary, no doubt, had her heart set on a horse. At least, I noted that David had begun to try to deflect criticism of Bertie's stuttering by speaking for him at times. As selfish as David could be — and as possessive of my time and attention — I was grateful for that.

"Mary will have her own governess soon," the prince announced. "And the three of you will be taking dance lessons in the coming winter. We've retained Miss Walsh to teach you, with about thirty others of your class who will learn also, when we are in London with special lessons or other times at Sandringham. You need to know the polka, the waltz, and the Highland schottische."

Though the boys knew to stand as stiff as

soldiers — as naval snotties, rather — I saw David's shoulders slump. I could read him, even if his parents could not.

"As for manly pursuits for you boys," the prince plunged on, "I want you to begin observing the game shoots and eventually to learn to shoot with the other guns, including the king and myself."

Both boys nodded.

That meant, I realized, that they would be near Chad again since he tended the game birds and often controlled the shoots. He had seemed to be so good for the boys. Fortunately, I would not be there, except perhaps to glimpse him from afar if Mary and I ever went out with the ladies to watch or partake in the luncheons the women guests attended. My mind began to wander, until I realized what else the prince was saying.

"And, I want each of you — Mary too — to know more about the fauna, especially the bird life, the natural beauty of Sandringham Estate, so I've retained Chad Reaver to instruct you on such. It was his suggestion and a very good one. Finch and Hansell may go too, but Lala should accompany Mary each time she is along."

The children's mother finally got a word in, which was a good thing, because I wondered if I'd imagined what he'd just said. Chad had suggested it. I had dreamed of him ever since the football game, wishing I'd had more time to talk to him, wanting to . . .

"Mary," her mother said, "we believe it's an important part of your education to know about a great estate, its flora and fauna, especially the birdlife. Your grand-papa may have a new, squawky parrot he spoils, even at the dinner table, but I mean the natural English birds, the partridge, woodcock, and grouse that your husband — far in the future, of course — may value and hunt, so . . . and, oh, yes, all three of you will, of course, eventually learn to ride."

"Eventually?" Mary echoed with a sigh.

But I was hardly listening again. I was go-ing to get to be near Chad — by royal order. Thank heavens, I wasn't to speak right now, for I fear I would have sighed with longing like Mary or stuttered like poor Bertie.

Although David and Bertie practiced load-ing and shooting guns at targets that au-tumn, the king's gathering of family and friends was to be the first shoot Mary and I would attend. It was this Saturday, the eighth of November, the day before the royal sixty-first birthday. We had just recently returned from Scotland, so the children had not yet had any nature walks with Chad, perhaps would not until spring. At least now Mary and I would see what the continual banging of the twelve-bore Purdey shotguns was all about, for the men's hunting sometimes made it sound as if we were at war.

Even more exciting, many guests, including the king's cousins, Kaiser Wilhelm of Germany, and Tsar Nicholas of Russia, were at Sandringham to celebrate the king's birthday.

And, to my amazement, the guest list also included Mrs. Alice Keppel and her husband, George. How the queen would cope I did not know, but Mabel, who was now underhousekeeper at the Big House, told me that Her Majesty was used to it. Mrs. Keppel had been in the king's life for almost eight years, and when the queen greeted her for this visit, Her Majesty had merely inquired how Mrs. Keppel liked her collection of Russian Fabergé animals.

Now Mary and I were in the day nursery playing with Harry while we awaited our summons to join the hunt group for luncheon set up under a tent beyond the village.

"Lala!" David cried as he burst in. "In

case Father makes me recite before the king or the Kaiser — I don't mean in German, like later tonight — won't you listen to my poem again?"

"Of course," I told him, though I too had long ago memorized the verses. It amused me that it was entitled "A Father's Advice," because it seemed to me that's all the boys had gotten lately. "Go ahead," I prompted. "And Mary, don't mouth the words with him this time."

I must say without much of the feeling both Hansell and I had coached him to put into it, David recited,

> Never, never let your gun
> Pointed be at anyone . . .
> You may hit or you may miss,
> But at all times think of this:
> All the game birds ever bred
> Won't repay for one man dead.

"Bully! Word perfect," I told him. "But don't forget to say it with emotion. Pause a bit, then emphasize those last two lines."

"Righto. Lala, wait until you see the kaiser. When he was born, he got a withered left arm somehow, but he hides it and still shoots well, that's what Papa said. See you later!" He was already out the door.

178

I was also excited about the luncheon, but I hoped not to observe the shoot today. I would like to see Chad but I wasn't sure I could stomach seeing all those beautiful birds driven out of their hiding places and brought down by crack shooters.

David and Bertie were long gone to the shoot when Mrs. Wentworth appeared at the open door and knocked on it once. "The shooting is over for the morning, Mrs. Lala, so you and Mary can go on out. You can ride the omnibus with the staff who are taking out more covered dishes for the lunch," she added and hurried back to her tasks.

I left little Harry behind in the under-nurses' charge. I must admit, I was almost as excited as Mary, but not for the same reasons.

On our way out to the luncheon site, a cluster of men and women brandishing pitchforks and scythes ran out of a woodlot and blocked the road. I pulled Mary closer to me on the inside bench of the omnibus. They had handkerchiefs over their noses and mouths as if they were highwaymen. Were we to be robbed right here? One of the footmen tending the boxes of food cursed, and one of the maids screamed.

Our driver pulled the horses to a halt and

ordered, "Clear the road!"

No one budged. I could see seven of them as I craned around but I did not stick my head out. One man among them shouted, "Tell 'em fancy shooters, king and prince too, that 'em groundskeepers and bird beaters been tramplin' our crops, usin' our land. We don't want all that open space with 'em bird culverts. You tell 'em, 'cause they don't listen to the likes of us, even Reaver don't much!"

Were they speaking of Chad? He'd taken over his father's duties several years ago. But didn't he get on well with the local people?

"I'll tell them," our driver promised. "Let us pass. We have women and children here," he said, stretching the truth a bit.

"So do we, and it's time the uppers knew it," the speaker shouted and strode back to look in where I sat with Mary. I shoved her behind me and stood at the rear entry to block his view of her as I looked down at the irate man. "You tell 'em all what we said!" he shouted up at me, waving his pitchfork like a sword. He wore a cap as well as the handkerchief, so all I could see were his pale blue eyes. He was very young, thin and lanky. I could tell that and no more.

"We most certainly will," I managed to

get out in a strong voice. "Every word. Now please let us pass."

Perhaps it was the word "please" or the fact I'd agreed or that I'd faced him without a blink, but he ordered the others, "Let 'em go. They heard us good." They backed off and disappeared into a nearby woodlot.

"Sorry 'bout that, Mrs. Lala," the driver called back to me as he started us up again at a good clip. "We'll have to tell the king and the prince, that we will. Just a rabble don't like the king's men what don't let tenants clear weeds and plant crops where the coverts for the birds are, where the drivers make the birds fly so the lords can get good shots. And the local folk not 'lowed to poach. They don't like the hares let loose to breed for the hunt neither, 'cause they eats the gardens."

"Yes. Yes, I see why they might be upset."

But, I thought, did they have to accuse their fellow countryman and neighbor, Chad Reaver, too?

Though still shaken by our encounter with the rabble-rousers on the road, I was absolutely astounded at the grandeur of the luncheon in an open-sided tent called a marquee in the middle of a field. Silver tureens held steaming hare soup, trays displayed beautifully arranged fish and cutlets, carafes and sterling settings on linen tablecloths covered a U-shaped table surrounded by padded, brocade dining room chairs. Monogrammed china and flower arrangements were everywhere, even at the children's table where Finch and I sat with David, Bertie, and Mary. I scanned the servants for Chad's wife but didn't see her.

After the main table was served, we too were offered food from a vast array of the king's French chef's dishes of cold salmon pâté, pigeon pie, tomato salad, haricots verts, Russian salad, and jellies. Tortes and cakes, pineapple ice cream and raspberry sorbet with tea or coffee finished the repast. The only thing we did not have at our table were footmen pouring wine and champagne kept on crushed ice in the makeshift serving area. Not my idea of a hunting picnic, but I reckoned I still had much to learn. And much to eat.

But I did glance over at the kaiser now and again. I'd seen photos of the Russian tsar, and he looked so much like Prince George they could be mistaken for brothers. However, the kaiser did not resemble his English relatives at all. He had a rounder head and a huge, handlebar mustache curled up at the ends rather than trimmed and turned down. Even for the hunt, he seemed extravagantly dressed and had two guards standing behind his chair. I saw that, indeed, David had been right, that he hid his deformed arm. His pompous stance and hand stuck in his bright blue jacket reminded me of a gazette picture I'd seen of Napoleon.

When the children went off to be presented at the big table, Hansell told me, "Now here's a good history lesson for you, Mrs. Lala. Forget the face that sank a thousand ships, the beautiful Helen of Troy. Forget Cleopatra and all that historical legend. In the here and now, which lady at the table do you think is the infamous Mrs. Alice Keppel?"

"The beautiful blonde sitting three persons away from the king?"

"No."

"The brunette with the huge pearl earrings directly across from him?"

"One more guess before we have the children back again."

"After that problem on the road, it's not my best day. Oh, but I do remember Rose told me she does not dress well, which narrows down the search a bit. But tell me then."

"The one in the russet gown and green

hat with ostrich feathers."

I saw who he meant. Alice Keppel, the mistress and advisor to the king of Great Britain and the Empire, was plain as could be. Rose was right: She did not dress elegantly as did the other ladies, including, of course, Queen Alexandra, near whom she was seated and who was decked out in fur and ropes of pearls.

"Well," I said with an exhaled breath.

"So, beauty is only skin deep, and maybe not even that. I heard His Majesty has portraits of beautiful court ladies in his sitting room, and he has a beautiful wife, yet, I wager, Mrs. Keppel is the love of his life. She is of such an amenable, affable disposition that even the queen has come to accept her, perhaps to like her. This will be history someday, so live and learn, yes? And, by the by, not to change the subject, but when do you plan to tell the king about those rebels on the road?"

"When he is not surrounded by his family and certainly not in front of the children."

"Speaking of which, here they come. Whirlwind time again."

"Lala and Midder," David said, as the children came back, looking quite triumphant, "we're to go watch the shooting, but we can't have our own guns. And I think

Grandpapa is wishing the kaiser didn't come, because they don't seem that friendly."

"That can happen, David," Hansell said. "Blood is not always thicker than water."

"The blood from the birds they shot? They say they brought down eight hundred already, mostly pheasants that got flushed out by the beaters from over there," he said pointing. "See those lads in the smocks, and I hear they make a pretty penny for their day's work."

Bertie put in, "They have to count the b-birds the d-dogs bring back to make a b-big bag. Chad has to write it d-down in his book for Grandpapa and Papa too. It's like a contest, like a little war the k-kaiser said, but his English is kind of funny, sort of like Mother's but k-kind of worse."

"Yes, well," Hansell said. "Perhaps we'd best not remark on how others talk. Let's just hope your and David's German is not funny when you talk to the kaiser, or Madame Bricka will want to shoot you."

That settled them down. Me too, as Mary came back to join us after she'd had a few minutes with her parents, being introduced to everyone.

"I whispered to Papa what happened on the road, Lala," she told me. "We women have to stick up for ourselves. Madame Bricka says so, and you did too. He's going to tell the king, but not now to ruin his day. That's what Papa said. 'Not ruin his day.' "

I was disappointed I hadn't seen Chad as the luncheon broke up and elegant carriages carried the lady guests back toward the Big House. But just before I mounted the steps of the omnibus, there he came, attired in a crisp, colorful uniform, striding toward us, followed by an entourage as if he were a king of his own domain.

Granted, the royal and noble men had looked fine in their tweed caps and Norfolk jackets, specially made to allow them to raise their arms to fire the guns their loaders handed them in quick succession. But I hadn't realized there were such fine uniforms for the gamekeepers and their staff. The so-called beaters or bird drivers wore smocks and black felt hats with bright ribbons. The keepers who patrolled the grounds — no doubt the ones the folk on the road despised — wore bowlers encircled with gold cords and boasting an embroidered golden acorn on the front. But Chad was all in red, coat and hat with breeches and gaiters, brass buttons and a silver hunt horn with a golden tassel to match the acorn on his green velvet cap. I froze and stared in awe.

He saw me then. He gave a quick nod and lifted a gloved hand to the brim of his cap and hurried on, but I think that was for me. I sighed like a silly green girl, before I forced myself up into the omnibus. As we pulled away, I craned my neck to look back, but the loaders and shooters were tramping off into the field again, with Chad leading, so he was quite lost from view. And lost to me.

As Mary and I rode back in the omnibus in the company of guards and the other carriages and wagons, the blasts of the shooters rent the air again. I saw Chad in my dreams that night, striding toward me, shooting hot looks at me and blowing his horn for me to follow him. We went into the woodlot where we struggled with each other and then fought ghosts wielding pitchforks. I woke quite exhausted, as if I hadn't slept at all.

As soon as I'd had breakfast with Mary and Harry, I was summoned to the prince's study and there stood Chad.

CHAPTER 14

I was upset to be summoned by the prince, to the very room where poor David and Bertie had suffered many a scolding. But to have Chad there with him, waiting for me, made my knees tremble.

Of course, they must only want to discuss what had happened on the road yesterday. Mary said she had told her father about it, and I had no doubt the omnibus driver had too. Did they tell the prince that Chad's name had been mentioned in the accusations, or was he here because he oversaw the workers who were hired to protect royal game coverts instead of the estate tenants' gardens and fields?

I began a dreadful blush, throat to forehead, but I curtsied under their gaze. Chad nodded as if in greeting or encouragement.

I felt trapped in a small, red box, for the walls were covered with red fabric. A massive oaken case with a glass door displayed the prince's collection of shotguns. A large desk and a worn leather sofa crowded in on me as did shelves lined, not with books to read, but rows of matching embossed leather scrapbooks which no doubt held the prince's precious stamp collection. Pictures of navy ships hung from the walls and cluttered the desk, with only one photograph of his children. I saw the large barometer on the wall, which David had told me their father often strode over to tap in the middle of a rebuke, as if he needed to know which way the wind was blowing. It was dim in here compared to the way I kept the day nursery. The air smelled of cigar smoke, and I suddenly felt faint.

I must have wavered on my feet, for Chad's hands were strong on my upper arms as he sat me on the couch and knelt on the floor, leaning close.

"Is she quite all right?" the prince asked.

"Charlotte?" Chad asked.

"I'm . . . I'm fine. Really. Just didn't sleep well last night."

I tried to rise for one must not sit in the prince's presence, but he held up a hand to keep me there and pulled over the chair from his desk. Chad sat beside me, and the prince's knees kept us both in place. Though seated, he did tower over both of us on the sunken seats of the couch.

"I can understand why you didn't sleep," His Royal Highness said. "What happened on the road yesterday was a disgrace and a shock. Perfectly beastly. The princess and I are grateful to you for taking good care of one of our children — again."

I nodded. I suppose he meant the time I'd rescued David and Bertie from their cruel nurse. "It did upset me, sir," I admitted. "And Chad, they mentioned 'Reaver' as being to blame too."

If Prince George was surprised at the two of us using our Christian names to each other, he did not let on, but said, "The driver told us, and Mary gave her excited version of it too. She said you hid her behind your skirts and faced them down and made them leave."

"They'd said their piece by then, but I wish they had done it without those sharp tools — which could have been construed as weapons."

"Most provocative and heedless. Can you describe any of the men? Perhaps the spokesman?"

"You've heard, sir, they all wore kerchief masks?"

He nodded but Chad spoke. "Height? Weight? Tone of voice? I suppose they were

190

all dressed for field work?"

"Their spokesman was young, but perhaps most of them were, because their elders would know better," I said, speaking slowly. I found myself strangely torn between wanting to help but understanding the pain of the farmers. "And tone of voice — angry and desperate. He always said *'em* instead of *them,* if that helps."

The two men looked at each other. The prince said, "That's local dialect, so I see you have been a bit sheltered here. Chad and his father have made a concerted effort to elevate their speech, as have others who work here or at the Big House."

A bit embarrassed, I could only nod. So Chad and I had that in common too, trying to better ourselves. How hard I'd worked back in London, even when I was a mere nursemaid, to rid myself of Cockney talk, which I easily fell back into the few times I visited at home.

"Well," the prince said, sitting back sharply in his chair, "as for that rude fellow sounding angry and desperate, aren't we all at times? But it must be seen to, Chad, lest the protest grow to a rebellion. I cannot have my children and staff threatened on this estate, so keep your ear to the ground and your back covered. Do not be going out in the coverts alone. Meanwhile, you and I will speak with a troublemaker or two."

Chad said, "If only the royal nursery could spare her when I go out, I would take with me the woman who talked them down, eh?" His words — *If only the royal nursery could spare her* — had come out bitter, and I understood that. Yet he had helped me here today, so perhaps he didn't detest me as much as I thought.

To my surprise, the prince smiled. "Mrs. Lala — Charlotte," he said, leaning slightly forward again, "I repeat, we are grateful. We are blessed to have you tend our growing royal brood as well as Chad tends the estate hatchlings. If you need a favor — an extra undernurse — more supplies, especially when the new baby arrives next month, you have but to ask. I owe you one — or two, probably three favors."

"I would just ask, sir, that you don't fence the children in because of that incident. The oldest are just starting to feel their wings. They long for horses and bicycles, friends, fun, and just a bit of freedom on the estate."

"How like you to speak for them and not yourself," the prince said, rising, so Chad and I got up too, as he steadied me by my elbow. "I assure you, their grandfather has bicycles coming, and we'll see to riding lessons, but we must instill discipline too. You just be certain that you are ever with Mary on the grounds and that Finch and Hansell go with the lads."

"Yes, sir. With two undernurses, I'm sure that little Harry and the new one will be well tended too."

When I was dismissed, Chad went over to open the door for me. How I wished I could pull him out into the hall to say the things that I'd wanted, that I was sorry — about the loss of his child, I mean . . . that I wanted to see him again, only to return the feather picture to him, of course . . .

He whispered, "Charlotte," and closed the door firmly behind me. I heard their voices from within, but the only words I recognized were Chad's ". . . also plans to stop those poachers, sir."

I turned away and hurried back to the nursery.

As if he were an early Christmas gift, a fourth son was born to the Waleses on December twentieth. His full name was George Edward Alexander Edmund, and he was a fussy, colicky baby. The poor princess suffered through another hard birth and was given ether to allay her pain. We all knew she hoped that was her last child, and so I tried to cherish him — which he worked against by squalling day and night. I took to walking with him at night like a ghost up and down the hall, thinking my own thoughts of doubt and regret. Chad had been right: What I had lost haunted me, though I loved these children and my position. Bless Princess May for insisting I take an extra half day off a week. Meanwhile, life and our patterned rotation of places went on. Now and again, I would take out the shimmering feather picture Chad had tried to give me as a betrothal gift almost two years ago. I cleaned the glass and the frame, then wrapped it and put it away with my foolish regrets and dreams as yet another year rolled by.

Thankfully, the next December, that of 1903, was mild, and I sometimes took short walks outside after the children were in bed, just to savor the quiet and clear my head. Mostly I strode round the outside of the house itself, filling my lungs with crisp air. I looked up at the stars in the dark heavens, which seemed to wink and glitter. Sometimes I walked to the glasshouse and peered in the windows at the green, growing bounty inside, lit by a single lamp at night, but I never went in now. From here I could see the Big House with its windows lit and the royal standard that flew on the roof when Their Majesties were here. Currently, the queen was in residence and the king in London for, in truth, they often lived separate lives.

I turned to head back, walking quickly and quietly toward York Cottage when something huge hissed over me and took me down. I tried to scream but the air whuffed out of me. On the ground, I fought a great woven spiderweb. A huge net? A man fell or jumped on top of me.

"Not a sound, you damned bastard or else — Charlotte?"

"Chad? What in the wor—"

"Curse it, woman! Keep your voice down. What are you doing out here in the dark? I was sure poachers were coming in this way tonight, even though the big gate is closed. Sorry. Lie still, and I'll fish you out."

"You're still after poachers?" I muttered as he struggled to find the edge of the net to unwrap me. "I've been out for a constitutional several nights and saw no one."

"You'll have to stop that. It's not safe."

"I very well see it isn't, because of Sandringham's own head gamekeeper on the loose."

"There," he said, lifting the heavy webbing from me and casting it to the side. "I said I'm sorry. They've been taking more birds this year than others, and I swear it's that rabble from Wolferton Wood, not West Newton. For all I can prove, it's the same brigands who stopped you on the road last year."

I tried to get up but had the heel of one wellie still caught in the snare and I fell again. He caught me partway down and sat on the ground with me. I vow, I don't know how it happened but we were suddenly in each other's arms, holding tight, kissing with open mouths, lying on the cold, wet grass. He rolled over me then pressed me down with his hard body. I could feel his muscles right through both of our winter coats. My petticoats smashed flat and my stays bit into my ribs to take my breath away.

I'd been snagged again and not just by a net. Oh, heaven help me, I'd never gotten over him, and now he'd know it. Nor had I ever kissed and held a man with passion as I did now. He clamped me to him, his strong arms hard around my waist while mine clung to his neck to keep his lips close. I could imagine we were back in the glass-house again and it was so warm and humid and — and I hugged him back, my tongue touching his, out of breath until one of us, not sure who, came up for air.

"Curse it!" he said and pulled us to a sitting position. "I didn't mean that — I mean, I did, but should not have. Forgive me."

"For that, then, but never for springing a marriage proposal on me the way you did once. I was too dense to know how you felt — back then, I mean. It all happened so fast that —"

"Fast? I'd been courting you for years."

"You had not! You had taken me here and there about the estate and were good to the boys!"

"I don't give a two-penny damn for that excuse! I didn't expect you to be so . . . so naive with a one-track mind!" He hauled me to a standing position, then bent down to pick my foot out of the net again.

"Chadwick Reaver! I had never been courted before, even though I had day-dreams I would wed my previous employer, but that was only a girl's dream because I did not want to leave his children."

"But you managed to switch your affections to other children. You would have certainly come to love ours. And how close were you to him?"

"It was all wishful thinking on my part while he searched for a woman fit to marry!"

"I'll bet. And now you've even won over

the Prince of Wales. Any dreams and wishes about him?"

"Don't be ridiculous. You knew from the first my loyalty to my children here — you helped with that, encouraged that. Loyalty and duty — Chad, what is it?" I cried as I saw a tear track down his cheek. I would never have noticed, but it shimmered in the light from the Big House.

He gripped my upper arms hard as if I'd run away. "Let's not argue," he said. "I've done enough of that these last years with myself over you. And with tenant farmers here, who can't understand the passion the royals have for game on the estate. Nor can I control my passion for you, Miss Charlotte Bill. I'm caught between the king and prince and my own people — and caught between what's right and wrong about you."

We stood, steadying each other, breathing hard, not speaking for a moment. My lips burned from his hard touch, and my cheeks flamed from his beard stubble. The winter wind was mild, but it wouldn't have mattered if it had been a howling North Sea gale. Finally, I found words I had wanted to say for so long. "Chad, I'm sorry I hurt you when you proposed. I . . . I hurt myself too. I know you will be a fine father, and I'm sorry you lost your child."

He sucked back a sob. "Not one, but two. She lost another not so far along, though it's something she doesn't want anyone to know. I told her we should not try again for it endangers her health, and the doctor agrees, but she seems desperate to show me we can — she can."

I thought of her words and that triumphant look she gave me in the glasshouse when I'd stumbled on her that June day. She'd thrown her boast at me: *I know who you are, but I'll make up for it now.* But to have lost two as if they were cursed . . .

"I'm so sorry, truly," I told him. "I know of no one, including the king and prince of all England and the Empire, who would be a better father than you."

"And you the best of mothers," he whispered, but he didn't sound bitter this time.

"I want to give the feather picture back for your family," I said in a rush. "I adore it, but its place is not with me."

"If you gave it back now and Millie learned where it has been, she would break it, break herself in two."

I didn't say I was sorry again. I was, but it seemed so sad and hopeless to repeat it. "I'd best go back inside," I said. "I hope you catch your poachers."

A light flickered in his eyes, but it seemed

to illumine his handsome face. Was a poacher on the grounds with a torch? I turned my head, thinking I would just kiss him a quick good-bye on the cheek and flee, when a shifting light in a window of the Big House caught my eye.

"Chad," I cried, "look there! That bright light in the window. Is it just a light?"

"Dear God, it looks like a fire! I think in the queen's chambers where Millie takes flowers!" he shouted and was off on a run toward the Big House with me right behind him.

Already out of breath from arguing with and kissing Chad, I was panting like a dog when we reached the side door of Sandringham House. It was a fire for certain, for we saw not only flames one floor above us but smelled smoke.

Mabel had said there had been a terrible fire in the Big House years before I came, but only the tapestries and treasures had needed saving then. All I could think of now was, *God save the queen!*

Chad pounded on the door while I yanked the bell cord. It was Mabel who answered, still in her day clothes. If the king were not in London, more rooms would have been lighted this time of night, more people on duty.

"Fire upstairs!" Chad shouted and pushed past her.

"The queen's rooms!" I cried and followed him in. "Get help!"

I could hear Mabel setting up a hue and cry for the servants, who never went to sleep as early as their betters. Soon we heard others, pounding up the stairs behind us, coughing in the acrid, spreading smoke.

As Chad and I reached the hall outside the private rooms, we saw that the queen's lady-of-the-bedchamber, Charlotte Knollys, had Her Majesty out in the hall, coughing, crying, with a robe wrapped around her nightgown.

"Oh, my picture," the queen cried. "My only picture of poor Eddie on my bedside table."

Eddie, her firstborn, I thought. The one who would have been Prince of Wales had he not died here at Sandringham. Once betrothed to Princess May, he had been the roué son no one but his mother ever mentioned.

Chad took off his coat, wrapped it around his right arm, pressed it to his face and plunged into the room through belching smoke. "Chad, no!" I shouted, but my words went unheeded in the growing hubbub.

"Don't go in," Lady Knollys shouted, as if Chad had not done so already. The smoke was thickening, and perhaps she had not seen him. "My room was just above, and the ceiling could fall in! I think it started in the chimneys."

My eyes streaming tears, I went to the bedroom doorway and peered into the gray cloud of blinding smoke. "Chad, come out!" I shrieked. "The ceiling might fall!"

That was all I could manage before I fell to coughing. The house butler and housekeeper tried to shoo us all down the hall and the stairs. "The volunteer firemen from the village have been called," the butler announced calmly as if he were just summoning us to dinner. "They're bringing the hand pumps. Everyone downstairs, if you please!"

I was ready to run in after Chad but I kept seeing the children's faces. I lagged behind the exiting crowd, led by the intrepid queen who had evidently slept through the first of the smoke, heat, and flames. With her deafness, perhaps she had not heard the crackling fire or first shouts from Lady Knollys.

Thank God, Chad came bursting out of the bedroom, though soot- and smoke-blackened and holding his breath. His hair looked singed, his eyebrows too, but he held in his hands a large, ornately framed photograph of a royal I had never seen but had heard scuttlebutt about for years, whispers that he had been a homosexual. That gossips had even suggested he might be Jack the Ripper, but that was utter nonsense, Mrs. Wentworth had said.

I rushed to Chad and put an arm around his waist to support him. The metal picture frame was hot to the touch. Chad held tight to me, an arm thrown over my shoulder, hacking, gasping for air before I tugged him away after the others.

Downstairs, when he gave Queen Alexandra the photograph, her tears matched those streaming gray soot from his eyes. "You," she told him, choking on her words, "are a dear, dear man for this, and shall be rewarded."

"My reward is that you are safe, Your Majesty," he barely got out before we heard a rumble from upstairs as the ceiling of her bedroom evidently collapsed.

"Outside," the butler's polite tones resounded again. "Outside until the firemen arrive and declare the rest of the house safe."

As we straggled onto the lawn, Prince George came running up out of the darkness, looking quite dazed and, for once, unkempt, for someone must have roused him and he'd dressed hastily. "Mrs. Lala," he said in passing, "you beat me here."

"It was the queen's bedroom, but she is fine," I called after him, not planning to tell him I'd been mistook for a poacher.

Chad and I stood aside, leaning against the sturdy tree trunk as the firemen's long wagon rushed in, pulled by six horses, loaded with two large hand pumps and a bell clanging. To draw water from the lake, the eight men tugged the hose like a long snake, putting one end in the water, and rushed inside.

In the dark, Chad put his arm around my waist, pulled me to him and kissed my cheek. He smelled like an ashy fireplace. He wasn't coughing quite as badly, but his voice was rough. I supposed my clothes and cheeks were soot-smeared too.

"So, we both have had thanks from the rulers of the realm, and offers of rewards, eh?" he said.

"Shall we ask them for the moon?" I tried to keep my voice light.

He ignored that and, with a huge sigh as we gazed back at the Big House, he said, "So those flames will soon be out, but I don't know about ours. Good night, sweetheart. And despite my mistaking you for a poacher and this near tragedy, some things did make this a good night."

He squeezed my waist and walked off into the darkness toward the village. And I — so relieved we had made some sort of peace with each other, but knowing it made things just as hard — pressed my shaking legs back against the tree so I would not fall down.

CHAPTER 15

The next summer we were all invited to the Big House for the celebration the king hosted for David's tenth birthday. Bicycles and ponies were in the offing for the three oldest children. Even Harry and little George were allowed to attend, so the king and queen could show off all their grandchildren to their friends. On the day of the great party, I could be found sitting against a wall in the Grand Saloon of Sandringham House, tending the youngest boys until they were summoned.

Although I had been in the Grand Saloon before, most recently when I was trying to find David and Bertie during a game of hide-and-seek with their grandfather, I had never seen it ablaze with lights and filled with gorgeously attired people.

Tears blurred my vision of the dancers rotating past. The entire room seemed to glitter. The jewels, silks, even feathers in the ladies' hair, were like nothing I'd ever seen before. The chatter, the background music of Gottlieb's German orchestra — brought in from London for the dancing — was overwhelming.

When I'd first entered the room with Princess Mary, we'd both gasped in awe. I'd handed Mary over to her grandmother, Queen Alexandra, who was not in the swirl of dancing with her bad knee and limp. But she presided over the glittering head table.

I'd promised to describe as many gowns to Rose as I could. The queen wore a rose-hued, gossamer chiffon gown with a flowing back and streaming gold ribbons. Then a mint green satin gown with a beaded bodice and gold cords from a gold lamé waistband swept by. I think those long ones were called bugle beads, but my head spun with trying to remember so much.

At the other end of the room from the orchestra, square, four-person, linen-draped bridge tables awaited players for after the meal, as this massive, high-ceilinged room served many purposes when King Edward entertained. I kept to a padded bench where I held George and put Harry right next to me. After their grandparents or parents showed them off, I would take both back to the York Cottage nursery, where Martha would watch them while I returned to wait for Mary, who, unlike her older brothers, was destined for an early bedtime.

Finch hovered too, though Hansell was on holiday. That, in a way, was another birthday gift to David, because their tutor drilled both boys mercilessly on things they hated such as historical dates and battles and places. But he had helped David write a speech of thanks to memorize for this evening. I'd heard it four times and found it sounded quite stiff — even pompous, hopefully just a reflection of Hansell and not David, for the boy was still insufferably selfish and willful, still resenting my attentions to the younger children at times.

David came over with Bertie in tow. "Lala," David said, "I think I shall have to shout to be heard when I give my thank-you speech."

"Everyone will be quiet to hear you. Do not shout, or you will sound angry. You will do just fine. And do not hang around your wrapped presents, ogling them."

"You were a good present to me once," he said flippantly and darted off.

I had to admit David's comment was one of the dearest, most clever things the boy had ever said to me. Perhaps he would someday be suave with the ladies. His compliment almost — but not quite — made up for the fact that I was sometimes as lonely as the children. I lived among the adults but was not part of them, just as I felt suspended between the upstairs and most of the downstairs staff.

Despite the noise in the Grand Saloon, my mind went back to my adventures of the day before. Chad had driven myself, the children, and Finch clear out to the fens near the bogs and the shore of the Wash, where he had shown us a sand plover nest with its speckled, grayish eggs, then pointed out the nesting pair themselves sitting in the grass nearby.

"Take a look at their short bills," he'd told the children. "That's how you can tell them from longer-billed waders like snipes."

"Why aren't they sitting on this nest with the eggs?" Mary had asked.

Chad had explained, "You see, here's something interesting about plovers. They are very clever birds and sometime sit on places not their nests so other birds — people too, I suppose — can't find where their eggs are. But I knew where to look, that's all."

David said, "Good idea, since some ladies like to take eggs, blow them out, and put them under glass domes just as if they were the real thing. I think that's as bad as if we blew babies out of mother's stomachs before they hatch and come out. Mama says she doesn't want any more in hers to worry about."

"Righto, my boy, but we won't go into all that right now," Chad said with a stern look at me. "Just remember, if you want to hide something precious, you have to stay away from it sometimes, so others won't know."

While Finch was staring off toward the distant sea, Chad had looked only at me, tipped his head a bit and narrowed his eyes. Sometimes it was like that between us — unspoken things that screamed so loud.

My mind was pulled back to the present as Little George fidgeted and started singing "Baa, Baa, Black Sheep" over the tune the orchestra was playing. I shushed him but I could not quiet my unsettling memories.

David's celebration had been a great success, and that summer my life was so busy that I could shut out memories of Chad for a few hours when things got chaotic — like right now on this hot, humid night, the twelfth of July 1905, soon to be a momentous date to me.

Princess May become pregnant with her

sixth child, but she was having a hard time "hatching it," at David liked to say. Now she had gone into labor, here at York Cottage, where she'd borne her other children — except David — and this time it seemed prolonged and difficult. The doctor had been upstairs with her for hours, while the prince smoked cigar after cigar and paced up and down the hall. Eva Dugdale, who was usually with her friend for her lying in and labor, had a sick child she could not leave, so was not here.

My voice wavered when I sang to little Harry and George to get them to sleep. The entire house seemed tense, waiting for a new infant's cry, when the entire staff felt like wailing.

I tried to tell myself that this baby's birth would assure that I could stay here longer, at least as long as it took this sixth child to leave the nursery. The princess had vowed that each of the last two pregnancies would be her final one. And this one surely had to be, for Rose had whispered to me that her monthly courses were quite erratic now.

I'd tried to buck myself up with the knowledge that I'd have another little one to tend, because Chad had told Finch and me that his wife was expecting again, and he'd seemed happy about that, so I tried to be too. I reckoned Chad thought Millie's losing their first child — and a second he'd mentioned the night of the fire — were far enough in the past that they could try again and all would be well.

I lay down in just a petticoat and chemise because my high-necked nightgown was too warm. As the hours of the night dragged on, I tossed and turned on my narrow bed, thinking of what must be going on down the hall. A feeling of darkest dread overtook me. I heard Prince George's feet pass by in the hall again, pacing — at least I thought I did. I remembered the tales of poor Scottish Kittie Rankie, the ghost of the witch who walked the Abergeldie tower stairs. I had told no one of the gray, swirling mist I'd seen when I'd peeked through the keyhole that day we were trapped there. David and Bertie were convinced she'd slammed the door on us, but I'd pooh-poohed it all and kept the vision to myself. But now, I even smelled the prince's cigar smoke through the door, so that was not my imagination, surely not a half-waking memory of the fire at Sandringham.

Annoyed at my disjointed thoughts, I tried to pray myself to sleep, then sat up and fanned my face just as Mrs. Wentworth's distinctive rap sounded on the door. It must be over — a new child to see, to help the doctor care for. I'd have to get dressed, but at least I'd left my hair pinned up.

I tiptoed to the door and opened it a crack. Then, when I saw it was indeed Mrs. Wentworth holding a partly shuttered lantern, I motioned her in and held my finger to my lips to remind her the little boys were asleep.

"Her Royal Highness is calling for you," she whispered. She had tears in her eyes, and her face was creased in concern. "You are sent for straightaway."

"The baby's born?"

She shook her head, and the lantern wavered. "I fear there's some concern. I am sent to fetch you. She wants you now."

My insides cartwheeled. Surely after five children nothing could go really wrong. Perhaps in her delirium — for I know they gave her ether each time — she'd thought the child was born and ready for my care. Or without Lady Dugdale to hold her hand . . . or worse . . .

"I'll be right there," I told her and let her out.

I dressed in the dark as I had many times when I had a sick child. But now, it might be worse than that.

As I hurried toward the princess's bedroom door, I nearly ran into Prince George, indeed walking the hall. His hair was slick with sweat, his face glazed with it. Yet he was formally attired.

"Oh, good, Mrs. Lala." To my amazement, he took my hand in both of his. He was trembling. "She's insisting she has something to say to you — that she's afraid it's . . . it's . . . it's" — he went on, almost stuttering like Bertie — "going badly. But she'll come through, always has. Comfort her, if you can."

"Yes, Your Royal Highness. Of course, I will, and I'm sure it will soon be over with a good outcome."

"Pray God," he said and opened the princess's bedroom door, then closed it behind me.

It was deathly silent inside when I'd expected bustle and much ado. The doctor came over to me, blocking my view of the bed. I knew Sir John Williams was much respected and trusted. He'd been here for most of the previous births.

"Mrs. Lala, Her Royal Highness has insisted you be summoned before the administration of the ether so we can deliver the child." His voice was a mere whisper. "It's a large baby with a big head, and that is causing complications. Can you speak with her and hold her hand as Lady Dugdale always did? Can you keep calm during a dangerous delivery? She's raving a bit, so I hope you can stay steady . . . be a comfort to her no matter what she says. Of course, I want to save the child but the mother's life . . . especially in this case . . . who she is . . ."

His voice trailed off. Imagine — a doctor, one dubbed "sir," and he was as terrified as I was. I wanted to burst into tears but fought for calm. "Yes, of course. I will do all I can to help her."

"Steady, then, my girl," he said and led me over to the big bed.

Princess May's skin glistened with sweat, her hair stringy and wild across her pillow. A woman I hadn't seen before, even when Harry and George were born — a medical nurse? — was wiping her face, neck, and arms with a wet cloth. Princess May wore a thin nightgown, ruffled up to under her breasts. A sheet covered her distended belly and spread legs. I saw a chair, which the nurse indicated with a nod was mine, but I remained standing, leaning over the princess to take her hand. I am not certain we had ever deliberately touched before. Just a moment ago, the prince had taken my hand — and now this.

"Your Royal Highness, it's Mrs. Lala," I said.

"Who?" she asked, then stared up at me through unfocused eyes. Her face was crushed in a frown that made her look like someone else. "Oh, Lala, yes, thank God. If I should die . . ."

"No. No, you will be fine."

She barely squeezed my hand and repeated, "If I should die, swear to me you will stay with the children until they are grown. I made the prince — ah, ah —" she cried, gasping for air as a wave of pain contorted her face even more. "You — promise — too."

My heart thudded so hard it shook me. "Yes. Yes, of course, I will."

"You love them. Protect them — ah, for — me."

"Yes, I swear it, but you will be there. We will have picnics in Scotland, and you will teach them more songs and —"

She screamed, gritted her teeth and reared up off the damp, wrinkled sheet, then collapsed again.

On the other side of the bed, leaning over

his patient while the nurse stepped away, Dr. Williams said, "All right, then, Princess May. Mrs. Lala has promised so we must bring this baby."

The nurse came back with a little wire mask and draped a small cloth over it, ready to cover the princess's mouth and nose. Ether, I thought. Not really newfangled since Queen Victoria had used it in childbirth.

The princess gritted out, "And if this baby lives and I . . . I don't . . . you will care for him or her too. Please, Lala!"

"Yes, I vow to you I will care for and protect this child with my own life."

She seemed to rest a moment from her agony as the nurse placed the mask over her nose and mouth and dripped liquid from a bottle on it.

"Sit back away from the fumes," the doctor told me. "Keep hold of her hand. This ether will help."

I did as he said, sinking into the chair, wishing Eva Dugdale were here but grateful I could help. The princess's grip on my hand and then her entire body went lax. The nurse kept the mask over her nose and mouth but dropped no more of the ether from the little bottle.

I jolted even more alert, more terrified

when the doctor drew back the sheet and lifted what looked to be metal tongs, large ones, in his hands.

I realized he was going to push those up inside her to grasp the baby's head and try to pull him or her into the world. My heart went out to our brave Princess May. And to this child who might not live and could kill our queen, its own mother; an infant I'd sworn, above all the others, to cherish and protect.

"This has to end quickly," Dr. Williams whispered to the nurse and moved the tongs closer. "With these forceps, God help us, it is now or never for them both."

■ ■ ■ ■

PART THREE

1905–1910
YORK COTTAGE TO
THE ISLE OF WIGHT

■ ■ ■ ■

CHAPTER 16

I held the princess's limp hand as the nurse steadied her hips and the doctor inserted the forceps. He was sweating now too, great drops off his chin and mustache, as he bent over, concentrating on delivering the child. The room was like an oven this July day with the windows barely ajar. If this went wrong for the baby or Her Highness, what would it mean for Dr. Williams? For Prince George and the children he was so hard on at times? And for the nation, all of our futures, should the Waleses ever be king and queen?

I saw now why Princess May dreaded childbirth. Oh, I'd heard my mother scream now and again through it, but it seemed to quickly end. Surely, this would be over soon and worth the agony and danger. Could I do this myself to bear a child? Chad was lost to me, couldn't ever stay with me . . .

"Stay with us!" Dr. Williams kept muttering. "This baby, nurse . . . I just don't know . . ."

So did he mean the baby was lost and he could only hope for Princess May? Sweat stung my eyes as I blinked back tears.

And then, a sucking sound. The princess's body shuddered. I leaned closer as a head appeared first, one shoulder, two, then the rest of a little body. Another boy, her fifth! Wet and messy, yet the most beautiful thing I'd ever seen. But not moving. Not crying. Not — not anything and turning blue.

I started to cry as the doctor bent over the baby and suctioned his nostrils and throat with a tube that had a rubber bulb on its end. Dr. Williams dropped that apparatus and, as slippery as the child was, draped him over one arm and patted, then smacked his back and bottom. No cry. No gasp for air.

"Nurse, see to the afterbirth," he said, then to my amazement, brought the little boy — birthing cord still attached — to me and lay the baby facedown over the apron that covered my knees. With both hands free he lifted the baby's hips and smacked his back smartly once, twice, while I stared aghast.

The little boy sucked in a big breath. He moved against my thighs and cried. Though

I didn't know if I dare touch him, I did, rubbing his wet, little back, his neck up to his sticky, short blond hair until the doctor tended briefly to the princess, then came back with scissors and turned the baby upright in my lap to cut and tie the cord.

"Never would have dared that on Lady Dugdale's lap," he muttered. "Keep him warm with these." He gave me several towels, and I gently covered him, then cleaned as much of the little boy as I could. He looked as if he'd been through a battle, and indeed he had. I murmured low to him, soothing baby talk, calling him "poppet, sweetums, my little one." Well, indeed, in a way, he was to be mine.

With a glance at Princess May, who looked unconscious yet, I spoke up at last. "Will Her Highness be all right?"

"And will he?" the doctor said as he bent down to stitch up the princess as if she were a sock that needed mending. "Like you, Mrs. Lala, Princess May has grit and go, and that lad had better too. Nurse can take him from you in a moment, clean him up properly, then we'll have a look at him, but I daresay you're getting on famously already."

"Thank God, he's breathing, but he looks a bit the worse for wear. I can even see the marks from the forceps."

"Necessity, or we'd have lost them both. It's best if you tell no one what a struggle this was. I'll inform the prince, of course. As soon as we have things set to rights here, I'll bring him in."

"The baby's trembling now, but no longer blue," I told him. I sounded breathless, as if I'd done all the work. "He's breathing but shallow. Despite these towels, we'll need a blanket even before he's all washed up to keep him warm."

For the first time since the birth, the nurse left the princess and brought me a blanket to wrap the little mite around the damp towels. But under it all, I kept my hand on his chest to be sure it rose and fell as he breathed. His tiny mouth was puckered, his brow creased, his nostrils flared as if this world was a shock and a struggle. I'd promised the princess I would take care of this child, as was my duty, but it was from that very first moment I held him, so helpless in my lap, that I loved him fiercely.

When the nurse took the child, my apron was such a mess that I removed it and left it with the pile of rags. I stood by as the nurse bathed the baby, put some sort of oil on his limbs, even washed his hair. He was so new, so wrinkled. He fretted and wailed as he was bundled, so I knew he was indeed kin to his siblings.

"Let Mrs. Lala hold him," Dr. Williams said, after he had put packing between the princess's legs. "I need you here."

I need you here. This child, even more than the others, needed me. He was special, and if I never bore a baby of my own, this one was mine.

Three days later, Finch and I escorted the five children down the upstairs hall, summoned to the queen's bedroom since she was more herself now. I would not say she was much recovered, though she usually bounced back quickly after a birth. I had seen her several times, and she had thanked me for my help and vow to tend the child, but I almost thought she resented the little one for giving her such a hard time. I would not feel she was really well again until the doctor and nurse, still here, left Sandringham.

Today would be the first time the other children would see their new brother, who took extra watching because of occasional breathing concerns. My nursemaids and I had the two younger boys all scrubbed up to meet the latest family addition and to hear their parents announce his name, or string of them, if the pattern held true. Unfortunately, Mary was pouting because her governess had scolded her for shoddy work, but Finch had David and Bertie in firm tow. Harry and George were still so young that all they knew was that they had another playmate.

I chided myself over how not only protective but possessive I felt toward the new Wales baby. So I gave extra cuddles to his siblings, lecturing myself that Mary Peters, the demented nurse I had replaced at Sandringham, had been overly possessive of David. I vowed I would not be that with this new child. Still, as I helped tend him on those first few days he was yet officially unnamed, I hardly saw the other children. On the way to visit their parents and new brother, David clung to me.

"Remember, I was first and I'll be king someday, even if I don't want to!" he whispered to me as if in warning.

"I love all of you very much," I assured him while Finch rolled his eyes and shook his head. He'd evidently been hearing much the same from David, maybe from Bertie too. "You are all different, and I love you in different ways."

"Well, Mary's different, since she's a girl," David said, seizing my elbow and bouncing my arm. I was carrying little George. "But now we have five boys, and I am still number one."

As we went in, I curtsied to Their Highnesses, for the prince stood near the bed where the princess lay, propped up on a pile of satin and lace pillows. The room looked so different from a birthing room, without the medical supplies but decked with flowers, letters, and cards. The familiar crib with its organza skirting and ruffled hood stood near the queen's bed. I had been helping the doctor and medical nurse off and on in the next room, which they had requisitioned to keep a watch over the baby, but, of course, they would have brought the new child here now.

I saw they were not in the room, perhaps resting after what had, no doubt, been an ordeal for them too. I was still weak-kneed at all that had happened. I edged a bit closer to the crib to glance in and — Dear God, it was empty! Had we been summoned for an announcement of another kind?

The prince must have heard me gasp. He looked so sharply at me that I feared a telling off, but he said, "The child is still with the doctor. As you know, some slight respiratory problems hanging on."

"What is res-pra-tory, Lala?" Mary asked,

turning toward me instead of her father.

He nodded that I could answer. "It means it's a little hard to breathe sometimes," I tried to assure her, though my heartbeat had kicked up. I longed to rush next door to see if the baby was all right. "Like when you have a cold and your nose is stuffy and you have to breathe through your mouth."

"Precisely," the prince said. "But you will all see him soon, and your mother and I want to tell you before it is announced far and wide that his name is to be John." He stepped to the side of the bed and took Princess May's hand as she managed a wan smile. "To be exact," the prince said, "his name is John Charles Francis in honor of my brother, who was lost."

"Lost?" little Harry piped up. "Like in the woods?"

"No," their father said. "Such as who never lived to grow up like all of you will, including baby John, who we will call Johnnie, right, my dear?"

Princess May agreed, and the children peppered them with questions about the uncle they didn't know they had, though the prince mostly put them off. As he prepared to shoo them out, each of the children went to their mother's bedside and kissed her cheek, I holding the two youngest in turn so they could reach her.

But I was as upset — even annoyed — as were the children, who were let down because the baby wasn't there and their questions weren't answered. I thought it was a terrible omen that a baby who had a difficult birth and was having trouble breathing should be named for a baby who had died. I'd seen the grave of Prince George's younger brother, John, out in the churchyard of St. Mary Magdalene a half-mile walk from here. It bore a white cross with the engraved words, *Suffer the little children to come unto Me.* Good gracious, I thought, though I loved and honored the Lord, I surely hoped He'd let us have Johnnie longer than he'd let Queen Alexandra keep her little boy named John.

The next evening, and I suppose it was a strange thing to do, when the princess insisted I needed a break from helping to care for Johnnie, I made a beeline for the deceased John's grave. Dr. Williams and his nurse were still with us, though he'd pronounced that the baby was getting stronger every day. Blessedly, I had seen that was true.

Daylight lingered in the sky, and the July evening was warm. Yet coolness wafted from the grass as I headed for the gray, rough-stone building with the white trim that stood out ahead. The Gothic windows lost the last rays of sun, and the face of the clock on the tower went dim. I cut across the rows of old tombstones straight for the white cross over the first John's little grave.

Remembering what I had heard from Mabel about this early death the last time I had visited her at the Big House, I stopped to read the carved words on the tombstone. JOHN CHARLES ALBERT had been born at SANDRINGHAM ON APRIL 6, 1871 and had died the very next day. Poor Alexandra to lose her sixth and last child, just as our Johnnie would, I had no doubt, be the Waleses' sixth and last. And she'd lost her firstborn Eddie, whose portrait Chad had rescued during the fire. Too many deaths here, but I vowed anew that our Johnnie would live and thrive.

I wished the biblical quotation the white cross bore didn't say *Suffer the little children* on it. Oh, I knew that word "suffer" meant "allow," but that didn't help. Queen Alexandra's lost sons — did they suffer? Our Johnnie seemed to sometimes when he struggled for a breath. If I was there, especially if I was holding him, I would shift him to lie upright against my shoulder, cradle the back of his head, and gently wind him as if he'd just been nursed because it seemed to help him breathe.

I jumped as I heard footsteps behind me. I spun around — Chad. Close. So near . . . We'd been together but always with the children and now to be so suddenly alone . . .

"Charlotte, I thought it was you. Why are you here? Isn't the new boy better?" Stopping two tombstones away, he snatched off his cap and turned it in his hands as he spoke.

"Yes, a bit better each day, though he struggles to breathe sometimes. They named him John, and I wish that they had not. It is good to honor those we've lost, but clinging to memories can make things worse," I said and pointed at the name on the tombstone.

"Ah," he said, frowning as his eyes went swiftly over me. When he looked at me that way, I always felt his gaze as if it were a physical caress. I hoped he didn't think my words referred to us — our loss of each other. "Yes, I've seen a baby fight for breath," he added, his voice breaking.

I realized he must mean that his own child — a son, I'd heard — had struggled that way too. I confided, "I thought I'd come here for a few minutes, grieve for this lost lamb, grateful my new, little charge is holding his own."

"I often walk here. At first, I didn't think it right to approach you so that we would be alone again — even without a net." One corner of his firm mouth lifted, but in a grimace or a smile? "I'm here also to . . . to remember my son," he said, his voice rough.

He gestured back the way he must have come, toward the simply marked graves with the low, crudely cut headstones, compared to these large, ornate ones that were tied to the royal family.

"Oh," I whispered, and tears burned my eyes. "I should have known he would be here somewhere."

He walked away from the church with a simple gesture that I should follow him. We stopped over a nearly flat stone, facing each other, looking down at it. The grass over the little grave seemed to be worn at the edges by footsteps. Chad's? His wife's?

The gravestone read BOY REAVER. "His name is — was — Matthew," Chad whispered.

I know it was foolhardy here in the open to take his hand, but I did. "I'm sure you will have another child," I told him.

"Would that I had you to tend him or her," he whispered. He sniffed hard, squeezed my hand, loosed it and walked away.

I stood there a moment, listening to a ruffed male grouse in the nearby woodlot make its distinctive drumming sound with its wings to attract a mate. Chad had told me of that the very day I first arrived at Sandringham, and I'd heard it many a time since these last nine years. I remembered too Queen Alexandra's agate grouse David had pilfered the first time I'd visited the Big House. He'd claimed it was to give to Chad. Poor David, wanting to please Chad as if he were almost a foster father at times, as was Finch to him.

I could only hope and pray that David and Bertie would get over their frustrations and fears, just the way I hoped and prayed that someday I would get past my hopeless love for Chad Reaver.

CHAPTER 17

In August of 1905, when Johnnie was a month old and fully in my care, all of us were told we would be summoned to Princess May's boudoir at midafternoon. That, of course, was not unusual, but the timing for it was — earlier than our usual promptly-at-four. I knew something was afoot, though she was much recovered, quite her old self. She went about during the day, corseted as tight as ever, though Rose said not with the same waistline. She held Johnnie from time to time, but treated him as if he were fragile. She would pass him back to me quickly, sometimes right after he settled into her arms.

I had a policy of always telling the princess the truth about her children when she asked. That Mary did not like to study, unless it was about horses. David still fidgeted and Bertie still stuttered. The prince and princess were dismayed that little Harry, now five years old, lisped, switching his *w*'s and *r*'s, so that he said his own name as Hawee. I had worked with him but felt as helpless as I did with Bertie's sad stammering. But most unsettling of all to me was that Johnnie still had rough breathing spells.

"Well, whatever will it be next with these children, who are given every benefit?" the prince had shouted one day at Finch, Mr. Hansell, Madame Bricka, Mary's governess, and me. I found him and the princess both short with me, despite their earlier appreciation, but then we all understood outside pressures as well as those within.

Despite the king's increasing popularity here at home and even in finicky France, Britain was wracked with unrest. Rural folk of my class had dared to organize a so-called March for Unemployed People to London, but the king had refused to meet with them. At least, thank God, he had not ordered the crowd to be fired upon as had his cousin Tsar Nicholas in a similar situation this January in Russia, an event that had been dubbed Bloody Sunday in the British press.

Also, women called suffragettes were demanding the vote, though most of the royals and nobles, I had heard, called them "New Women." I rather liked that title, for I had lately come to think of myself as a "new woman," one whose vocation was to be her life, one who would not marry and have children of her own. I thought it strange, though, that the word "suffrage" sounded as if it had to do with suffering, but meant having the vote. And hadn't women, even in these modern times, always suffered?

Sadly, Chad's wife, Millie, had miscarried again, and I'd only seen him from afar. I guess the prince had decided Chad's field trips and nature lectures to his eldest children were over. At age thirty, I knew I had best be my own woman, if not exactly a new one.

Here at Sandringham, Princess May and Queen Alexandra were still not getting on. Mabel, Rose, and I were among the few to realize this had all come to a head in a sort of unspoken contest over which woman could collect the most Fabergé agate animals. It was a sort of joke between Mabel and me to keep count of our respective mistresses' new birds and beasts.

I'd learned much about the little carvings in these last years, such as Fabergé was not a Frenchman but a jeweler and artist who lived in Russia and was mostly patronized by the Waleses' cousin, Tsar Nicholas II, and his Romanov family. But what the queen and princess coveted now was something called Fabergé eggs. Mabel and I had a bet on which of our mistresses would come up with one of those first, and then a new competition would be on.

One day Mabel and I sat on the bench by the lake in our few hours off that we could coordinate. Mabel told me, "Agate animal number twenty-one, a rooster, no less, has appeared right on the table next to the piano. When someone plays it loud, the rooster scoots across, and I'm afraid it will fall off. Well, I tell the maids when they dust there, like I did for years, move it back away from the edge. I heard Her Majesty tell Milady Knollys that Princess May doesn't have a rooster or a tally of statues that comes even close to hers."

I didn't say it, even to Mabel, but with so much upheaval in the country, didn't the queen have more to worry about than besting her daughter-in-law's stone animal collection? But I did confide to Mabel, "I heard the princess is getting things she fancies from homes she visits. She admires something so fervently that they can't help but offer it to her. Lady Dugdale had the pluck to tell her that her hostesses will start hiding things soon. Princess May lived in Italy once, you know, and learned all about great art and such."

"Which the queen finds boring. Not that those agate animals aren't fine art. Char, why do you keep looking up at the window of York House?"

"I made your sister promise that she'd wave a handkerchief at the window if Johnnie has a spell, that's all."

"That's all? You worry about him all the time. He's better, isn't he?"

"Yes. Difficulties fewer and farther between. It's just he expects to see me when he wakes. He's . . . he's different from the others, even the ones I tended as babies. A bit more sensitive. Well, I've got to run, my dear. And will Sandringham House still be standing without you? There's something big coming at the little house, I can smell it in the wind."

"Big, like what, Char?" she asked, stopping to turn to me. "Come on, tell true!"

"Some sort of announcement from the prince and princess. I only pray the king is not ill with all this national ado, because — just like little David doesn't want to be king, so he says — I don't think the prince ever wants to be king either. And don't you dare even tell one of the queen's agate animals I said so!"

We hugged and were on our ways, Mabel cheekily humming "Rule Britannia" and I, glancing up at the window again. It was the one from which I used to watch for Chad down by the lake, the one now where little Johnnie slept.

"Your mother and I have something to tell you," the prince announced to his children and their staff as we stood behind the five of them and I held Johnnie in my arms.

To my surprise, rather than letting him do the talking, the princess spoke. "We had such a triumphant tour of the empire the year your grandfather became king, that we are being sent to India in mid-October, and will be away until April."

Mary said, "But that's — why, that's nearly half a year!"

"My dearest ones, I know you will miss us, and we shall miss you all greatly, but this is very important for your grandfather, for Britannia, and us too."

Princess May beamed as she explained it all with a smile and sweeping gestures as if showing them exotic India itself. I recalled how the previous tour had given her a lift, more self-confidence, to be so welcomed and cheered — and how the children had hardly known her when she returned home.

She went on explaining the places they would visit, "Indore, Benares, Bombay —

239

we'll send you wonderful postcards, of course."

All that meant little to any of them, though David and Bertie would soon have Hansell making them memorize details about those sites. These two oldest would run rampant again, with the blessing and abetting of their royal grandparents. I could read Bertie's face and demeanor: He was happy to escape his father's correcting and scolding him for his stuttering. David would be even harder to control, but it would give me more time to work with Harry's lisp. And in those six months of Johnnie's delicate infancy, the precious child would be more mine that ever.

Few could pry me away from Johnnie while the Waleses were gone, but one glorious late autumn day while they were in India, Hansell and Finch dragged me outside, though I protested that I didn't want to ride a bicycle. If they did their lessons well, David and Bertie with Mary right behind, were allowed to go flying down the slant of road toward Wolferton Station on the two-wheeled wonders of freedom.

David had told me it made him feel the "very, very best ever," so I was all for it. Bertie stammered less these days, especially when he came in from rides. Like Mary, the boys rode horses, but not with the love she did. It was their bicycles that were their escape from lessons and worries, and, at time, loneliness.

"Come on, then, Mrs. Lala," Finch insisted, hustling me outside before I even had time to pin on a hat. The cool wind lifted my skirts, and the sun felt like a warm caress on my pale face. I did manage to untie my apron, so it wouldn't be soiled. It was a new one with fine trim, sent to me by Dr. Williams to replace the one that had held Johnnie — which I wish I hadn't discarded now. That baby on my lap was perhaps the closest I would ever come to childbirth.

Finch went on, "There will be a good lot of us, and you won't have to fret for the children. We'll do that, eh, Mr. Hansell?" he asked with a wink at his coworker.

"But I don't really ride," I protested. "I've watched it often enough, but I never had a bike of my own, and Finch has only given me two lessons on Bertie's bike, and that was months ago."

"We'll get you started. No fretting," Hansell insisted in his best tutor's voice. "And someone will be with you."

We walked out to the cluster of bicycles,

leaned against the side wall of York Cottage. I believe the king had purchased every one of them though he never rode himself. David and Bertie grabbed theirs and began riding in circles, impatient to be off. Mary held on to her handlebars strangely, as if they were a horse's reins. I saw one bike was built for two. Were Mr. Hansell or Finch planning to ride with me? Was that why I had nothing to worry about?

I hesitated only a moment longer, thinking the children deserved this fun while their parents were off cutting ribbons in faraway India. I was just enough in the "new woman" mood to give this a try. Dr. Williams had said I had grit and go, and I supposed I was out to prove it today.

Hansell steadied me as I climbed onto the backseat of the bicycle built for two. The seat seemed oh so small, but I managed it despite my skirts. Balance was the hardest thing. I remembered that from my maiden voyage and another attempt on one of these contraptions. Truly, I had the hang of it but was yet a bit afraid to ride downhill as the others always did. I feared the so-called brakes wouldn't break my headlong hurtle clear to the railway station.

"You ready, Chad?" Finch bellowed, looking behind me. "We got her out, and she's set to go!"

"What?" I said, twisting to see Chad jogging around the corner of the cottage. "They didn't tell me you would be here. I heard you helped Bertie when he fell off near the woods but I'm not sure . . ."

"I am," Chad interrupted and mounted the same bike on the seat ahead of me. "You need to get out now and again, and today's the day."

I leaned forward and said to his broad back, "Are you certain this is wise?"

"No. But life is even shorter than I ever realized, Charlotte Bill, so here we go!"

David, Bertie, and Mary were long gone, with Finch and Mr. Hansell riding after them. "Finch owed me a favor," Chad threw back over his shoulder as — I'm sure without much help from me — he righted the bike and started off, while I struggled to stay upright. Had I just been abducted? And by the man I'd adored for years? It seemed wrong and yet so right.

"Hang on!" he called back and pedaled even harder as we started downhill.

I had no choice. I hung on for dear life. And it was fine with me.

Chapter 18

The wind ripped long strands of my hair loose behind me. Pine trees lining the road whizzed by. I found my pedaling had to match Chad's, and he set a fast pace. This ride downhill was foolhardy, outrageous, and quite grand.

He began to sing, which I'd never heard him do before, from that song about Daisy, written about King Edward's previous mistress, no less: *"I'm half crazy all for the love of you . . ."*

Peering around his shoulder, I could see the others ahead of us, racing toward the station. We passed some village workers on the road, trimming trees. Chad shouted a *halloo* to them. I would have waved, but my hands were gripping the handlebars for dear life. Had this solid, reliable man taken leave of his senses? Wouldn't it spread like wildfire that Chad Reaver, the head gamekeeper, a married man, was riding madly with a woman not his wife? It was my duty to guard my reputation too.

"Chad, this is a lark, but we should turn round and go back," I called over his shoulder.

"You and I can't go back, my love. Too late."

"Don't call me that. Your duty —"

"Yes, I know. Duty calls, but I'm not listening."

Despite the fact we were hurtling downhill, he somehow applied the brakes and we came to a slow stop. He put one foot down to steady us as we tipped a bit.

"Get off," he said.

"What?"

"Charlotte, get off the bicycle and stand beside it. I need to speak to you and we can stand here, looking at the bike as if there's a problem with it."

"There is a problem with it. We shouldn't be together like this, in private at night or in broad daylight with half the estate folk watching."

"Get off the bicycle."

I did while he held it steady. As I stood beside it on the side of the road nearly to the station, he bent over it, looking at it, not me. I should have waited for him to speak, but I blurted, "I wanted to write a condolence message for the loss of your second child, but I thought it unwise, that Millie might take it amiss. I see you buried the baby next to her brother."

Not looking at me, he nodded. "Did you leave the bouquet of flowers there about a week after?"

"Yes."

He looked up, frowning. For one moment I feared he was angry with me for interfering. "Thank you," he said. "That was kind. And like some silly, love-struck swain, I kept one of the roses, dried and dead as it is now."

"Oh. And, how is she — Millie?"

"Hell-bent on being a mother, while I fear for her — and us. The doctor said it could kill her, so our . . . our relationship is difficult. I'm finding it hard to take the bad with the good."

Tears prickled behind my eyes, but I didn't cry. "Like Princess May and Prince George now. No more children, I think, but perhaps it isn't even possible after Johnnie's difficult birth."

"And how is your newest charge?" he asked, going back to fussing with the bike.

"Better at breathing. Growing some, but not as he should. Slow to roll over. He should have done that about a month ago."

"Well, you would know about those things. You're more mother to him than Princess May," he said, straightening and clapping his hands as if ridding himself of dirt.

"You mustn't say that."

"Only to you. I just wanted to talk, though I admit I'd rather kiss and caress you."

My cheeks flamed with heat, and my lower belly began to flutter. "Talking like that doesn't help."

"I know, but I dare hope you feel somewhat the same. It helps me to be honest with you. No more rolling around on the ground together, but I didn't want you to think I was angry with you. Life is precious and short — too short for some," he added, his voice bitter. "Whatever happens, I just wanted you to know. And now, we shall say the bicycle is fixed, and we'd best catch up with your three eldest children before David and Bertie come charging up here to help us. Here," he said, taking my elbow and helping me to get back on. "You'll have to really work hard, sweetheart, when we pedal back uphill. Milady Lala, you have a man who shall always love you from afar. No, don't say a thing. Here, your skirt is going to be caught." He pulled my hem from the pedal and mounted ahead of me.

We whizzed on down the road, though my

heart was thumping as if we already rode uphill. I hoped no one would see my tears and trembling lower lip, but the truth was I didn't need this bike, for I was flying. Still, the pain of being so near and yet so far from him was renewed agony.

"Isn't it great, Lala?" Bertie called out when we joined the others. "I can say words like 'big, beautiful bicycle' and not stutter one bit, so when they get back, I want you to tell P-Papa!"

"David beat me here," Mary interrupted, "but I'm getting closer! Girls can ride fast too!"

So I was back with my own little family, the only one I would ever really have.

My ninth Christmas at York Cottage, the year of 1905, with the prince and princess in India, seemed different. That day, the children's grandparents were with us, and later we'd be going to Sandringham House for the gala celebration. Perhaps I was getting used to the glamour and generosity that had once amazed me. I would not say the glitter was off the tree or the shine off the candles, but this year Christmas did make me strangely homesick — not as much for my own family as for a home of my own.

I'd heard Princess May say last year that

Christmas at Sandringham was like the world of Charles Dickens wrapped in an exquisite package. It was becoming a new tradition that Mr. Hansell, using broad gestures and different voices, read Dickens's *A Christmas Carol* to all of us assembled at York Cottage before we went to the Big House.

As ever, the children were on pins and needles to have to wait so long to open their gifts. Yet my charges, even David, sat as if entranced from the very first lines "Midder" Hansell read: *Marley was dead, to begin with. There is no doubt whatever about that. The register of his burial was signed by the clergyman, the clerk, the undertaker, and the chief mourner. Scrooge signed it . . . Old Marley was as dead as a doornail.*

"But he still comes back as a ghost," Bertie whispered, twisting around in his chair ahead of me. "Remember that ghost who locked us in the t-tower in Scotland?"

Holding the sleeping Johnnie in my arms with George beside me on the same seat, I motioned for Bertie to turn around and pay attention. But the ghosts of Christmases past were in my thoughts, happy memories tinged with sadness. I hadn't gone to London to see my parents this summer because Johnnie needed me. Then there was the haunting of my heart with memories of the Yuletide with Chad the year he gave me the gloves, the time we made snow angels, the time . . .

Johnnie sucked in a breath, and his eyes flew open in surprise. I knew a rough breathing spell was coming, so I immediately tipped him up against my shoulder and patted his little back. His velvet-soft head tilted against my neck. He cuddled in, the little gasps not so bad and quickly past.

I jumped when David and Bertie shouted "Bah! Humbug!" the first time Mr. Hansell read those words. I wished they would quiet that down, for Johnnie jumped each time, so I rose and, bouncing him against my shoulder, walked him out into the hall. Even with the door barely ajar, I could hear how they chimed in — now with their grandfather's booming voice — each time "Bah! Humbug!" was said until the happy, tearful ending when Tiny Tim cried out, "God bless us every one!"

Applause, of course, for Mr. Hansell. At this point Princess May always led the children in singing carols in the sitting room, but without her, there was no one to lead. I loved to sing and could have done it, but I would not presume. Chad might have once implied I was more mother to my charges than was Princess May, but I dared not think such thoughts. Besides, with their grandparents here, that helped to fill the gap of their parents' absence.

A bit later, I left Johnnie sleeping heavily in his cradle with his undernurse Jane watching him and traipsed outside to the coach house near the stables to watch the presentation of Christmas gifts to the York household and estate staff from the king and queen, in place of the wandering Waleses. In a curved queue, about three hundred folk waited outside in the frosty but snowless night, gardeners, foresters, stable hands — including Chad and his wife with his game-keeping staff.

Since his parents were away, David, who was nearly twelve, had the honor of sitting just inside the coach house door with Their Majesties. While the rest of us stood behind their chairs, I kept a good eye on George and Harry. I and the nursery staff had received new outfits and a holiday stipend, the latter of which I'd sent home for my parents' gift.

In turn, the household, then the estate staff, many of the latter who were married, stepped forward with their mates and were each able to select a large, wrapped joint of beef and wished "A Happy Christmas!" by the king.

I held my breath as Chad and Millie Reaver stepped forward. Like the others, Chad doffed his cap and made a slight bow while Millie bobbed a quick curtsy. Chad's gaze met mine, lingered, then darted away. Millie stared at me and when she turned sideways to move on — just as that time so long ago when we had talked in the glass-house — I was certain she was slightly pregnant. Well, I mean one can't be a little bit pregnant, but she could not be too far along. Maybe she had conceived about the time Chad and I had our last privy chat, that day on the bicycles. If that was the time — somehow, that hurt.

As if I'd caught Johnnie's malady, I gasped and sucked in a throat of chill air. I started coughing and gestured to Mary to watch the two youngest boys as I moved to a far corner of the coach house. No way was I going outside, so that Chad and Millie might think I was following them.

Despite the evident danger of another childbirth for her, I had to admire her pluck. She was desperate for a child at the risk of more grief, and I understood that. I would die for Johnnie, and he wasn't even really mine.

"Char, are you all right?" Mabel asked as

she came up beside me. The king and queen had brought some of their staff with them, including Mabel. Bless her, she extended a little flask of something in her hand, and I took a swig from it.

"Spiced cider," she whispered, "nothing like the toffs drink. I've got to hurry back to the Big House, see that the tree candles are lit for the children in the grand saloon. I oversaw the decorating of the tree, with the queen standing right beside me. A Christmas tree is one of the few things Queen Victoria's Prince Albert liked that the king abides."

"I remember," I told her, my voice sounding raspy. "King Edward redid Buck House and got rid of the old queen's beloved Osborne House. Must the royal offspring always resent their father?"

"Char, you think too much. Come on, it's Christmas. Oh, by the way, you should see the wrapped gifts — some for your little Johnnie too. I guess you'll have to open those for him this year with the princess gone."

She took back the flask and darted off. *Your little Johnnie,* she had said. Yes, unlike with the other children, I felt that he was mine, though someday, I supposed, I'd have to give him up. But not to death's cold hand, not like Chad and Millie had to do, and the king and queen also. That indeed would be a haunting far worse than any fiction of what poor old Scrooge went through. How sad the story of Tiny Tim being crippled, and Johnnie had problems too. By next Christmas Eve, I vowed, he would be stronger, better, if not normal, in his own way, just fine.

But, after the York Cottage festivities, I could not help but think that sometimes the royals nearly abandoned their children. Not only would Johnnie's parents be in India for months, but almost as soon as they returned, I'd been informed, they were heading for Norway, and Mary was to be prepared to go along. The event was the coronation of the prince's sister Maud, as queen, and her husband, newly named Haakon as king of Norway.

Mabel had also told me that Queen Alexandra thought all that a farce because the new Norwegian king had been elected by a popular vote, no less, and it set a dreadful precedent. I rather thought that sounded fair, though a bit too American. But Mabel had whispered that Alexandra was also incensed that her daughter-in-law May must have convinced Prince George to sanction such an event. Well, the only thing about all that which really bothered me — besides the children being without their parents longer — was that the Waleses were going to miss David's twelfth birthday.

I hurried to catch up with the children piling into the horse-drawn omnibus for a traditional ride to the Big House. The estate workers had greatly dispersed, but a few stood about. Not the Reavers, thank heavens, for it yet bothered me to see them together. But a lanky man was calling to a woman who was maybe his wife. He was calling her Lil and telling her to keep back from the omnibus full of " 'em uppers." And there was something about his voice . . .

I jerked my head around. That man. It had been over three years, but I could have sworn he was the leader of the pack that had halted this very omnibus and threatened us as we were heading to a picnic with the kaiser. And yet, it was Christmas and the prince — even Chad — were not here to tell right now. Nothing else had come of that for a long time, so the rebellion must have died down.

Still, if anything untoward happened, I'd have a better description of the lanky man. I would be able to say, at least, that he had a wife named Lil. If I ever had another chance to talk to Chad, I'd warn him, though. I looked around, craning my neck to see if there could be any of that man's cohorts hanging about to stop us again, but I saw only darkness.

With a jolt as the horses started to pull, we headed toward the Big House, ablaze with lights.

CHAPTER 19

On a lovely day the next spring — it was 1906, amazingly, six years into the new century — I kept Harry and little George out of the way of flying feet and darting undercooks and two scullery maids in the main kitchen of Sandringham House. Johnnie was taking a nap, watched closely by both of my undernurses, and this was my afternoon off. I planned to meet Mabel and take the boys for a walk with us. The leaves were fully budded and the robins and skylarks sang, so why not?

Poor Harry, recently turned six, had been put in splints like Bertie had, but Harry was also in heavy boots to help straighten what his father called knock-knees. Despite his difficulty walking, the boy always wanted to go along, but I felt so sorry for him as the contraptions made him seem clumsier than he already was. Right now, he and three-year-old George knew they'd be in for a treat from their grandparents' kitchen and Mrs. Grey, the head cook.

I told her, "I hope we're not in the way if we just stand here and smell those wonderful aromas."

"Never in the way," the sprightly woman called to me as she supervised pouring and stirring and oversaw the arrangement of several silver food trays. "Not the queen's grandchildren! Edwina here will fetch the little ones some biscuits. It's the lemon sauce for the sponge cake you smell. Her Majesty has three friends and, of course, Lady Knollys to lunch.

"And how's that youngest little angel now?" Mrs. Grey asked as she fringed china plates with springs of parsley. The plates held displays of cold meats; asparagus tips; cucumber; egg sandwiches; cheese canapés with pickles; a salmagundi salad with spring flowers round its rim; and — oh, my — scones with strawberries and clotted cream, my very favorite.

"Johnnie's doing much better now, Mrs. Grey. Still not sitting up well at nine months but breathing easier."

"Well, good news all round about little ones, since Chad Reaver finally got his child."

The stone tiled floor under me seemed to

tilt. "They — The baby is all right?" My heart thudded in my chest. Finally, a child. How happy Chad — Millie too — must be. Finally, Chad had some good after the bad.

"A girl, what's that name they gave her?" Mrs. Grey asked yet another cook, one who must be new from the village since I hadn't seen her before.

"Penelope, nickname Penny," the girl said, stirring something on the huge iron stove. "Still so sad, such a price to pay."

"What?" I cried, thinking of Johnnie's breathing problems. "Is the child all right?"

I caught a look they gave each other just as Mabel appeared from down the hall with three tall, white-gloved footmen. The men carried the trays out of the kitchen while a third stood like a sentinel in the corner, evidently waiting for the tray with the dessert.

"Sorry I'm tardy, Char," Mabel called to me over the bustle. "Did the lads get a treat?"

Mrs. Grey was pouring lemon sauce over the sponge cake, set among rosebuds on its own round, cut-glass tray. When I nodded, wide-eyed but didn't speak, Mabel hustled the three of us outside and propelled us over to a bench by the back door herb garden.

"They told you about the Reavers, didn't

they?" she asked.

"Yes, just now, about Chad's little girl."

"I wanted to be the one to let you know. Can you have these two go play by that little horse head swing Her Majesty had built for their sister?" she asked, pointing to the weather-worn swing that dangled from the branch of an old apple tree. "Maybe Harry can swing George."

I told the boys, "Harry, you watch George and don't swing too hard, then we'll go for our walk."

"It's swell, Lala," Harry said, ever the little helper. "I know it's your time off and you brought us anyway." With his mouth still half full of a biscuit and dragging his feet in his boots, he took George by the hand and tugged him over to the old swing.

Mabel grasped my hands, which I had gripped in my lap.

"There's something wrong with the Reaver baby, isn't there?" I asked. "What if they lose her after all they've been through?"

Mabel's lower lip dropped. She squeezed my hands tighter. "They didn't tell you all of it then. Well, I mean it just happened yesterday evening. Char, their baby's thriving, has a wet nurse even, because Millie died giving birth. They're burying her day after tomorrow."

■ ■ ■ ■

Mabel walked the boys back to York Cottage for me. I sat on the bench, queasy and crying, watching the wind move the empty horse head swing that creaked as if a ghost sat there. And maybe it did. Not Millie's to haunt me, but strange regrets. Grief for Chad. Torment that maybe I should have married him. Agony over whether to try to write him, comfort him, attend the funeral or just stay away.

And could this mean another chance for us? He'd said he still loved me, but my way was set now with protecting Johnnie just as he must care for his Penelope. I'd vowed to Princess May I'd never leave Johnnie, and I felt fierce about protecting him.

I sat there until Mabel came back, pulled me off the bench and made me walk and talk. She and Rose were the only ones who knew my feelings for Chad, but I'd not told them that he had declared he loved me yet after all these years. The first day I'd met him, he'd said one had to learn to take the bad with the good. *The Lord giveth and the Lord taketh away,* my mother would have put it, though she would have had my head on a platter with lemon sauce if she'd known I loved a married man.

But he was not married anymore.

The next year, the king decreed that David was ready for the Royal Naval College. "Midder" Hansell had objected, Finch was stoic about it, and I was appalled. Since David was so immature and shaken, I had tried to enlist the support of Princess May to appeal to the prince for more time. But she had said she could not interfere with his decision that "The Navy will be the making of him." In her own words, she had added with a sad smile her usual comment, "After all, Lala, we must keep in mind that his father may someday be his king."

The poor boy passed a three-day battery of grueling tests — of course, dare they deny a future king? — to become a cadet. This morning, his family and the staff who had been close to him were assembled outside York Cottage to bid him farewell for the months he would be away until Christmas.

At least, I had said to buck him up, the college was on the beautiful Isle of Wight, at Osborne House, though that held no fond memories for him. Soon after Queen Victoria had died, King Edward had given her beloved place to the nation, so David had no ties to it. I had been hoping the king would overrule his son about sending David off — with Bertie and the other boys to follow when they also turned thirteen — but the carriage was waiting to take David to the railway station.

I could see the poor child was trembling. He dreaded leaving here, and I could not blame him. What ties had he ever had to "regular lads," as Finch called them? And, even more than his brothers, he had chaffed and suffered under his father's strict rules and regulations. For their whole lives, it seemed to them, they had already had a strict commander, and today Prince George was decked out in his full uniform as if reliving his beloved naval days.

By contrast, David looked as if he were pained by his blue jacket with its brass buttons, stiff white collar, and sharp navy cap. Under his parents' watchful gaze, he went down the line of the house servants, then to his personal staff, Finch, Mr. Hansell, even Madame Bricka, with whom he had never gotten on. Then me. I held little Johnnie in one arm, a full family member though the sweet, little blond boy had no notion of what was going on or what lay ahead for him. When I gave David a one-armed shoulder hug, for we had said our tearful goodbyes earlier, he threw his arms around me and held tight.

But he knew better than to sob as he had earlier, "Lala, I don't want to go! I don't want to leave here, leave you and Finch, and what will Bertie do without me? But I'll write, Lala, I will write!"

Then, silent, still trembling, he loosed me, stepped back, and squared his shoulders. He hugged his sister, then shook hands with Bertie, Harry, and George. But I did regret the fact he didn't so much as pat Johnnie on his head or grasp his little hand. The more I'd tried to get him to warm up to Johnnie, the more coldly David had treated him. It both angered and hurt me.

His face looked pinched and pale as he mounted the carriage steps. His father, who had surprised us all by deciding to accompany him from here to London, then to Portsmouth, climbed up and sat beside his heir. The prince had a large traveling trunk, but David only his single packed dressing case. As they slowly pulled away, I saw Chad had been standing on the other side of the carriage.

I gasped and clutched Johnnie closer. For months I had only laid eyes on Chad from a distance — including when I stood far back in the crowd of villagers and estate workers at Millie's funeral, and I'd never glimpsed his daughter, which I longed to do. He still wore a black mourning band round his shirtsleeve. He looked thinner, older, sadder, and yet strong and solid. And he'd finally grown a fashionable mustache, one tinged with silver I could see in the slant of sun.

"Chad!" I heard David cry out as the boy twisted around in the carriage. "When I get back for the holidays, I can help you again with the grouse! I didn't mean to break the latch on the cage so the fox got some of them. I —"

His father pulled him back in his seat as the carriage rolled away, down the road where we had all once ridden our bicycles so happily to the railway station.

My gaze locked with Chad's before Princess May called to me and I had to turn away. Here, I thought, Chad had lost some of his fledgling chicks to a fox, and today, I knew just how he felt.

David's first letter to me was dreadful, and I could only pray the ones to his parents were not of that ilk:

Dearest Lala:
My bed is hard iron, but that is the least of it. We live in huts, thirty of us

packed in round what was once the Osborne Mansion. We rise at six and rush about. It is so cold. We have to take a wash in icy water in a pool.

I do get ragged on by the other cadets. I am just not used to their type. I should have played more with village lads to get the hang of things. The senior cadets are pretty hard on us. I'd take a scolding from my father and lessons from Madame Bricka in place of this. I suppose you are helping Bertie with his "stammers" and "Hawee" with his lisps. And when you hug Johnnie, don't forget your first care, and I hope you still care for me, David

That Christmas, when Johnnie was two and a half and starting to come into his own as a sweet, slow, and stubborn self, poor David returned home with a sealed, bad report for his first term. Of course, when his father opened it, he was enraged. I could not keep from crying as I knew David was being fiercely scolded in the library. I heard later from Finch that the prince had hired one of the toughest teachers from the naval college to tutor him over the holidays. Worse, he had told David he would do his extra studying during the time the boy had hoped to spend with his grandfather at the Big House.

I respected and honored Prince George, but, I swear, I could have told him off that day. When I laid Johnny down for his nap, I bundled up and rushed outside to vent my anger away from people, and ran into Chad Reaver at the side of the house where he was leaning an animal cage doorframe against the wall.

"Oh!" I cried out, sounding so stupid to myself after all this time when I wanted to say so much to him.

"Hello, Charlotte. I thought it might divert David — make him feel better, because Finch told me he hates navy life — if he could repair the door he left damaged so the fox got in. I fixed that long ago and bred more chicks, but he needs to know he can set something right, so I'm going to have him fix this one."

"Yes, he does need to know he can set something right. I've had letters from him, bad and sad ones."

"How is the youngest lad then?"

"Much better than I could have hoped at first. Johnnie has a naughty streak, not that they all don't."

"Not my shiny Penny!" he said with a quick grin that lit his face. "You should see her, looks like my sister, her aunt Winnifred, who is helping to tend her when I'm out and about like this."

"I never said how grieved I was for you, but Millie left you a great gift."

"I do blame myself for her loss. We should not have tried for a child again. I've been punishing myself in a way and trying to keep from blaming Penny."

"Oh, no, you wouldn't do that."

"You think you know me? Charlotte Bill, you and I haven't exchanged a word for ages, namely twenty-five and one-half months. When Millie died, you see, I vowed I should not have still cared for you all those years, so I steered clear of you. Millie and I weren't meant to be, but neither were you and I, even though I wanted to think so. Well, as they say, 'Water over the mill dam.' Excuse me, but I was told I could see David for a few minutes now, and if he spots you, I won't get this done."

"Yes," I said, my voice breaking. "I'll be on my way then. You know, Mr. Chadwick Reaver, you told me there would be bad mixed with the good that day you picked me up at the train station some ten years and I don't know how many months ago — an eternity, I guess. Thank you for caring for David. He needs that . . ."

I turned away, hurrying, not looking back,

then realized too late I was heading for the glasshouse his wife had tended, the place where I had once turned him down and had lived these years to regret it — except for my children, all of them, especially my Johnnie.

CHAPTER 20

"Johnnie! Johnnie, you come back here, you bad boy!" I cried and chased him down the hall toward the study where I knew Prince George was poring over his stamps. That room was off limits to the children, for the vast collection was all neatly labeled and ordered. This time of day His Royal Highness liked to spend time looking through his albums and placing new stamps in them in their proper places.

When I took Johnnie outside, I'd learned to rope him to me, my wrist to his middle, so he would not dart off. In the house, he was easier to watch but he'd given me the slip this time.

His nickname was "the Imp," and that well earned. Even I was forced to agree that there was something different and difficult about Johnnie. He seemed to live in a world where the only rules that mattered were his, as if he marched to some special music within. He'd been slow to talk, but when he did, he observed the world uniquely and spoke as if he commanded his own planet. His parents loved him dearly, and I adored him, but not right now!

The Imp managed to turn the doorknob of his father's sanctuary, which I had not entered since the time I'd spoken of the rabble-rouser. Since then, and with my information about the man, the Prince had located him. To avoid my — or Mary, truth be told — having to testify against the rebel, named Barker Lee, His Highness had threatened him with prison but had given him the choice of leaving the estate. Thankfully, he did, taking his family with him to who knew where. I did pity the man. I was glad he was gone, but how I would hate to have to leave Sandringham — almost as much as I hated having to chase Johnnie into the prince's inner sanctum.

"Papa! Papa! Stamps! See?" Johnny cried before I could get to him as he stomped round in a circle, laughing.

I groaned inwardly. Harry and George had been teaching him how to march with a paper hat and wooden sword, and Harry had explained the marching to him as "stamping." There was always a sort of clever reasoning to Johnnie's foolishness.

"Lala, what is this?" the prince exploded, rising from behind his desk and pointing to his son as the boy whirled about with his arms extended. Unfortunately, the breeze he made sent several stamps flying off the corner of the desk onto the carpet.

"He darted away, Your Highness," I said, out of breath, as I scooped Johnnie up in my arms, then realized I must retrieve the stamps. No, Johnnie must. The child had to learn to behave, to take orders if he was to live in the real world and not one of his own making.

I pinned Johnnie's thrashing arms to his sides and turned him to face me, risking ignoring his sputtering father. I supposed I would be in for a dressing down but I was not giving up on this lesson.

"Johnnie!" I said, kneeling and putting my nose right to his. "This is Papa's room. These papers are his. They are a different kind of stamp. They fell on the floor. Pick them up for Papa."

Johnnie twisted in my arms to regard his father towering over us. It had taken me two years to get the child to wave good-bye. You might know, he did it now, lifting his wagging fingers toward his father. I couldn't decide if Prince George would explode in anger or in laughter, for Johnnie was one of the few who could make him smile these days.

I was there on my knees, holding Johnnie when Princess May came in. "Oh," she said as she saw the six stamps on the floor. "Oh, my."

Johnnie shrugged loose, and I let him go. The child was smiling, as if he had not a care in the world, which he probably did not, though I fretted over his peccadilloes all the time. The boy bent and picked up a stamp, looked at the picture on it and handed it to his father. The next one he gave to me, then to his mother and so on until all six were off the carpet. He always had loved counting things, arranging things — his way.

"Thank you, my boy," Prince George said. "But next time you must knock on the door. Wasn't that good that Johnnie picked up the stamps, my dear?" he asked Princess May, who stood there with tears in her eyes.

Johnnie had baffled her too from the first. She seemed almost afraid of him and what he would do next, and I can't say I blamed her.

"Yes, thank you, Johnnie," she said. "And Lala too."

"If you'll excuse us, please," I said, getting to my feet and handing my two stamps to

Prince George. I took Johnnie's hand, and we headed for the door. "I am sure Johnnie will knock next time, Your Highness."

At the door, the boy turned, tugged his hand free and knocked on the wood *rat-a-tat* as if he was some drummer boy in the army — or navy, around here.

As I took his hand again and hustled him out the door and up the stairs, I heard Princess May say to her husband, "He does rather have his own sort of logic, doesn't he? I don't know how she deals with him day and night."

How did I do that? I loved the boy.

That spring that Johnnie was four, I took him out to see Chad's chicks — mostly partridge, this time — in the closest cage where he kept them until they could be released into the fields and coverts he so carefully tended. Last year, he'd sent a grouse chick to the house for Johnnie for a pet, though he hadn't brought it himself, and I feared he was avoiding me again. When the bird had grown too big to keep inside, we'd let it go in a part of the grounds where the hunters seldom shot, because — though Johnnie didn't know it — I couldn't bear to think "Peeps" would be brought down by a loud, twelve-bore Purdey shotgun like the hundreds of other birds Chad had reared.

"Peeps," Johnnie cried when he saw the birds. "Lots peeps! On a walk, Lala."

I gasped. A few were in the big cage, but most were loose, running all over the ground. The cage door stood ajar, perhaps the same one David had once left open to allow a predator in.

Johnnie chased them, laughed, and scooped two up to cuddle. It was then I thought I saw Chad behind a bush, glaring at us. But as the man darted away, I saw it was a stranger. No, he looked like the ruffian who had stopped the omnibus and scared Mary and me long before that, but I knew he was long gone. Or was he? At least the man had turned tail and run, but it was obvious who had loosed the chicks.

I picked up Johnnie, chicks and all, in my arms, riding him on my hip with his legs clasped around me. I hurried away from there and went out into the road by the church, the way we had come. Thank God, the man was nowhere in sight. It was almost as if I'd imagined him, but the loose chicks were real. Still holding Johnnie, I rushed back to York Cottage and told the prince's butler, who said he'd send someone to fetch Chad. I told him the man had looked like

Barker Lee.

"And tell him we have two of the chicks here!" I called as he hurried outside.

We waited in the downstairs hall with all the doors closed so the two partridge chicks couldn't go far. I thought Johnnie would chase them, but he was so good, petting, calming them — and they calmed him. I sat on the next to lowest stair, watching, wondering if Chad would come for these two.

I heard his boots as he came in the side door. Even his tread was familiar, as if I'd dreamed his coming for me. Foolish girl, I scolded myself.

"You say it looked like him, Barker Lee?" he got out before he spotted Johnnie.

I stood and clung to the carved banister. "I realize he's been sent away and his hair looked shorter, but yes, the one married to Lil."

"I'll have to tell the prince straightaway. He should have been locked up. If he's sneaked back in to cause trouble, maybe someone's hiding him on the estate. If he's doing this, it could be worse — and serious poaching has started again. Anyhow, with help, I've scooped up most of the chicks."

To my surprise, his tense stance, his anger seemed to evaporate as he squatted next to Johnnie. I was certain they had never met before, but the boy seemed to have a natural curiosity about strangers. "Good boy," Chad told him. "Thanks for taking care of these partridge babies."

"Partridge," Johnnie repeated perfectly, though he sometimes didn't like strange words and usually made up his own. "Peeps."

"Yes, peeps. If Mrs. Lala says it's all right, you can keep these two, and I'll send you some feed for them. They'll need water, just like you do." He looked up at me, then stood. "I'll send some wire so you can make a sort of cage. Wouldn't do to step on peeps in the middle of the night."

"Oh, yes. Very kind. Johnnie had another one, but when it got big we had to let it go."

He nodded. As in the past — it seemed like a thousand years and yet just a few moments ago — his gaze held mine, then swept over me, taking me all in, making me want to throw myself into his arms. No, no, I told myself. Not this again. Not this hopeless hunger, this longing that could keep me awake at night, however exhausted I was. No!

Chad said, "Best if you don't take the boy back there or off anywhere alone. Let me know, and I'll show him as many peeps as he wants, keep a watch on both of you. If Barker Lee's come back, he may mean more than mischief."

"Thank you. You've always been so kind to the boys, Mary too."

"Have you heard from David?"

I lowered my voice. "His letters are so sad. Chad, they make fun of him and call him 'princey.' They dumped red ink in his hair and taunted him. I swear, I thought it would be the other way, that they would be stand-offish with him."

"Then he's got to learn to stand up for himself. I just hope it doesn't turn him against us commoners in the future. Maybe it will help when Bertie goes too."

"Which he will as soon as he's thirteen. And it will be even harder for him — the bad without much good, I fear."

He nodded, then bent and ruffled John-nie's hair as he used to do to David's. "I'll send wire for the cage," he said and started away, but he turned back and smiled when Johnnie's high-pitched voice piped up.

"Papa says I can't make a peep," the boy announced, "but I like to keep these peeps."

It was the longest sentence the child had ever uttered. I was so happy — so pent up — I leaned down and hugged him and cried.

That same summer, much later, nearly July, York House was abustle with preparations for all of us to visit the Isle of Wight for a family reunion with the prince's cousins, Tsar Nicholas and Tsaritsa Alexandra of Russia. All the Wales children would be there, and Their Imperial Majesties were bringing their four daughters and their heir, Alexey, the young tsarevich, a boy about Johnnie's age. The older children were learning a spattering of Russian words, though their cousins were said to speak perfect English.

I was overseeing my undernurses' packing of my three youngest charges' clothes when Mrs. Wentworth rapped on our open door. Usually, she sent one of the maids up with messages or to fetch me if I was needed downstairs or in the princess's room. Princess May and I had come to an understanding to speak freely — when we were alone. She fretted that something was wrong with Johnnie, but it only made me want to protect him more. I know I made excuses for some of the things he did and overlooked others.

"Mrs. Lala," Mrs. Wentworth said, "you

have a visitor."

My stomach did a little cartwheel.

I motioned for Martha to keep an eye on Johnnie, who was playing with one of the peeps, one that was getting much too big already and must be released soon — perhaps just before we headed for the royal yacht and the Channel.

"Who is it, Mrs. Wentworth?" I asked as I walked out into the hall with her. "I'm not expecting anyone."

"Came in on the train and walked all the way up the road, a Mrs. Margaretta Eager." She handed me the woman's calling card.

I wracked my brain. I knew no one by that name. Could she be a friend of my mother's? Did this mean trouble?

Mrs. Wentworth went on, "A lady who runs a boardinghouse in Holland Park in London, so she says." Mrs. Wentworth was obviously enjoying doling out her information when I was nearly champing at the bit. "A friend of your family, I take it, but she says she brings no bad news, kind of her to say that right away, I thought. I put her in my sitting room, and you may join her there. I'll have some tea sent in."

"Thank you so much," I said as I fingered the card. It did not have embossed letters, so it was not an expensive one.

I followed Mrs. Wentworth down the back servants' stairs, smoothing my hair, stiff white cap, and my skirt. Too much chasing Johnnie and playing with him on the floor, which I'd never done with any of the others at that age.

The door to Mrs. Wentworth's sitting room, with her small bedroom beyond, stood ajar. I went in and closed the door. When I saw the woman in a straw hat with a flower band that looked the worse for wear, I realized I didn't know her.

"I hope you don't bring bad news," I blurted, no matter what Mrs. Wentworth had said, as I sat in the other chair across a small, cluttered table. "I'm sorry, but I can't place you, Mrs. Eager."

"Actually, Miss Margaretta Eager," she said with a nervous nod at the card I still held in my hand. "Thank you for seeing me, Miss Bill — or I hear they call you Mrs. Lala here."

Probably in her mid- to late thirties, she had a round, flushed face. The walk from the train station had put pink in her cheeks, and she was perspiring through the dark blue jacket of her walking suit. Her handbag and parasol lay on the floor. Her fading reddish hair was speckled with gray, and her blue eyes looked faded or sad. Though she had said little, I picked up a slight lilt to her speech — Scottish or Irish, I thought. So whatever could this stranger want from me?

She clutched her crocheted gloved hands tightly in her lap and, keeping her voice low as if we shared a secret, said, "You see, Mrs. Lala, I was royal nanny to Tsar Nicholas's children in Russia before I had to leave, sent away, I was. Today I spent the fare to take a railway carriage clear out here because I hear you will be seeing them soon and I am desperate for your help."

CHAPTER 21

"Then we have much in common as head nurses to royal children," I said, as Mrs. Eager shared her identity and her past. "Russia — what an adventure! But then, why are you here?"

"To ask a favor," she said, leaning forward. "Small, but so important to me." She glanced down at a square piece of metal that just filled her palm. It looked to be silver, perhaps a facedown picture frame. "But, if you have a few minutes," she went on in a rush, "for I know how busy you must be, I would like to explain a bit first."

"Yes, of course. The favor you mean, because I and my charges will see the Romanovs soon? I know it's been in the London papers that Prince George and his family are going to meet with them on the Isle of Wight."

She nodded. She understood. It was so comforting to meet a stranger with whom I had much quickly in common.

"Oh, the tsar's visit has been in the London papers, all right," she said with a disdainful toss of her head and slight frown.

I told myself, that despite my instant sympathy for her, the woman was obviously of Irish background and that England always had an "Irish problem." She seemed not to like the tsar, so should I trust her or did she have some bone to pick with that royal family?

"I tell you," she went on, "Parliament and the press have been screeching like banshees that the tsar is a brutal dictator. They've never yet let up about Bloody Sunday five years ago, no they have not. I was there when it happened, and it shouldn't have, and I don't forget what those in power do to the ones who prop up their thrones, for certain I don't. Why, some don't think Prince George should even meet with his cousin, but then, doesn't family count for something? But Bloody Sunday . . . I can see why the Russian people are angry about that. Nearly a hundred dead and a thousand injured! I'm Irish, you see, so I can understand that, at least."

I knew Bloody Sunday was the day that the tsar's Imperial Guard had fired on a march of unarmed Russian protestors in

Moscow. Many, I'd heard, were displaced peasants and urban workers, who had come to present a petition to the tsar for better wages.

"As I said, I was in Russia then," she said, lowering her voice again and leaning closer across the small table. "It was the year little Alexey was born, the son the royal family and the nation had waited such a long time for, through four female babies." She sniffed and fumbled for a handkerchief in her handbag. "My little girls," she said and blew her nose. "And how blessed you are that you will see them, how they've grown and how they are getting on."

There was a knock on the door, which opened on Tessa, a kitchen maid, with a tray of tea and some biscuits with jam. "Please thank Mrs. Wentworth, Tessa," I told her as I made room on the table between us. I could tell the girl was hoping to overhear something about my mystery guest, for she lingered a bit, eyeing Mrs. Eager.

"Shall I pour then, Mrs. Lala?" she asked.

"Thank you again, but I will manage."

When the door closed behind her, my guest went on as if we had not been interrupted. "The grand duchesses were my charges for nearly five years."

"You miss them, then? Do you have something for them?"

She didn't answer my question, but plunged on, "I'd go back in a heartbeat, though I was fearful at first. Even though it was lonely in Russia — well, I could hardly mingle with non-royal family nannies there. It's always hard for the likes of us — you and me — caught between the royals we serve and the other servants. The imperial family is quite secluded for their protection, you see, protected by the Imperial Guard, by the tsar's own security police and plainclothes men within and without. My dear girls were lonely too, but we got on so well, and then, finally, the heir came along while I was still there, the boy everyone had prayed for."

"If you don't mind my asking," I said as I poured her tea and put two spoonfuls of sugar in hers, which she indicated, "why did you leave? Did the girls grow too old for a head nurse — a nanny?"

"Oh, no. I was their companion too, chaperoning them on walks or rides. But their parents sent me away just when their precious heir needed a nanny. He was given into the care of a woman named Mariya when it should have been me, it surely should have been. After all, English nannies are all the rage in Russia among the rich.

But Mariya wasn't opinionated like me, that's what I overheard once. Oh, no, she'd never dare to so much as ask a question."

I looked up from my teacup. "So you were asked to leave?"

She nodded as tears filled her eyes. Her teacup rattled in its saucer in her lap. I prayed she would not faint.

"Dismissed, after all those years," she whispered, "with no warning . . . because I was curious." Again, she could not go on.

"Don't speak for a moment. Can you drink some tea?" I urged her.

She managed that. "It's not that I was replaced exactly. I think the tsar decided and Tsaritsa Alexandra said no more nannies. She did bring in another Russian woman to watch them too, a Sofya something or other, I heard, a sort of governess. And that woman stopped the girls' letters and gifts to me. Sofya, I hear, is a stickler for discipline and is like a spy on the girls. Oh, yes, their parents dote on them, but now they have to protect Alexey. He is their only hope that the Romanovs can keep the throne, that is, with the unrest and rumors flying about all the time — the bad, dangerous feelings against the tsar. And the tsaritsa never was well liked with her German and English ties. She is often ill," she said, whispering again as if the walls had ears. Finally, looking angry now instead of stricken, she took a sip of tea, then another. She downed the rest, and I poured her more.

"Sad to have to live that way," I said, "so isolated from and hated by one's own people."

"The children surely can't play with those lower than themselves — which is everyone."

"I do understand that," I admitted, remembering poor David and Bertie at that football game with the village lads that was a disaster until Chad came along.

"I tell you, Mrs. Lala, they are wonderful girls, spoiled, I suppose, but not snobbish. They sleep two to a room in narrow beds and wash with cold water in the mornings. They always teased me that they were starting to pick up my Irish brogue. Oh, they can be a handful, even boisterous, that they can."

My heart went out to her, a sister under the skin. I thought of poor David with his iron bed and cold baths at naval college and how I had been teased that David and Bertie had picked up some of my Cockney accent. And I thought of my boisterous, little Johnnie.

"So, the favor you would ask?" I said to her in the lull as we both seemed steeped in our own memories.

"Two, really. If, when you return, I might visit you again so you could tell me what you saw, what they said. The girls, I mean, since Alexey was never really mine and is severely guarded to keep his secret."

"You have hinted at such before. What secret?"

"I wager your employers know it, but it is so sad, and I only guessed it. That may be why they dismissed me so summarily, despite the pleadings of their dear daughters. The rumors fly about that the tsar's heir may be anemic, but that's not true. It's worse," she said so low that it sounded like a hiss. "He has the bleeder's disease that is in the royal families descended from Queen Victoria. King Edward's brother Leopold had it, I heard. Hemophilia, but no one is to know. I only tell you so that you will be aware what you see, why they coddle him outrageously, not just that he is their only son and heir. I swear, however much they love their girls, because I guessed that about Alexey — it's why they let me go."

"I can see why they don't want word on that out. After all those years waiting for a son, like our own King Henry VIII who went through all those wives and got a boy who didn't live long."

"Don't even say such! But, oh, yes, I even feared for a while, and the tsaritsa did too, I could tell, that Tsar Nicholas would have to divorce her to get an heir — like Napoleon divorced his love Josephine, they said."

I sat still, balancing my teacup on my knees, not drinking, my mind racing. "And besides telling you what I see of your precious, lost girls, what else then?" I asked her. "You mentioned a second thing."

Without breaking my steady gaze, she put her teacup back on the tray and fumbled for the silver square in her lap. She extended it to me. It was a framed photograph, one of her with the young grand duchesses, such pretty girls. They wore hats that looked like half moons and sashes over what appeared to be white, ruffled chiffon dresses. Pearls round their graceful necks — and Mrs. Eager in a plain dark dress. All so happy, arms entwined around each other. And most amazing, they were all smiling when it seemed no one, royals and commoners alike, ever smiled for photographs. She pointed each one out to me by name and told me of their personalities and prefer-ences.

"Mrs. Lala," she said, "I have few treasures

where I run a boardinghouse in Holland Park in London, just making ends meet now, no stipends or allotments from my days of service or my medical nursing days in Belfast. I know I could get a pretty penny for this silver frame. But — and I wish to be honest with you about what I'm asking you to do — it's the only one I have that has a place to hide a note behind the picture. I am asking you to give this to the girls as a remembrance of me — Olga or Tatiana, the older two — and tell them I love them all and miss them. And whisper to them I have written a note secreted here, since I fear the ones I wrote them lately have been destroyed before they were read — or else they aren't allowed to answer. Please."

I reached over to touch her gloved hand. "If I can. I will try. Surely, their guardians won't mind that."

"No, you must do it in secret! You may have to outwit their watchdog Sofya, and don't let Mariya see you either. And please, tell no one what I've shared with you about their heir. That, I think, is dangerous knowledge, so maybe I should not have told you. But I so wanted you to understand that I wasn't let go for something bad I did. I think it was because I knew too much and — well, like my four Russian girls, I chatter too much. And so, in a kinder way, they have silenced them too with even more isolation, spies, and guards. I swear, you will see guards all about, and so you must be wary. If this is impossible, I will surely understand."

We held hands a moment in a silent pact, then drank our tea. She suddenly seemed hungry, so I let her eat most of the biscuits and take the rest for her trip back to London. I probably overstepped myself to ask the footman who sometimes drove the children's pony cart to take her to the train station in it.

I hid the picture of Margaretta Eager and Russia's beautiful grand duchesses until I was ready to pack it — then decided to wrap it in a handkerchief and keep it in my handbag with me at all times. I wondered what the note secreted within said, but I didn't look. I had no way of knowing if I would have the chance to give it to Her Highness Olga or Tatiana, or what would happen if my passing it to them would be discovered. I only knew how desperately I understood and sympathized with this other royal nanny, for I knew not what risks I would take if they sent me away and cut me off from my dear children.

■ ■ ■ ■

I was soon to learn that security for the tsar's arrival on English soil was so difficult that the two related royal families would first greet each other at sea from a distance to give the tsar's forces time to establish themselves on the island. In the Channel off the Isle of Wight, the tsar's favorite yacht, the *Shtandart,* was protected by two Russian cruisers, three destroyers, and ships of the British Fleet. Besides all that, it was the week of the race at Cowes leading up to this second day of August 1909, and the sea was peppered with small English racing and pleasure craft of all kinds.

I stood on the deck of the royal British yacht *Victoria and Albert,* with a firm hold on Johnnie, who was also roped to me, while the rest of the family waved to the Russian royals from the railing. That is, the rest of the family minus Bertie, poor boy, who had the whooping cough and was in sick bay at the naval college, which he too now attended, and David, whom we would meet up with on shore.

Even the king's white-coated, long-haired terrier named Caesar barked a welcome. How Johnnie loved that dog with the stubby tail that flicked back and forth at the mere sight of the boy. Although he liked to watch the queen's thirty or so elegant-looking borzoi dogs be fed off silver plates, he adored little Caesar. One of the first things he had learned to read were the words engraved on the dog's Fabergé collar: *I am Caesar, the King's dog.* Johnnie talked to Caesar sometimes and, I swear, the dog understood his roundabout logic better than I did!

I squinted in the sun and stiff breeze to pick out Tsar Nicholas and the Empress Alexandra with their four daughters, the beloved girls Margaretta Eager had not been eager to leave. I fought to shove aside the nightmare I'd had last night about her, for it was pure foolishness.

I'd dreamed the former Russian nanny had handed me a photograph of myself standing and smiling amidst the six Wales children. It was all I had left, because they had been sent far away from me. It was dark, but I searched for them everywhere at Sandringham House in the places David and Bertie had liked to hide, and in the glasshouse amidst dying flowers, inside a cage with little chicks running hither and yon, and beneath the white, linen-covered tables under the huge marquee at the hunting party. I wandered through the cemetery of St. Mary Magdalene, calling for them amidst the graves.

Then I found all six of their names on white crosses, each with the inscription, *Suffer the little children . . .*

I jerked alert as a welcoming cannon boomed and crowds cheered.

Johnnie was cheering too, jumping up and down. "Big noise, Lala, big noise!" he cried. "Papa shooting guns at Chad's birds. They all fall down dead, but not my peeps! Not me neither!"

I knelt and hugged him. He clung to me, and I was so grateful to God to be here and to have my boy healthy, unlike the little heir to the Russian throne, a secret I was willing to take to my grave for poor Mrs. Eager. The silver frame with her photograph and note felt heavy in my handbag until I could safely slip it — I hoped — to her dear, lost girls.

CHAPTER 22

Waves crashed on the beach and seagulls screeched overhead. Harry, George, and the "Tsarevich Alexey" shouted as they chased plovers and ran from the reach of the breakers. Mary, though I knew she'd just as soon dive into the waves as watch them, followed the lead of the four grand duchesses and kept her feet dry in her high-button shoes. David, nattily attired in his cadet naval uniform, escorted the five girls.

He did so proudly, which warmed my heart. He was in a fine mood, not only to have escaped the naval school he detested for a day or two, but to have been able to see his grandfather, though the king and queen stayed mostly on the *Victoria and Albert* and let some of the activities come to them. After all, it was Prince George and Tsar Nicholas who were heading up this royal visit.

I kept Johnnie on a tether, for I wasn't

sure what he would do and I was not in the mood to fight the surf to retrieve him. At least, I thought, little Alexey could run about a bit, though followed closely by his personal one-man guard. I noted that the entire Russian retinue had been so protective of him when they first came ashore.

Despite all that worry, Johnnie lifted my spirits. I was happy to see him so entranced by the many shells scattered on the sand.

"If these she shells, Lala, where the he shells, the boy ones?" he asked me, turning each one over, evidently searching for its private parts. Well, I'd had no answer for that one, not now at least.

He was also fascinated by the Brownie box cameras the Romanov sisters carried, snapping pictures of each other, even of us. Soon Johnnie picked up a piece of driftwood and aimed it at me, then at the others, chattering, "Click, click, click." The grand duchesses even posed for his imaginary camera, so sweet and kind of them, but then they were used to obeying their brother, barely a year older than Johnnie. For one moment, when the oldest two girls, Olga and Tatiana, posed, flashing lovely smiles, I almost dared to slip the photograph in my handbag to them. But their guards stood too close, and we were quite exposed to view.

"Our *dyadkis*," Olga explained to Johnnie when he aimed the driftwood at the men with a *click, click.* If any of the Russians had been told Johnnie was a different sort of boy, they were not acting like it. "It means uncles, but they are just our companions, our own private shepherds of the flock, yes, Tati?" she asked her sister, and they shared a little laugh before moving on again.

There was one opportunity missed, I thought, and clutched my handbag closer, praying I'd get a chance to secretly pass them the picture. I could see how Margaretta Eager had loved these girls, so full of life.

The entire beach was cordoned off and patrolled by the tsar's many security men, just like the whole island, as far as I could tell. Some of the guards rode bicycles, so wait until I told that to poor quarantined Bertie. Margaretta had been right that Tsar Nicholas — the adult British royals called him "Nickie" — was guarded like no one else I had ever seen.

Despite the beautiful day, it began to cast a pall over me. Just as the royal Russian children's guardians kept an eagle eye on them, so they did on all of us. I began to despair I would not be able to pass on the picture and note. After all, their visit here was to be only four days, and my young charges, Harry, George, and Johnnie, were not to be included in most of the activities on the royal yachts or at Barton Manor, where the British royal hosts would entertain ashore. So today could be my last chance.

I hustled Johnnie along behind them again, hoping for a moment the guards or the watchful Tsaritsa Alexandra or Princess May, who sat in deck chairs on the sand, would not notice a quick explanation and exchange. Finally, the Russian children stopped so that little Alexey could skip clam shells into the waves.

"Oh, you be careful," Olga, the oldest girl, told the boy. "Don't pick up sharp ones. Let's all find good ones for Alexey to throw!" she cried.

The four Russian girls, attired in light gray matching sailor-styled dresses and ribboned straw boaters tied on their heads, formed a protective barrier around their brother, and a beautiful barrier it was.

Olga, thirteen, David's age, was a pretty blonde and seemed kindhearted, even when she ordered her sisters about. I'd heard rumors that she would be a good match for David someday, but I could tell he was much enamored — for the first time in his life, I believed — with the second sister, Tatiana. Imagine, someday possibly a Russian queen for England! But there was too much bad feeling toward their country, I thought, just as the Russians, so Margaretta had said, detested the Tsaritsa Alexandra for her English and German blood.

Speaking of blood, it was obvious that the four grand duchesses and the unwitting David and Mary were working hard to find shells that wouldn't cut Alexey. I assumed his sisters knew the reason for that, but nothing untoward seemed to occur to the British royals.

"Lala, Lala!" Johnnie interrupted my thoughts, training his piece of driftwood at me. "I want pictures of you and Mama."

And not his father, I realized. Sad that the fear of Prince George had to start so early for the children. In Russia, it seemed the other way round, for I had seen the tsar hug his son and, laughing, tell Prince George, before they went off somewhere together, that the boy's nickname was "Alexey the Terrible."

"I say," Prince George had told him, "I have five of those, including the little one with his nanny."

The tsar's sharp, blue gaze had sought Johnnie, and there I stood, under the scrutiny of His Imperial Majesty of All the Russias. I was tied to the boy, perhaps the way the tsar would like to have his precious heir tied to someone for his safety. I bobbed him a curtsy. He resembled Prince George so much, to the shape of their heads and faces, their sharply trimmed beards, navy jackets, caps, even their build and height. Indeed, the two looked more like twin brothers than cousins, even to the blue color of their eyes.

But right now, I was watching David, noting his eyes were all too obviously for Tatiana, who was twelve. Though graceful and lively, she seemed delicate, a stunning girl with her curly, auburn hair and huge, gray-blue gaze. If I drew attention to myself — and they learned I had a message from Margaretta, which said I knew not what — would I get in trouble? Worse, could this seemingly kind royal family, who obviously trusted no one, think I was a danger? I dreaded being dismissed the way she had.

I'd considered too giving the picture to one of the two younger Russian girls to give to the older ones. Maria and Anastasia seemed to venture out on their own a bit more. Maria had been especially beloved by Margaretta. She'd been described to me as a bit shy and clumsy, so maybe we nannies favored the ones who weren't so talented, outgoing, and bright.

The youngest, blue-eyed Anastasia, at age eight, seemed to fear nothing, even be a bit naughty, so she reminded me of Mary. And little Alexey had brown curls and huge blue eyes and seemed a daredevil, one who liked to order others around too. I'd seen him salute the guards so that they had to salute him in turn. No wonder his father had that little nickname for him.

Suddenly missing my own father, who had called me "Lottie," I sighed and sucked a deep breath of tart sea air. When I licked my lips, I tasted salt. It was hard to walk on the soft, dry sand, and the wave-washed area sucked my steps down a bit. Such a lovely day and here I had knots in my stomach over trying to secretly give the girls a gift and keep Johnnie, Harry, and George in sight, though Finch was watching the two older ones too. But what really made me glad, even more than Johnnie's joy, was the fact that the prince had said Harry could go without his braces today, and the child was running free.

How I wished the same for the tsar's guarded children, who had to sleep on the protected yacht, stay together in a group — and make it hard for me to get so much as one private word with them.

That afternoon, a gift from heaven! Princess May informed me that the two oldest grand duchesses, Olga and Tatiana, were to be allowed to shop on the high street in West Cowes, and would I take Mary ashore and accompany them?

So here was my chance, my last chance, I thought. I left Johnnie taking a nap under Martha's watchful eye aboard the *Victoria and Albert,* though he had fussed when he heard I was going out. Mary and I took the tender ashore and hurried past several rows of Russian guards to wait for the tender from the *Shtandart.* I'd heard their yacht had a crew of 275 sailors, and we saw six of them were on the boat with the grand duchesses. But, oh no, I saw two women who hadn't been along on the beach this morning stepping onto the dock with the girls.

We greeted the Russians, and our little shopping entourage started up toward the high street, where many of the fancy London stores had summer shops during the yachting season. Grand Duchess Olga began introductions. I had to smile when she called Mary a duchess too. "And this is our governess, Sofya Tyutcheva, and our friend Mariya Vishnyakova," she told Mary.

Aha, I thought, the villainess who had cut off Margaretta's letters to and from the girls, and the one who had become nanny to Alexey. So, on this little excursion, when I thought I'd find an excuse to pass the photograph, there would be more hostile, watchful eyes on us than ever.

I too, like my new friend, Margaretta, fell in love with the lively, lovely grand duchesses. They were so excited to be shopping on their own, buying gifts for friends including someone they called "dear Grigory" or "Rasputin," someone I knew nothing of.

It didn't take any of us long to realize we were at the center of a fishbowl with vacationers, yachtsmen, and natives to the isle following us and pressing in to get a glimpse of the tsar's daughters and Princess Mary. So perhaps the guards were needed after all.

The Russian shoppers bought souvenirs and some luxury goods, including perfume for themselves at a shop called Beken and Son. Even the shopkeepers acted like starstruck worshippers, crowding us together. More than once, I told myself, now was the time to pass the photograph, but one of their "uncle guards" or the two hawk-eyed women were always watching. But I saw Olga had brought her camera and was having trouble balancing it with her purchases tied in paper and strings, so I stepped in to hold the Brownie for her before the others could.

"Here, Your Grace," I said. "Before we go out in the crowded street again, please let me take a photo of you and Grand Duchess Tatiana with Lady Mary."

Their guards, the *daykins,* or whatever that word was, nodded permission and stepped back. Olga and Tatiana stood on either side of Mary. I had not the slightest notion how to use a Brownie camera, but I recalled how Johnnie had pretended with his piece of driftwood, so I peered into the glass eye, centered the tiny images, and pressed the button. I took one more. Then, rather than giving the Brownie right back, I risked putting the picture frame from my handbag under the camera and handing it to Olga, pressing the small frame into her hand.

"What is . . ." she began to say, before I interrupted her. Thank heavens, everyone had started chattering again.

"A frame you can use if you could send the Princess Mary a copy of the picture as a memento," I said in a rush. Then, I whispered, "It's from your dear friend Mrs. Eager, for the four of you, no one else, a note in back of it. She misses and loves you all."

She looked at me, wide-eyed, then glanced at the photograph in her trembling hands. I could almost hear her brain click like a camera, remembering, thinking.

"How kind of you," she said, passing the camera to Sofya who had edged close to us, while Olga slipped the frame unseen into the small paper bag with her perfume. "Could you please carry my camera, Sofya? I may want to take more."

Frowning, the woman nodded and stepped back. "Tell her, we shall cherish this," Olga whispered to me, not looking at me now. "Tell her we miss her too."

"Miss who?" Sofya was back that fast, leaning in, for she'd evidently passed the camera off to someone else.

"I don't want to miss another shop before we must head back, dear Sofya!" she said and turned away, then back to me. "And thank you for that photograph on our grand shopping tour," she said to me. I saw her blink back a tear. She was as bright as she was beautiful. "The photo you took will be very dear to all of us, and I shall send you a copy — you and Duchess Mary."

She hustled out the shop door to join her sister amidst the growing crowd of gawkers outside. Oh, yes, I saw again why Margaretta missed her Russian girls. My handbag felt much lighter and my heart too. What a perfect, blessed day. Surely, nothing bad could happen now.

That evening, during an elegant Russian-British family dinner ashore at Barton Manor, to which Harry, George, and, of course, Johnnie, were not invited, I sat with my three youngest charges on the deck of the *Victoria and Albert* and watched the sun set. I felt at peace for the first time since Margaretta had asked me to pass the picture to the older Russian girls. Except for Bertie's not being here, all seemed right with the world.

I reclined in a canvas deck chair with a sleepy Johnnie tight beside me. Harry and George shared the one next to us, as we watched for the tender that would return their parents and Mary, for David, poor boy, was heading back to his cadet training, when he wanted so to go back to the mainland with all of us.

Johnnie sat up straighter. He'd seemed nervous, even after his nap today, and yet so tired his eyes seemed almost to cross.

How grateful I had been that, compared to the poor little tsarevich, he was doing well. Margaretta had mentioned rumors that Alexey was ill, but the truth of his even darker secret I had not heard whispered once today.

"They're coming back!" Harry called to us and went to the rail. "Papa and Mama's boat and the Russian one too. We'd better get down to bed, Georgie, because Papa made us promise."

They scampered in, where I knew Martha and Jane would be waiting to put them to bed, then I'd tuck them up soon. This moment with Johnnie on the yacht, gently rocking, was so sweet.

"That boat," he said, pointing at the well-guarded Russian tender. "Girls in cloud dresses."

"Yes, beautiful dresses that looked like clouds, satin, tulle, and chiffon." I amazed myself that I could pick out not only patterns now but yard goods, materials, after listening to Rose for so long.

She had almost dived over the railing into the sea today when she got the slightest glimpse of the summer gowns with blue satin sashes the tsaritsa and her four girls wore as they were rowed ashore to Barton Manor. Earlier, she'd made me describe their simple, sharp gray sailor suits to the last stitch and pleat. It was so good to be traveling with Prince George and Princess May this time instead of having them take Rose and be gone for months. She was down in Princess May's cabin now, laying out her nightgown and preparing to unlace her from layers of garments.

"Come on, my boy," I told Johnnie, as I stood him up and struggled to rise from the canvas chair that sagged like a hammock. "Time for bed, and we'll have a story about girls in cloud dresses."

"And boxes of pictures."

"Yes, with Brownie box cameras. That's what those were, and we'll ask your grand-papa for one for Christmas for all of you. Come on then, before Papa and Mama find you still up."

"Up in the clouds," he said, holding my hand.

But as we went over the raised step into the companionway, he gripped my hand so hard he hurt me.

"What is it?" I asked, turning to him and looking down. "It's not dark below. Lanterns, see and —"

His eyes rolled up into his head. His features went slack, then twisted. His body shook, convulsed. He fell against me, and, catching him, I sagged against the wall under his weight. Dead weight!

■ ■ ■ ■

Part Four

1909–1914
YORK COTTAGE TO
BUCKINGHAM PALACE

■ ■ ■ ■

CHAPTER 23

I managed to catch Johnnie partway to the floor. He was breathing, unconscious, yet moving his rigid limbs. I lowered him to the wooden deck. Why didn't someone come along? Should I scream for help? But I could not bear for someone to see him this way. I knew the court physician, Sir Francis Laking, was ashore and on call in case the king took ill, but . . . but what was happening to my boy?

His limbs flopped so hard, they beat out a fierce rhythm against the floorboards, even his head, which I tried to steady. His teeth were clamped shut yet saliva flowed from the corner of his mouth. If he should die . . .

"Johnnie. Johnnie! Can you hear me? It's Lala."

I needed help but could not leave him. After what seemed an eternity, he went quiet, still breathing, thank God. He had a pulse but seemed to sleep like the dead.

"Johnnie! Johnnie!"

He opened his eyes, then closed them again. I wiped his sweaty brow with my skirt hem and held his hands, cold and clammy. Finally, a sailor came through the companionway.

"Did the lad fall, then, ma'am?"

"Yes," I told him, not wanting anyone to know what had happened until I told the queen. "Can you help carry him to his cabin? Carefully, please. He hit his head."

The young man scooped the boy up as if he were weightless, and I led him to the cabin I shared with Johnnie. Finch was next door with George and Harry, but I didn't want to alarm them. Like most of the cabins on this deck, our space was small, with two narrow bunks squeezed in. I gestured at one and the sailor lay Johnnie down.

"I am grateful," I told the man. "Would you wait outside in the hall so you can take a note for me?" I tried to beat down raw panic. I felt the desperation of the Russian royal family to protect and shelter their ill boy.

I scribbled a note to Rose, asking her to bring Princess May, and sent it with the sailor. I sat on the edge of Johnnie's bed, loosened his collar, unbuttoned his shirt, and bathed his face and neck.

"Did I fall in the sea?" he whispered. "I'm wet."

"It's all right. I think your mama's going to come to tuck you up. Not dizzy? No belly or headache?"

"I was swimming. I hurt my head — on a seashell."

It seemed as if I held his hand for ages. I could hear Harry's and George's voices next door through the wall, and occasionally, Finch's. Finally, a knock on the door. I rose to open it.

Princess May stood there with Rose behind her. The princess was evidently ready for bed. Her hair was down, and she wore a full-length, striped brown and beige silk robe wrapped around her body with no skirts or petticoats beneath.

"What happened?" she asked and came in with Rose in her wake.

"As you can see, he seems well enough now," I tried to assure her. "Could Rose sit with him for a moment, and I could explain in the hall?"

"Don't leave me, Lala," Johnnie whispered.

"You just rest. Mama and I will be right back, so we're not leaving."

Rose shot me a desperate look. Mending clothing, not children, was her love. But the princess and I stepped quickly out, and I closed the door. As I explained it all to her, sugar coating nothing, the yacht began to rock, so we were evidently under way.

"Something he ate?" Princess May asked, frowning. "Are you sure he didn't just trip and hit his head?"

"I am sure. I am sorry, but I am sure."

"Running around with the Russians?" she went on as if asking herself, instead of me. "Could he have caught something ashore? There is something strange about little Alexey."

For certain then, she didn't know about the Romanov heir! None of them must know. But I knew the tsarevich's malady was nothing contagious. I almost told her what I knew, but I honored my pledge to Margaretta.

"Could we have the royal physician look him over?" I asked. "Did he come aboard?"

"No, the king felt well enough that he told him to stay ashore for a few days. But we'll have him visit when we can. Lala, as alarming as that must have been for you and Johnnie, I have heard of cases where children had convulsions and it came to nothing. They outgrew it. Too much excitement for him with all these new people around, I fear. We shall just keep a good watch on him

— as you always do. I'll go in and see how he seems to me. As ever, thank you for being there with him, and I'll inform his father in the morning, as he's in with the king right now."

She pulled her robe closer and went back into the cabin. I leaned against the wall to steady myself, and not because the yacht was rocking. I was rocked to my core by her reasonable response when I feared the world had just tilted.

Even back in the quiet routine of Sandringham, I feared another "attack," as I came to think of it. Yet things had returned to normal. There was not another falling fit, as Rose, who had been sworn to secrecy, called it. No more "childhood convulsive reactions to stimulation," as Dr. Laking termed it after he had examined Johnnie. I hovered and watched the boy like a hawk and was grateful each day that it seemed to be a "onetime brain disturbance," as Prince George had dubbed it.

Finally, by the end of November, I began to believe them and relax a bit, and my growing group of female friends helped with that.

Last week, Margaretta Eager had visited me for the second time, and we frequently corresponded by post. She had been so relieved to hear every little detail about how her Russian girls were getting on — and my repeating how graciously and cleverly Olga had accepted the photograph. Of course, my friend Mabel Butcher was still dear to me, as busy as she was as head housekeeper at the Big House.

Today I was enjoying sitting in Rose's sewing room off the kitchen while Johnnie took an afternoon nap upstairs and I had tea with Helene Bricka and Rose.

"You should see the gown Princess May is wearing to the queen's birthday party at the Big House next week!" Rose told us. She had an eager audience, for Helene dearly loved the princess and anyone who supported her. I yet felt as if I were an understudy of sorts for the sartorial styles of the Marlborough House and Buckingham Palace set.

"I hope," Helene, chatty as ever, said, "it's quite grand, because the queen is always trying to upstage her. Why it even annoys her that May has such good hearing she can pick up on distant conversations, while the queen can't catch things said right at her, let alone their quite pointless race to see who collects the most Fabergé agate animals and those ornate eggs with the surprises hidden in them! Why, the queen, I hear, has two large electric lighted cabinets full of those carved creatures and bejeweled eggs — eggs, no less!"

I didn't want to hear all that again, so I asked Rose, "So what will the gown be like?"

"English-made as usual, not imported from the Frenchies like some I could name."

Helene gave a sharp nod. "When she is queen, she will promote British fashions, not foreign. Oh, I know in the olden days it was treason to so much as think about the current sovereign's demise, but the king is not well. Too much wine, women, and song, not to mention those gargantuan meals he puts away and those dreadful cigars."

There was a moment's silence as Rose and I glanced at each other.

All three of us knew the Prince and Princess of Wales did not covet their fate to be next in line to the throne. They dreaded and feared it.

"Oh, well, about the gown," Rose went on. "Of course, it is on the cutting edge of the shift in women's styles. Raised waistline, less tight, the hips smaller and the skirts less full. Frills and flounces are so passé now. But I guess "passé" is a French word, is it not, *Madame* Bricka?"

"Hmph. Too much change too fast is

never good. Someone had best tell Prime
Minister Lloyd George that. All those liberal
ideas! Pushing through that so-called Great
Budget with pensions and national insur-
ance for the masses, as if people cannot put
in an honest day's work for themselves
anymore. The very idea! No wonder the
royal family doesn't like or trust him. Give
the man on the street too much power, and
we'll have more protests and riots, like in
Russia. But I didn't mean to interrupt. I
daresay, Charlotte will be the only one of us
to attend the gala party with the children,
so best you tell us of the gown, Rose, and
she can report on the other ones later."

Rose put down her teacup as if she needed
her hands free to describe it. "It's striped
white and gold silk with tassels in the
Egyptian style. Neckline and sleeves
trimmed in gray chinchilla. And," she
whispered, though we were quite alone, "the
corset hardly pulls in the waist, though it
does push up the bosom, which will be dripping with diamonds below a six-strand
choker of pearls in that look the queen has
made her own."

"Touché," Helene pronounced with another nod. "Dear May knows how to hold
her own, even fight back, but with beauty
and dignity."

I thought about that as we chatted on. Beauty and dignity would stand her well at this elaborate party. Finch and I were to escort the three youngest boys so their grandparents could show them off as if they didn't belong to Prince George and Princess May at all. But, sometimes, I too felt they were more mine than theirs.

How I often wished Princess May would worry more about her children. Mary had turned stubborn about her studies, however much the prince harangued her. David and Bertie were both desperately unhappy at naval school.

And last month I had stood horrified in the study to hear His Highness tell Harry, "You are a boy and not a little child, so stop that sniveling. Do not behave like a baby or I shall send you somewhere else." And now he was doing just that. Harry was to be sent away to live and study at York Gate Cottage, Broadstairs, the seaside home of the court physician, Sir Francis Laking, when the doctor would not even be there, because the boy needed the sea air and to be built up, the prince said. Soon it would just be George and Johnnie in my care. George was a handful, even as clever and charming as he was for a boy who would be seven next month. And Johnnie — I always worried what he would say or do, even though I'd finally relaxed my fear he'd have another convulsion.

Rose's voice sliced through my thoughts. "Charlotte, whatever is it? You look as if you've been sucking on a lemon, my dear. I'd give anything to see the fabulous creations at that party, so you'd best take good mental notes for me. Oh, I know, you're more worried about the children behaving there."

With another of her signature sniffs, Helene put in, "With that Mrs. Keppel in attendance, and all the hanky-panky that goes on during and after these gatherings, I just hope the adults behave themselves."

For the celebration of Queen Alexandra's sixty-fifth birthday, the Grand Saloon of the Big House was absolutely aglitter with lights and jewels, silks, satins, crystal, and china — and filled with chattering people. I wore my best gown, chocolate silk with beige ruching and a touch of lace, though I'm afraid it was of the old cut. Earlier in the day, Rose had piled my hair up and made some ringlets with her heating iron, and I wore tiny, single-pearl earrings. As Finch and I walked in with the children, I saw something that made me think of Helene's words about the adults behaving themselves.

For the first time, I saw the women were also smoking, not just the men. No cigars, though. Including the queen, they were puffing on thin cigarettes they took from flat, gold and gem-encrusted cases before one of the gentlemen swooped in to light them for them with a lucifer. The air beneath the chandeliers was quite blue with the smoke.

"Makes me dizzy," Johnnie said. Immediately, I loosed his hand and stooped to look him in the eyes.

"Want to sit down? Does your head hurt or is it spinning?"

"I feel good, really."

"Ha," George told his younger brother. "You are hardly ever acting good, really. You're always into something."

"No bickering, either of you. Smiles and manners, or you'll get reminders from me and Finch later."

Finch put in, "I always did like your name for that, Lala."

"Better known as punishments," George said with a roll of his eyes.

"But not for Johnnie," Harry dared to say. "Just Georgie and me."

I gave the nine-year-old a pat on the head. Did they really see it that way, that I was harder on them and coddled Johnnie? "I love all of you just as much, but in different ways," I told them. And then I was saved from trying to explain more by Johnnie pulling his hand away and dashing off toward the lighted cases of the queen's Fabergé animals.

I lifted my hems and tore after him with Finch and the other two in my wake. I'd decided against tying Johnnie to me, thinking it would look bad, but that might have been a mistake.

"Look, Lala," Johnnie told me as he gazed up awestruck at the lighted cases. I couldn't help but think the expression on his face must have been what I looked like the first time I saw the royals' tall Christmas tree. "A zoo! But pretend animals."

"Yes, that's right," I told him, pleased by that comment, for he often merged the real world with his imaginary one. "Pretend animals, not real ones."

George said, "But I'll bet Grannie's Russian dogs and Grandpapa's little Caesar are here. Still, the ones in this case would skid great on the floor in the hall, or be bully chess pieces."

George was the cleverest of the Wales brood, even more than David had been at that age. Sharp-tongued but kind, he sometimes helped me with entertaining and watching Johnnie, and I was grateful for that.

Harry tugged at my sleeve. "But there are some real animals over there, Lala! Goldfish! See? Right on the big birthday cake!"

I grabbed Johnnie's hand so I didn't have to chase him again, and we went over to the six-tiered, elaborately decorated cake on a table of its own. Between each of the layers, next to the small pillars that held up each tier, were round crystal bowls with three goldfish circling in each. The boys watched mesmerized, and it was Johnny who spoke first.

"They are going in circles but they want to be in the sea. They want sand and shells."

"Ah, there are my lads!" a familiar voice boomed out as King Edward approached. I curtsied as the boys, Johnnie too, swarmed him, hugging his legs, nearly knocking him over. I was amazed at how much he had aged since I'd seen him but two months ago. Heavier, fleshy jowls and a bit bent at the spine. A cigar in one hand, of course. "All right," he said, "before we have any more of this grown-up chitchat folderol, let's have a butter pat race on Grandpapa's pant legs, and you can all bet on the winner. Now, don't you worry, Mrs. Lala, they'll be fine with me!"

As Finch and I backed off, he told me, "I'll keep an eye on the lads from over there in the corner."

"I'm going back by the door. It's closer if Johnnie needs me."

Off the boys went to the head table while I held my breath, but it did give me a chance to look around. Princess May's gown was stunning, and I'd tell Rose so, but the queen herself, sitting at the head table, dripping in diamonds and greeting guests, had outdone herself with the decorations in the vast room. She always loved ornate displays and, although it was December first, the room had a harvest theme with swags of grape leaves and pheasant feathers decorating windows, tables, and the massive picture frames on the walls. I supposed the feathers were from Chad's birds, ones maybe the king, prince, and their cronies had shot. I scolded myself for thinking of such far too much lately — that lovely things had to die so that the royal and rich set could live this way.

Under a burst of wheat stalks tied with a gold velvet ribbon on the wall, I sat in a tiny jade-green silk upholstered chair and kept my eye on the boys, praying Johnnie would not act up or say something outrageous. But

I blessed his grandfather from afar for taking time to play with them, even in the midst of all this.

I could see one of the beautifully scripted dinner menus, propped up against the array of goblets next to each silver table setting. I squinted a bit to read it. Oh, my, eight courses. First Course, Oysters and Stewed Trout; Second Course, Green Pea Soup or Grouse Soup. I thought of that agate figure of the grouse David had filched so long ago on my first visit to this house. I'd seen it in the lighted case tonight. I sighed. As spectacular as was this grand display, as much as I admired it all, I no longer felt in awe of these people and places. Instead, I saw the excess here as well as the excellence.

The Third Course was Poached Salmon with Mousseline Sauce — whatever that was — and Cucumber. The glasshouses out back always grew summer vegetables in the winter. And where were those fish coming from with the ponds newly frozen over? You'd think they should serve Prince George's daily lunch fish called Bombay Duck. Not duck at all, but crisp-fried and highly seasoned fish imported from India. And I had seen he was quite out of sorts if something else was served to him at York Cottage promptly at one.

The Fourth Course had a variety of choices, or did they eat them all? Roast Saddle of Mutton, Roast Duckling with Apple Sauce, something called Parmentier Potatoes or Broiled Rice and Creamed Carrots. The Fifth Course was shorter: Roast Partridge Squab with Cress. I was glad Johnnie couldn't read yet. Those just as well could be some of his pet peeps.

The Sixth Course was Cold Asparagus Vinaigrette, though I could not fathom why they didn't just have that with the main Fourth Course. The Seventh was Pâté de Foie Gras — how the king loved French food — and Celery, no less. Finally — and here my mouth started to water — Cheese Tarts. Also Peaches in Chartreuse Jelly. Did that mean they would be colored green? And, with the cake, French Ice Cream.

My stomach rumbled at the mere thought of cake and ice cream, though I had already supped back at York Cottage with Johnnie on mutton, potatoes, and, for dessert, custard. I was quite used to nursery fare, though I did occasionally eat what the downstairs staff were having.

As I glanced up from that amazing menu, I saw Chad, dressed in his hunt master uniform, looking so handsome. It was almost as if I'd imagined him. He was indeed standing in the doorway nearest me, frowning, looking over the crowd. When his gaze snagged mine, he smiled and walked over as if he'd been searching for me alone.

CHAPTER 24

"Shall we dance?" Chad asked, his voice teasing as he took my hand, kissed the back of it, then let go. "Or shall we just stare into the fishbowl — the entire room, not the ones holding up that huge cake."

"Johnnie was entranced. Forgive me for being surprised, why are you here and in your formal hunt garb?"

"The king is going to have a few of the queen's borzois paraded in with gifts in leather pouches they will wear and he wanted each dog collar — I mean, Lady Knollys thought that up — to have a feather in it to go with the room. I was asked — told — to bring nearly a hundred feathers for this. Frankly," he said, not glancing around but still staring at me, "I would have used fir boughs and pinecones in December."

I had to laugh at that. As if he were some sort of interior decorator instead of an outdoorsman. But he was right: some sort of solid simplicity would have moved me more than all this gleam and glitter I had now become so used to. It was so good to see him, as those times were few and far between, though he did materialize sometimes with a new pet chick for Johnnie when the others got too old.

"But I couldn't say no to the feathers," he added. "The king's already out of sorts that it's going to rain and ruin the hunting tomorrow, so he'll have to entertain the men inside all day. I think Johnnie looks good."

"Speaking of the Imp," I said, "I'd better check on him." I leaned slightly to the side to be sure things were going well with the king and the boys. Just in time, for the king was evidently scanning the crowd for me and Chad was blocking his view. I excused myself and hurried over, into the little circle of guests who were cheering on three melting butter pats running down the sharp crease of His Majesty's black silk pant leg.

Pointing at a pouting Johnnie, the king told me, "The boy says he doesn't like butter but jam, and we're not racing jam tonight, Mrs. Lala. It's set him off a bit. Best take him back for now, eh?"

I decided a walk out in the hall was in order. I didn't see Chad where I'd left him, but he was in the corridor. Six elegant-looking borzoi hounds — the queen owned more than I could count — were lined up with little ribboned saddlebags on their backs. One of the king's equerries was sliding wrapped gifts into each bag, more Fabergé animals I surmised. At each holiday, birthdays too, gifts seemed to proliferate as if they were breeding under the huge tables.

I held on to Johnnie's hand so he wouldn't charge the dogs and upset things. But, as Chad looked up at us, winked at Johnnie — or me — and began stuffing pheasant feathers in each collar, the king's fox terrier Caesar appeared from somewhere and ran yipping at the waiting, larger dogs.

They ran, scattering feathers and gifts along the corridor, barking madly, while Johnnie laughed and clapped and Chad swore. Then the boy seemed to go very still amidst the noise and chaos. His eyes took on that dull, dead look I had seen only once before. Oh, no, not here amidst all these people!

The king came out into the hall with an entourage and shouted, "You bad, bad boy!"

For one moment, I thought he meant Johnnie, but Chad rushed to retrieve Caesar for the king as more people spilled out into the hall to see what the ruckus was.

Johnnie wavered on his feet, then seemed to come to attention, standing stiff. Panicked, I pulled him against me. With him pinned to my side, I half-lifted, half-dragged him down the corridor away from the growing crowd, searching for a place to shelter him before the horror began.

Panting, my pulse pounding, I tried the knobs of several locked doors beyond those for the Grand Saloon before one opened on a small, narrow room with floor-to-ceiling empty shelves, perhaps ones for the silver and china now on the dinner tables. I prayed my boy would not go into another convulsion. However grand the day and great the people, everything could be ruined, and it was Johnnie who mattered above all else.

I had no choice but to lay him on the floor. I searched for a light, saw no pull cord or switch, but when I closed the door, a light overhead came on. My heart thudded as hard as the rhythm my poor boy beat on the wooden floor as his limbs convulsed. I held his head steady, horrified at the dazed, contorted expression on his face. Tears coursed down my cheeks and dropped on his.

The noise in the hall quieted, even as Johnnie eventually did. How long had this seizure lasted? Endless. He opened his eyes, though he didn't seem to see me. Dazed. Not quite there.

I heard the door handle turn, felt the whoosh of air. I tried to block whoever was there from seeing, but —

"Charlotte? Is he all right? What happened?"

Thank God, it was Chad.

"He had a sort of seizure. Convulsions."

"Should I get a doctor? I think there's one always near the king lately."

"If you do, then maybe they won't say it's nothing this time."

He closed the door and kneeled beside me. I leaned against his strength. He put one arm around my shaking shoulders.

"He's had this before?"

"Once, months ago. August, on the royal yacht. They decided it was a onetime event, but I feared it wasn't."

"They'll have to face it now."

Johnnie's eyes flickered open. "Chad," he said. "My head hurts. But can we play with the new peeps?"

"Not right now, my boy. I think we need to get you home in bed, right, Charlotte?"

"Her name is Lala."

"Yes, all right. You two stay here for a moment, and I'll tell Prince George, see what he says. I have a cart, but we'll need the omnibus to get him back home. It's here too."

"I want to stay for the party!" The sudden volume of Johnnie's voice startled me. "Ice cream and fish cake. I want to put them in the sea."

Chad and I exchanged swift glances. At least Johnnie was talking, remembering. He was slick with sweat and seemed to keep drifting off, no doubt exhausted.

"We'll be sure you get ice cream and cake later," Chad told him with a squeeze of his shoulder and then a squeeze of mine. "I'll be right back."

"Chad," I called after him. "Tell only Prince George. They don't want people to know."

He frowned, nodded, and closed the door.

I wiped Johnnie's face with my skirt as I had that day on the yacht. I hummed to him, thinking how many times Chad had helped me over the years. He was, no doubt, partly doing this for Johnnie and the royal family, yet I was so deeply moved, comforted and grateful.

But the horror of something I'd overheard Dr. Laking tell Prince George outside the door months ago when they no doubt thought I couldn't hear them had haunted

335

me like no ghost ever could: "If it's only one incident, Your Highness, we can just be watchful, and he's fine with such a dedicated nanny. But if there are more convulsions, we will have to consider epilepsy, and that's a whole different kettle of fish."

"Epilepsy!" the prince had cried. "But if Johnnie gets worse, that . . . that doesn't mean he's an imbecile, does it? I know he's different, a bit slow, but we can't have that sort of stigma for the royal family on view or even whispered about."

"I can imagine, sir, what effect this might have on the public — and on your other children. We could isolate him, send him away somewhere. Indeed, time will tell."

Chad carried Johnnie on his back, horsie style, as the older boys had always called it. I held the side door of Sandringham House open for them, and, wrapped in rainwear, we went out where the omnibus had been brought round and left for us. Chad was going to drive it himself, as we needed no others to talk about Johnnie taking ill. The team of two horses waited there, stamping impatiently. It was starting to sprinkle, and thunder rumbled nearby. The coming storm made the blackness of the night even darker.

Chad laid Johnnie inside on the seat closest to the front with his head on my lap. The child was exhausted, drifting in and out of sleep, fighting that because he loved being with Chad, and rides in any vehicle around the estate were one of his favorite things. Chad said he had talked to Prince George, and we were doing the right thing. In the morning he would summon the doctor again. I dreaded that. I would fight to the end for Johnnie to stay with his family — with me.

Chad patted Johnnie's head and squeezed my shoulder again, but before he could climb out to go round to drive, Prince George appeared up the back steps of the omnibus and climbed in.

"He's quite all right now?" he asked me. Or he might be asking Chad.

"Papa," Johnnie said, his voice sounding weak now. "I want ice cream and cake."

"And you shall have some tomorrow, my boy," he said and, despite his elegant evening suit, bent down to look closely into Johnnie's face. It almost seemed he was bowing to us. In the muted glow from the house windows, I could tell his coat and stiff white waistcoat were raindrop-spattered.

He looked up and asked me, "Like the other one on the yacht?"

"Similar, Your Highness."

"What other one?" Johnnie asked. "Harry and Georgie get to stay at the party, and I don't."

"We'll have our own special party later," I told him, and the prince, bless him, nodded.

"I will tell Princess May that things are under control," he told me. "You are both in good hands with Chad. Now I'd best get back before I'm missed."

His feet sounded on the floorboards as he made a hasty exit out into the quickening rain. I remembered the day I had protected Mary when the rabble-rousers led by Barker Lee had stopped us on the road in this very vehicle. Afterward, Prince George had thanked me and said he owed me a favor. Queen Alexandra had said much the same to Chad — that he should be rewarded — when he had saved the picture of her dead son from the fire. If the doctor diagnosed that Johnnie had epilepsy and must be sent away, could we call in those favors so that he could stay? Would Chad agree to help with that?

His voice jolted me from my agonizing: "Hang on! Before the rain gets worse, we're on our way."

Off we went into the storm. Away from

the protection of the Big House, rain thudded harder on the omnibus roof. Thunder rolled, and lightning lit the sky. I held tighter to Johnnie. A huge crack sounded nearby and then some sort of gigantic crunching noise.

"Tree went down on the road ahead!" Chad shouted, his voice barely discernible over the thunder. "Prince George said the guests and their servants have taken most of the rooms back there, so we'd best go on! I'm turning off, away from the forest, across the football field."

I was amazed he could even see, but he must know every inch of these fields and forests. How long ago that football game seemed when Chad had helped David and Bertie play with the village boys.

"Can we take shelter somewhere?" I shouted to him, not certain he could hear me in the drumming of rain on the roof.

"My house 'til it lets up!"

My house. Simply words. The place he had lived with Millie. The house — the home — that could have been mine with him. I wasn't even sure which one it was across the field with its front on the village green of West Newton and its garden gate on the field. Would his daughter Penny be there or was she with his sister, who was helping to raise her?

"Lala." Johnnie's shrill voice pierced the din. "If we get wet, I won't have to take a bath."

Tears burned my eyes, but I had to smile at that. Thunder echoed again like mad applause at the way this child's mind worked. A "brain disturbance," Prince George had called the earlier seizure, but it seemed Johnnie's brain was slightly disturbed all the time. I felt the same in all sorts of ways, and not only because I feared for Johnnie's future.

I did not know whether to laugh or cry at the fact that, twelve years after I had first met Chad Reaver, though now under wretched circumstances, I was finally going to his home.

Chapter 25

It wasn't the best of welcomes to what must be a pretty cottage. Sheets of rain poured off the tile roof and washed the ivied, red-brick walls. Lightning stabbed the sky, and thunder growled above the downpour, like wagon wheels going over cobblestones. Chad pulled the omnibus nearly up to his doorway, got down and tied the horses' reins to a hitching post. The team stamped and snorted at the noise.

He ran round to us and clambered in the back. "I'll take him," he shouted over the din.

I helped Johnnie sit up, but he clung to me. "Let Chad carry you," I told him. "I'm coming too."

The boy transferred the clamp of his arms to Chad, and we climbed down. The front door opened, and a square of dim light threw itself across our path. With all the newfangled electric in the royal houses, I'd forgotten the dimness of lantern light.

A woman stood silhouetted in the doorway with a child peering from behind her skirts. I thought of poor Millie. Did her ghost still haunt me? She'd borne her baby and should be here now, on this threshold.

"Chad, whatever . . ." the woman cried as we hustled past her and in. Chad was soaked to the skin; I was almost as wet, but at least Johnnie was mostly dry.

"Winnie, this is Charlotte, the royal children's nurse, and Johnnie, the youngest Wales. Charlotte, this is my sister Winifred and my daughter Penny."

"Oh. Oh, yes," Winnie cried as she closed the door behind us and gaped at us a moment while Chad put Johnnie in the rocking chair by the lighted hearth and then stoked up the fire behind the firedogs and iron grate. I swear Winnie almost dropped me a curtsy. Though I couldn't quite manage a smile, I nodded to her and hurried over to perch on a stool Chad pulled up for me.

"I can't hug you right now, precious," Chad told his daughter. "I'm really wet. How is my girl?"

"I don't like thunder, Papa. I'm glad you're home. And brought me a boy to play with."

"Not right now. He's a wee bit tired."

Though I kept my hand on Johnnie's arm, I turned to look closer at Chad's Penelope. In the flickering firelight from the hearth, it was as if a little angel had come to greet us. She had curly, white blond hair, wide blue eyes, and a guileless face. Only her gingham dress of blue-and-white print — and the lack of halo and wings — marred the illusion.

"Penelope, I am so happy to meet you and your aunt," I told her. "Johnnie doesn't feel well right now, but he'll be better another day. Maybe the two of you can play then."

Though her aunt Winnie made a grab for her, Penny came even closer to peer down at Johnnie. "I got wet swimming with fish," he told her.

She nodded as if that was the most logical statement in the world. Chad hurried away, then back to us with a blanket for Johnnie, and Winnie darted off only to again appear with mugs of steaming liquid and two towels. I quickly dried Johnnie's face and hair, then put the other, dry towel around his neck and shoulders. When Chad saw that, he put the one he'd evidently fetched for himself around me.

I put my free hand up to cover his on my shoulder. We linked fingers. I wager the four

of us made a silent tableau with Penny leaning close over the other arm of Johnnie's
rocker. Winnie ahemed, then said, "Chad,
I'm going to put my shawl over my head
and go next door to see all's well with my
two, despite this downpour. Will all be well
here?"

"I can't thank you enough for staying with
Penny tonight when you have your own to
care for," he told her.

"Well, they are not four years old and . . .
and it was lovely to meet you, Nurse Charlotte and Sir . . . Johnnie."

She shot Chad a look somewhere between
I don't believe they are here! and *What should
I call this royal boy?* She kissed Penny on
the top of her golden head and hurried to
the door. Flapping her wool cape open
above her head, she plunged out into the
rain, closing the door behind herself.

So there we sat before Chad's crackling
hearth like a little family.

We drank our tea, and Chad fetched slabs
of bread with honey. It seemed finer fare
than Poached Salmon and French Ice
Cream. I still sat by Johnnie's rocker — he
dozed off and on — and Penny climbed on
Chad's lap in the other hearth chair.

"As soon as the rain lets up, I'll get you to

York Cottage," he told me.

Penny said, "Papa, I don't want to stay here alone."

"No, you can go too," he promised.

"Did you put those feathers on the walls and on the dogs?" she asked him with a huge yawn.

I jumped as Johnnie spoke instead of Chad. "He used a lot of them. Lala, did the queen's dogs run around and bark?"

"Yes. I'm glad you remember," I told him. "The king's little Caesar scared the bigger dogs, the queen's dogs."

"If she has bigger dogs, she should be king."

Penny giggled. And bless her, Johnnie smiled before slipping back into sleep again. I took the empty cup from his limp fingers and rose to get theirs from Chad and Penny too, then realized I should not take over like this. But it seemed so . . . so very right.

I glanced around the small, cozy, low-ceilinged room with its wooden table and four chairs. Fir boughs and pinecones made a pretty little centerpiece. From the windows hung white curtains, looking starched and ironed. The cottage was plainly furnished with no upholstered pieces, though there were plump chintz pillows along the window seat. Two well-worn woven rugs covered the floor. On the whitewashed wall behind the table hung a feather picture, perhaps the mate to the one I'd had for years, the one I should give to Chad for Penny now. This one was of the lake near York Cottage, very pretty, with waterfowl amidst the gentle waves and aloft in the air.

I went into the kitchen alcove, for it was not a separate room. I put the cups down on the smooth oak counter. The iron stove was a small one, but neatly blackened. A corner cupboard displayed rose-patterned bone china, which looked unused. The daily dishes were heavier brown-and-blue pottery ware. As accustomed as I was to fine, expensive things, I still felt right at home here. It all made me homesick for the house where I'd been raised.

As I turned back toward the hearth, I saw two bedroom doors across the parlor and open steps that must lead to a loft or attic. That was all. But somehow it was — I know it would have been — enough.

Penny had fallen asleep in Chad's arms, and Johnnie was dozing. As I walked back toward the hearth, Chad held out his free hand to me and I took it. I standing, he sitting, we held hands, and it made me want to cry — either that or the fact I feared I'd have to fight for Johnnie in the morning if the prince and the doctor wanted to send him away. That seemed to be what the royals did to their own flesh and blood, to a boy who cried too easily, to the heirs who hated naval school, but not to my Johnnie!

I knew we had to get home, though the queen's birthday celebration could go on for hours. The raindrops on the roof were dwindling now. I blinked back tears at the precious beauty of this moment and this place. Johnnie, ill though he was; Chad, though he'd never be mine either; little Penny born but one month after Johnnie, both of them angels unaware.

I sucked in a sob and pulled my hand back. Chad rose and put the sleeping girl in his chair, then came over to me and drew me back from the hearth a bit. I threw myself into his arms before they encircled me, and we both held tight.

"Whatever happens with the boy," he whispered in my ear, "I will try to help."

"You do help. You always have, and I appre—"

The kiss was mutual and fierce. I might as well have been back out in the storm. He was so strong, and I felt swept away. I needed him and always had. Propping my knees against his, I pressed to him, flattening my breasts against his chest. Why had I said *no* to him years ago? But then there would not have been his beautiful Penny, and I would not have been here to help my Johnnie. No, surely I had done the right thing and I must hold to that. But now I only wanted to hold to him.

All thoughts blurred as I opened my lips to return his crushing kiss. His hands not only held me, but moved over my back, waist, and bum, crushing my gown in back. He tipped me in his arms and began to trail hot, openmouthed kisses down my throat to the lace at my neckline and my collarbone. The entire world turned upside down and began to whirl.

"Lala, a fire!" Johnnie's shrill voice sounded. Chad jerked alert and released me. Penny woke up. I rushed to my boy so he didn't tip out of his chair.

But it was only a fallen hearth log that threw sparks and burned brightly anew. "It's all right," I comforted Johnnie as I stooped to hug him.

"It's all right, for certain," Chad said. "And, I agree there *is* a fire, one that's been smoldering for years. Now let's bundle up Penny, I'll put the screen over the hearth, and we'll take you two home."

Funny, I thought, but I had felt at home.

■ ■ ■ ■

The next day, wringing my hands, I paced in the corridor outside Prince George's study, waiting for a summons to join him, Princess May, and Dr. Laking, who'd been in there over an hour after he and two medical colleagues had examined Johnnie — without me in the room. I kept rehearsing what Helene had told me. Some famous, brilliant men had been victims of the dread disease of epilepsy: Socrates, Alexander the Great, Julius Caesar, and Britain's onetime enemy, Napoleon. And they had done well enough, hadn't they?

But I scented raw royal fear that news of the Waleses' strange, "different and difficult" son would leak out. I guess it just didn't do for Britain's royal family in these tenuous times of liberal policies and social unrest to have an epileptic boy. Some said that meant he was an imbecile, when he was not!

After what seemed almost forever, Dr. Laking opened the door and nodded to me. I felt as if I were walking into the lion's den. The prince and princess were standing — Prince George by his desk, Princess May by the window. The other two doctors I had not met huddled near the sofa, looking as if they would like to sink onto it. I curtsied to Their Highnesses.

The prince said, "This is Johnnie's nurse and nanny, Mrs. Charlotte Bill, whom the children call Lala. I have told you all she has conveyed to me about the two seizures the boy has suffered."

"Two, but months apart," I dared to put in.

"However," Dr. Laking said, "we believe they will come closer together, and you — all the family — need to be prepared. It sounds to us as if the child is having grand mal convulsions — epilepsy — and there are no cures, only treatment for that. So do you know, Mrs. Lala, if he has had any petit mals before the big ones — a fixed, blank stare, for example. Maybe his eyes rolled up, muscles twitched, or there was a sudden forward slump of the head?"

"Yes, a bit. And now that I know what to look for, it will be easier for me to get him into a private room before anything else happens."

My stomach knotted as the doctors glanced at each other. Again I prayed that these medical men would not counsel sending Johnnie away from his family and from me.

"His parents want us to try to treat the malady, and we hope you will help with that."

"Oh, yes, anything to keep him here with us."

"Well, then, we shall have it all explained and hold you to it. We realize that your title of nurse means caregiver, a nanny, not a medical nurse, but the prince and princess feel we should try that first — keep it in check. But they also say you are so dear to the child, and he to you, that you may not be able to administer the doses. It can be rough going."

"Better me than someone who comes in he doesn't know."

With a single clap of his hands, the prince said, "All right then. I knew Mrs. Lala would help, for she's done it often before with the others."

I nodded, relieved I did not have to call in any favors. As much as I longed to be near Chad, I silently vowed again to keep Johnnie close to me, no matter the cost.

The first time the doctor showed me how I must "dose" Johnnie, as he had put it, it was not only rough going but a horror. Worse, it occurred after a third attack, within a week of his second seizure. Back came Dr. Laking from London with his black leather valise of so-called treatments and cures.

As he explained their administration to me, keeping his voice low, since Johnnie was in the room, I was appalled. I had fought so long to protect the boy and now felt like a traitor, holding his arms at his sides as he screamed. "Lala, help me! No, no!" as the doctor took over.

He dosed Johnnie with croton oil, a small amount, but one that caused painful, violent vomiting and diarrhea. I kept my hand on Johnnie's forehead as he threw up into a basin and I tried to talk soothingly to him.

Dr. Laking then stirred a tablespoon of mustard powder and a teaspoon of salt into warm water and made the boy drink it, holding his nose. Johnnie was too weak to fight by then. He hung almost limp in my arms. I felt sick to my stomach too. I was sure the child thought I had betrayed him.

"Note these exact dosage amounts in this pint of water," the man told me, while tears ran down the boy's face and mine too. Though Johnnie was too sick to talk anymore and was only weakly holding my hand, I was not too weak.

"Doctor," I told the man, as imposing and stern as he was, "this chance cure is worse than the disease. Is there not some other way?"

"I warned you, and you agreed. As soon as he's emptied out, he will have a double dose of bromides. It's a white powder in water, tastes sweet, so he won't mind that as much. It's a sedative to calm him and his brain activity, an anticonvulsant, and that's what we want, so you must do precisely as I say. We are no longer so ignorant as to believe in something as superstitious as demon possession for epilepsy. The Lord may have cured the epileptic boy in the Bible, but this is left to us."

When it was all over and I put Johnnie to bed, he was limp and trembling. His naturally rosy skin looked gray. I felt I had not seen him in such dreadful shape since he was born — not even during his convulsions. He fell into more of a stupor than sleep, his head back on his pillow, mouth open, breathing hard.

As the doctor headed for the door, he turned back and said, "Believe me, Mrs. Lala, these anticonvulsive therapeutics are the best we have. It may lessen his attacks, but I must warn you it sometimes causes confusion and abnormal speech for a while."

Still stunned at the brutality of it all, I followed him out into the hall and exploded,

"It *may* lessen his attacks? He already has trouble with reality and speech, as Prince George and Dr. Williams must have told you, doctor."

"Be that as it may, this is all we have in modern medicine, that and keeping the patient from becoming too excited or stimulated."

"Both of which he is now to a dreadful degree!"

His eyes widened. His lower lip dropped under his black mustache. I feared he would bring someone else in or convince the prince to send Johnnie away, but I could not abide tormenting the boy like that.

We stared unspeaking at each other for a long moment.

"In this case," he said, "the ends must justify the means." He narrowed his eyes, turned away from me, and strode down the hall.

Week-kneed, but feeling fierce, I had a moment's insanity where I longed to send for Chad and plan an escape for the two of us, taking Johnnie and Penny with us . . . to Scotland, even America, to the ends of the earth where the brilliant doctors and powerful people of this planet would never find us.

Oh, yes, mind you, I knew I had overstepped. He was the king's court physician and came here at the request of His Majesty. But if I had to fight him — the king and prince too — over this, I would do just that.

CHAPTER 26

Although Prince George had once promised me a favor, I thought my best hope to fight against the so-called treatments was Princess May. If that did not work, I intended to lie about giving Johnnie those dire treatments. I would dose him with the bromide but never empty his small body out fore and aft the brutal way the doctor had done.

"Yes, Lala. Come in," Princess May said as Mrs. Wentworth opened the door to her boudoir for me and left the two of us alone.

I curtsied and stood beside the daybed where she had her silk-slippered feet up. She wore a warm-looking mauve satin robe lined with chinchilla, which Johnnie loved to pet as if it were the feathers of one of his peeps.

I cleared my throat. I was not usually so nervous when I spoke to her. "As I'm sure you heard from Dr. Laking, Your Highness, Johnnie had a real setback from the strenuous treatment after his latest seizure. The doctor admitted as much when he checked on the boy before he left for London the next day. It did more than take the starch out of Johnnie. He cringed and turned away from me twice as if I'd struck him, though the next night he sat on my lap while I sang to him and rocked him to sleep. You know he's delicate anyway with such a loving, trusting personality. I . . . I fear such brutal treatment will harm, not help, him in the future, Your Grace."

Her eyes misted but she did not cry. She pressed her lips tightly together. "It was — is — a decision his father and the doctors made, and I felt it was the only hope for a cure, Lala. Nip it in the bud, so to speak."

"But if the bud breaks — is crushed . . . Please, Your Grace, help me to convince the doctors, the prince too, that the result is harmful. He's skittish, and he's never been that way, your dear little Imp. I know how much you love your children, long to protect them, and he needs that more even than Bertie or Harry and —"

She held up a hand at my outburst. Though I wanted to scream at her, I stopped in mid-thought, madly blinking back tears.

"You have been — are — a godsend to my children," she told me, gripping her hands together in her lap. "I know you vowed you would protect Johnnie with your life. But you do see the difficult situation I find myself in. Their father is not only head of this household but will — that is, may — soon be their king, my king. The prince and I, well, we find it difficult to speak about emotional things, but I will write him. That is what we do to keep things well between us."

My eyes widened. Somehow I kept myself from saying, *Write him? Write your husband about the most important, emotional things? Like Johnnie? Write him?*

I decided then I might have to somehow go it alone to help Johnnie. Indeed, if he had another seizure, I would lock the door and make a game of drinking the bromide and throw the dreadful other poisons and instruments of torture in the chamber pot where they belonged.

I heard David's loud voice the moment he came into the house. He and Bertie were home for the holidays. They bid their parents a proper hello in the front hall at the bottom of the stairs, then thudded up the steps to the nursery.

"Lala, what do you think of my new cadet blues?" David demanded as they charged into the room. I gave him a mock salute, and he hit into me so hard for a hug I almost went off balance.

"You look very handsome," I said, holding him at arm's length. My, he was getting tall, Bertie too. "Perhaps Dartmouth Officer college suits you better than Osborne, David."

"B-But I'm still there, Lala!" Bertie said as I hugged him too. "I miss D-David; miss you."

Johnnie came over, all smiles, and Bertie hugged him too. David gave him a pat on his head. "Oh, we're going to have so much fun," David announced, smiling at me. "I can't wait to see Grandpapa! You know, he said I could drive his motorcar when I'm sixteen, and I'm not so far from that. I'll give you and Bertie rides in it, at least round here, even if they don't let me drive in London."

"Me too," Johnnie put in. "Rides just like Chad and me."

David ignored that. "And the girls will like it too. How I wish that pretty Tatiana was not off in Russia."

"I didn't think you meant your sister and your mother," I told him with a smile. "You know, my boys, it wasn't so far back you were both longing for bicycles."

"I have a pedal car," Johnnie put in. He

did indeed, an early gift from his grand-father, sent from London. It was all I could do to keep him from dragging it in the house so he could ride inside.

"That's nice," David said just as Bertie spotted Finch down the hall and both boys ran to him.

I felt deflated at the way David had treated Johnnie, who had always adored him. But, I tried to tell myself, it was just that the two oldest were happy to be home for a while. But no, Finch had said he'd explained Johnnie's condition to David when he'd taken some supplies to Dartmouth. The boy's letters to me were less frequent than when he'd first been away, but he never asked about Johnnie. Well, Christmas always put love in the heart. Before Mr. Hansell read *A Christmas Carol* aloud this year, I'd remember to tell David that Johnnie was like our own Tiny Tim and was to be especially loved and protected.

As winter turned to spring, anyone who knew the king was worried for his health. From Christmas on, he'd had a deep-chested cough that shook his big, barrel-like frame. He was hardly ever jovial now. Even little things annoyed him, so I knew better than to risk asking him through the queen for help with Johnnie. His Majesty was especially on a rant about the dangers of socialism.

On a warm day, when I had the nursery windows open, I overheard the king talking to Prince George. "That man!" he'd ranted, "is preaching class war! He's a danger to the monarchy and the stability of this nation, and don't you forget it. I'm ashamed to have him bear the names David and George, royal names!"

"That man" was Prime Minister David Lloyd George, and he gave all the Waleses fits. They were fearful he would ruin the monarchy and cast them out, though I doubted after centuries the British would give up their kings and queens. But I knew from my mother's letters that my father had marched in a river workman's parade for more rights and better pay. The other well-argued idea, that of women possibly getting the vote someday, my father said was quite insane. Women's suffrage, they still called it, and over these last years I'd come to think it a very good idea.

"And," the king had ranted on to Prince George, "I won't abide that sort of socialist unrest on this estate. There's been some rabble-rousing again. Chad thinks that clever bastard Barker Lee might be back, sneaking in, poaching too. We cannot have that sort of thing again, and I've told Chad Reaver so, told him to keep an eye on Lala and the children, since we can't lock them up the way I'd like to do with Barker."

"Chad's always been staunch and loyal and —"

"Precisely. I'm tempted to make him estate manager but he's so good with the birds and what would you and I do without our shooting, eh, so . . ."

His Majesty had begun one of his terrible gasping and coughing fits, and I closed the window half wishing I had not wanted spring air inside and smelled cigar smoke instead. But it was good to know they admired Chad. But had he been so protective of us lately because of a royal order and not his own desire?

Later that month, I heard that Mrs. Keppel had convinced the king to "take the cure" with her at Biarritz in his beloved France, and afterward, they came straight to Sandringham. We all knew he'd collapsed while in France, but had rallied.

The queen had been informed of his ill health, but she was off in her homeland of Denmark with her daughter Toria and her sister. The king and queen had a strange marriage, I thought, but then so was one in which the husband and wife wrote each other about important things instead of discussing them face to face. Not only did the royals rear their children in unique ways, but their own relationships seemed to be laws unto themselves.

Well, I mustn't complain because Princess May had managed to keep Dr. Laking far from Johnnie, and if he had a seizure — he had one at least every fortnight — I dosed him only with bromide dissolved in apple juice, as well as tenderness and love, and no one had again mentioned sending him away.

Sunday, May Day, 1910, Chad, Penny, Johnnie, and I took a lovely walk together on the estate. It was a rare treat. The two children got on famously — as did Chad and I. I hated that he now carried a pistol and was more nervous — watching for Barker Lee, I surmised. I didn't want to ask, for I feared he wouldn't go round about with us if he believed I thought we were in danger. I could not fathom that man would dare show his face in daylight, in the forest or not.

Somewhere in the bushes, we heard a dog barking over and over. We saw a squirrel scoot up a tree.

"That doesn't sound like one of the

queen's borzois," Chad said, "though I've seen the whole lot of them taken for a walk on paths here while she's in Denmark."

"She's coming back soon, I hear, since the king's been so ill. Imagine, a legal, royal wife far away and —"

"And the illegal, scandalous, and real one staying in the Big House," he finished for me. He lowered his voice, though the children were ahead of us on the path, looking for the dog. They'd been picking daisies, for both loved flowers. Johnnie had permission to have his own garden this year. I had not tethered him to me today, for when Penny was along, he quite readily stuck with her.

"My definition of a wife," Chad went on, "is one who sticks by in hard times, and that's Alice Keppel, not the queen. Still, I can understand that Her Majesty resents his long string of lady friends."

The dog turned out to be the king's terrier Caesar, trotting smugly toward us on the path with the silver tag on his collar jingling. That meant the king — and, no doubt, Mrs. Keppel — were not far behind. Johnnie and Penny called to the dog, who came over, happy to be petted. The king almost exploded around the turn in the path, walking fast, though looking wobbly, swinging a walking stick. A few steps behind, hustling after him as best she could, came Mrs. Keppel, using her closed parasol like a cane.

"Well, well, little Johnnie!" His Majesty bellowed. "Ah, Mrs. Lala and Chad out for a walk."

He was out of breath, so I couldn't fathom why he'd been going at such a clip. But it was as if Mrs. Keppel had read my mind. "Must you do everything so fast?" she scolded the king. "I can barely keep up."

Chad and I bowed and curtsied, but Johnnie just hugged his grandfather's knee. Chad whispered to Penny to curtsy, but misunderstanding, she hugged his other knee.

The king shouted a laugh, which turned in a coughing fit that seemed to shake him. When he stopped hacking, Mrs. Keppel, as if nothing were amiss, smiled at Penny and told him, "You always did have a way with pretty girls, sir."

He turned to me and asked, "How is the lad getting on then?"

"Still some problems, Your Majesty. Mr. Hansell is going to begin working with him soon, so we shall see about reading and writing. But he is — well, a bit better. And being in the arms of his family does him wonders."

"And in your tender and capable arms, I

don't doubt, Mrs. Lala."

"I'm better," Johnnie said. "Not butter like on your knees."

"Good memory, my boy. We will have to do that again someday, won't we? I see you've been gathering flowers."

"For you and the lady to give to Grannie," he said, and offered the long-stemmed, ragged bunch of wilting flowers to Alice Keppel.

"Why, thank you, Johnnie," she said, not reacting to the mention of the queen at all. "How very kind of you."

"A prince of a boy," King Edward said. "And good day to you all. Chad, keep an eye out for local socialists, like Mrs. Lala keeps an eye on the boy."

He was off at a fast pace again with Mrs. Keppel in his wake. What he'd called Johnnie — a prince of a boy — stuck with me the next few days after the king had gone back to London with Mrs. Keppel, and Queen Alexandra returned from Denmark to Buckingham Palace.

The king's cough got worse, and his boisterous grip on life faded fast, we were told. We were all summoned to London, including David from the Dartmouth Naval Academy and Bertie from Osborne, though Harry was still at Broadstairs. Just four days after we had seen him on the forest path at Sandringham, King Edward VII suffered a fainting fit at the palace and took to his bed.

All this made me remember what the king had said last to Johnnie. After all, if His Majesty died, Prince George would be king, Princess May queen, and my Johnnie a prince of a boy indeed.

CHAPTER 27

At Marlborough House in London, we spent the time the king was on his deathbed watching the crowds of people on the Mall. They did not know that the king was dying. Unlike us, they were not continually glancing at his lighted windows in the palace or at the royal standard flying on the roof. Instead, they were hoping to see the fiery tail from the pass of Halley's Comet this historic day of May 5, 1910.

Finch and I were with the two oldest and two youngest boys because Harry was still in what I considered cruel exile at Broadstairs. Mary was with her mother in the palace.

"His Majesty must be getting a good night's sleep," Finch announced, "and you boys might as well too. It's late."

"But the lights are all still on at Buck House," George protested. "Do you think he sleeps with the lights on?"

"Never you mind. To bed, all of you," Finch insisted, with a clap of his hands. "If there is any news, anything to be done, your father will send it."

Bleary-eyed, George obeyed, and I took Johnnie's hand to head him toward their bedroom. David and Bertie lagged behind, exchanging furtive glances and whispers. As reluctant as their parents were to inherit the throne with its public and private problems, a summons to discuss their grandpapa's departure would not be good news either.

"David, Bertie, let's go!" Finch ordered. "Set sail toward bed, you two cadets. Haven't they taught you to take orders yet?"

As they finally budged, David said, "I'm looking forward to the day I will give the orders — when I'm an officer, I mean."

David and Bertie were in the next room with Finch, while I tended George and Johnnie. I let the two youngest boys chat for a while before tucking them up, not that Johnnie had the slightest notion what Halley's Comet was that George chattered on about. But he was always happy to be with George, since Finch had pretty much taken him over now, leaving me with just Johnnie. It was, I knew, both his parents' and Finch's way of letting me give full-time care to their youngest child, and I considered that a victory. The family and household staff all knew of his epilepsy but were sworn to secrecy. Dr. Laking had been right about one thing: Even seeing their little brother's eyes glaze over and me hustle him from the room and lock myself in with the child upset them. And I absolutely dreaded the possibility that Johnnie might have a seizure in front of his father.

I'm sure we all slept fitfully that night. I know I did. I was barely dressed at dawn's first light when I heard David's and Bertie's voices in the hall. Johnnie and George were still in heavy slumber, so I opened the door and went out just as Bertie was telling David, "I saw it out the window! The royal flag on the p-palace roof at half mast!"

The two of them tore down the hall into the sitting room to the window from which we'd watched the palace last night. I followed just as Finch was coming out of the next room. "What's the ruckus?" he asked me. "I told them to be quiet." My heart thudding, I gestured for him to follow.

As Finch and I stopped in the doorway, David and Bertie stood shoulder to shoulder at the window. Bertie's thin frame shook. David hung his head, then put his arm around his brother. I stayed put, but Finch went to stand behind them and placed a hand on their shoulders.

"Gr-Grandpapa is . . . g-gone," Bertie whispered. "That's what that means."

"I fear so, lads," Finch said. "A sad day for all of us — the country and the empire. You must both be brave and help your father now."

David choked out, "My best, very best friend ever, not Papa, but Grandpapa — besides you, Lala — and Finch too."

Tears blurred my vision as David and Bertie turned toward me. While Finch comforted Bertie, David came to put his head on my shoulder as if he were small again. The two youngest boys, still in their nightshirts, must have heard us and came out and down the hall. Johnnie wedged in between David and me and hugged my waist while David held to my shoulders.

He looked down at Johnnie. "You didn't really know him!" he told the child and stomped off. He went into his and Bertie's room and slammed the door.

That echoed in the hall and in my heart.

Dragging their feet at their father's summons, David and Bertie went downstairs at Marlborough House while the city and nation plunged into mourning. Mary came back from the palace and filled Finch and me in on everything.

"At least now that I'm an adult, I could be a help to Mama," she told us. She looked exhausted and suddenly older than her thirteen years.

"I'm proud of you, Mary," I told her. "Remember, I told you once that you would be called upon for important tasks."

"But strange now to think she is not only Mama anymore, not even Princess May, though she said Papa will always call her May. She's decided to take the name Queen Mary at the coronation. She's really Victoria Mary, you know, but she could never be called Queen Victoria. Papa — I mean, King George — says there could never be another one of those. But in all this, I think it's Grannie they are worried for. Papa says she's adrift without the king."

Finch said, "And a shock not to be queen anymore."

"Well," Mary said, leaning forward as if the walls had ears, when it was only Johnnie playing with a toy wooden wagon and painted horses across the room, "Grannie is insisting she's still queen and should take precedence over Mama. And she won't give up Sandringham House, because she says the king left it to her. She may even refuse to give up the palace. Papa's very upset that she closed off Grandpapa's bedchamber where he still lies and won't let others in."

"Oh, no!" I blurted when I should have kept calm, because Johnnie looked up and came over.

"Yes," Mary said, mouthing the words now. "Papa says just like Queen Victoria did with her Albert, and Grandpapa hated that, but it is all rather romantic, isn't it?"

It wasn't my idea of romantic, but I kept quiet.

"Something bad happened," Johnnie informed us solemnly. I reached out to put an arm around him, and he leaned his elbows on my knees. "Did someone get sent to his room? I hope it's not me."

"It's not you, my good boy," I told him with a quick hug. "And how are the horses?" I asked him with a nod at his toys on the floor.

"Not afraid. The ones Chad drove Lala and me to his house — they were scared of the storm." He went back across the floor to shove his horses around again.

Mary's comment about it all being rather romantic still bounced through my brain. There was a moment's lull where Finch looked at me with one eyebrow raised and Mary tilted her head. I felt my cheeks flush. Chad and I had told no one we had stopped at his house the night of the queen's — the former queen's — birthday party. It was our secret, as were our feelings for each other. He knew I couldn't leave Johnnie, but he also knew I loved him. Despite that dilemma, for now, we had to be content.

"And that's not all," Mary said when I added nothing. "I overheard that Grannie invited Mrs. Keppel in to say good-bye to the king and when she left his bedroom, she — Mrs. Keppel, not Grannie — was so distraught she could hardly walk or breathe! I heard she cried and cried!"

Who needed the London gazettes, I thought, when we had Mary — Princess Mary — on the scene?

"So sad too," she whispered with such a serious look on her face, "that little Caesar followed Mrs. Keppel out of the room and then the king died, as if his pet had been his spirit leaving. What if Grannie tries séances that are all the rage, that's what Papa said. And Caesar's going to be in the funeral procession, walking before the heads of state, because that's what Grandpapa wanted."

Johnnie stopped giddyapping his horses long enough to put in, "If Caesar's in a parade, I will be too. With my peeps."

On that note, David and Bertie came into

the room, both looking somber. "Tomorrow," David said, "we are all to stand at attention from designated places here at Marlborough House while Father is officially proclaimed king from the balcony of Friary Court at St. James's. Even the new king and queen will watch it from the window here, because that's the best view, but Bertie and I will be in our cadet uniforms, watching from the courtyard below. And George and Johnnie — with you and Finch at the back of the courtyard," he added, with a "that's where Johnnie should be" glance at me.

David went on, "When we told Papa about the flag on the palace flying at half mast, he said that the nation's flag must fly at full staff for the new king — him. Then he ordered a flag to be flown on Marlborough House, right on the roof above our heads, to show everyone that . . . that . . ." He faltered and tears sprang to his eyes.

Bertie put a hand on his arm and said, "That the king is d-dead, but long live the king!"

I couldn't help but blink back tears at all I'd heard — and at how grown up my first three children were now. I was proud that Mary seemed to be coming into her own. Poor, beleaguered Bertie had shown both compassion and strength. David stood strong, and his voice, but for that blast of emotion, suddenly sounded older than his years. Though he'd often declared to me that he never wanted to be king, he looked, at least, like someone who could be Prince of Wales. The way he treated Johnnie, I could only hope he would learn to be a compassionate one.

As a group of men assembled on the balcony at St. James's Palace, I held Johnnie tight before me and Finch kept his hands on George's shoulders as the boy stood ahead of him. How I wished Harry could be here, but things were happening too fast. Ministers and privy councillors were in uniforms as were the king's heralds and others clad in costumes of scarlet, blue, and gold. The King of Arms began to read the decree in a loud voice that echoed down to us and gave me chills up my backbone.

"The high and mighty Prince George Frederick Ernest Albert is now, by the death of our late Sovereign of happy memory, become our only lawful right Liege Lord, George the Fifth, by the Grace of God, King of the United Kingdom of Great Britain and Ireland and of the British Dominions beyond the Sea, Defender of the Faith, Emperor of India, to whom we acknowledge all faith and constant obedience, with all hearty and humble affection, beseeching God, by whom Kings and Queens do reign, to bless the Royal Prince George the Fifth with long and happy years to reign over us."

I heard George say under his breath, "I hope we don't have to call him that long name now. Do you think someone might think I've just been named king?"

My clever, funny George. And, despite the momentous occasion, I nearly laughed when Johnnie said, "Happy years in the rain sounds good, if we don't all get wet. I'm always getting wet when I have my fall downs, and I don't want to do that anymore."

We all jumped when the trumpets sounded and distant guns boomed. I watched Johnnie closely to be sure he would not have a bad spell — a fall down — as he'd come to call his fits, but as loud as it all was, he seemed to like the music. I'd been teaching him "God Save the King," which he hummed when someone in the crowd began to sing it and the anthem was picked up by others until it swelled the skies.

My boy raised his hands and seemed to rhythmically conduct the music. I only hoped, now that we had a new king, he would not want to send Johnnie away and that we could indeed have a reign of "all hearty and humble affection" and "long and happy years" to come.

On May 20, 1910, the formal funeral procession seemed unending as it headed out from the palace to Westminster Abbey. Finch and I watched with George and Johnnie from the window. David, Bertie, and Mary rode in a coach with their mother, though Queen Alexandra's coach would take precedence when they reached Westminster Abbey. Insisting that he looked "just fine," lying there in his bed, it had taken the widowed queen nearly a week to allow the king's body to be placed in a coffin and moved to the throne room of the palace. Though she had been a bit dotty at times, his death seemed to have unsettled her thoughts even more.

Music came and went from the massed bands, the endless, solemn drumbeats and wailing bagpipes below. Johnnie directed each mournful or majestic melody with his hands and even marched in place. Amidst the tight ranks of blue-jacketed sailors in straw hats, we saw the coffin on its bier roll past. It was draped with the royal standard on which were perched Saint Edward's gold crown at the head and the scepter and orb at the feet.

The king had been such a life-force and I had seen him so few days before he died that I almost thought he would sit up, throw back the coffin lid, and grab the crown again. Maybe that's why his poor widow had tried to hold on to her unfaithful husband. After all, lying there dead in his bedroom, the loud, dynamic man was, at the end, hers alone, not Mrs. Keppel's, not his friends'. In death, "King Teddy" seemed to be as beloved as he had been in life. I wondered if old Queen Victoria would, at last, have been proud of her son. And I prayed our new king would be proud of his and let them know so.

When we saw a kilted Highland soldier walk past with little Caesar on his leash right behind the symbolic riderless horse, Johnnie shouted out to the sprightly little terrier, "If you are in the parade, I guess you are better than Grannie's bigger dogs! I'm smaller than all my brothers, Caesar!"

Of course, no one below heard him. Would they ever hear his voice? I wasn't even certain people knew he existed.

Behind the coffin walked kings, presidents, and heads of state, including Kaiser Wilhelm, whom we heard was furious to be placed behind a pet dog. Former President Theodore Roosevelt, as ambassador of the current American president William Taft, was there too, in plain black, carrying his coat because the day was warm. He was dressed more plainly than the dignitaries in uniforms, laden down with ribbons and medals and wearing ornate hats or shiny helmets with fluttering feathers.

Soldiers in black bear fur hats and red tunics rotated past us for nearly a quarter of an hour. I felt quite dizzy with it all, but, thank heavens, Johnnie seemed only entranced by the sound of boots, horses' hoofs, and the occasional shout in the crowd of "God Save the King!," which he sometimes echoed.

I was so proud of him that day for his interest in the parade, his relatively good behavior — and the fact he had not had a seizure with all the excitement and distractions. But the next day, he made up for that by running away from me in Marlborough House and rushing down a flight of stairs when I knew some of the high-ranking foreign guests were staying on the floor below. I picked up my skirts, grabbed the marble banister, and rushed downstairs after him.

The little imp, thinking it was some great

game, opened the first door he came to and plunged in. Two men were inside, neither of whom I recognized when Johnnie shouted out, "Let's play hide-and-seek, and Lala is it!"

Horrified, I made a grab for him. He hadn't given me the slip for the longest time, and I'd stopped tying his waist to my wrist.

I saw we were in some sort of sitting room. He ducked under the table where the two men sat with papers and maps spread out between them.

"Well, Winston," the bigger man said, "looks like the Germans or Russians have sent two unlikely spies."

The younger man laughed. "Colonel Roosevelt, we who have run our navies must stick together at all costs, spies or not. I was just going, ma'am," he told me as he scooped up some papers, shook hands with the other man, and headed for the door. "And, sir, tell President Taft we are grateful he sent you for this important event."

"Bully right, Churchill. We'll be in touch, but I'm sailing for home tomorrow. African safaris wear me out, shooting all that game."

"Better than having to shoot at Boers. And who is this rowdy young gentleman, miss — ah, Miss Lala?" he asked me, politely ignoring that I'd sucked in a sharp breath when I'd heard the names of two American presidents. As for this man, I had no notion who he might be.

"Forgive us for intruding, Mr. Winston," I told him.

"Mr. Churchill. Winston's the first name, and I'm stuck with it."

"Mr. Churchill and — and sir — president. I'm Mrs. Bill, Prince Johnnie's nanny, so —"

"Ah, so he's not just a rumor," Mr. Churchill said as we both watched the former president pluck Johnnie from under the table and put him on his knee. I prayed the boy would not do something dreadful.

I stared into Mr. Churchill's face with his assessing stare that so demanded truth. But my upset stomach cramped again. Was Johnnie, now a prince of the realm, indeed a hidden boy — a secret as I had feared? If so, it would make it so much easier for his father to send him away.

"Ah, so you're his nanny?" Churchill pursued when I hesitated to answer. "I can't tell you how much a good nanny means. I loved mine so, so very much," he added, and his eyes misted. "Good day to you, Mrs. Lala Bill, and to you, sir. I heard you had a way with children — and nations," he called over his shoulder to the American and was out the door, which he left open.

So, having no choice, I turned to face Johnnie, sitting smugly on the knee of the big, ruddy-faced, square-jawed man with a large mustache and pince-nez glasses who had been in the funeral parade with the dignitaries and . . . and had once been president of the entire United States of America!

Former president Theodore Roosevelt was a bear of a man but so gentle with Johnnie. "You're a corker, you know that?" he asked the boy. "I've had a couple like you, but they're quite grown up now."

"Oh, there's more than me, but they're all older."

"Yes, I've met the oldest ones."

I wondered if Johnnie seemed so content because this man reminded him of his grandfather. I should take him and go, but shouldn't I give way to a president as I did the king?

"Sit, sit right over there, Mrs. ah — Nanny, while I talk to this fine lad."

I sat ramrod straight in the chair Mr. Churchill had vacated while President Roosevelt talked to Johnnie. The boy explained to him how he'd watched the parade out the window and that Caesar was his favorite marcher. I suspect it didn't take Mr. Roosevelt long to realize the boy was different, but I was awed at their easy, sincere conversation. Then I was panicked as Johnnie told him, "Lala and Chad — he takes care of all the birds — are like another Mama and Papa to me, so I have two of each."

I sat up even straighter in the chair. Johnnie had never said that to me. I was touched but appalled again. Would he announce to servants and world leaders alike about Chad and me?

"I see," the big man said, though I doubted that he did. "You know, my boy, I watched the funeral procession of our great president, Abraham Lincoln, from a window in my grandfather's house on Union Square in New York City when I was about your age. They figured I was too young to be out in the crowd. People felt sad that day, just like they did for your grandpa."

"I think of him a lot, unless I have a falling fit. Ep-lep-sies," he said.

I had to bite back another gasp. Little pitchers must indeed have big ears as well as bigger mouths than I'd imagined. Here I thought he had no notion what to call the malady that troubled him. Perhaps I should share more of it with him than I had.

"Which," I put in, "is known only within

the royal family."

"I understand," Roosevelt said, shooting me a serious look. "Now let me tell you something else," he said to Johnnie with a little bounce of his knee. "I don't share this with many, and we kept this in our family too, but when I was about your age I had severe asthma attacks. That means I had trouble breathing. I'd wake up at night so scared, feeling like I was being smothered — like a pillow was over my face. The doctor said no cure, but I worked it out, got rid of that curse."

"But how?" Johnnie asked as if he grasped every word of what was being said — and, since he'd come up with "ep-lep-sies," perhaps he did.

"I worked very hard to build myself up. Took walks and runs and swims."

"Righto. I do that, but the swims only in the tub. I wanted to swim in the sea when we were with the royal Russians, but Lala said no."

"Ah, got to keep an eye on those Russians, and I'm glad to hear your Lala keeps a good eye on you."

When we finally stood up to leave — I realized I'd been gripping my hands together so hard in my lap that my fingers had gone numb — Mr. Roosevelt asked me, "Is he being schooled at home, ma'am? I was in the beginning when I wasn't well."

"Yes. They are all with tutors for a while, then out into the world, but I teach him things too — his handwriting."

"My lad, I can tell you are a square, bully boy!" he said and ruffled Johnnie's hair. And then, to my great amazement, he extended his hand to me for what must be a very American handshake. His hand was huge and warm.

"I can't thank you enough," I told him. "We shall not forget you, right, Johnnie? Thank your new friend."

"Righto. I won't forget you and I will write you a letter when I learn how."

"I will look for that letter. You just have it sent through one of your father — the king's — equerries or secretaries, eh?" he said with a look at me.

I took Johnnie's hand, and we went out. "He was very nice, just like Grandpapa was," he said, looking up so earnestly at me. "So if I'm not king someday, president would be fine too."

CHAPTER 28

In his new reign, poor King George had trouble from all sides, including from his mother. She didn't want to give up her "sweet, little crown," Sandringham House, or Buckingham Palace. He had problems with Prime Minister Herbert Asquith, who tried to restrict the power of the House of Lords. The Suffragettes took their motto "Deeds, not words!" to the streets in protests and vandalism and went on hunger strikes. That strike was matched by workers' unions and protests: a railway strike, a cotton industry strike. The coalfield strikers in South Wales and other places refused to work too. As ever, the Irish were demanding home rule, and I know that worried him.

Though the king had always been a short-tempered man, he was even more so now, and I lived in fear that something Johnnie did might get him sent away. I dreaded what Mr. Hansell's judgment of the lad would be when he began to tutor him. Hansell was a toe-the-line sort who wanted yes-or-no, down-the-line answers, and that was not Johnnie. If Hansell compared Johnnie to clever George, Johnnie was such . . . well, such a dreamer, creative too, in his own way — but definitely not down the line.

Ordinarily, I would not have been so strict with the dear boy, but I was afraid that his love of the king's beloved pet parrot would cause a problem too.

King George, so unlike himself, now gave that squawky, colorful macaw free rein in York Cottage, where we yet lived so the Queen Mother, Alexandra, could have the Big House. But even when the king took the bird there, she flew hither and yon, landing on ornate flower and fruit centerpieces or even people's plates — fortunately, usually the king's. Johnnie had picked up on a piece of doggerel that George had composed, and chanted it all the time, no matter who was near: "Charlotte the parrot / Rules in the palace," over and over.

"Lala," the king said to me one day when I was chasing Johnnie who was chasing Charlotte down the front staircase, "if the boy can learn that little poem, can't he learn simple sums? Hansell says he thinks it's hopeless. I don't need outsiders in these dreadful times thinking my son believes a birdbrain and not a king rules in the palace."

"Yes, Your Majesty. I will see to it that he doesn't chase the bird and say that — if I can."

"Ah, Mrs. Lala, I do remember your first name is Charlotte, so perhaps I unwittingly named that grit-and-go parrot after you. It sometimes does as I want but usually goes its own way."

Grabbing Johnnie's wrist, I came down the last two stairs so that I didn't tower above the king. "I do what is best for your son, as you have bid me, sir."

He sighed. "I know you do, but tough times are ahead with many enemies. Best he not come to London to wave us off for the tour of India, best he stay here where he's safer. Charlotte the parrot's not going on our trip either, my boy," he added, stooping slightly. "Charlotte's staying in London."

"Not this Charlotte Lala," he said. "She stays with me."

"Yes, of course," he agreed, but I didn't like the trend of all this. A parrot could go to London but not his own son? Worse, the king was shrinking Johnnie's world when I longed to expand it, to teach him things — oh, not sums — but about the world, birds and flowers and . . . and life. As my father used to say, I felt caught between the devil and the deep blue sea.

I walked a tightrope after that, with events blurring by in my efforts to help and amuse Johnnie and keep him safe from being sent into exile as his father had done with his other sons. In the early summer of 1912, when Johnnie was seven, his brother George was sent away to school at St. Peter's Court for summer term. That was about the time David got the mumps and wrote me a sad letter from Dartmouth about how lonely he still felt and how he wasn't ready to go for a two-year stay at Oxford, though he would take Finch with him.

But the David I saw the next year in May, while the king and queen were at a wedding on the continent, with Kaiser Wilhelm and Tsar Nicholas in attendance, wasn't sad at all. He drove into Sandringham, Finch by his side, honking his horn, roaring along in his new gray Daimler.

I was proud that the king had invested David as Prince of Wales on his seventeenth birthday last year, but it had gone to his head. The *I serve* motto of the heir was more like *I must be served* under David, though he dare not act that way before his parents. He'd taken to ordering even his brothers and sister around, although Mary mostly ignored him.

"Isn't it a beauty, Lala?" David shouted to me. "Get in and we'll take a ride. But it might be too dangerous for Johnnie. Finch can stay with him."

"David, he'd love to go if it's safe."

"Safe? Of course it's safe, but he and Finch will have a fine time here. Lala, the Prince of Wales is speaking," David declared as Finch climbed out and held the door for me. I hesitated. I couldn't bear to look at Johnnie, and I was angry with David, but I had promised him.

"Can we go round once and then collect Johnnie and Finch?" I asked.

"All right then."

Finch picked Johnnie up, something I could not do anymore. "We'll be right back, Johnnie. Right back," I called to my boy.

But we weren't. We sped through the village, where I saw Penny playing with some other children. We roared down to the train station and back, but whizzed right past York Cottage where Finch and Johnnie were throwing stones in the lake.

"David, you said you'd stop for them," I protested, however much I admired his motorcar and driving skills.

"And we will. I may even take Grannie for

a ride. She's becoming too much of a recluse, I hear. Poor Aunt Toria has to wait on her hand and foot, and Grannie won't let any suitors near her."

"We visit her sometimes. Yes, her mind wanders a bit."

"Then I'll bet she and Johnnie get on famously."

"Take me back right now. It's been a lovely ride, but I need to go back to the cottage."

He smiled and shrugged, but obeyed me, though he did not have to anymore. We pulled up in front in a cloud of dust, but I saw only Finch. My heart leaped out of my chest faster than I leaped out of the motorcar.

"Finch, where's Johnnie?"

"We're playing hide-and-seek. He's just back round the side of the house. He's not near the lake."

"I didn't see him. I hope he didn't take one of those bicycles. He's a good rider now. We — I taught him."

David evidently thought the boy would appear if he made noise, so he leaned on the horn. Finch and I tore around to the side. Thankfully, both bikes were still there, but so was a ladder a workman must have left behind.

I looked up to see Johnnie on the slanted second-story roof above our heads, peering over, waving down. That dratted David was still laying on his horn.

"Johnnie!" I cried above that noise. "Don't you lean over! Don't you move! Finch is coming up to get you."

"Not Finch," he said. "Not David. Only Lala. You took a fast ride but the birds are flying up here. I think I can see Chad's house too. It would be so fun to fly."

Dear Lord, I feared he would fall or even jump — try to fly. Pushing Finch aside, who acted like he was going up anyway, I picked up my skirts hems to my knees and started to climb.

I talked as I went up, holding to each rung of the ladder, holding to hope that Johnnie would not jump. "You sit down!" I told him, despite the fact he often did not obey. "You stay right there!"

"But Lala," he said, leaning over the eaves, "Georgie told me men can fly now. He showed me pictures. He reads me books."

"They cannot fly unless they have wings, and you do not. Sit down!"

I'd been so proud of George's early reading skills, just as I'd grieved Johnnie's lack, but I'd never imagined this. I'd hated heights ever since we got locked in that

Scottish tower. I was so high now that I could look across the upward slant of roof, but I was only at the height of the boy's feet.

"Sit down," I ordered again. "Sit down right there. I want to talk to you."

At last, he obeyed. Finally David laid off sounding his motorcar horn. Evidently, he had not even climbed out of the Daimler to help. I was angry with him, with Johnnie, with George, with the king — with the world. At least Finch had the brains to just steady the ladder beneath me. Well, he'd better, after letting the boy out of his sight.

As if nothing was amiss, Johnnie chattered on. "Do you know stories about men flying, Lala? You don't read me those. *The War in the Air,* that was one book. Airships in the sky. Georgie said so, and I want to see one."

"All right, all right. But we have open fields here to see the sky. It's more important to have open space on the ground than to sit on a roof. Scoot closer to me — slowly — and we'll go down the ladder, then watch the sky from the lawn. We'll ask your grannie to let us go up to the top floor of the Big House and look out the windows. We'll be higher than this then. Come on, Johnnie."

"And don't be mad at Georgie."

"I won't. Not much."

"If Papa sends him away to school, you can read those books to me."

"All right now, I have a hold of you. Turn over on your tummy and scoot this way so I can put your feet on the ladder and we'll go down together."

He did as I bid but kept talking. "You do believe it, don't you, Lala? Men fly in aircraft and shoot at each other in the sky."

"In books, Johnnie. Just in books. And in our minds. We don't want war in the air any more than on the land or sea."

"Papa said to Mama there might be war if Cousin Willie builds up his arms. But I heard he has one really small arm, and he hides it."

I must keep him talking, but I wanted to scream — and get back on solid ground. Ah, I had him now, on the ladder, his back pressed against me, his feet on the rung at my waist level.

"I'm going down one step at a time, then I'll bring you with me," I told him. "But you keep hanging on with your hands all the way down."

"That's what else Papa said about bad war — we have to hang on."

"I know what you're going to say," George told me when he came into the empty drawing room after supper that evening. Jane was watching Johnnie upstairs, who was still going on about flying, and I had asked for George.

"Then tell me what I'm going to say, George. If you knew already, why didn't you think ahead when you filled your little brother's head with ideas of men flying and shooting, no less?"

"But that's just it, Lala." He looked so in earnest, standing as if at attention before me. "I am thinking ahead and not about the navy where Papa is determined to send me. I want to learn to fly an aeroplane. I've read and read about it in H. G. Wells's *The War in the Air* and *The Sleeper Awakes* and Jules Verne's *Master of the World.*"

"Yes, well, I am proud of your reading and your intelligence and imagination, but as for those shooting battles in the sky, please don't involve Johnnie. Thank you for reading to him, but you do know he can't always tell the difference between truth and pretend, don't you? You have him looking up at the sky all the time, and he bumps into things. He nearly fell in the lake yesterday, let alone he could have fallen off the roof."

"Yes, but you watch him well, and Finch didn't."

"The way you present your case, perhaps

you should be a barrister someday, George Edward Alexander Edmund — when you are not fighting the enemy in aeroplanes."

"It's not all in books and imagination, Lala, really! In the 1890s, both Germany and the United States patented rigid flying machines called Zeppelins. And guess what? They are filled with gas that makes them float, but it can burn too if they are not careful. A little hard to steer in the wind, but there's a cabin at the bottom with a crew. How I'd love to fly in one. Wouldn't you?"

"I admit that would be quite something, but I prefer to keep my feet on the ground — and Johnnie's too."

"Don't be angry, Lala. I know you are at David but not at Bertie or Harry — never Mary or especially Johnnie. So don't be angry with me, please. Should I not read to him then? He can't just listen to that gramophone music all day. I thought I was helping him — and you by amusing and tending him at times."

Ah, my clever and brilliant George. I had meant to scold him but I hugged and thanked him instead. But what nonsense — what pie in the sky indeed — about war, especially in God's beautiful heavens.

■ ■ ■ ■

PART FIVE

1914–1919
YORK COTTAGE
TO WOOD FARM

■ ■ ■ ■

CHAPTER 29

I was so tragically wrong about aeroplanes and men shooting at each other. All too soon, England and all of Europe swept toward war. It wasn't King George and Queen Mary's triumphant Entente Cordiale visit to France to strengthen ties that made the kaiser, "Cousin Willie," angry. It wasn't even that the so-called Autocrat of All the Russias, "Cousin Nicky," mobilized a huge army. It was the assassination of Archduke Ferdinand and his commoner wife Sophie, a couple who had once visited Their Majesties in England, in little Serbia that set off the powder keg. Austria then declared war on Serbia, and everyone else took sides.

King George had written a personal appeal to Kaiser Wilhelm, but Germany still declared war on Russia and then on France, so England as a French ally was all in. Ultimatums and tense replies flew back and forth. Talk about family squabbles: Since so many of Queen Victoria's descendants ruled Europe, family fought family.

I heard about all this — sometimes, when the king and queen made time for brief visits to Sandringham, but I could never quite understand it. Why? Why war? And why was everyone acting, this August 1914, the month Germany declared war on England, as if that was a reason for celebration?

When Johnnie and I got to the village green to hear the small brass band, Chad appeared from the crowd, ruffled Johnnie's hair, then twirled me off my feet while Johnnie clapped and laughed. Chad put me down and kissed my cheek. He was beaming as Penny, newly turned nine just like Johnnie, ran to us and was swept up in Chad's arms. She had a little Union Jack flag that she sweetly gave to Johnnie as she beamed at me. Clusters of cheering local folk seemed to bubble up around us, and I'd seldom seen Chad so jubilant.

"The local lads and men are enlisting in the King's Own Sandringham Company," he told us. "I have too, along with Winnie's husband, Fred, and many neighbors. We'll be in the Fifth Battalion of the Royal Norfolk Regiment. We just hope to get to France before the war is over. The only thing that worries me is I still haven't managed to find and stop that damned poacher and thief Barker Lee, and I'd hate to leave this estate at his mercy. I swear he's the one skulking around at night over by the marsh, poisoning birds and stealing what Johnnie calls peeps."

"If he hurts peeps, he's a very bad man," Johnnie agreed.

"Stealing them to sell as well as to get back at you for tracking him, the beastly wretch," I said. "It's gone on for years, like a deadly game with him. Perhaps he will finally step forth to enlist, where he'll have to give his name and address, and you can find him and have him arrested."

"Not that sneaking coward, but he does know I'm after him." Yet, for once, Chad barely frowned over the wretch who had been the bane of his life these last few years. "But let's talk about better things," he insisted. "See that poster over there?" he asked and pointed at a large chestnut tree with a stiff piece of paper nailed to it. From the poster, a mustached man in a billed and decorated military cap pointed a finger straight at us. The big printed words read, BRITONS. JOIN YOUR COUNTRY'S ARMY! GOD SAVE THE KING!

"Who's that man?" Johnnie asked Chad.

"His nanny should tell him it's not polite to point."

Chad hooted a laugh. "Then he didn't have a nanny as good as yours. That's Lord Kitchener, lad, your papa's secretary of war."

"But," I put in, "it means you'll be leaving, Chad. Going into war . . . into danger."

"With our powerful navy and fighting force, it will be over by Christmas. Everyone says so," he assured me and gave Penny a bounce in his arms before he put her down.

The band started in again with "Land of Hope and Glory." Many of the villagers sang along and then went right into "God Save the King." Though I still didn't much like the idea of war, a short one would be good.

The four of us sat on a tree stump, bum to bum while Penny and Johnnie chatted. She was so good with him, as kind as George but without the high-flying ideas. Such a dear girl. Johnnie had told me just the other day that he liked her as much as he did the "girls in cloud dresses," for somehow, his memories of the tsar's daughters were as vivid as were mine. The good deed I'd done for their former nanny, Margaretta Eager, had gotten me a friend in her,

404

though we corresponded more than we saw each other. How upset she would be that the tsar was taking his country to war too.

"Any word from the Prince of Wales?" Chad asked me over the increasing noise of yet another patriotic song.

"He still writes on occasion, though less and less. I believe," I told him with a wink, "I can read between the lines that he has found some females much more exciting than his old nanny to confide in. But he did write that he's miffed that his father has enlisted him in the King's Guard for ceremonies at Buck House, since he thinks he should go to sea after all that naval training. Now that there's to be war, he'll really be champing at the bit. But I think he's mostly fretting that at five feet seven inches tall he'll be a pygmy, as he put it, since the regulations for the King's Company is six feet."

"Then," Chad said, "they will have to get him a very tall bearskin hat. Besides, doesn't being a prince and the heir add immediate height?"

"I like bearskin hats," Johnnie put in. "I'd like to have one, if the bear wouldn't come looking for it."

Penny made a face and growled at Johnnie, which he thought was hilarious. I just looked at Chad, smiling despite my worries

405

over the war, lost in his steady gaze amidst the brass music and the cheers.

He mouthed to me *"Meet me outside at nine?"*

I nodded. Suddenly, in my head, my own band played, and in my heart, I cheered.

Though a nursemaid or even a nanny could be dismissed for having "a follower at the door," Chad and I did meet to walk and talk sometimes after I tucked Johnnie up and one of the maids sat with him a while. Our days were so busy, Chad was so busy during the day and I too, but this was our time, when Johnnie was safe in bed and Penny was with her aunt Winnie.

I had told Chad's sister more than once not to curtsy to me, but she still bobbed me a quick one now and again, as if the fairy dust of royalty had rubbed off on me like in that new book I read Johnnie called *Peter and Wendy.* I liked it well enough but it was annoying that a nanny had let those children fly away to Neverland. I had to continually explain to Johnnie that children could fly only in books.

Sometimes in the evening, Chad and I strolled through the gardens of the Big House. Queen Alexandra and her daughter Toria still lived there, as the former queen seemed quite unwilling to give it up, which King George allowed for his "Mother dearest." If it was chilly, Chad and I stepped into the glasshouse to keep warm, but we never went down the aisles that Millie used to tend or where I had turned down his proposal years ago. We just hovered inside the door, kissed, and whispered as if the plants had ears.

But this was late August with a warm breeze and slice of moon in the sky like a slanted smile. It almost made me believe that war did not exist — at least that it would never take Chad and the other men away, nor touch these places and people I had loved for so long. I could not believe this man would be leaving. I fervently wished that he would not.

"I don't know when we'll be billeted out or where we'll be sent," he told me, tucking my arm through the crook of his and keeping it close to his ribs. "But I'd like to know you will be right here when I get back. Well, you'll hardly run off with Hansell, since I hear he's enlisting too," he teased, suddenly sounding nervous.

"Yes, poor man. He was never really happy here. When he tried to take on Johnnie, it was the last straw, but I'm working with my boy to write a good cursive hand, even though his reading will never be as it should."

"You've been a godsend for him, especially with his fits."

"More and more of them, worse and worse. But so far never at night when he sleeps, thank God. That would mean the poor child would have peace nowhere. Still, it scares me that the king hints at sending him away from the family, and I could not abide — could not allow — that. Still, just knowing about his seizures upsets the other children. His Majesty fears it would hurt the royals if the public knew Johnnie had fits, as if he was an imbecile, and that's so unfair because he isn't! Chad, I couldn't bear it if he tried to have him put in some sort of asylum."

We stopped before going in the door. He hugged me and whispered against my ear, "Shhh. Let's talk of happier things. Let's talk about us. Speaking of a commitment for life, we both get on well with His Majesty. Do you think we could make him see the wisdom of not sending Johnnie away — at least not far away — but of appointing you, of course — and maybe me — as his guardians, so that you and I could make a commitment — I mean to each other when this war is over?"

He was almost speaking as jerkily as Bertie did sometimes to keep from stammering. We stood, gazing into each other's eyes in the pale moonlight near the spot where he had snagged me with a net so long ago and we had rolled on the ground, kissing, which is just what I wanted right now.

"All that sounds wonderful to me," I said.

"Better late than never, as they say."

I smiled up at him through my happy tears. "Righto, Chad Reaver, for I have loved you for years, I vow I have."

"Then, God willing, there are vows in our future and —"

But to my utter amazement, Chad's head jerked, and he thrust me away hard and shouted, "Run! Go!"

What? A man leaped from the darkness with a raised pitchfork. Chad jumped back, then tried to kick the long tines away, but the attacker stabbed him with it, twice, before I could even react.

CHAPTER 30

I screamed. Screamed again. In the night, black blood — Chad's blood — splattered and spurted over the grass and my skirts.

Chad had said to run, but I could not leave him, not like that. The man — Barker Lee, I knew who he was even in the sparse moonlight — merely scowled at me. He must have decided I was worth nothing, that he wanted to finish off Chad, who, groaning, tried to roll away on the ground.

I picked up a rock, big as both my hands, that sometimes propped open the glasshouse door. It was heavy, but I threw it. It hit the man hard in the back of the head. He turned toward me, cursing, holding the pitchfork in Chad's leg, pinning him down. I lifted and heaved a clay pot at him from the stack of them, then another. But the rock had done its duty. He staggered toward me, crumpled to his knees, then fell onto his face about five feet away. Was he dead?

It didn't matter because Chad lay stabbed and bleeding. I pulled the pitchfork from his leg and cast it away. I kneeled and bent over him. Had I made a mistake to pull it from him? He was bleeding worse.

"Go . . . for help," he said. But in his shock and agony, he gripped my hand so hard I could not run if I'd wanted to.

"You're bleeding too hard — your leg. I have to stop the bleeding first. I'll scream. Someone will hear."

"My belt . . . round my leg."

Like a madwoman, screaming, "Murder! Murder! Help! Help!" I tugged my hand from his grasp, then unbuckled and struggled to pull the belt from under his weight. Slippery with blood — grass, belt, my hands. The bleeding punctures — tears in his trousers — seemed high, near his hip. Stop the blood, stop his lifeblood.

I thought I heard someone coming but didn't look up. At least Barker Lee lay still. God forgive me, I hoped he was dead. He had maimed Chad's leg and hip horribly.

"Chad, you asked me to wait for you," I told him as I tightened his belt around his thigh. "Now you have to wait for me . . . for Penny. Stay with me here. Don't you give up!"

"Too late. Love you — tell her . . ." was

so faint and then I think he passed out. Or worse.

But, thank God, footsteps came close. Someone from the Big House — Mabel and two men.

"Barker Lee stabbed Chad with a pitchfork!" I shouted. "Get Queen Alexandra's doctor! He's losing blood, too much. I don't want to move him!"

That sent the men running, but Mabel stayed with me, kneeling, helping me hold the belt tight while I pressed my right hand flat and hard over his thigh wounds. When Barker Lee groaned and moved, she took off her apron and with its ties bound Barker Lee's wrists. The doctor came at a run, carrying his satchel, then Hansell arrived with others I knew. But everything except Chad was a fading blur, even when Penny's Uncle Fred, Winnie's husband, bent over us to ask what happened, but when he saw, he kneeled and prayed.

The constable came, more people he kept back, while I still knelt there, holding Chad's limp hand. His blood soaked my skirts, warm, then cold, stiffening the material while the doctor worked on the unconscious man — my unconscious man.

Finally, the doctor spoke. "His pulse is stronger now, but that leg will have to come off, I fear. I think your tourniquet saved him, but we shall see. Men, bring that stretcher, for we'll have to move him to Sandringham House. Pray he stays unconscious. A real blessing you found him out here," he added to me in a quiet voice and, blood-splattered himself, stood to supervise the men who would lift Chad.

I too rose at last, stiff, sore, heartbroken. And angry. Furious with the monster who had tried to murder him. I watched as the constable took Barker Lee away, conscious now. I began to tremble and felt so very cold.

If Chad had not been looking so intently into my eyes when that demon struck, wouldn't I have seen or sensed him? Had I answered that I would marry Chad? Had I imagined some of what he'd said and would I ever know that if he'd died? I had feared he'd die in the war, but this . . .

Mabel walked on one side of me and Mrs. Wentworth on the other, holding me up between them, steering me back toward York Cottage. I fought fear and grief, but at least I had not run, even when he'd told me to. I had stayed and fought for him, for us.

Two days later, dry-eyed but feeling fragile and broken, I sat in the king's study, being questioned by Sandringham's Constable Markwood, with King George present. Barker Lee had died of a blood clot to the brain after they'd taken him from the scene of the attack. No doubt, the rock I threw had killed him. So the wretch's blood had clotted while Chad bled. So far, my dear love was still alive, fighting for his life in a bed, instead of on a battlefield for England in the grand war as he had planned. Queen Alexandra's doctor had considered something called a blood transfusion, but decided it was too risky since Chad was "holding his own." How I wished that he was holding me.

Constable Markwood continued questioning me about Barker Lee's demise. "Mrs. Bill, the point is, this ruffian Lee had several blows to his head and body. Was Chadwick Reaver able to fight back?"

"Chad was taken by surprise and went down under the initial stabbing blows to his leg," I said. "I'm sure that man was aiming for his chest or head, but Chad leaped back after he thrust me away. Mr. Lee seemed quite demented, and he came out of the dark — out of nowhere. I believe he must have been planning more thievery on the estate, but he went far beyond that this time — obviously."

My voice sounded flat and hollow, but I'd hardly slept since the attack. The king hovered, perhaps thinking I would faint again as I nearly had under duress and questioning long ago in this very place — and over the same villain too.

"My point is, Mrs. Bill," Constable Markwood said, "who struck the blows on him with the rock and crockery that did him in?"

"He looked at me, then went back to stabbing Chad, and then I —"

"In other words," the king interrupted, "self-defense or the bastard would have tried to kill her too as well as my estate manager. Just write down self-defense and be done with it, Markwood. The man got what he deserved for longtime poaching and destroying wildlife and property. He threatened my daughter, Mary, years ago. His well-deserved demise has saved Sandringham and Norfolk a good deal of expense and time for a trial when we have larger trials than that looming."

I thought the constable would argue or continue his questions, but he put his paper and pen in his jacket pocket. "That's exactly what I'd surmised, Your Majesty. Just tidying things up since the deceased could not make a statement of his own. I just pray your estate manager lives."

"As do we all," the king said as he showed him out and closed the door just as I started to rise.

"Stay a moment, Lala," he said. He came back and perched on the arm of his old worn sofa and looked down at me. "Did you stumble on Chad or were you out and about with him?"

I raised my chin. I would not fudge about or lie to the king. "Out with him, sir. Walking. He was leaving soon with your regiment. I'm sorry if you don't approve."

"I didn't say that. I realize the two of you have been friends — honorable friends — for years. Lala, I need to rush back to London, but I want you to visit Chad. If he is conscious, tell him I have commanded that he remain here during the war to oversee this estate, the sooner the better he can get back on his f— that is, manage with a false leg or whatever it takes. Tell him he will be serving his king in that way, for he knows I love Sandringham even as he does. Do what you can to comfort and console him. The queen and I do not know what we would do without your caring for Johnnie — and though it is different — for Chad too."

"You won't send Johnnie away from York Cottage, sir? He's sheltered here."

He rose and put the chair back into its place by his desk. "Decisions must be made, even ones with far-reaching consequences." His usually stentorian voice quavered. "I must do what I think best. I don't know. There is so much I don't know in these terrible times."

When I headed toward the Big House the next day to see Chad, who was still being cared for in a guest room there after his leg had been amputated three days ago, I approached Winnie and Penny on the path as they walked toward me. Winnie nodded — her latest rendition of a curtsy.

"We could only see him for a few minutes," she told me. "But he opened his eyes and moved his hand when Penny talked to him, held her hand and talked a bit to us."

"I'm sure that gave him strength," I told them, but my voice was shaky. I put my arm around Penny's shoulders. The poor girl was trembling, and I hugged her to my side.

"Lala, they had to cut off his leg!" the girl blurted and sucked in a deep breath. "To save him because it was going green and bad. But I told him he's still my whole papa."

Tears blurred my vision of her sweet face.

"That was a wonderful thing to say, my dear."

"Did you tell Johnnie?"

"I told him his friend Chad was hurt, and he said he was going to write him a nice note. I've been teaching him to write letters in cursive. He's going to put some flowers with it."

The child nodded. There seemed nothing else to say. I took a deep breath and told them, "The good news is that the king has asked me to tell your papa he is to be the estate manager here when he is well. He is depending on him to help in that way."

"Oh, thank the Lord," Winnie said as her posture seemed to deflate with her sigh. "Of course, we would take Penny but their house — his birds — so we're over the moon about that kind offer from the king, right, Penny?"

"Righto," she said with a smile despite the tears tracking down her flushed cheeks.

I stooped to hug her again, and she held to me. "Don't be afraid," I told her. "Your papa is a strong man."

But when I saw him lying there, under a sheet with but one leg, his left one, his hip bandaged hugely, outlined nearly from his hip on down, I hesitated at the door. God forgive me for the thought, but so much of him seemed missing. The medical nurse sitting there nodded to me, then got up and left us alone. So pale. My ruddy man was so pale. He looked to be asleep, but he moved an arm and opened one black-and-blue, swollen eyelid.

"I don't want you to see me like this," he whispered. His voice was rough, not his own.

"Well, I am seeing you and grateful for it, my love. Besides, you cannot ask me to leave because I come bearing a message from the king." I went closer but didn't sit in the chair the nurse had vacated. I stood, leaning over him a bit on his . . . his side with the leg — taking his hand in mine. He seemed a bit cold, though the day and room were warm. "Don't you want to know what the king said?" I asked, fighting my impulse to burst into tears.

"That I failed to stop that bastard. That I can hardly do my duties anymore with one leg, so he's retiring me, replacing me?"

I leaned closer. "Just the opposite. He expects you to get your strength back as soon as you can so you can run this estate while he's so busy. Nothing has changed, here at Sandringham, that is."

"Charlotte . . . sweetheart," he choked out as if it hurt him even to speak, "everything has changed. For me, for us —"

"No! I will not let you —"

"Just listen. Can you see me leading a hunt party or tramping through the marsh grass after pheasants or grouse? And what we were beginning to believe could come true — impossible."

"It isn't."

"It's enough you wear yourself out taking care of Johnnie. You don't need another difficult case on your hands. Now, don't argue as I can't bear it. I'm tired, so go on now. Take care of your boy, and the doctor and nurse will take care of me. Don't come again to see me like this, because . . . because I didn't see him coming and I couldn't even protect you, let alone myself. I'm exhausted and heartsick. Go."

"Chadwick Reaver! Is this the way you would treat me if that blackguard had stabbed me and nearly killed me? You have a new war to fight now, and I — and His Majesty — expect you to fight it. Now you'd better get some sleep because I think you are delirious, and you are going to need your strength."

I marched out into the hall, then burst into tears, leaning against the paneled wall. A footman scurried past with a tray, averting his eyes from the scene I made, no doubt the way they were taught to avoid their betters. But Chad's nurse was there, and I supposed she'd heard all that was said.

"Bravo!" she whispered and, putting her arm round my shoulders, steering me farther from Chad's open door. "I've seen other men just give up, and it's the worst thing they can do. He's still facing possible infections from that pitchfork, but the doctor hopes to pull him through. Well, the old queen's physician — who could do better, though he seems unable to convince Queen Alexandra that the Germans aren't coming here."

I blew my nose and stood straight, then swiped madly under both eyes. It seemed good to think of someone else's problems, even dear, dotty Queen Alexandra's. I cleared my throat and told her, "She's hated the Germans ever since they attacked her homeland of Denmark years ago."

"So I've heard from her, I assure you. She mixes up times and places, waved to cows in the field the other day. But she does love it when you bring her youngest grandson here."

"I will do that again soon," I told her, perking up a bit. That would help Queen Alexandra and give me an excuse to visit Chad. But his healing, a possible infection, his broken spirit, his thinking he should cast me off now — he just had to pull through all that.

Chad's recovery was long and grueling, stretching nearly a year. Johnnie's visits, as well as Penny's, helped him back to health a bit, but he remained adamant that I must not consider a future with him. I read him David's letters — another excuse to see him, though the latest ones worried and angered us both. The Prince of Wales was now twenty-one, but always a boy to me. When British men were dying in the trenches of the war, David had the gall to complain that Paris, where his beleaguered father had finally sent him to be part of the war effort, was dull and boring. Yet Finch had sent a note that said, despite the dreadful trench warfare and men missing their wives and families, David was *feeling his oats and had a* very good *friend, a Parisienne woman who seemed very fast and was evidently teaching him all the right — or wrong — things.*

I kept waiting for the old Chad to show himself, but only with the children did he make an effort. He had been back in his house for several months, and though he walked with crutches, he kept insisting he would tell the king he could not do his estate duties. When I told His Majesty, he would not even see Chad because he refused his resignation and told me to tell him to "get cracking." However rough and demanding the king yet was on his sons, I was grateful that he treated Chad the same way.

At least when Queen Mary was at Sandringham that meant my dear friend Rose was here too, for I missed her sorely when she was in London so much.

"Her Majesty is doing yeoman's work in bolstering the war effort," she told me as we sat in her mending room off the kitchen one evening. "She visits hospitals and cheers soldiers heading for the front. How much I miss all the grand events though — dressing her for them, the lovely gowns and all. We're on food rationing at Buck House just as strictly as you are here, not so much as a nip of wine either. I tell you, belowstairs as well as up, it's dreary and dreadful."

Actually, hearing of the casualties our men had taken early in the war — lists posted in the papers were terribly long — I was rather put out at Rose for complaining about no fancy dresses. Everyone was suffering and having to do without, so why should the royal family not set the example and share in their people's trials? My brother Ernest had gone to war, and my parents were desperately worried about him. As for rationing, perhaps I'd been so inured to nursery food over the years that I hardly noticed the difference.

I was just going to scold Rose when the door burst open and Princess Mary stood there in tears. We both leaped up. "Whatever is it?" I asked.

"Oh, Lala, I just knew you'd understand! Can you talk to Papa about it? Mama just goes along with whatever he says!"

I was appalled to see my tomboy Mary like this. "What's amiss?" I asked, pulling her into my arms. She seemed so young again, needing me.

"It's perfectly awful, all that's happening. Londoners breaking windows of German shops. Someone even stoned a dachshund to death in Green Park! And now I have to send my dear Else back to Germany, and everybody loves her. You both know her! After I left the nursery, she's been my maid that long! This whole war is not fair! Troops billeted here, when no German soldiers can march clear to Norfolk! All the flowers in Grannie's gardens are going to be pulled up and go to awful things like Brussels sprouts and turnips!"

I let her talk, then quieted her down.

Sheltered as she was and reared in a family with German kin, how could she grasp how much the Brits hated the Germans and how bad it looked for the royal family to bear the last name Saxe-Coburg-Gotha. I'm not sure her parents realized it either.

"Look, Mary," I told her, "it is very sad about people hating the Germans, but you can see —"

"They call them the Huns, but we — my family — are related to them over and over. My Else is hardly Kaiser Wilhelm, you know, any more than that little dog people killed was piloting those horrible Zeppelins that are bombing London!"

"Shhh. There are many burdens for English folk right now, and for the royal family with their blood ties to the Germans. Many people are having to give up things and people they love. And some Britons just don't understand German descendants, like your family, can be true blue."

"I know Bertie wants to do his part and now he's having more abdominal attacks. And David — well, I heard he's tripping the light fantastic in Paris, and here I am, just asking to keep my dear Else. It was enough to lose you, Lala, but . . ."

She exploded in tears again. When she pulled away and stomped out, I was reminded again that my dear children were growing up and my days as royal nanny could well be numbered.

CHAPTER 31

Paris, July 1915 — Dearest Lala from David.

Finally I've been allowed to see some action, that is, I helped interrogate a few prisoners. My German helped out, bless old Bricka! There is a shortage of munitions, which are going to the Dardanelles instead of coming here!! We hope to receive more soon!! But things can be tedious and dull, a bloody bore, even on my 21st birthday. I hear the tsar is having troubles in Russia. War, war, war! And the dances when I was summoned back to Buck House just before the war were tedious affairs too. Why the old quadrille dance when we could be doing the hoochie koo and the tango? My best to Chad — the king says he's navigating well on crutches and uses a horse cart to get about. I assure you I am making up for my wretched childhood — except for you and Finch, well Bertie too. I hear the Sandringham Company is in the Gallipoli campaign in Turkey. Damn Turks siding with the Huns! I'm sure those Zepps harassing London wouldn't bother with boring Norfolk — but you keep looking up.

"Keep looking up, indeed!" I told Chad as we sat on a bench by the lake while Johnnie threw stones into the placid water. I still made an excuse to read Chad David's letters, for he mostly avoided me, and we'd had words about our . . . his situation. Avoiding me was easy enough while he was occupied overseeing the estate, especially since most of his staff was now untrained women and boys. More than once, I had told him his injuries didn't change how I felt, but he insisted they changed how he felt.

Now, when he said nothing, I went on, "Isn't he giving away war secrets in this letter? I mean, I'm hardly going to telephone the Huns, but shouldn't some of this be kept secret?"

"His father would throw him in the brig. David's always been naive, but that's dangerous in wartime. On the other hand, his mail does come here with the king's letters to Queen Alexandra, so they must be safe."

Chad almost smiled but he still didn't look at me. The old Chad, sturdy, secure, and supportive had not come back. So I had to bide my time to make him realize he could be everything I ever wanted again.

"Keep looking up," Chad repeated with a nod at Johnnie, whom I'd been watching too. "Your youngest prince does that. Is he still looking for George's aeroplanes in the sky?"

I shuddered, as whip-smart George had been prophetic. The huge German dirigibles, the Zeppelins, were dropping incendiary bombs on London. They blew holes in buildings, started fires, and killed citizens. George had been right about something else: Men were in training to be pilots who would shoot each other down in the air.

"Johnnie's also looking for girls in cloud dresses up there," I added. "He's never forgotten meeting the tsar's daughters, but he looks up to find them. They were such beautiful, charming young ladies almost ripe for love and marriage."

Chad grabbed one of his crutches, heaved himself up, half balancing on it, then stooped to grab the other off the ground where it had fallen. What had I said? I was always walking on thin ice with him now.

"Chad, I could have helped with th—"

"Don't you get it?" he told me low enough that Johnnie couldn't hear. "I don't want your help, picking up my crutches or myself. I want you. I want us to be the way we were, when I had two good legs and I hadn't quite proposed a second time, which is all water over the mill dam now." He started away, walking fast despite the thick grass, then spun back to me. "You'd better watch the boy because if he wades in too deep, I won't be a bit of help to save him, and if he has a fit — hell, it doesn't help to hear about the others fighting . . . or know David's chasing women. Let's face it, even when I had two legs, it was you who had to stop Barker Lee!"

He mounted — by pulling himself up over the wheel after he heaved his crutches in — the small, one-horse cart he used to get round the estate and left me with tears in my eyes that blinded me like the sun off the water.

The war was not going well. The battles that were to be over by last Christmas waged on. And to make things worse — and worse than Chad's temper — the king fell off his horse in France when some guns boomed.

He broke his pelvis in several places. He was in constant pain, physical as well as mental, in his anguish over dead British soldiers and the ruination of the royal families of Europe. I overheard him say once that Queen Victoria would be rolling over in her grave to know her descendants were at war and many were losing their thrones. At least His Majesty was on the same side as Tsar Nicholas. He even named him an honorary field marshal of the British Army for fighting the kaiser.

As in the old days when I was grateful that King George left the estate, the entire staff at York Cottage breathed easier when the king had convalesced and went back to London. Prime Minister Asquith's insisting "It just didn't do to have a king in a cottage" annoyed him, but he still refused to take Sandringham House from his mother. Again, I feared he'd send Johnnie away, for I knew I'd beg to go with the boy. And then, what would become of Chad and me?

I did not think things could get worse until that summer when horrendous news reached us. The king's own Sandringham Company had been massacred to a man in the Turkish campaign. What a good idea it had once seemed that they could serve together with their kin and friends. But it meant, if they were attacked, they could all be wounded or killed. New weapons called machine guns had mowed them down when they were ill-supplied. One hundred fifty local men were lost. At first, Sandringham folk held out hope that some had been taken prisoner, but we learned those few had been shot too. Of course, if Chad had had his way, he would have been among those slaughtered.

I, like many of the local grieving women, hurried to the church to pray and comfort others. The long list of men's names was nailed to the church door, some familiar to me, some not. At least Hansell had been in another company. Inside, Winnie sat, crumpled over in a pew across the aisle from me, for her husband, Fred, was among the dead. Her two daughters and Penny were with her, all sobbing into handkerchiefs, so they didn't see me.

But no Chad here where I thought he'd be. All I could think of was that he must surely see the hand of God in his salvation from this massive loss of men. And then, could he not be more content with his lot?

But later, when I found him outside, at the fringe of the graveyard, leaning against a tree, I sensed that he would rather have died with his brother-in-law and friends than be the last man — well, standing.

I walked slowly toward him, not certain what to say.

"I should have been there with them," he told me. He stared off across the tombstones as if he'd seen a ghost — ghosts.

"I thank God you were not. Things happen for a reason, Chad."

"Do they? This godforsaken war? All these deaths? Remember that football game when David and Bertie were young? Every one of those boys who played that day but the two royal ones are on that list."

I sucked in a sob.

"They died heroes. I'll be sure my nieces know that, Penny too. They say someone named Winston Churchill, First Lord of the Admiralty, took the blame for not sending in more troops, getting them supplies in time. I hear the Lancashire fusiliers lost half their men, but not — not all — to a man. What?" he asked, turning toward me. "Why did you jump when I said that name?"

"I met him once — Churchill — about five years ago at Buck House. He seemed forthright and honest."

"At least he took the blame like a man. But this loss will do him in for his political future, a fatal mistake like that. All I know is, if I was there — one more man — it might have made a difference. I could have been with them, done something to help."

"Or died too. But you are helping here. Helping the king, being kind to Johnnie, keeping things going, and —"

"I'm a charity case. I couldn't help those men, couldn't save you — couldn't even save myself. Don't look at me that way, Charlotte! See you at the funerals, where we'll have to bury empty boxes, because the king's equerry says we won't get bodies back, just like I'll never get myself back."

Again, as times before, he turned away from me and moved faster than I could have run, through the tombstones, toward his horse cart. I stood there, praying fervently for the families of the lost and for my lost Chad.

Johnnie's epileptic attacks grew more frequent, but I knew better now how to handle them. I read the warning signs and managed to get him away from others in time, and I never gave him the dreadful doses the king's doctor had. Instead, I put a pillow under his head so it didn't bang on the floor, slipped a padded leather strip between his teeth so he didn't bite his tongue, and gave him a sip of apple juice with bromide when he quieted.

But there were some happy moments I tried to cherish. Queen Alexandra was good with him. When the women gardeners began changing the flower beds to vegetables, she'd told them to leave a place back by the gazebo for a patch of flowers, where Johnnie could plant seeds. She'd also had Winnie, who now oversaw the vegetables in the glasshouses, plant some already sprouted flowers in Johnnie's spot the next morning.

"Results right away," the old woman said as Chad, Johnnie, and I stood there, admiring the miraculous flowers. She seemed a mere specter of herself, terribly frail, gaunt, white-haired with two huge, bloodshot eyes peering from a wrinkled face. I fancied she looked like that haunted Miss Havisham presiding over the ruins of the glorious past. Before George was sent to naval school, he had read Johnnie and me Charles Dickens's *Great Expectations.* Sadly, any sort of great expectations were in short supply during the dreadful war years.

"That's what we should have in this war," Queen Alexandra went on, "the results of victory full and fast. But all we get are longer lists of the wounded or dead and those beastly Zepps bombing London and the coast!"

■ ■ ■ ■

One thing about having troops now billeted at Sandringham was that it seemed safe even after dark. The few times Their Majesties were in residence, I could see why the men patrolled here. But, I swear, the rest of the time, like now, they were just out for strolls because they were so bored guarding a dull country estate and the dowager queen. If only the men who ran this war would have let the Sandringham Company perform these duties.

One fine night that fall, moonless, cloudy, and quite windy but still warm, Johnnie and I sat in chairs in the gazebo behind the Big House with Queen Alexandra, her spinster daughter Toria, and the ever faithful Charlotte Knollys. We were eating, talking, enjoying the air while Johnnie went between eating goodies and taking one of the three lanterns and walking a few steps away to admire his private flower bed in bloom.

"My, aren't the stars lovely tonight," the old queen said, fumbling for her small ear trumpet she was willing to use in the dark when she thought no one could see it. "Now wherever is that?" she asked, and for the fourth time this evening, her ladies and I began to look for it. To my surprise, Johnnie spoke up.

"I know where it is, Grannie!" he called out, coming back to us.

"What? What did he say?"

"Johnnie, where is it?" I asked him, moving the plate of currant and blackberry scones away from him, for he's been eating far too many, which made me miss Bertie all the more.

"I hid it until I can have one of my own," he told me. "Papa won't let me. I want a big one like Mama has. A gramophone."

I gasped, took his hand and pulled him away from the others. He was eleven and growing fast, but I didn't let his height and weight cow me when he needed to be scolded. After all, he still reasoned and acted like a four-year-old, and maybe it would always be that way for him.

"Johnnie, that is the ear trumpet so your grannie can hear better. It looks a bit like the big bell of a gramophone that plays music, but it's different," I tried to explain, though once he got something in that head of his, often, that was that. "You show me where you hid that right now."

"She listen to it, Lala," he said, pouting. "So it has to have something in there, like music. I put it in my flowers. And I hear something right now. Music. Don't you?"

I was not to be put off, so I marched him a short distance to his flower bed. But a hum did vibrate in the breeze, a sort of buzz like distant music, a thrumming. We both looked up. It was too late at night for bees. Maybe someone at the church was playing the old pipe organ, but this was more like a distant droning, one I'd never heard, not a railway engine.

I glanced back toward the gazebo where the ladies were still looking under the table and chairs for the ear trumpet. But they too stopped to walk out from under the gazebo roof and look up into the windy darkness. Nothing. Nothing to see but big, shifting clouds.

Besides Johnnie's lantern, the lights from the house windows threw pools of gold upon the lawn and vegetable beds with his few special flowers nearly at our feet. "Now you find that and bring it right over to Grannie," I ordered and went back to tell the women I knew where it was.

The droning hum was louder. Not a motorcar. I looked up again, craning my neck. Was that cigar-shaped thing a cloud? That sound wasn't distant thunder.

A voice I knew well shouted so loud, I nearly tripped as I hurried toward the women. Chad. Chad yelling. And farther away, men's voices, strident, panicked, a gunshot or two. At what? Into the air?

And then I knew.

Chad shouted, "Get the lights out! A Zeppelin's overhead! Take Queen Alexandra inside! Now!"

The two women nearly picked her up and hustled her away between them. I ran to the gazebo, unhooked the two lanterns from the roof, and thrust them in the door of the Big House after the women — then remembered Johnnie had the third lantern.

I turned around, expecting to see him with that and the ear trumpet, but I saw only Chad, emerging from the night. Where was that boy? His war in the air had come here, and if he was still out there, looking up . . .

"Johnnie! Come here!" I cried and ran past Chad only to find the lantern by the flowers but no boy. I tipped it over in the soil so it went dark. I screamed over the increasing drone that was now a roar, "Johnnie, we have to go inside!"

Chad moved swiftly toward me, swinging his body between his crutches.

"Where the hell is he?"

"He was just here!" I shouted. I lifted my skirts and started to run across the dark, dewy lawn with Chad behind me, just as an incendiary bomb hissed, then hit, blowing the gazebo where we'd just been sitting into a booming fireball.

CHAPTER 32

Chad hit hard into me, knocking me down. The air banged out of me. I tasted grass. He covered me with his body as another bomb hissed and — I believe — one of the glasshouses on the other side of the house blasted shards of glass that did not come this far, though they made a crackling, tinkling sound like a wind chime as they rained down in the distance.

Shingles and wooden planks flew, then thudded to the ground just behind us, while the bonfire of what was left of the gazebo lit the night. Glass windows along the back of the house shattered from the bomb or the heat. God forgive me, I gave not a moment's thought to those inside but only to finding Johnnie.

"He's out here somewhere!" I yelled, trying to get up despite Chad's weight and hold on me. "If he's under that thing, looking up, following it . . ." I choked out,

"John . . . nieee!"

Chad swore. We stumbled to our feet. For once he let me help him, though in the blackness of the night, I handed him a piece of blown gazebo wood instead of his second crutch before I found it. Together, we stumbled on farther out on the lawn, then back toward the house, picking our way through debris in the flicking flames of the gazebo fire.

"It's circling back," Chad shouted as the monstrous thing pivoted and its grinding hum grew louder again. "Johnnie, you come right here!" he bellowed, balancing on his crutches and cupping his hands around his mouth. "Where are you? Lala and I need you!"

What if Johnnie was . . . was hit . . . was gone, I thought, as we ran under the beast into the blackness away from the house again. No! Not my Johnnie. He'd fought so hard to be born and could not die like this.

"John Charles Francis, you come here right now!" I shrieked just before another booming blast split the air ahead of us near where the lawn met the trees.

We went down on our faces again, then stumbled to our feet. Despite the droning, I heard my boy's voice. Or did I imagine it?

"Lala, did you see that?" Johnnie shouted,

but I still couldn't spot him. Chad and I ran in the direction of his voice. "I don't like the big booms though and what made that fire, and . . ."

He emerged from the dark, looking straight up as the Zeppelin hovered overhead. If he didn't weigh as much, I would have swooped him into my arms and run for shelter.

Chad got to him first. "We have to run to the ravine over there!" he shouted, grabbing his arm. "I think it's going to drop more bombs!"

Just as the two women had hustled the old queen inside, Chad gave Johnnie a yank in the right direction, then I took the boy's other arm and half pulled, half shoved him toward the ravine. The little glen, hidden from the house, had a stream that had cut into the rock. We had explored it together what seemed years ago, in the spring, looking down from a little cliff at this level above the slippery rocks where a family of ducks played. But there were places to cling, to be sheltered by the rock overhang.

I was astounded Chad could move so fast, and I too with my dratted long skirts. At least the beast had passed over us now, heading away from the Big House, maybe toward the Wash, toward towns there or back toward whatever horrid German place had birthed it.

Then again it hovered, pivoted as if it would make another pass. I glanced back at the Big House, which now lay in darkness. I was grateful the moon wasn't full. The increasing winds were inward from the sea. Was the Zepp going with the wind or of its own devising?

The three of us, Johnnie between, quiet now at last but breathing hard, scrambled down and huddled below ground level on the upper rock ledge of the ravine. How Chad managed that, I don't know. It was cold here, but that's not why goose bumps skittered across my skin. I realized I was crying, from fear and from gratitude that Chad had managed to get safely over the edge and had his arms around both of us. Over the whine of the wind, the rustle of dry leaves, and the rattle of water below, we realized the dreadful droning was gone. Yet Chad's strong arm still circled my heaving shoulders, pressing me tight to the rock face. I felt his touch stronger than mere stone. As horrible as this attack had been, to be held by him here with the three of us safe, together — at least for a moment — was almost worth the terror.

■ ■ ■ ■

The next day, Their Majesties rushed back to Sandringham to view the destruction themselves and requested that Chad, Johnnie, and I be there. The king, bless him, tousled Johnnie's hair, then shook hands with Chad. The queen hugged her son a long time — indeed, she always did love him — and squeezed my hands, blinking back tears of relief.

Both of them were aging. The war was wearing everyone down, everyone but David on the loose in Paris, it seemed. The queen's dark hair was streaked with gray, and her hands shook. Creases etched themselves deep into King George's face, and dark circles shadowed his eyes. His hair was flecked with silver, and his movements were stiff rather than sharp as they had always been.

"Papa, the gazebo's gone, and the glasshouse broke!" Johnnie told them. "But we hid in the rocks. Georgie will be so sad he wasn't here to see that big aeroplane!" That said, he was content to go back to playing on the floor of the old queen's sitting room with the Fabergé grouse piece his eldest brother had filched years ago.

During all this, Queen Alexandra continued to sip her tea. "I told you those Germans were evil to the core," she said to her son.

"Yes, Mother dearest. I fear you're right. Now if you and May will keep an eye on Johnnie, I'm going out back again, just with Chad and Lala this time."

"And we ought to fine those bloody Huns for the price of a good gazebo!" she called after him. "Your father first kissed me out there under it!"

Ever since his accident when his horse fell on him, King George had walked slowly, with a bit of a limp he tried to hide. He led Chad and me toward the back door. It was dark in the back hall, for several windows that had blown in were temporarily boarded up. We stepped out onto the stone porch that overlooked the pile of burned rubble.

"Thank God, the winds were up," the king said. "That made their aim a bit erratic or they could have hit the house or cottage. But this is nothing compared to the devastation I've seen in France, or London either." He cleared his throat and frowned, gazing out at the busy soldiers picking up debris and looking into the two huge craters on the lawn. "Your hiding in the ravine was better than trench warfare our lads are going through. So, Chad, how did you happen to be here when the guards I assigned to the estate should have been closer, though we never thought a damn Zepp would come here."

"I was nearby because I wanted to be sure Prince John and Charlotte got back safely to York Cottage. I know it's safe with the guards here, Your Majesty, but I follow at a distance if they go out at night."

"I see."

I didn't see. I had no idea Chad was secretly protecting us, but I bit my tongue. Why he had he never told me or walked back with us? It would have given me much comfort and hope.

"The queen and I," the king said and cleared his throat again, still looking at the ruined, burned-out gazebo, "are overwhelmed with gratitude to both of you for taking care of Johnnie — and for warning my mother and the women. I've chosen not to let that be public knowledge, to let on or encourage the ungodly Huns that they almost hit one of the royal family."

He spun to face us. I had expected a dressing down for letting Johnnie temporarily out of my sight and was prepared to face a scolding. I was sure Their Majesties would not dismiss me, since Johnnie needed me so much, but I was terrified that something was coming that he hesitated to say.

"Chad, I want you to know that you have served your country and king to the utmost, despite not leaving here. I have something for you to express my — our — gratitude."

From his pocket, he pulled a dark red-and-blue ribbon wrapped around something. "This is a gallantry award," he said, handing it to Chad. A medal with four white enamel rounded arms set in silver with a laurel wreath and gold crown in its center dangled from the ribbon. It was one he could pin on his chest, though the king just pressed it into his palm.

"But Your Majesty, I . . . I don't deserve — this —" Chad stammered.

"My man, never say that and not to your sovereign. It's a D.S.O. awarded for an act of meritorious or distinguished service in wartime and usually when under fire or in the presence of the enemy, and you bloody well deserve it."

Chad bowed his head and held it close to his chest as the king turned to me. "I know how hard you try, Lala," His Majesty told me, "but is Johnnie too much to care for now that he's growing up? He would have left the nursery long ago. So far, you have made it possible for him to remain with us, in the heart of his family."

"He can't leave. He needs me," I blurted as all my worst fears exploded. "Please don't send him away, Your Majesty. No one else could care for his epilepsy as I do. The only medal I will ever want is that I can still care for him."

King George narrowed his eyes. Above his neatly trimmed mustache, his nostrils flared. I feared the worst, but he nodded and said, "Charlotte Bill, you have always been a great blessing to us and our children. I don't know what Johnnie — or his mother and I — would do without you. So far, you have made it possible for him to remain with us."

So far? What else was coming? Did the fact the boy could have been killed last night because I wasn't watching him closely enough mean the king would yet send him or me away? I almost blurted out that there must be somewhere I could go with him — not to a hospital or asylum as the royals had sent others who failed somehow — not . . .

"Well, enough said for now," His Majesty added. "By the way, the queen and I didn't want to tell you this in front of Queen Alexandra, but that same Zepp or its cohort did deadly duty last night, so we got off easy here. I never thought the kaiser would send Zepps to Norfolk where he was welcomed and entertained more than once, but he's stooped that low. Six British citizens are dead in the attack at Woodbridge not so far from here, and King's Lynn has been hit. Houses were bombed in Wolferton Flats near the Marsh, and craters and devastation are at Dodshill. But the strikes in London have been much worse, so Her Majesty and I intend to visit those places to keep up spirits. Meanwhile," he added, turning to face Chad again, "I leave the care of this dear place and people in your hands, both of you."

"We will do more than our duty, sir," Chad promised as the king left us there and limped out onto the lawn, weaving his way among charred debris. He spoke to some of the soldiers who were cleaning up the mess.

Tears sprang to my eyes, and I reached for Chad's offered hand. Together we looked at the medal. He turned it over, and we saw the engraving on the back of the suspension bar: *Chad Reaver from his grateful King.*

Though we both blinked back tears, I sensed in Chad a lifting of his spirits, some of his old self returning. He stood straighter, and his eyes had that old fire in them when he looked at me.

I told him, "You no doubt saved my life and Johnnie's, and I am grateful too. From your grateful Charlotte," I whispered and lightly kissed his cheek. "So I don't want to hear anything about how you didn't save me from that demented poacher. You saved me from a German Zepp attack because I would have gone right out there after Johnnie, and we would both be at the bottom of that farthest crater now, in a very big German-made grave."

"We did win our own little war last night, didn't we, love?"

"I hope we also won the one between us."

"Truce? Better relations?"

I smiled and blushed. "Truly? I will sign that peace pact with my life."

"The old queen said the king first kissed her out here. The gazebo's gone but we aren't, and one kiss deserves another."

He took my hand and led me back inside so we would be out of sight of the king and the soldiers. Just as we went through the battered doorway amid the broken windows, he kissed me, hard and long.

CHAPTER 33

"Queen Alexandra insisted there not be so many candles this year," Mabel whispered as the two of us stared at the tall Christmas tree while Johnnie kept walking around it, looking up at the angel on the top. "I hope Johnnie and the others won't be disappointed. I mean, I understand, since so many of our men are stuck in wet, cold trenches, feeling homesick and with lice and all — and our poor lads from Sandringham gone for good."

Mary, ever with her ears open, came up behind us and said, "Funny saying, *gone for good,* isn't it, when things are really going from bad to worse? Mama says the injuries she's seen when she visits the hospitals are horrible and that dreadful chorine gas the Hun beasts are using . . ." She shuddered.

"I didn't hear you come in," I said and gave her a hug. She was also chilled to the bone from her trek to the Big House where we were to celebrate this Christmas Day, 1916, with the family — except for David and Bertie. But George and Harry were happy to be back together, and Johnnie was thrilled to have George home for a while. Here came Harry and George now, stomping off snow while one of the footmen waited for their coats and hats.

"You might know," George told us, as Mabel hurried back to her duties, "David's living it up in Paris."

Mary said, "He can't be living it up in a nation so beleaguered by war. France is even worse off than we are."

"I'm not talking about the war, but about David. I hear he has a tootsie-wootsie there and —"

"George," I interrupted, "not here and not now."

He cocked his head, shrugged, and grinned as if he were the cat who'd eaten the canary. I'd expected Finch and David's superiors, especially his father, to keep control of David during the war. But apparently that was impossible.

Mary and I went over to the tree, and she studied the packages there, looking for a large one with her name on it. I knew she had her heart set on a gramophone. David had one, and she figured she should too.

And Johnnie — I dread to think what he'd do if he got the one he'd asked for, because whenever he heard a lively tune, he always took my hands and jumped around as if he knew how to dance — as if I did too.

My mind skipped back to when I used to recite nursery rhymes or singsongs to my little brood. How David and Bertie had loved *Rock-a-bye, baby, on the treetop,* but I'd stopped using that after their little world fell apart with cruel, crazy Mrs. Peters — and now the big world was falling apart with the war.

Later, when the adults arrived, we ate a lovely but not sumptuous Christmas dinner as we had in the old days. It was a simple beef roast with potatoes, carrots, Yorkshire pudding, then just tea, no wine, but a lovely plum pudding brought to the table with its brandy coating all aflame, which pleased Johnnie mightily. I realized I much preferred this fare to the opulent array of dishes I'd seen served here before, wartime or not.

We were a much smaller group than other years when friends attended, for Their Majesties felt everyone homeside should be with their own loved ones this year. Even Queen Alexandra's loyal Charlotte Knollys wasn't here, nor were Eva Dugdale and her husband.

It was the first holiday dinner I sat at the same table with the family, so I could watch Johnnie. Imagine that, me at the table with the royals, but times were changing. Even here, the traditional barriers between uppers and lowers were coming down a bit. Queen Alexandra also broke tradition by giving the children their gifts immediately after we finished dessert. Both Mary and Johnnie opened big boxes with gramophones from their grannie, despite the fact the king had said that the one in their mother's boudoir was quite enough for one house and family.

But I think he too joined in the children's joy, perhaps putting his war worries aside for a few moments. Things were not going well, and I knew from what Mary and George had said that he was quite upset that anti-German sentiment had turned against anyone who had a German last name. Spy mania, some called it, and here was the royal family with that heritage and name of Saxe-Coburg-Gotha.

Johnnie kept cavorting with Mary and George to some sort of ragtime tune on Mary's new gramophone. I knew their mother felt we should all be singing carols or even saying prayers, but I was glad she let the children spend their pent-up energy.

However, I told myself, I would have to be sure my lad was careful with his new gramophone. *Gently, now!* was the motto I had to recite to Johnnie repeatedly as he had grown tall and didn't know his own strength. Sometimes it seemed that Chad, Penny, and I were the only ones who could keep his high spirits reined in — even shortly after one of his spells.

"Look, Lala," he told me as he buzzed past, circling the tree, making me almost dizzy. "The angel on top looks like the girls in cloud dresses high in the sky!"

Harry got into the fun, organizing the four of them to make a "choo, choo" railroad round and round the tree. Finally, it was too much for the king, who announced, "Enough! You are tiring your grandmother out, and I would appreciate some peace and quiet."

The moment I popped up from my seat behind the royals to snatch Johnnie away, I sensed George was going to say something flip. I pointed at him in warning, but he was not to be denied. I prayed he wouldn't sass his father. At least, he said only, "Peace on earth, good will to men. We would all like that, so we'll quiet down. Too bad Hansell isn't here to read us his *A Christmas Carol* story, right, lads?"

"And we all yelled 'Bah! Humbug!' right along with him," Harry said, sobering too and lifting the needle off the record so the music stopped.

As I walked behind the tree to collect Johnnie, I gasped. My pulse pounded: he was wavering on his feet, his eyes rolling back, going to his knees. *Oh, please, dear Lord, not here. Not now!*

I could hardly carry him from the room or even drag him out. At least we were behind the tree from the adults, but —

"Lala," Mary cried, "whatever is it? He looks — Oh, no!"

Someone said something else, but I shut it out, the sounds, the voices. I broke Johnnie's fall as he pitched forward nearly into the tree and kept him from going facedown on the polished wooden floor. I rolled him on his back and put between his teeth the top of a velvet-lined gift box in which Mary had received a single strand of pearls. I seized a flat, unwrapped box labeled for David and thrust it between his head and the floor as his convulsions started.

Mary: "Can I help? Oh, dear! Mama, Johnnie's sick — you know."

I: "Mary, get back, all of you. It will pass. He will be all right. Go sit down."

The king: "What? Here? All of you, come

back here!"

Yet not only Queen Mary but Queen Alexandra joined me and helped to stop the endless thrashing of his legs and arms. I think the king took the others out into the hall — I don't know what I thought.

Then, finally, it was over. He stopped shaking and opened his eyes.

"I wanted to bring my peep," he said, looking up, dazed, at the high ceiling.

"We'll take you back to your bed and you can see your peep," I promised.

Queen Mary helped her mother-in-law rise. I saw both of them were crying, then realized I was too.

"I have a nice peep for you," the old queen said, "one that won't get too big so you have to get a new one like all those times before." She tottered off, and I paid her no heed, for she could say things as far afield as Johnnie.

But when the king sent in two footmen to help Johnnie get back to York Cottage "from his fall," the dear old woman came over and pressed the Fabergé grouse into the boy's trembling hands.

"I know you want real peeps, my dear, but you keep this one too, all right? Your brother David liked it, and I know you do too."

"Thank you, Grannie. If Lala says I can

keep it — only one peep at a time."

"My, he seemed lucid," his mother said from behind me when I thought she'd walked away.

"For a few minutes — then exhaustion — sleepy time, right, Johnnie?"

"But what about my gramophone?"

"They will bring it to you, but now, off to York Cottage, off to bed," I told him.

I did not realize until the king appeared to supervise the footmen putting Johnnie and me in a motorcar outside that I was both sweating and chilled. I was terrified that this epileptic seizure of the many I had tended in private was going to upset my world just as surely as had that first fit on the royal yacht nearly seven years ago.

I was surprised the next week when Lady Eva Dugdale arrived at York Cottage and asked to see me in the queen's boudoir. The king and queen were in London, and Lady Dugdale usually attended Her Majesty. I went down the hall, nervous, even fearful, for I'd been waiting for the other shoe to fall — a talk from the king about not letting Johnnie get so excited at best — perhaps a real scolding for me — though my being dismissed would be the worst.

I curtsied to her and tried to buck myself

459

up. Twice this kindly woman had done me a service, in hiring me to tend the royal children and in helping me rid David and Bertie of Mrs. Peters. I saw that she had ordered tea for two, and she let me pour. I was usually more adept at that, but my hands were shaking.

"Is Her Majesty quite well, milady?" I asked.

"Exhausted from visiting hospitals and waving the troops off to France. But I hear Johnnie is still not well. As large as he is now, are his seizures not more — noticeable? More dramatic?"

I tried to keep my teacup from rattling in its saucer. "As you may have heard, but for a single incident, we are handling it well. He is happy here at Sandringham, and he's even learned to write his parents letters in a large, but very legible script. He loves it here and knows no other life, so it would be wrong to change anything."

"Charlotte," she said, leaning closer and reaching out one hand to cover mine, "you have been the best thing in the world for these children, from the first, with that terrible woman I mistakenly sent here. But you must know how distressed the other children were by Johnnie's seizure on Christmas Day, other times too, though they didn't see his problem full face until then."

I could have shattered the thin bone china in my hand. The queen — no doubt, the king made her do it — had sent this woman to tell me Johnnie was to be sent away. Perhaps that I was to be let go after all these years.

Trying not to shout, I told her, "Johnnie would be greatly set back should he lose his family. Forgive me for speaking true, milady — if he would lose me. The king knows that. He cannot mean that his youngest son should be hidden, be sent away from his family and all he knows."

"His Majesty greatly admires your stalwart service to Johnnie and would like to reward it."

"The only reward I want is for Their Majesties' youngest son not to be sent away." I nearly burst into tears. I knew the king had a war to fight, but could he not tell me this in person, so that I could deal directly with him? Would he not grant me a favor for taking good care of his children for all these many years? He gave me no medal when the Zeppelin attacked, but he'd said he owed me much.

"Charlotte," Lady Dugdale said again, pulling her hand back from mine and sitting up even straighter, "have you heard of or seen Wood Farm on the estate? It has a nice cottage, brick, two stories, I hear, quite snug with fields and forests nearby."

Her words barely punctured my fear and fury. "Wh-What? Nearer Wolferton?"

"Yes, before the marshes and bogs begin, closer to the railway but in a secluded spot on the estate."

"This estate. Nearby."

"Three miles, I believe, or so Chad Reaver told me when he brought me here in a carriage from the station today." Wood Farm but three miles from here. Dared I hope it wasn't total exile for Johnnie or me? But it was still wrong that the king of England and the Empire would banish his boy from his family. So wrong!

"Now," she said, taking what was her first sip of tea, "I've arranged for Mr. Reaver to take you, me, and Johnnie there to have a look at the house straightaway. The wind's a bit nippy, and snow is on the ground, but we'll manage."

"But it's still exile from his family . . . from his parents." I gripped my hands tightly together around my teacup. "Milady, I want to understand what you are saying. The king — and the queen, of course — are suggesting — I mean they have decided —

that Johnnie and I would live at Wood Farm?"

"With some staff, a house maid, cook, and one of the few footmen — of course, the last nursemaid you have here, if you wish, as I understand rooms have been readied for them in the spacious attic and there is a good-sized kitchen at the back."

"But York Cottage, his family, and this staff are all he knows. Would he be banished there or able to visit and have visits from the family?"

"As I said, the other children suffer when they see him the way he is. But of course, they could visit."

"But would they, if their parents didn't approve such? And if Johnnie was not to be hidden —"

"Hidden? He's to have freedom to move about the entire estate."

"But his family are gone so much already. And would it not help others who have children in the nation with such problems if the royal family did not banish him?"

"Best not protest, even though you argue like a clever lawyer. Charlotte, these are terrible times for European rulers. Monarchies are endangered or going down. Our royal family needs to look and be strong, united, capable in all ways."

I just stared at her but I was seeing Johnnie's parents, the stern king and pliable but loving queen. They were banishing my boy so they could present a perfect picture, and Johnnie did not fit that.

"Besides," Milady Dugdale went on, "this place has always been a bit crowded, hasn't it, and you'd be absolutely knocking round in the Big House. Queen Mary says she and the boy's grandmother will visit. You see, Their Majesties could not get away right now to explain all this, nor did they want to just write or telephone."

I knew how busy and bereft Johnnie's father was, fighting a war, and yet I considered him a coward not to tell me this himself. And for not keeping Johnnie with the family. His mother, at least, should have fought for him — or written a damned note to her husband — to have the boy stay at York Cottage, which had been his home.

But a strange little voice in my head said quite clearly, *But you are his mother, except by blood. You have reared him, helped him, protected and loved him. And they are letting him, thank God, stay in your care . . .*

"Charlotte," another voice, perhaps a real one, broke into my head. "Are you quite all right? You look . . . well, dazed. Do you understand what I've said?" Lady Dugdale asked, leaning close and shaking my wrist as if she needed to wake me up.

"Yes. Yes, all right," I managed, as I told myself this could have been worse. I steeled myself to be calm when I wanted to scream and break things for this was wrong, wrong, wrong. And cruel, though I would fight to keep Johnnie from thinking so. At least it would not be for me like poor Margaretta Eager who had been sent away from her royal Russian girls. And Chad was waiting to take us there.

"I am glad they sent you," I told Lady Dugdale, shaking myself back to reality. "It's best their Royal Majesties didn't do it, for I fear what I might have said. You have ever been a friend to me, if you don't mind my saying so, milady."

"I not only don't mind, but I am honored," she said, looking much relieved at my change of tone.

I let out a big breath, and my shoulders slumped. My heartbeat quieted a bit. I'd seen Wood Farm once from afar, years ago, riding round the estate with Chad, but I could picture none of it now. Perhaps it would be almost like a house of my own.

I wanted to hate Wood Farm but I could not. The farmhouse was much smaller than even York Cottage, of course, but it was broad enough across the front that twelve windows could be opened to the breezes from the fields and forests in fine weather. It was all sturdy, muted redbrick with a covered doorway and a small garden in front surrounded by a low, square wall, though right now snow lay on it all like vanilla frosting, including the two chimneys and slanted roof. In truth, it was a charming house.

"We can keep peeps in the yard," Johnnie announced, for I'd spent the way over here explaining to him that, now that he was growing up, he could live away from York Cottage just like his brothers did.

"Only one peep at a time, remember?" Chad told him as we got down. "Peep George would be unhappy if you got more right now, but I know he'll like this new place."

Chad winked at me over Johnnie's head and behind Lady Dugdale's back as he opened the gate for us. Yes, I thought, with Johnnie here and Chad but three miles away, this house could be a home. Already I could imagine Penny swinging on the gate with Johnnie.

The rooms were comfortably furnished and spic and span. The scent of lemon oil and — could that be? — baked bread filled

466

the air. It was a bit chilly but we could soon build up the hearth fire in this main room and the kitchen. It had electric lights and a telephone on the wall.

"Of course," Her Ladyship said as we walked from room to room on the ground floor, "you can bring Johnnie's furniture and things he likes."

Johnnie chimed in, "Especially my new gramophone and Peep George — and Lala too. But where will Papa and Mama sleep when they come here? Don't they want to live with me anymore?"

My gaze slammed into Lady Dugdale's, but we turned away from each other. I had much work to do, far more than just packing and arranging.

"We'll talk about all that later, my dear," I told him. "And Chad and Penny will visit and I'm sure your family will too."

Chad waited below while the three of us went upstairs and even looked into the attic with its single hall and four small rooms for servants. The views out the upstairs windows were good. We could watch the seasons change the trees from here and even see the smoke from the railway station on a clear day. The bedrooms upstairs were spacious compared to the nursery and rooms at York Cottage. In a way, it seemed to me a step up, but I would have lived in a mud hut to keep Johnnie with me.

Chad was waiting downstairs, turned sideways so that, despite his crutches, it looked as if he had two legs and was whole again. But he would always be whole to me, all I ever needed, if I had Johnnie near to protect and tend.

"Well," I whispered to Chad, "at least Their Majesties have bought me off at a pretty price — and place."

"I was hoping you would accept the inevitable," he told me as he held my arm and I stepped up into the carriage. "Including expecting a caller at the door, one Mrs. Wentworth will not give the eagle eye to when I appear with another peep."

"I can have another peep?" Johnnie asked as he piled in next to Lady Dugdale.

"I'm afraid peeps don't like the gramophone played as loud as you do," Chad said, climbing up into the driver's seat and putting his crutches under his leg. "Except Peep George doesn't seem to mind, so I think he's it for now."

"Lala said it's not a boy but I'm not changing its name!"

"Not a boy?" Lady Dugdale said with a laugh. "But how do you know, if I dare ask?"

"Peep George laid an egg," Johnnie told

her. "Only girls do that, like when I was born, right, Lala?"

"More or less," I told him, patting his shoulder, "but we'll work on all that too."

Johnnie bounced in his seat, Her Ladyship smiled, and Chad nodded before he turned back toward the horses. So, instead of total desolation and defeat, I felt I had won a little war to get to stay with Johnnie. But that didn't mean I wasn't still going to fight for my little prince.

CHAPTER 34

Whenever we could steal away from our duties, Chad, Penny, Johnnie, and I spent time together, as we did one spring day in 1917, on a Sunday picnic to a wooded area called Cat's Bottom. I'd already explained to Johnnie that there would be no cat to see.

"I do feel a bit guilty sometimes for being so content," I told Chad as we sat together on our blanket and watched the children pick flowers and then, laughing, throw them at each other.

"That's how it's been for me, not being able to fight the Huns. I know you understand. It's amazing the war has gone so bad for Russia that the tsar has been forced to abdicate. Another big blow to His Majesty. One royal cousin causing all this mess and the others the victims of that."

I sighed. "Uneasy is the head that wears the crown, as I've heard said. But with all their appearances among their people and their bravery during the war so far, I think Their Majesties will weather this storm. But I . . . I can't believe it either about Tsar Nicholas. I've never seen a ruler so protected and so powerful. Even on holiday, nothing but guards, guards, guards. But maybe that means he was never really free. I'm hoping England grants asylum to the Romanovs. Johnnie's never forgotten the tsar's four daughters and the poor little tsarevich . . ."

"Poor because he won't ever rule now? They'll probably leave Russia with enough wealth to build themselves a palace right here on these grounds and one near London. But you have seen enough rulers to know more about them than most, haven't you, my love?" he asked and pelted me with some purple columbine Penny had brought him before she was off again.

"Including an American president," I said. "It's been a more amazing life than I could ever have dreamed, and yet — despite seeing all the glamour, the food and fashion, yachts and travel and important people — it's being someplace simple like this with you, Johnnie, and Penny that means the most to me. I do feel I've succeeded with the children — except David."

My big, stalwart man reached over and

squeezed my hand. "Any more letters from him?" he asked as he stroked my arm, wrist to elbow. His merest touch was enough to electrify me, and he knew it.

"One last week, delivered right to Wood Farm's door. He was very sarcastic about his father, terribly. He referred to his war appearances to boost morale as stunts . . . stunts! I should burn the letters, all of them. But, you know, he's been so callous toward Johnnie —"

"Jealous of your love and attention for his younger brother, whom he considers damaged and unimportant compared to him."

"I forget you know David well too. But I thought — when and if he becomes king — if he tries to belittle Johnnie or lock him away, I would just remind him I had some letters that would not make him look too good."

Chad looked surprised, then hooted a laugh. "Why, Charlotte Bill, alias Lala, a blackmailer."

"I wouldn't do it, of course, just suggest it to him, that he treat Johnnie better. I'm grateful his mother and grandmother still visit and care for him, but he does feel he's been sent away at times — for being ill or naughty. I try to talk him out of that."

"I have always loved your backbone —

and the rest of you," Chad said. "And I am proud to help you with Johnnie. Who could not love him? So, since you've said you will marry me, let's ask Their Majesties' permission together the first chance we get — when they're visiting here and the time is right with all this death and destruction. Maybe it would be best when the war is over. Surely, he will think we'll both be good for his boy, and Penny can live with us too. And, of course, I will write to your parents."

"Yes, Chad Reaver, again I say that I will marry you and somehow, someday, we will live happily ever after."

Finch appeared one evening at Wood Farm when Johnnie and I were working on his writing a letter to his parents. I hadn't seen the man who was David's valet for over a year — and here he was in a spiffy uniform!

"Finch, it's so good to see you! Is David here too?" I asked when I opened the door myself and glanced out at David's motorcar.

He gave me a light hug and patted Johnnie's back as the boy ran up and hugged him.

"How are you, Johnnie, my boy?"

"Fine, but I think I'm really Lala's boy. Since I don't live at York Cottage anymore, I was sad but mostly not now."

"Oh, I see. But you are still a fine lad, and a prince of a boy."

I shook my head at Finch and frowned behind Johnnie's back, for I'd gone round and round with the boy about whether he was still a prince. He'd finally declared on his own that he'd rather be a farmer and help Chad with the peeps than go back to London again because there were too many noisy people there. But on some deep level — I prayed he had not sensed it from me — he must have felt he'd been betrayed. And yet he seemed happy here.

"So how is David?" I asked as I put my arm around Johnnie's shoulders.

"He's in London," Finch said, "much enamored of a new lady and generally raising Cain. I motored down to collect some things for him. He's officially moved out of York Cottage now."

"Haven't we all? But not another French girl, I hope. Come in, sit down by our very own hearth and tell us all you know."

"All right to tell . . . both of you?" he asked, with a roll of the eyes toward Johnnie, who came up to his shoulder now. "Prince John is growing fast, but —"

"Yes, all right. Johnnie, why don't you go to the kitchen and ask Cook for some tea for us — and feed Peep George before you come back too, all right?"

"I will have tea with you, because Finch is on our side in the war."

"Yes, he is," I assured him as he went out.

"Another peep?" Finch asked. "Isn't this peep the sixth about now?"

"He's named this one after George, whom he misses terribly. He won't give it up so it's much too big. Chad had to clip her wings so she won't fly away."

"Ah, Chad. And has he clipped yours?"

"I'm not leaving Wood Farm as long as Johnnie needs me." I lowered my voice. "His spells are getting worse as he gets older, when I hoped it would be the opposite."

"But about David. He's taken by — and taken up with — a married woman of his set, Freda Dudley Ward. Her husband knows it, but is quite amenable and prefers to look the other way."

"Oh, no. Do Their Majesties know?"

"More or less — mostly less, since he tells them she is just one of many friends, but it's much more. But the thing is, she dominates him, and he seems to love it. Bloody damn — sorry for that language," he whispered, "but he's lost his mind. He likes her to order him around and talks baby talk to her sometimes. I swear, he lisps worse than Harry used to. The thing is, there has been an Inspector Palmer snooping around."

"Trying to get something about all this on David?"

He shook his head. "Just the opposite. Trying to clean up after him in a way, cover his tracks. With this awful, endless war and the way royal houses are falling, I think the king is trying to — as the Prince of Wales describes it — 'put the skids' on him. So the prince just wants you to know that dealing with Inspector Palmer, in case he comes here, can be a two-edged sword. It looks like he's trying to help, but he may report to the king."

I heaved a huge sigh. "As if King George doesn't have enough on his mind right now. Thank you for the warning but I doubt any inspectors will come here to talk to a nanny from years ago."

"The prince admitted he's sent you letters — and he's sent some that could be black-mail fodder to the French mistress he had. At least Freda Dudley Ward is not some gut-tersnipe and knows how to keep her mouth shut. But the prince regards you highly. You were like a moth—"

I held up my hand to stop what he would say, but Johnnie bounced back into the room then too. "Finch," he said, "I want you to meet Peep George out by the back

476

door to the kitchen."

"I'd be honored, sir," he said and stood.

"My name is Johnnie here at Wood Farm where I am happy. But if I go anywhere else, my name is Prince John."

The two of them headed toward the kitchen. I went to the front window and frowned out at the distant pine trees, which looked as if they were spearing the racing clumps of clouds. My mind raced too. Finch had properly called Johnnie "sir," though how often I thought of him as my boy and tried to forget that he was a prince. Now, David, heir to the throne, was running amok in these terrible times. We'd heard just this week that the tsar was actually under arrest with his family, though I had not told any of this to Johnnie.

"Now that's a smashing peep!" Finch told Johnnie as they came back in. "You take good care of him."

"I do. Chad and I take good care of Lala too."

Finch shot me a look over the boy's head. "I'm glad to hear that. Which reminds me, after a spot of tea, I've got to go back to taking care of another of your brothers, namely David."

"David doesn't like my peeps or my papa. And I don't think he likes me. But Lala does, better than she likes him."

I gave a little gasp. From the mouths of children — even Johnnie's — but I should know that by now. It hit me full force then: David had been permanently damaged by his first nanny. When I rescued him, he thought it his due to be cherished above the others. Even before Johnnie, he'd fought for that. But my necessary and obvious love for the youngest royal child had angered and hurt him too. I dreaded how his relationships with his two nannies might shape and shake his future as prince and king. Was it true that *the hand that rocks the cradle rules the world*?

God forgive me, I was happy when Finch left. He'd brought the outside world with him, brought out Johnnie's buried feelings that he'd been abandoned by David and his family. But it had also emphasized Johnnie's love for the life I had built for him here.

As if to celebrate that dream of mine, the four of us went on a picnic that very afternoon, not far from the house. Because we were all together, it seemed a wonderful outing as we headed toward the meadow. We could have been on a desert isle and we would have felt that way. Chad must have been thinking the same, because he began

to sing the lively, old Boer War song "Marching to Pretoria."

Walk with me I'll walk with you,
And so we will walk together . . .
Dance with me, I'll dance with you
And so we will dance together . . .
We are marching to Pretoria . . .
Pretoria, hoorah!

"And Wood Farm, hoorah!" Johnnie
shouted.

I looked at the boy as he went back to
singing lustily, swinging his arms and
marching along. It reminded me of that day
he had marched and stomped on his father's
precious stamps. But Wood Farm and this
lovely surrounding area on the great estate
were his home and now mine too. The four
of us were a little family of God's making
and our own.

I recalled the old tune "When Johnny
Comes Marching Home," an American
Civil War song Queen Mary used to play on
the piano at York Cottage: *We'll give him a
hearty welcome then, hurrah, hurrah!*

Johnnie not only felt welcome here but
was surrounded by love. It was a bit daunting how perfect and precious our lives
seemed to me in that moment, a million

times better for my boy than living in a palace or a grand house amidst power and position. Oh, yes, I resented that the king and queen had seen fit to exile him, to hide him, but I vowed to make up for that.

Johnnie looked at me again and grinned. "I'm going to grow up to be just like Chad, Lala," he told me. "And someday I will have hundreds of peeps, and no one will steal them or shoot at them from the sky either! I will keep them safe here, take good care of them, and they will be happy just like me! Am I like a peep to you, my Lala?"

"Yes, my dear," I told him as Chad smiled at both of us. "Only, always, I love you so much better than that."

Finally the king was coming for a brief respite from the war, and Chad and I were going to ask him for permission to wed. My father had written back a lovely letter — in my mother's handwriting, for his had never been good. If we could stay in Their Majesties' good graces, we would be married in the church here, small, private with just Johnnie, Penny, my parents, and my friends Mabel and Rose. I even decided to be daring enough to hire Rose to make me a new gown.

Thank God, things were looking up a bit.

The Americans had entered the war at last and had given all of us a great boost in morale and men. Meanwhile, speaking of sending letters, poor Margaretta Eager poured her heart out to me in correspondence, especially when the assurance of British asylum for her dear girls and their family seemed to move so slowly — and then halted when King George privately admitted he feared bringing the once autocratic despot here to England when his own powers were under fire by some liberals in the government. How I wished I dared plead with His Majesty to help his Russian cousin's family, for I could not stand the idea of those five lively children imprisoned all their lives.

"Mrs. Lala," Victor, our elderly Wood Farm footman, announced with a knock on the open upstairs schoolroom door, "a male visitor to see you, not Mr. Reaver or Mr. Finch this time, but an Inspector Palmer, says he's from a government Special Branch, that he did."

Johnnie looked up from laboriously writing a "Welcome Back" letter to his parents. "A special branch of a tree?" he asked.

"Thank you, Victor. I'll come down to see the inspector if you will sit with Johnnie here."

"Oh, yes, miss. Johnnie and I get on smashing, don't we, sir?"

My heart was pounding. Was I to be interrogated, as Finch had suggested? I steadied myself by reviewing what he'd said, that Special Branch was working to protect David and, in a way, perhaps the king too.

As we sat across from each other — I did not call for tea — the red-haired, broad-shouldered man complimented the summer gardens and the well-kept estate. "But, of course," he said at last, tugging at his shirt cuffs, "I'm here on official business. Mrs. Bill, I need to inquire if you still have the correspondence the Prince of Wales has sent you over the years since he has lived away from Sandringham."

"Letters to me, yes, but I consider them personal and private."

"His Majesty's government would like to ask the greatest of favors, Mrs. Bill, that you allow me to take those letters into custody for the good of all. I'm sure the notes are sentimental to you, but as time goes on, we must be certain the private correspondence of the heir to the throne does not fall into the wrong hands — and I surely don't mean yours, for the prince trusts you implicitly and thinks of you with admiration."

"Into the wrong hands, here, in this secluded area on the king's rural estate?" I asked, getting into even more of a fret. I must admit, I was ashamed and angry at myself that I had thought to use those careless comments if David ever tried to hide or harm Johnnie, so I understood what he meant. But if Special Branch shared those letters with the king, His Majesty would have a conniption.

"The Prince of Wales said you had grit, but this is wartime, Mrs. Bill, and I would *greatly* appreciate — as would the prince and the king — if you would entrust all of those missives to me."

"Yes, I see," I said and rose to fetch them. I was annoyed again. Never had I felt more like one of those suffragettes both my father and the king tried to dismiss and keep in their place. "But please tell David," I added, "that this should be a nanny's lesson to him — not to put anything in writing or do anything in his life he will regret."

Inspector Palmer rose too. "I will tell him. Good advice for all of us, especially for our Prince of Wales."

Chad and I were at sixes and sevens, waiting for Their Majesties to come to Sandringham for their twenty-fifth wedding anniversary on July 6, 1918. It had been over a year since we'd formally pledged to each other and, though being together was a joy, it was getting terribly difficult to wait. More than once we'd thought of writing the king, but Chad believed our chances were better to face him in person. I too feared his answer, for nannies were always single women — yet, was not Johnnie's situation, almost hidden from the outside world, different enough that an exception could be made?

But we grew bold as the war seemed to be winding down. The German navy had refused to fight, and it was rumored that the kaiser would flee to a neutral country. The royal family had dropped their German last name and formally had become the Windsors, named after that most British of castles. Enough things seemed to be going well that they had decided to risk a week away from London — and we would risk asking them as soon as we could.

It was very windy for July, and it had been raining, but I could have flown as high as the kite that Queen Alexandra had given Johnnie. Penny was visiting her mother's family over in the village today, but Chad had taken a few hours off to greet the king when he arrived — and to be with me.

Our boy had insisted on bringing Peep George, but the old bird was tethered by one leg and was pecking for insects in the slight depression where a Zeppelin bomb crater had been filled in and sodded, while Chad and Johnnie wrestled with the wind to keep the kite aloft.

Johnnie shouted to me, "The other George, my brother, would like to see this kite flying, Lala! I'll write him about it."

"You are getting very good with your handwriting," I called to him. Johnnie was ecstatic, and Chad was managing to keep himself upright and let the boy help to control the kite.

"Righto!" Chad told Johnnie. "But now tug on the string and run a bit with it when it starts to come down."

"It's as high as the clouds, Lala!"

"Don't run too far!"

He screeched in his excitement, which made Peep George try to fly. Somehow the grouse's tether came off. Despite her clipped wings, she managed to get aloft for a few feet and flew right into the ravine where we'd sought shelter from the Zeppelin.

"Oh, no!" I cried.

Chad saw it too and started over. "Stay with him," he called back to me, "and I'll see where she is. Maybe just down on that first ledge."

Hoping Johnnie didn't notice Peep George was missing, I went over to him and helped him keep the kite from diving into the ground when he yanked it too hard. I looked back at Chad. The bird must have been reachable, because I didn't see him. He had managed to get to that ledge in the dark, no less, under attack with Johnnie and me that terrible night, so I just went back to watching Johnnie. Chad would be here with the bird soon.

But where was he? His crutches lay in the grass near the rim of the ravine. Surely, he hadn't gone down too far for that bird.

"Johnnie, leave the kite where it hits this time. Look, here comes Mabel, maybe to tell us your mama and papa are here or it's time for lunch. Go tell her about the kite, all right?"

"But . . . where is Peep George?" he demanded. "Did he fly away?"

"He's fine. He's with Chad. Go with Mabel now," I ordered, gesturing to her. "Chad and I will bring Peep George into the house."

I strode right for Chad's crutches. I looked down onto the first ledge — no. I held to a sturdy, young tree and leaned out, looking down — down to where Chad lay sprawled and unmoving far below by the little stream, down into the depths of my soul.

CHAPTER 35

So we had a funeral instead of a wedding. Many local folk attended because so many had known and admired Chad. Despite my dazed state, I came to grasp that in burying him, a real body in an actual casket — a rather fine oak one the king purchased — for the villagers, it was like having one of their once strong fathers, brothers, and sons, who were buried in France, home again to lay in Sandringham soil.

At first, I could barely risk being with Johnnie, not that I blamed him, but I was so distraught that I upset him. I could not stand to look at Peep George, though she didn't live much longer from her injuries, which made Johnnie more difficult too. Bless her, Queen Alexandra and Toria kept him for a few days, with Mabel's help. But when I heard Alexandra's sister, Maria Feodorovna, the mother of Tsar Nicholas, was staying there, I knew I had to pull myself together and get Johnnie back.

Queen Mary and the king had attended Chad's funeral. Also, they sent me a condolence note, so I guess they knew how much Chad had meant to me, though I never told them we had hoped to wed. My parents said I should come home for a visit, but this was home to me now.

Besides, it was more shocking deaths that made me go to the Big House to take Johnnie back again, for in that same July of 1918, word came that the tsar and all his family had been slaughtered by Bolshevik revolutionaries in some dreadful cellar in the dark of night.

"Everyone here is crying," Johnnie said, when Mabel brought him down to me with his little satchel. "I guess it's for Chad and Peep George going away. Grannie knows they went away."

I could tell Mabel had been crying too. I was not sure that I'd ever get over Chad's loss, but to think of the tsar's children, so full of life, those lovely, sweet girls — oh, but Margaretta would be devastated. She'd actually been able to exchange some letters with the girls during the first months of their exile. And I had a feeling she would never quite get over their fates. "I will explain to Johnnie," I told Mabel, and we hugged each other.

"I overheard," she whispered, "that the king blames himself for not taking them in, but that's to remain private. He and the queen are going to the London memorial service for the tsar, though the prime minister advises against it. So much loss . . ."

"I hope no one is mad at me for anything," Johnnie told me as he carried his satchel and we started out for York Cottage, where Victor was waiting for me with a carriage, the same one in which Chad had driven us to see Wood Farm for the first time. I needed the walk to steel myself to explain things to Johnnie as best I could, to find the words not only about losing Chad but those beloved girls in cloud dresses. We walked a ways and sat on the bench at the edge of the lake where Chad and I had sat, once angry with each other, while Johnnie threw stones in the water. Today, as if he sensed something, he did not speak or jump around, but looked up at the sky, a habit he'd never lost.

"I want you to know," I told him, "that Chad did not want to leave us and did not want to leave Sandringham."

"Where is he then? Out by Cat's Bottom or in the woods? Penny said he's gone and that's all she was supposed to say to me, but she was pretty sad."

"You know that people die sometimes."

"Grandpapa died. Grannie said so and said did I remember him."

"And do you?"

"Did he put butter on his pant legs, Lala?"

I smiled. "Yes, to make you laugh. He liked to make you happy, and I do too."

"Did he know about my falling fits?"

"No, he died before that. Johnnie, Chad fell down in the ravine and hit his head and died, but he didn't want to leave us. He went to heaven now, far, far up there, somewhere, but his body is buried — like we buried Peep George — in the ground. But we'll always remember him here with us, won't we?"

"I will and bet I can find him somewhere in the woods or by the Wash where he showed us birds that fly."

I sighed, but his not really grasping all this was for the best. Should I even tell him about his girls in cloud dresses? No, that was beyond his understanding, and, frankly, beyond mine.

"Grannie said you were sick but you'd be better soon," Johnnie said, putting his hand in mine. "You still look a little sick."

I forced a smile and sniffed back tears,

when I thought I'd cried out all that I would ever have. To each his or her own way of grieving for those we love and those we lose, and God help us if that is the same person.

"And, Nanny Lala, I have a present for you," he announced and opened his satchel to dig out a folded piece of paper. "To make you feel better, make you well, 'cause you taught me to write and lots of things."

I opened the note. In pencil, in his best handwriting, though a bit on the slant, with the paper giving off the sweet lilac scent his grandmother often wore, I read, *NANNY — I LOVE YOU. JOHNNIE.*

That note and that child kept me going, though his seizures were increasing in frequency and length. I treasured the visits from his grandmother and sometimes his mother, who loved him dearly and visited when she could. Penny came often too, to play with Johnnie, but it lifted my heart to see her getting on without her father. She lived with her aunt and two cousins, but we saw a great deal of her.

And through Penny as well as his grandmother, Johnnie played with many of the local lads, openly and easily, in a way David and Bertie never had. Johnnie was not lonely as they had been — as I still was for

Chad. It pained me that I imagined him everywhere we went on the estate and hurt me too when Johnnie sometimes insisted he was looking for Chad. And when he stared up at the clouds and mentioned the pretty girls in cloud dresses . . .

I tried to buck myself up, despite wind and snow, that January 18, 1919. The Armistice bringing Europe peace, the Treaty of Versailles, was to be signed that day in France, though that would bring no Sandringham boys home. I almost snapped at Johnnie for playing his favorite record of American war songs repeatedly that day: "Over There" with Enrico Caruso and "When Johnny Comes Marching Home Again," because his name was in that song. How that reminded me of one of our last days together — as a family with Chad and me. Today my boy had been marching about and here we were cooped up, and I could have screamed.

"Johnnie, can we turn that off for now, or change the record?" I asked in my best I-mean-it nanny voice.

"I can put on 'I'm Always Chasing Rainbows,' " he told me. "I like the words, *watching clouds drifting by.* Lala, are you still sick?"

Just heartsick, I thought, but I said, "I'm

fine. If you're fine, I'm fine."

"Oh, I am," he said, but he lifted the needle from the record and came over and sat next to me on the sofa. "Lala," he said, so seriously, "the music has stopped."

I nodded and took his hand. After these fourteen years we'd been together, once again he was trying to comfort me. I tried to look only at the bright side of things: I regretted nothing but, of course, Chad's loss — Johnnie's banishment from his family home and David's increasingly reckless behavior over the years.

"We are going to dance!" Johnnie declared, jumping up to put the music back on. It was another of his favorites, "After the Ball."

"This is about a game bouncing a ball," he told me as he pulled me to my feet, held my hands, and bounced around the room, pulling me after him.

Many a heart is aching . . . *Many the hopes* . . . *vanished* . . . The words on the record echoed in my heart.

I didn't tell him it wasn't about a game, not that kind of ball. I never told him that I was going to go on even if I sometimes felt my life was over, but for him. Because right then, his eyes rolled back into his head, and he collapsed, and I screamed for Cook and

Victor and we managed to get him upstairs before the worst of the seizure began.

"You can leave us now," I told them as I scrambled for his mouthpiece and his pillow. "Just another one. He'll be better in the morning. Thank you both for being so loyal. Close his door, please."

I was grateful he was in his own bed. The seizure was worse than usual, but when it ended, I managed to get some water with his bromide powder down him. At least Their Majesties had agreed that we should forgo the more brutal cures, and I wasn't even sure this helped.

Johnnie wasn't a bit chatty afterward as he often was. He just whispered, "I'll find Chad. Don't worry, Lala," and fell into an exhausted sleep.

I sat by his chair, nodding off now and then as he slept, wishing my world was like his, that I had hopes of finding Chad and could see girls in cloud dresses in the sky.

Then, in the early evening, I jolted alert and realized my boy wasn't breathing. I jumped up, bent close over him, tried to shake him awake.

"Johnnie. Johnnie!"

I felt for his neck pulse, his wrist pulse. Nothing. No. No! But he felt cold, his eyes closed in sleep. Limp, unconscious, that was surely all. It had been a more violent seizure than the others, but he always woke up — he must talk to me again! He'd said he'd find Chad!

And perhaps he had.

I telephoned the queen, and she and the king motored to us straightaway from London. She came up to his bedroom where he lay, pale as a ghost on the bed.

"My dear boy," she said, bending to take his limp hand. "And my dear Lala." I had tried to stay strong to console her, but she embraced and comforted me. "Perhaps the Lord wanted to care for him now, despite the fine job you have done," she told me.

It was only then I noticed the king had not come up, though I'd seen him get out of the motorcar and had heard his voice downstairs. "Does His Majesty wish time alone with —"

"He can't bear to see him . . . like this. He wants to remember him handing him stamps off the floor and jumping about when he was supposed to be quiet, that's all."

"Yes," I said, blotting at my tears that had dropped on the shoulder of her coat, "that's all."

On January 21, 1919, we buried Johnnie in the Sandringham churchyard where Chad lay. I had his *NANNY — I LOVE YOU* note and the Fabergé grouse stuck in my muff and I held tight to them the entire church service and burial. Bertie and David were still away, but Mary stuck tight to her mother, Harry to the king, and dear George to me. But after everything, it was frail, old Queen Alexandra and I who lingered longest at the fresh grave, despite the bitter cold.

"Should I return the grouse statue, ma'am?" I asked her.

"You keep it, my dear. And you come here to live in the Big House with your friend Mabel until you are ready to . . . to get on with your life. I hear Mabel might go with you, and I will miss her too. Missing people we love — it is still better to have loved and lost than not to have loved, as they say, isn't it?"

"Yes, ma'am. Thank you for reminding me of that. So many losses here, but love means we wouldn't want to blot the memories out, even if they hurt."

"Precisely. My sister says the same, and she's lost her son, his wife, and those lovely

Russian children to those black-hearted Bolsheviks! I know my memory is not as good as it once was, dear Lala, but I won't forget our Johnnie. Now you're trembling from the cold. I'd best get back in my motor and go home — and you too — to Wood Farm. But if it is too empty and awful, you come to me."

Erect, beautiful, despite her feeble frame, she patted my arm and turned toward her waiting motorcar. I blinked back tears at the array of fresh flowers left to freeze on the grave and hurried to take her arm so she wouldn't slip. I wanted to stay here at Sandringham, near Johnnie, near my beloved Chad forever, but they would both want me to go on — go on and keep looking up.

CHAPTER 36

April 6, 1959
The Sandringham Estate

"Lala, dear," the Duke of Windsor cried as he entered my flat. He looked as boyish as ever, though he was nearly sixty-five. I still saw the child in him, jumpy, unsure, trying ever so hard to please and charm — and cling.

"Sir, how wonderful to see you and how good you look," I told him. I bobbed him the slightest of curtsies. At least my temptation to box his ears for letting us all down had passed.

"Now, don't you 'sir' me. I won't have it," he insisted as he gave me a quick hug and stepped in past me, then flourished the big bouquet of pink roses I had seen he was trying to hide behind his back. Never had that boy been able to hide anything from me, though, Lord knows, he tried.

"Oh, how lovely and thoughtful," I told

499

him, inhaling their scent. I closed the door, and we went into the living room. "I'll put them in water straightaway." He sat where he'd been twice before in my comfy chair while I popped the roses into my only large vase and ran some water from the tap in my kitchenette. I hurried back in to put the roses on the telly. I caught him staring, almost glaring, at my large framed and tinted picture of Johnnie, but he looked back to me with a beaming smile.

"I hope the duchess is well," I told him, sitting on the chintz sofa directly across from him.

"Hearty and happy. But to business. Despite your silver hair, you still look like the Lala who saved us all — ha!"

"Ha, is right. I'm eighty-four, my boy."

"My boy — I'll always be that to you, won't I? But for Mary and Harry, I'm the last left of your brood of the six of us and the last of all the royals you knew when you were in service with us." He heaved a huge sigh. "But here's my task at hand. I'm writing a second memoir, things I didn't get to in *The King's Story,* which did quite well by the way, especially in America. This one's to be titled *A Family Album.* It will have some photos — of you too, that one with the nursemaids where Bertie and I are in the

500

sailor suits Father insisted on."

"Did he ever! And shouted at me to sew up your pockets when you put your hands in them. Anyone who slouched or didn't dress proper he called a cad, and we couldn't have that with his two oldest boys, and you the heir."

As he slowly shook his head, creases furrowed his brow. He fussed with his collar and tie. "Shouted at everyone, didn't he? But my grandparents and you were my refuge."

We were silent a moment as the bad times as well as the good seemed to hover in the room. He fidgeted, pulled out a gold cigarette case, then slid it back into his pocket as if I'd scold him if he smoked here. I spoke to break the tense silence.

"I thought your first book was masterful, sir — David. Even Mr. Hansell and Mademoiselle Bricka would have been pleased. You have a way with words. May I fetch you some tea before we reminisce?"

"Thanks, but I'm okay. I've taken to American coffee."

"And speech. Then ask away for your book."

From his suit coat pocket, he took a small pad of paper and unscrewed a gold fountain pen. "Lala, you'd never consider writing a

501

book, would you? I daresay, you've seen a lot of us from the inside out."

"Me? Hardly. A retired and tired nanny. Absolutely not. My correspondence with your mother after I left service was as far as my writing talents go."

He looked relieved. I could still read him after all this time. Something else was coming. His expression was half pout, half fear. How tragic that he and Bertie were so abused in the beginning and that I couldn't quite love that out of them the way I had protected Johnnie.

"You did give back all my letters to Special Branch when they asked for them during the first war, didn't you?" he asked, trying to sound nonchalant. "I mean, if you had kept any of them, I'd like to give them a glance to see if they'd be of any use for the new book. I don't want others scaring things up, misrepresenting me, foibles and all."

"David," I said, leveling a stern look at him but resisting the temptation to shake my finger, "you asked me that once before." In a stern voice, I told him, "Special Branch sent an agent to ask that I hand them over, and I complied."

"Well, then," he said, slapping his knee, "on to *A Family Album*. Any memories of when you first came to Sandringham?"

As we talked, the only thing I mentioned of his childhood nightmare was that his nurse when I arrived used to make him cry so she could have him all to herself. He frowned and nodded. No doubt he had buried deep those dreadful days.

"Yes," he said, scribbling fast with his pad perched on his knee. "The third nanny was the charm, eh? Someone told me that the first one got sacked for calling my maternal grandmother fat. Well, everyone called her 'Fat Mary' behind her back, and she was." He looked up at me. "The duchess and I watch our weight. She has a throw pillow that says, *'You can never be too rich or too thin,'* and she means it, never lets me over-eat. She runs a tight ship, and I love her for it, gives me a good whack now and again. Good thing I had strict naval training before she became my captain — eh?"

He forced a laugh, and I smiled, but the biggest puzzle of David's adult life hit me hard. He had always been attracted to women who resembled the worst person he had ever known — not counting Adolf Hitler, of course. Wallis Simpson even physically resembled the woman who had been so cruel to him. Terrible that the poor boy had married Wallis, forsaking his heritage and kingdom for her! Worse, that, even in physical resemblance, I swear, he had sought out women who reminded him of that sadistic Mary Peters — and then, more or less, had married one of them.

He looked up at me. "I've tried not to lord it over others because of being born with a silver spoon in my mouth, Lala, one, I daresay, I've managed to tarnish now and again, though I did dearly care for my people, those down and out especially."

But for your own little brother, I thought, but I said only, "I know you tried, David." I was pleased he could be so insightful, but rather than pursue that, off we went again, sailing through memories, some good, some bad. Despite what he'd said about not lording it over others, he clung to the idea he was special. As firstborn son, the golden boy, the internationally charming and adored Prince of Wales, of course, he had been. But he was never strong enough to overcome. Bertie eventually did. Mary, Harry, and George coped. Even my dear Johnnie, bless his soul, did in his own way. But not the heir.

"I won't hide Johnnie in this book, like they tried to do," he promised, putting pen and paper away. "Full disclosure in these modern times." When he rose, I stood to show him out. He seemed in a hurry now, glancing at his watch, probably needing to report on time to his wife, just as he used to do to his father. "Yet I am always surprised to see you still have him here," he went on, in lecture mode now, gesturing at the portrait, "reminding you of the tragedy. You should put up that feather picture from Chad over the hearth instead."

"It's in a place of honor in my bedroom."

"At least I see you have a photo of the rest of us too on the mantel."

I did indeed, but it was normal-sized, not life-sized like the framed one with Johnnie as a baby all decked out — from his layers of muslin, cambric, and lace to his white stockings and buttoned shoes. I'm sure it would have pleased David mightily if I'd taken it down while he was here, but Johnnie wasn't going anywhere, not from over my mantel and not from the memories of my years with the royal Yorks, the Waleses, the Windsors, my own family album.

I have been content these many years since Chad and Johnnie died, I told myself as I strolled the Sandringham grounds alone after David's chauffeur drove him away. After I left service, Mabel and I ran a boardinghouse in Slough, and later we traveled the world. We both put a bit of money into Rose's tailoring shop in Piccadilly, for she never became the designer she longed to be. I still enjoyed her company from time to time. Margaretta went back to Ireland but never quite recovered from her losses and died early. I warrant that I could have done that too, but I was too stubborn and built of sterner stuff.

I see my siblings in London, and I've coddled their children and grandchildren. I live near Mabel in the grace-and-favor flats Bertie arranged for when he was king. He used to visit too, so Sandringham no longer makes me sad, only sentimental. I often rehearse for myself memories of my little brood. Johnnie's happiness and Chad's love gave me the strength to do that.

But I never forgave David for giving up the throne when his father died. And I never forgave him for one more thing: shortly after Johnnie died, David wrote his mother that his youngest brother had not been much more than an animal and it was a blessing he died. Rose had told me that the queen had sent her son a scathing letter, forcing him to apologize.

Queen Mary never told me that, although the two of us corresponded and occasionally saw each other here. I believe she was a better grandmother than she was a mother, for Bertie's daughter, Queen Elizabeth, treasured her so. Queen Mary has been gone now for eleven years, and I do miss her. One Christmas at the Big House, Queen Elizabeth told me she did too.

And now that David has just visited me in my old age, I feel softer toward him, but I still need this walk on the grounds today. How many more times will I be able to do so? And, still, everywhere I look, I see Johnnie, Chad, the others — and my younger self.

I visited Chad's grave today and then walked to Johnnie's. I put one of the roses David brought me on my boy's grave, then went on, past the Big House where the queen and her family still celebrate their Christmases. I like her immensely, because she reminds me of Bertie with her kind eyes and kinder heart. She knows her duty as did the Saxe-Coburg-Gothas, the Yorks, the Waleses, and the Windsors — all but David — before her.

How proud I was of Bertie, picking up the pieces of David's derelict duty to his country. Bertie married a fine woman and found a way to stop his stuttering, though the few of us who knew his struggles noticed that he carefully paused before attacking a sentence.

Princess Mary, Countess of Harewood through her marriage, was named Princess Royal in 1932 by her father. Harry, Duke of Gloucester, did well for himself and served as regent for the young Princess Elizabeth until she was of age, lest Bertie die early. My dear Prince George, Duke of Kent, married Princess Marina of Greece and Denmark and had three lovely children, while Mary and Harry each had but one. Sadly, George died in the Second World War at age thirty-nine in a military aircraft, which crashed in Scotland. He had been a proud RAF captain. It is the way, I consoled myself, he would have chosen to die.

How I mourned Queen Alexandra when she passed away here in the Big House in 1925 at age eighty. David once called her wonky, and I knew her thoughts often went astray, but, good gracious, so do mine at times . . . back to that first day I stepped off the railway car on the Wolferton platform and there was Chad waiting for me, and now I wait to see him again. Pictures of him flying a kite with my dear Johnnie or pointing out a bird in flight, even throwing a net over me and knocking me to the ground where I too shall sleep someday . . .

But now I see someone coming toward me on the path near the village, a young woman with a baby in her arms. It is as if I am seeing myself, young and eager and happy again, but I recognize who it is. Our dear Penny was wed here years ago and moved to King's Lynn seven miles away. I've helped tend her four children, but she's a new grandmother now, and dare I hope . . .

"Lala, there you are! I had to show you my first grandchild, and can you guess his name?" she said as we hugged with the baby between us.

"Oh, he's just lovely. Is he to be called Chad?" I asked, blinking back tears. "They don't dare call him Chadwick the fourth because your father didn't like that name. Too pompous."

"Yes, meet just plain Chad Johnson," she told me. "Isn't he perfect? Someone said they'd seen you walk this way, so let's go back to your flat and you can give him one of your famous cuddles. Once a nanny, always a nanny, even a royal one."

"Yes," I told her, smiling down at the new little one. "Yes, indeed."

P.S.
INSIGHTS, INTERVIEWS
& MORE . . .

AUTHOR'S NOTE

I have been intrigued by Britain's royals since I was ten and had a British pen pal who used to send me magazine photos of England's "young queen," Elizabeth II, who, of course, recently had her sixty-years-on-the-throne Diamond Jubilee, as did her great-great-great-grandmother Queen Victoria in this story. Over the years I have enjoyed such great BBC series as *Upstairs Downstairs* and *Downton Abbey,* but it is my many trips to England that set me on the path to write about the Saxe-Coburg-Gothas, who changed their last name to Windsor. During my most recent visit, for a meeting of the Historical Novel Society, I toured Buckingham Palace and researched at the Victoria and Albert Museum for this novel: the places do help to reveal the people.

Not only did the late Victorian, Edwardian, and World War I eras teem with fascinating people and worldwide upheaval, but I have always been astounded by the fact that, among the British upper classes, parents seldom tended or reared their own children, the future of their nation and their once great empire. As we know today, those early formative years in children's lives can make or break them.

Women who tended young children were first called nurses, but that term slowly changed to nannies to differentiate them from medical nurses. (In earlier years, they did much of the nursing of babies and toddlers.) In my research, I came across numerous examples of these Victorian and Edwardian servant women who had far-reaching impact on great people and so on history. This could be a tragedy — as it was with the true case of David and Bertie's terrible nanny, Mrs. Peters — or a blessing, as with Charlotte Bill.

Besides "Lala," another great example of a supportive nanny is the one who reared another famous person. The first five years of Winston Churchill's life were totally impacted by his nurse, Mrs. Everest, who was his constant companion while his parents were busy elsewhere. Churchill visited and supported her financially for years, was with her when she died, and when he died years later, the only photo he had next to his bed was of her.

Another incident illustrates the fact that servants reared noble and royal children: Mrs. Sly, a nurse employed by Queen Victoria, once fell ill on a trip and, despite a retinue of nursery maids, maids of honor, and servants, Queen Victoria and two of her ladies found that, by accident, they were in charge of two royal children, both under age three, in a railway carriage for a journey of several hours. The women had no clue how to entertain or control them. The children ran around, broke things, yelled, and would not settle down. "The Queen became irritated, then furious, finally exhausted, despairing and helpless" (*The Rise and Fall of the British Nanny* by Jonathan Gathorne-Hardy).

Since I have written several Tudor-era historical novels, I must mention that it is not unusual for earlier royals to see that their nannies were well taken care of in old age. Both Henry V and the notorious Henry VIII supported their nannies for years. Although I have no doubt the British monarchs loved their children, they were often absent and distracted parents. Royal librarian Owen Morshead once told British diplomat and politician Harold Nicolson:

"The House of Hanover, like ducks, produce bad parents . . . they trample on their young" (*Edward VIII, A Biography* by Philip Ziegler). From that book also, the royal private secretary Alec Harding is reported as observing, "Why George V, who was such a kind man, was such a brute to his children [is unknown]."

Although it is obvious that Prince William and Duchess Catherine are excellent caregivers of Prince George and their new daughter, Princess Charlotte, I noted that they originally planned to have no nanny — then realized they certainly needed one with their firstborn. William's own nanny, Jessica Webb, helped out briefly. When she retired, at age seventy-one, they hired Maria Borrallo, whom the press has nicknamed "Supernanny" for her martial arts and defensive car driving skills. That's a far cry from just hiding a royal child behind one's skirts in a potentially dangerous situation.

Helene Bricka's quote about the inequality of the classes in Britain at this time comes from a letter she wrote. I have tried to stay true to the characters in the novel who actually lived, which includes the royals and nobles of that day. Bits and pieces are recorded about Charlotte Bill, and there are several fine photographs of her, all but two with her royal charges. Still, this novel is what Alex Hailey, the author of *Roots*, appropriately dubbed "faction." It is based on factual research but has fictional dialogue, situations, and some characters that would fit the facts. I did not put President Theodore Roosevelt in the story simply to name-drop. It is recorded that the former president met Johnnie and was greatly amused by him.

Chad Reaver is an amalgamation of two men on the estate, the village schoolteacher and the gamekeeper, both of whom King George admired. Being a romantic, I would love to have written a happier ending for Lala and Chad, but that would be tampering with her life story too much. Yet I could not resist giving her loyalty and a love life beyond her young charges. Chad's daughter Penny, although she is fictional, represents a young girl who was often Johnnie's companion on the estate during his Wood Farm years.

During the era of this novel, little was known about epilepsy (the actual treatments, as described here, were brutal) and nothing about autism, which is of such interest today. Johnnie was definitely epileptic, but I believe what they called "different" and "strange" meant he was autistic also, probably a child with Asperger's syndrome, although it is wrong to diagnose him from such a distance even if he fits that general pattern.

Some who knew Charlotte Bill wrote her nickname as Lalla with two *l*'s, but I chose to use the shorter spelling that others have used also. Lala was a minor character in the 2002 BBC production *The Lost Prince,* which told Johnnie's story from his point of view. I could only locate that on videotape but I intentionally did not watch it because I did not want to be swayed by the casting or the actors' portrayals. I did, however, read the screenplay by Stephen Poliakoff. His foreword gives an excellent overall view of the characters and their tumultuous times.

For those interested in the tragic story of the Romanovs, there is a YouTube feature called *The End of the Romanovs.* Be sure to have plenty of tissues when you watch it, but these were sad times.

The letters David sent Lala were just one example of his naive, indecorous correspondence to women. His letters to Freda Dudley Ward and especially to his first flame, the French courtesan Marguerite Alibert, have come to light. Marguerite, who was later accused in England of murdering her husband, threatened Prince Edward (David in this story) with blackmail and exposure. Special Branch was involved to collect the letters and keep Marguerite quiet (see *The Woman Before Wallis: Prince Edward, the Parisian Courtesan, and the Perfect Murder* by Andrew Rose).

I was amazed how Lala's story touched huge events and personalities. She intimately observed not only the royal family of Britain but such movers and shakers as Kaiser Wilhelm and Tsar Nicholas and his family. I love the little details of Victorian/Edwardian life, including the actual collection Queen Alexandra (and Queen Mary) had of agate animals. Take a look at them, many from the Sandringham House collection, at http://www.pinterest.com/fslewis1 faberge-animals/.

Sandringham has several places of interest on the large estate. Sandringham House, of course, is where the royal family still celebrates Christmas. Today, York Cottage serves as offices for the estate. Wood Farm is still intact and occasionally inhabited: The Duke of Edinburgh has used it during shooting weekends. The younger royals have had private parties there. Divorced spouses of royals such as Sarah, Duchess of York, are sometimes housed at Wood Farm during the holidays so they can be near the royal children without staying at the Big House. Diana, Princess of Wales, was born at Park House on the estate. And although it played no part in this story, it's interesting to note that a future king and queen have property on the estate: The ten-room Georgian mansion Anmer Hall was given to Prince William for his thirtieth birthday so he and Duchess Catherine could have a Sandringham retreat. It must be a great getaway spot for a growing family, since it has a tennis court and swimming pool.

Please visit my website (www.Karen HarperAuthor.com) and my facebook page (www.facebook.com/KarenHarperAuthor) where I will be posting pictures of Lala and the royal children and the Sandringham Estate, and, of course, of Johnnie.

Special thanks, as ever, to my husband, Don, for putting up with an obsessed Anglophile and for proofreading my manuscripts, and to Dr. Roy Manning for advice on inherent dangers in birthing practices.

Besides the books mentioned earlier, others that I relied on for this story include: *Sandringham Days: The Domestic Life of the Royal Family in Norfolk, 1862–1952* by John Matson; *Matriarch* by Anne Edwards; *The Real Life of Downton Abbey* by Jacky Hyams;

Pocket Guide to Edwardian England by Evangeline Holland; *Upstairs & Downstairs: The Illustrated Guide to the Real World of Downton Abbey* by Sarah Warwick; *Four Sisters: The Lost Lives of the Romanov Grand Duchesses* by Helen Rappaport; *Epilepsy, Hysteria, and Neurasthenia, Their Causes, Symptoms & Treatment* by Isaac George Briggs (1892); *World War I, The Definitive Visual History,* ed. Richard Overy; *The Century* by Peter Jennings and Todd Brewster; *Sunrise and Stormclouds,* ed. Roger Morgan; *A King's Story* by Edward VIII, Duke of Windsor; *A Family Album* by Edward VIII, Duke of Windsor; *King Edward VIII* by Philip Ziegler; *Edward the Uncrowned King* by Christopher Hibbert; *The Rise and Fall of the Victorian Servant* by Pamela Horn; and *A Spoonful of Sugar: A Nanny's Story* by Brenda Ashford.

On-site and on-line research also helped fill in the gaps, including a well-made documentary on Johnnie's life available on YouTube called *Prince John, The Windsors' Tragic Secret,* which includes many photos and Johnnie's *"Nanny, I love you. — Johnnie"* note to Lala, who died, unwed, at the age of eighty-nine in 1964.

— Karen Harper

READING GROUP
DISCUSSION QUESTIONS

1. Do you think it is true that "The hand that rocks the cradle rules the world"? If so, why did the upper-class ethic during the Victorian and Edwardian eras allow servant women to rear their young children? And what sort of people did this practice produce? How has that thinking changed over the years to now?

2. Really, what is the definition of "motherhood"? Is it strictly biological or is it more?

3. A study of the royal Yorks/Windsors reveals a lot about the relationships of fathers to their children. It's obvious that the dynamic between Prince Albert, later King Edward VII, and his son George, later King George V, was dysfunctional. Can you read between the lines to say why? And how would you assess the

relationships of George, Duke of York, to his six children?

4. Likewise, the royal marriages of Edward/Alexandra and George/May have unique arrangements. Is this just because "the royals and very rich are different," is it the result of arranged marriages, or is it just a product of a stricter, different time? Have you seen modern marriages with similar problems?

5. David, later king and Duke of Windsor, is a fascinating study, a man who gave up the throne for "the woman he loved," a twice-divorced American who pretty much wore the pants in their marriage. Do David's early years with the strict and cruel nanny really explain this, or is his family to blame also for his later lack of duty?

6. Many of us saw the movie *The King's Speech.* Does this book throw more light on why Bertie stuttered and had a bad digestive system? Yet where did he find the strength to rule and take the British nation through the trials of World War II?

7. Perhaps the Yorks/Windsors coped with Johnnie as best they could for that era —

or did they? Autism was not known, and epilepsy was feared. Did they handle their youngest child well? Did Lala?

8. As a reader, what do you think of historical novels that are what Alex Hailey, author of *Roots,* dubbed "faction" — that is, well-researched books that have fictional scenes and dialogue and some invented characters? Does faction work in a way a straight history book would not?

9. Is it "better to have loved and lost, than never to have loved at all"? Lala loses much in this story, but is she better for having known, loved, and helped those who have died?

10. Would you become a British royal of these eras (or Russian royalty) if you had the choice? (And for the Russians, if you didn't know the revolution was coming?) Or would you like to be part of the British royal family today? What are the pros and cons of such a life?

11. Charlotte Bill and other nurses and nannies like her were some of the first "career women" who gave up their own romantic and domestic futures for their duty. Are

they caught between the past and the future during this early "suffragette" movement? Are they to be admired or pitied?

12. There has recently been much world-wide upheaval over big-game hunting and the overhunting of species in general. How do you feel about the massive number of game birds killed by the upper class of this era? Why do you think this sport was such a passion?

13. As dreadful as World War I was for the British (and others), did any good social movements come from so many men being lost? How so?

14. Those of us who have enjoyed such BBC series as *Upstairs, Downstairs* or *Downton Abbey* have had a peek into understanding England's servant class at this time. Were there both joys and sorrows, triumphs as well as tragedies in this lifestyle?

ABOUT THE AUTHOR

New York Times and *USA Today* bestselling author **Karen Harper** is a former university (Ohio State) and high school English teacher. Published since 1982, she writes contemporary suspense and historical novels about real British women. Two of her recent Tudor-era books were bestsellers in the UK and Russia. A rabid Anglophile, she likes nothing more than to research her novels on site in the British Isles. Harper won the Mary Higgins Clark Award for *Dark Angel,* and her novel *Shattered Secrets* was judged one of the Best Books of 2014 by *Suspense Magazine.* The author and her husband divide their time between Ohio and Florida.